PRAISE FOR **a s y l**

"Alexis is funny, wry, has a great satirical eye. . . ."
— *Windsor Star*

"There is sex, violence, betrayal and the most devious grand-mother one could ever hope not to have. . . . Ottawa itself is a character in *Asylum*. . . . It is [Alexis's] asylum. In both senses of the word."
— *Ottawa Citizen*

"A Russian doll of a book, thick with layers and twists."
— CBC

"The Great Ottawa Novel has landed."
— *Toronto Star*

"Constantly surprising, so rich and affecting. . . . Its imaginative reach is thrilling. . . ."
— *National Post*

"Beautifully crafted characters, as real as anyone you might meet on the street . . . the story is intricate, many-layered, and thought-ful. An excellent novel."
— Halifax *Chronicle Herald*

"Some of the most beautiful prose I've read in years. . . . For me a great novel is one that satisfies three criterions: First, it must be a story told well. It must also be written as if every word has just been handed down from style heaven. And lastly, it must have at its centre a truth that skirts the frayed edges of your own philosophy until it weaves its way into the way you look at the world. André Alexis's *Asylum* is a great book."
— New Brunswick *Telegraph-Journal*

BOOKS BY ANDRÉ ALEXIS

FICTION

Despair and Other Stories of Ottawa (1994)

Childhood (1998)

Asylum (2008)

PLAYS

Lambton Kent (1999)

FOR CHILDREN

Ingrid and the Wolf (2005)

André Alexis

a s y l u m

EMBLEM
McClelland & Stewart

Cloth edition published 2008
Emblem edition published 2009

Emblem is an imprint of McClelland & Stewart Ltd.
Emblem and colophon are registered trademarks of McClelland & Stewart Ltd.

Library and Archives Canada Cataloguing in Publication

Alexis, André, 1957-
    Asylum / André Alexis.

ISBN 978-0-7710-0670-8

I. Title.

PS8551.L474A89 2009   C813'.54   C2008-904196-8

We acknowledge the financial support of the Government of Canada through the Book Publishing Industry Development Program and that of the Government of Ontario through the Ontario Media Development Corporation's Ontario Book Initiative. We further acknowledge the support of the Canada Council for the Arts and the Ontario Arts Council for our publishing program.

The epigraph by Ibrahim Ag Alhabib is a lyric from the song "Assouf" (Longing).
Words and Music by Ibrahim Ag Alhabib.
© 2007 EMMA PRODUCTIONS SAS and EMI BLACKWOOD MUSIC INC.
All Rights in U.S. and Canada Controlled and Administered
by EMI BLACKWOOD MUSIC INC.
All Rights Reserved   International Copyright Secured   Used by Permission

The lyrics on page 165 are from "Ramona," written by Mabel Wayne and L. Wolfe Gilbert (EMI Music). The lyrics on page 464 are from "Perfidia," by Alberto Domínguez (PEERMUSIC).

Every effort has been made to contact copyright holders; in the event of an inadvertent omission or error, please notify the publisher.

Typeset in Dante by M&S, Toronto
Printed and bound in Canada

ANCIENT FOREST
FRIENDLY

McClelland & Stewart Ltd.
75 Sherbourne Street
Toronto, Ontario
M5A 2P9
www.mcclelland.com

1 2 3 4 5   13 12 11 10 09

In Homage to Harry Mathews

ⵏ•∵•ϚE ⊏•⁞Ϛ#•⁝ ⋦• •⊙--][Ϛ⁞‖•‖•ⵏ

What can I do with this endless longing?

IBRAHIM AG ALHABIB

TABLE OF

CONTENTS

BOOK I

A BITTER AFTERTASTE

I 've been living in Italy for fourteen years now, here at Santa Maddalena.

Santa Maddalena has been good for me, I think. It's taught me discipline and humility. I wake early in the morning. I go to sleep in the early evening. My day is spent caring for the grounds, churning butter, helping to tend the bees, or in prayer, meditation, and worship. In the evening, I read or I translate text from the German. My fellows are, most of them, pleasant company. There's little time for long conversation, and no time for idleness, but I do appreciate the amity of thoughtful men. In fact, until recently, I've been rather immersed in monastic life.

I don't know why exactly my feelings shifted. But one day, I felt such a longing for Ottawa, and for my country, it was as if I'd been in Italy for only a week or two, recently exiled. Was it nostalgia? Yes, I suppose, but it was more than that. Nostalgia, as Fra Philippo says, is a bitter aftertaste that follows the sweetness of leaving the world. I was accustomed to it. Over the years, I've felt intense nostalgia, and wondered if I'd been right to leave home at all. This recent feeling, however, was closer to bewilderment or panic. It was like being lost in the woods, anguished at the thought of all I might never see again.

Why at that moment? Hard to say. Perhaps it had taken four-teen years for Ottawa to catch up with me. Or, again, it may be that, on the point of losing the last scraps of my old world, I felt a resurgence of the past, the last gasp of home as it expired within me. Whatever the answer, my bewilderment brought with it the most vivid and unpredictable memories. While sweeping my cell, I remembered a kitchen on Cooper Street, its yellowed linoleum tiles. Stooping to pull a weed from the rows of cavallo nero, I imagined myself by the side of the canal looking down into its grey water. And one morning, while praying for a greater capac-ity to believe, I had a vision of a fire hydrant near the corner of Somerset and Percy.

At times, Ottawa overcame me, leaving me momentarily help-less. And yet, though my memories were of a variety of details (unusual or banal), faces (well known or not), and houses (familiar or not), they all had one thing in common: most every detail, face, house, etc., was from the time after I left home and before I came to Santa Maddalena. Little came back from my childhood: no homes, schools or schoolmates, and few memories of my parents. Once I realized how bounded my memories were (from finding a place of my own to the decline of the Conservative Party), it felt as if my psyche were trying to tell me something crucial, though, for the life of me, I couldn't make out what it might be.

I suppose I could have waited this storm of memory out. I could have drowned my memories in work or prayer, as Fra Philippo advised me to do, but I have chosen instead to meet them head-on, to write them down, faithfully, for as long as it takes. This way, I will make of my predicament, if memory *is* a predicament, a spiritual exercise. Perhaps, through this discipline, I'll find something out about myself. So much the better. There may be comfort in self-discovery, as there may be comfort in seeing how much (or how little) of my city remains within me.

The one thing that troubles me: I wish, above all, to be truth-ful and, to accomplish that, I may have to invent as much as I remember. There seems no way around it. Much of the context of my last years in Ottawa is now clouded or gone. I can't recall all the tones of voice, the way the sun or a sudden fragrant breeze distracted from a conversation or influenced a thought, the sound of the city (its specific pitch), the anxiety of life in the capital. But truth is meaningless without context, without an environment. So, in the end, it's either recall what I can and invent what I can't or give nothing but detail, detail, fact and detail.

Although, on second thought, why should I be troubled by invention or even hearsay? For truth's sake? Yes, of course. But how many times have I stood in front of a Gozzoli or a Pontormo and felt a truth, though all before me was invention? Just the other day, in fact, I stopped at San Marco to admire a panel by Fra Angelico: Christ, victorious, enters Hell to free the righteous trapped in Limbo. It is a wonderful work, of course, but I was struck, as always, by the demons, two of whom hide in an alcove while a third lies crushed beneath the door Christ has knocked down. Evil has been going about its business (chastising sinners, stoking fires, keeping the place foul, etc.) when, out of the blue, a door bursts open and Christ enters to redeem the righteous. The work shows no overt sympathy for the demons, but il Beato Angelico manages to suggest a pathetic daily grind: evil startled in the midst of evil routine. Though there may be no Hell, no demons, no Adam, no Christ, still something true is caught.

So, to begin . . .

In 1983, I was twenty-six and increasingly at odds with my parents. My father would stop me in the hall or come into my room to say
   – The crunch is coming, son. And what are you going to do when it comes? You've got to have something to fall back on.

I understood. "Something to fall back on" meant a profession, but I could not find the right road. None of the professions meant anything to me. Worse, they all seemed the same: doctor, lawyer, accountant, politician . . . I could not even find a tendency in

myself. After a while, I began to blame my parents for my lassitude and indecision, and I resented their concern for me. They
wanted me to find work, to do something more than stay in my
room and read? Fine. I took work at a bookstore and moved out
of my parents' home.

It was, at first, exhilarating to live on my own: everything was
new and interesting. With a small loan from my father, I rented
an apartment on Percy and made my entry into the world. But,
paradoxically, I stepped away from it at the same time. From the
first moments on my own, there was, along with exhilaration, a
vague disappointment. I was not at ease. I did not quite belong in
my city. I thought too much. I wondered about every little thing.
What was this world to me? What did I want, exactly? What could
the people around me tell me about myself? Though I had
changed domiciles, I was still adrift. Independence, such as it was,
brought no answers.

Though I didn't know it, I was already moving towards Santa
Maddalena.

It wasn't all ambivalence and doubt, however. Among other
things, there were the Stanleys, who had been our neighbours
when I was young, and, of course, there was the Fortnightly Club.
One of the most pleasant memories I have is of a particular
meeting of the Fortnightly. I'd been to a number of Fortnightly
evenings, evenings at which we (its members) met to discuss philosophy and ideas. At *this* meeting, we were to discuss the life and
work of Thomas Aquinas. Aquinas did not interest me at the time
(and interests me little, now) but, newly liberated from my
parents, I believed I was the kind of man who should be *able* to
discuss Aquinas. I suppose I thought Aquinas obscure, dull, and
difficult to read, qualities that afflicted all the "serious" reading I
did at the time: from the brief passages of Hegel I managed to
digest to the bits of Mallarmé I couldn't keep down. Reading
Aquinas was, to me, a sign that *I* was "serious," and I consoled
myself with it.

So, armed with a paperback edition of the *Summa Theologiae* (abridged) on which there was a portrait of St. Thomas by Carlo Crivelli, I met up with the other members of the Fortnightly Club.

2

NINETEEN EIGHTY-THREE

On the last evening of the Conservative leadership convention, the Fortnightly convened in Walter Barnes' backyard to talk about Aquinas. The subject had been chosen by Walter himself and, as happened when Walter chose the subject, it was a little obscure. Still, for three hours, the conversation was engaging. It began with the Arabic philosophy Aquinas had appropriated (Averroës, Avicenna, and al-Ghazali), touched on an ancient recipe that called for a loaf of bread to be buried for thirty days, and then moved lazily on to other things: viniculture, books, travel, Italy.

Someone asked someone

– Have you been to Florence?

and that prompted a round of collective recollection.

Walter had been, on several occasions, but he admitted he did not love the city. It was filled with dour people, not at all like Siena, which, though not as blessed culturally, was wonderful and mysterious.

François Ricard described his and his late wife's honeymoon in Tuscany. He and Michelle had spent three days in Florence, and they had eaten so much ice cream, the city would always remind him of peaches and pistachio. And, it's true, the Florentines were mean and petty, but one could forgive a city anything for San Miniato, the only church in which he had felt the presence of the sacred.

– You speak as if God exists, said Mr. van Leuwen.

– No, no, even if He doesn't, said François. The *place* is holy.

Mr. van Leuwen smiled. He himself had never seen Florence, but he was an admirer of architecture, and he could understand how the curves and angles of a room might themselves be sacred. Wasn't it the Lollards who destroyed Catholic churches for that very reason?

– The Lollards didn't destroy churches, said Walter, but they hated the smells and bells.

– There you go, said van Leuwen.

Then there was me. I was fascinated by Florence. I'd learned Italian and memorized whole passages of Machiavelli's *Istorie Fiorentine*. I'd never seen the city and hoped I never would, because I had once dreamed it was the place I would die, but Florence seemed to me the embodiment of an ideal. (As I write these words, years later, some twenty kilometres from Florence, I no longer believe in the swift and brutal end I had, rather romantically, dreamed for myself.)

We might have talked about the city the rest of the evening, but Louise Dylan brought the matter to an end. She quietly said

– What does all this have to do with Thomas Aquinas?

Not that she was interested in St. Thomas per se, but she was feeling defensive, for Walter's sake. He'd been kind enough to host the evening. Why shouldn't we stick to his chosen subject?

– Well . . . Aquinas was Italian, said François.

– So he was, said Walter.

And we began again to think again about the era when Truth was God and God was Truth.

A gentle wind ruffled the tablecloth and the paper napkins. Walter's backyard came briefly to life. On the other side of his picket fence, the cypress trees shook, while the grass, daisies, and trefoil on his lawn moved as if trod by someone just denser than air.

I'd been invited to join the Fortnightly Club by Henry Wing, a friend of my father. Henry thought it a shame I should waste my education on clerking, and my father agreed. As one of those Trinidadians who could recite pages of Herbert, Homer, or Horace just to demonstrate the superiority of a British education, my father loved the idea of intellectual society. One of his biggest fears was that I should waste my intelligence on frivolities and, to a lesser extent, I feared the same thing. I joined the Fortnightly because I thought it would do me good to talk to men and women who were (or seemed to be) at home with ideas.

Naturally, things were not as I supposed. I gradually learned that the members of the Fortnightly, thoughtful though they were, were often unreasonable. Walter Barnes, for instance: a mind so filled with amusing details (Hegel's parenting, the Greek origins of the word *paideia*, the invention of talcum powder . . .), it didn't always have room for the big picture, or for the obvious. Walter was a pleasure to be around. He was a vivid companion and one of the most attractive men I've known, but you could not have said that Reason and thought were his strongest suit. *Au contraire.*

That evening in '83, the first or second I attended after leaving home, we sat in the yard, in near darkness, telling stories and talking about Aquinas or medieval matters: would the soul of a rat ascend to heaven? No. A bird? No. What about a mermaid, half-woman, half-dolphin? Well, according to Peter of Ghent, only half of her would enter paradise: the half that sang.

Later, as the conversation gently and irrecoverably lost direction, each of us grew more pensive. Walter thought about his travels. Louise, whose husband was away on business, imagined the tail of an armadillo. François Ricard recalled a night in Positano when he and Michelle had gone out to the stone porch of a house they'd rented, out to see the stars over the Mediterranean. Mr. van Leuwen was reminded of pins shaking in a box as a breeze passed through the trees. And, finally, there was Henry. He'd said little all evening, but he was thinking about Aquinas.

After a while, Mr. van Leuwen looked at his watch: nine o'clock.

– It's getting late, he said.

The sun was just beneath the horizon and there was a pale blue glimmer at the bottom of the sky. All rose from their chairs.

– Thank you, Walter, said Henry.

Walter answered

– No, no. Thank *you* for coming.

Though it wasn't her place to ask, Louise said

– Should we have coffee?

But each of us declined, and we all (Louise included) walked out of the house and into the evening. It had not been a successful gathering where Aquinas was concerned. But, as usual, there was a spirit to the proceedings, a conviviality that came from good humour and, where I was concerned, the hope of belonging to a tradition, however ungainly, of intellectual pursuit. Besides, it was interesting to imagine paradise filled with bits of mermaids and halves of centaurs. How strange, I thought, the Middle Ages must have been.

––––––––

As she (covertly) returned to Walter's house, Louise thought about her husband, Paul. He was in Texas, in Amarillo on business, and it suddenly seemed odd to her that she was married, that she had a husband.

What is a husband, anyway? Is it someone with whom you have a relationship, a relationship that evolves, because time passes and one changes? Certainly. But one could say almost as much of a house or a dog, even when one feels, if only instinctively, that a husband is more than a house, more even than a dog. Is a husband love, then, or desire? Yes, but love and desire are too inconstant to make anything at all. Today, your version of love, your version of desire, may include your husband; tomorrow, it may not. Then they will, and then they will not, and then they will . . .

The man you love . . . a constant presence . . . a shadow . . . a version of yourself . . . an idea you nourish . . . a habit . . . a nuisance . . . a voice, a face, a hand . . . Or, perhaps, "husband" is a story you tell yourself, a story about a house in which there is another presence, faceless, who moves with you, beside you, strong at times, gentle at others, and you are yourself surprised when, one day, you recognize a man you have never met, a man who holds within him something of your own story.

Whatever a husband might be, Louise's was in Texas. What's more, she would have said, if asked, that he loved her, and he provided for her as unselfishly as he provided for himself. Paul Dylan was love and precision, and so he had been since high school where they first met. He was not perfect, but it wasn't Paul's imperfections that tempered her feelings for him. It was, she believed, something in herself, a restlessness.

She and Walter had been having an affair for months, and she was beginning to think him inexhaustible: not physically so much. It was rather that her own fascination was inexhaustible. It was physical, as well, of course. Walter was tall and broad-shouldered. His skin was smooth as a woman's, and it was a pleasure to watch the play of his muscles as he sat up in bed or as he undressed by the bedside, illuminated by the candle that burned on his night table. So graceful for a man who spent so much time leaning over books or lecturing on sociology, not what you'd expect beneath the rumpled clothes he wore. (So much about him was unexpected. There was, for instance, a joyous intensity to their love-making, a shared adventure. You mightn't have thought a professor of sociology capable of such abandon, but Walter was that rare thing: a man who actually loved fornication.)

At times, she felt awkward and vulnerable, but that wasn't his doing. Walter was playful, considerate, and attentive. No, Louise was intimidated by her own recklessness, and it seemed to her she would have done anything for Walter. In comparison, her feelings for her husband were tame. And that was it, that was the point, for her: she should have felt overwhelmed by her emotions for Paul while feeling real friendship for her lover. In that sense, she had married the wrong man.

Wasn't it time to tell her husband so?

Walter was still in his evening clothes: white shirt, grey tweed jacket (with navy blue elbow patches), beige corduroys.

– Louise, he said

and opened the door.

– Please come in, he said

and left her in the doorway as he returned to the backyard.

For a moment, Louise felt ashamed to be left at the front steps. This wasn't like him at all. Perhaps he was disappointed. Perhaps the evening had not gone as well as he might have liked. She walked through the house. Walter was sitting in a garden chair, his back to her, looking over his shoulder towards the picket fence. He was handsome in profile, distinguished, though his broken nose made her feel as if he had difficulty breathing. It looked more intriguing straight on, when his eyes (blue) and eyelashes (long) were a distraction.

It was strange to regard him so dispassionately but this, too, gave her pleasure: as if he were a landscape as alluring from afar as at close range.

– It was a lovely evening, she said.

She put a hand on his shoulder, the fingers of the other hand played with the hair on the back of his neck.

– Should we go inside? she asked.

– No, he answered, it's a perfect evening. You can see the stars.

It was still warm, the breeze still played in the branches above, and, from time to time, the smell of pine was so sharp it was as if they'd rubbed their fingers in spruce gum. Louise sat in the chair beside him, and though the evening was beautiful and the sky was soft and it should all have been soothing, she felt uneasy: something of his tone, something in the way he looked.

Walter interrupted her disquiet.

– I think we should talk, he said.

– About what?

He leaned his head to one side and said

– I wish there were an easier way to say it. The last few months have been wonderful, but I can't go on like this.

– Like what?

– Lou, please don't make it more difficult. I just can't stand the subterfuge.

– What did I do?

– You didn't do anything.

– Is it Paul? Do you want me to leave him?

Now that was a surprise, but Walter answered

– No

and added

– I want us to be friends. I'm not sorry about anything, but I can't do this any more.

His words were clear. He was resolved, solicitous, melancholy, but Louise felt she must have done something wrong.

– Was it something I did? she asked.

– No. You've been wonderful.

For a moment, she panicked. It made no sense to beg, but she considered begging. Then, as if it were all she wanted of him, all she wanted in the world, she said

– Could you bring me tea?

– Of course, he answered.

He stoically rose from the chair and left the yard.

How clear he'd been, and conscientious. Yet, although he hadn't lied, Walter had been almost entirely dishonest.

From the moment he met Louise, he'd felt strange stirrings. His feelings weren't simply sexual. They were primarily sexual, but, as he was compulsively heterosexual, it would have been strange if this had not been so. In fact, he rarely felt anything *more* than desire, and most of his relationships had been too brief for him to "get to know" the women with whom he fornicated. But with Louise, there had been, from the beginning, a compulsive curiosity as well. He wanted to know things about her that should not have mattered: where she was born, who her parents had been, what she thought about Byzantine art. What didn't he want to know? That was bad enough, that and the fact she was married to an acquaintance, but besides the curiosity there was, when he was with her, an inexplicable ease and a longing for another life.

Most men would have taken these things for premonitions of love, for love itself, or for some version of love. But because he had never felt such things for anyone, Walter was fascinated in an almost scientific way. He tried to isolate what it was in Louise that brought his feelings out: her hair, her voice, her eyes, her long and lovely back? He figured each of these things to himself, trying to see which moved him most. Unfortunately, they moved him equally and, worse, he could not imagine one aspect without imagining the whole. Unlike other women, of whom he retained only fragments, Louise could not be broken down in his imagination.

If, in the end, he'd pursued her as concertedly as he knew how, it was, in part, because he was perplexed by his own feelings and, in part, because he assumed his fascination would fade, as fascination had always faded, once they fornicated. Sadly, his emotions would not cooperate. Once they began a relationship in earnest, his desires and longing increased to the point of distraction. He could not stand to be away from her, could not stand himself when she was away, could not think, became forgetful, became someone he did not know.

And so, having had no previous experience of love, having no idea if he would ever recover himself and his life, feeling like a man whose house is overrun by mice, Walter did the only thing he knew how: he ended the relationship.

What was it he'd said?

– *I just can't stand the subterfuge?*

That had a noble ring to it, as if he could no longer bear to be dishonest.

He prepared a cup of green tea. He avoided Louise's eyes. He kept his answer brief when, in despair, she asked again what she'd done.

– Nothing, he said. You've been wonderful.

He watched as she cried, gave her one of his own handkerchiefs, waited until she had calmed down before walking her to his door and wishing her good night. He did everything a man who does not love would do, exactly as if he were not in love. A strange accomplishment, and one he would regret.

3

TAHAFUT AT-TAHAFUT

Around the time Walter turned his back to his own feelings, Messrs. van Leuwen, Wing, and myself were looking for a place to drink. We were also, now that we weren't obliged to, talking about Thomas Aquinas: his belief that manustruption is a form of murder, his misuse of Aristotle, and his dependence on Arabic philosophy, Averroës in particular.

– What was the name of Averroës' book about philosophy? asked Henry.

– *The Incoherence of Philosophy?* said Mr. van Leuwen.

– Yes, said Henry. It was something like that, but that doesn't sound right.

The three of us were walking south, which, as we all lived north, was inconvenient, but the inconvenience went unremarked because the company was pleasant. The city was lit up against a darkening sky, and the night air was slightly cool. We were on the bridge above the canal when van Leuwen said

– Is Paddy's okay?

And Paddy's it was: a small tavern, dimly lit, the stench of ale, the fog of cigarette smoke, and not enough tables. There was place at the bar: three stools near the end where the waitress stood, waiting for her orders. Van Leuwen spoke to the waitress.

– Busy, isn't it? he asked.

She answered, coolly

– Yes. It's always busy Saturdays.

She looked up at van Leuwen and was surprised to see him redden: a stocky, pale man in an orange shirt, neat as could be.

– More money for you then, eh? he said kindly.

Kindly, but without a hint of encouragement, she answered

– Maybe

moving away from the bar with a tray of beer.

The noise of the tavern, the sound of so many voices chatting in so many registers, was pleasing, but one needed beer (the first mouthful cold enough to rattle your teeth) to bear the smoke, to feel part of the conviviality. So, for a while, we made only sporadic attempts to talk, paying more attention to the beer than to each other.

(How odd it was, at times, to be in the company of men so much older than I was. They treated me with respect, as if my intelligence made us contemporaries, and this was at the root of my discomfort. My own contemporaries treated me with a certain disdain. I did not often drink, did not often go to movies, did not attend rock concerts or football games. As far as my contemporaries were concerned, my ideas were stale. Men like van Leuwen and Henry Wing – who, perhaps, thought of me as a younger version of themselves – became my contemporaries, and I was not always grateful for the exchange.)

At last, Henry said

– *Eheu fugaces, Postume, Postume . . .*

Van Leuwen smiled.

– It's too early for Horace, he said. Besides, you never quote the good ones, like *Quod ut superbo provoces ab inguine ore adlaborandum est tibi.*

– Another round? asked the bartender.

– Yes please, I answered. Three more Old V.

– Speaking of Horace, said van Leuwen, did you notice anything . . . strange between Wally and Louise?

– Like what? asked Henry.

– I'm not sure . . . like he's doing her.

– Walter's a good man, said Henry, but he usually does his
students.

– That's true.

– Here you are, gentlemen, said the bartender.

I paid and, enthralled as I was by all things sexual, asked

– Does he really get so much poon?

– He has a reputation, said Henry. I don't know where it comes
from, but it's not incredible. Have you seen him around young
women?

– I have, said van Leuwen. He's a ferret.

– A ferret?

– Yes, a predator. You know, there were so many ferrets around
my uncle's farm, you had to take a rifle with you to the outhouse.

So began a conversation about the wilds of Ontario, a debate
about wilderness, civilization, men, and ferrets. After an hour,
Henry went off to the facilities. He stepped down from the stool,
leaving his glass at the bar. The tavern was now almost impossibly full. It took some skill to move about, but Henry did it gracefully, vanishing into the Men's, shrouded in cigarette smoke.

– Here you go, said the bartender.

Van Leuwen, who'd ordered the round, paid for the bottles. He
was about to thank the bartender when a darkly dressed man
took Henry's place at the bar. He was short and had a distinctive
nose: long, with a bump near the bridge.

– That chair's taken, I said.

– Yes, said the man. I'll get up as soon as Henry's back.

– You know Henry?

– No, but we overheard his name while you were speaking. An
interesting conversation it was too. My friend and I . . .

He tapped the shoulder of a man beside him.

– We were really interested. And I'm with Henry: Man and Nature are not the same. If they were, there'd be no ultimate difference between Athens and an anthill. Listen, you don't mind our butting in, do you?

– Not at all, said van Leuwen. I'm surprised you could hear us, but we weren't speaking seriously.

– I see, said the man. You take your ideas lightly.

– Yes, said van Leuwen smiling. We're, uhm . . . intellectuals.

The man smiled politely, but his companion looked glum, as if he might have expressed his dislike for intellectuals but felt constrained.

– My name's Franklin Dupuis, said the man. And this is Edward Muir.

Edward tipped his head forward and back, without looking at anyone in particular, but Franklin shook hands with van Leuwen and me. His handshake was firm, his hand cool, and I liked him immediately.

When Henry returned, Franklin got down from the stool. By way of introduction, van Leuwen said

– Henry, these gentlemen don't like intellectuals.

– Don't they? asked Henry.

Edward said

– We've got too much respect for ideas to respect intellectuals.

Edward's hair was black and short. His face was puffy, his lips full, his eyes slightly oversized behind the lenses of his glasses. There was something priestlike about him: a black jacket, a white shirt, top button buttoned, and black pants.

– Ideas, Edward added, are too important to be thrown around like, like . . . fish or something.

– What he means, said Franklin, is that we admire people who mean what they say. Don't you?

– Yes, said Henry, but ideas are peculiar things. You can't really mean an idea until you've thought it through, played with it.

– That sounds like sophistry, said Edward.

– No, said Franklin, it isn't sophistry, but the problem is we none of us live forever. Who's got time to turn ideas over and over? An honest man knows a good idea when he hears it, instinctively, yeah? If the world was run by intellectuals, Henry, we'd still be in caves arguing about the wheel.

– He's got you there, Henry, said van Leuwen.

– Another round, gentlemen? asked the bartender.

– Allow me, said Franklin.

He paid for the round. This one was taken slowly, as was the one that followed, but the one after that, which came at eleven, was not so much taken as discovered, because the point had come when one forgets who has ordered what and the tavern itself begins to lose its identity. At least, after five of six pints, Henry and van Leuwen had come to that point. Franklin and Edward seemed unaffected by the draughts they drank. Edward was more personable, perhaps, but Franklin spoke coherently on about ideas and civilizations long after either Henry or van Leuwen could appreciate his wit. So, when Henry got up to leave, pleading somnolence, van Leuwen got up with him and they left the bar together.

I stayed to drink with Franklin and Edward.

Outside the tavern, van Leuwen said

– Should we walk?

– Certainly, said Henry.

But as soon as he saw a taxi, van Leuwen flagged it, apologized to Henry, folded himself into the backseat, and went off.

Henry walked on, unperturbed by his friend's departure. He walked back, not unsteadily, in the direction from which they'd first come: north, north over the bridge, contemplating the night sky, the black water of the canal, the lights along the promenade, the hard emptiness of Landsdowne, thinking again of Aquinas, of black metal railings, stone bridges, maple trees, tarred roads, the city and his contemporaries, his contemporaries all wandering through the same warren.

He thought, too, of women, of a certain woman, and of love, a subject never far from his thoughts. Tonight, for instance, it seemed to him that Aquinas, if he'd speculated less about what God wanted and more about what He *is*, would have anticipated all the philosophers of love who came after him. But, then, who were these philosophers of love? The only one who came to mind (as he crossed MacLaren) was . . . Sartre, an atheist. So, if he'd thought more about what God *is*, would Aquinas have come to atheism? Really, if it came to that, the only *true* "philosophers" love had were poets, and *they* brought almost as much confusion to love as philosophers did to the world. The problem, as Henry saw it, was that poets replaced one incoherence with another. Then again, the poet's incoherence was easier to bear, wasn't it?

It often was for him, at least.

––––––––––

When van Leuwen and Wing had gone, Franklin Dupuis held court on his own. He was, it seemed, an intellectual with little patience for intellectuals, a man who did not take himself seriously, though certain moral notions and political ideas were important to him. He was, for instance, devoutly Conservative, liberalism being to him a vile cast of mind. (It had its purpose, of course, what with democracy being, at very least, a two-stroke engine. Still, there was something about the word that suggested a deluge, a deluge of false emotion, hypocritical concern, and endless squirming.) This was not an unusual opinion in Ottawa, but Franklin expressed it with such élan it had the force of original thought. At least, it did for me, that night. For me, it was illuminating to hear belief rather than consideration, feeling before thought.

Edward was a different story altogether. He was as quiet as a shadow, until late in the evening when he'd drunk enough to let himself shed a few opinions. Above all, one felt Edward's devotion to Franklin, his admiration. The only time he expressed an idea that was not an echo of Franklin's, Franklin himself said

– You've been drinking, haven't you, Eddy?

and both men laughed. I felt, in that moment, as if I'd missed something important, but Franklin waved his hand, as at a fly, and returned to the conversation I'd begun: Art, *true* Art, as a civilizing influence, as a way to take joy and depth of feeling from Nature, which, without Art, was nothing but twigs and violence.

Later still, when we'd drunk enough to make us wobble, the conversation grew less abstract.

– Don't forget we're going to Reinhart's studio, said Edward.

– Oh, yes? said Franklin. I haven't seen him for years.

– You saw him last week, said Edward.

– That's true, said Franklin.

And then, to me:

– Reinhart is Edward's closest friend.

– He's your friend too, said Edward.

– I admire Reinhart, said Franklin. He's a real artist, but aside from you, hI 'aven't 'ad a close friend since hI was a hinfant.

– Where you from? I asked.

– I'm from Québec, said Franklin. Can't you tell?

– You don't have an accent. Montréal?

– No, said Franklin. I'm from Baie des Brumes, the Bay of Fog.

– Where's that?

– Far away, said Franklin.

Which is all he would say about it that night, insisting he'd had such a happy childhood his past was obliterated by the warm glow. Really, he remembered very little, save for a handful of impressions (cold grey water and deep blue skies, mostly) and meaningless occasions. For instance, there was the time he pulled a pot of boiling chocolate down on his arm or, again, the time he visited the Kingston pen with his father and couldn't sleep for days, disturbed as he'd been by the harsh lights and the smell of bleach.

– Yes, I said, prisons just aren't civilized.

This was the best my wit would surrender after a tenth beer, but Franklin laughed. (Edward laughed as well, though he didn't seem to know why he was laughing.) So, there was no reason to think my comment had any serious significance. And yet, in retrospect . . .

After we'd had another round, and talked about nothing in particular, after we'd walked homeward, and talked of nothing specific, after I'd suggested Franklin join the Fortnightly Club, his intelligence having impressed me, and long after I'd passed out, head down on my kitchen table . . . The following day, in other words, it seemed to me that my errant comment about uncivilized prisons must have had *some* significance for Franklin, his last words to me having been thanks for my "observation."

– You're absolutely right about prisons, Franklin had said.

4

FRANKLIN DUPUIS

Franklin Dupuis had, in fact, been born in Anse Bleu, not Baie des Brumes, in 1938. Anse Bleu (of which Franklin was ashamed) was newly minted, no more than a year old when his parents, Dr. and Mrs. Dupuis, settled there. It was a scattering of houses by the mouth of the St. Lawrence River: trawlers in the harbour, nets draped over prows; seagulls, seagulls, and sparrows. Whales passed in the St. Lawrence, their grey backs like a school of wandering shale. To the north, the modest mountains held back the world, and the waters of the Manicouagan ran to the sea. Anse Bleu was, in its way, a version of the country itself, holding all of Canada in a few strong lines: trees, rivers, mountains, birds, fish, winter.

It was not, however, a place for Franklin. To begin with, there was the matter of language. His father was francophone, spoke little English, and belonged to the community as the community belonged to him. Dr. Dupuis was not at odds with himself or his world, but his wife, a woman from Neguac, was an outsider who found it difficult to live so far from New Brunswick. Mrs. Dupuis was francophone, but she spoke English to her son, creating for herself a smaller world she shared with her son alone. So, although Franklin grew up in both languages, one (English) was intimate, the other (French) communal.

Franklin could recall his mother's accent, her thick eyebrows, a mole on the side of her nose, her shade of nail polish, and the dress she wore (long and red) on those evenings his parents went out. It wasn't much, but each detail was vivid, and they were, along with English, her only conspicuous legacy because, when Franklin was seven, she died giving birth to a second child, a child that followed her into nothingness, dying fitfully, hours after she did.

Franklin's mother died before he'd learned to live without her, but Anse Bleu lived mindlessly on, flowering into a new self, with aluminium works, hydro-electricity, and whale watching. Dr. Dupuis gradually receded into a second family, marrying a young woman named Hélène, siring a few more children, all girls, a new family that had no special place for a Franklin who, at eleven, spent much of his time in his room speaking English to himself.

Around this time, Dr. Dupuis took his son with him to Kingston, Ontario (the name *Ontario* sounding to Franklin like that of a mysterious and hidden waterfall). It was the doctor's last serious effort to bridge the distance between himself and his son. They drove first to Montréal, where they spent the night, and then on to Kingston where Dr. Dupuis' sister, Hortense, had moved. The road took them through the heart of Québec: passed the swollen bay at Chute-aux-Outardes, along the highway by the wide, blue St. Lawrence, onto the ferry at Les Escoumins, and then to Montréal, at the sight of whose ramshackle outskirts Franklin felt a thrill. Dr. Dupuis tried to engage his son in conversation but, Franklin being quiet, silence overtook them at Trois-Pistoles. And from La Pocatière to Montréal, no further efforts were made by the good doctor.

The following day, Dr. Dupuis was more persistent. Putting discretion aside, the doctor spoke of whatever came to mind. He spoke of everything – except, naturally, of Franklin's mother, a subject neither ever mentioned to the other. He asked about Franklin's plans and Franklin's hopes, but although Franklin appreciated his father's efforts, he could not bring himself to answer with anything more than a few opaque words. (Well, the father having taught the son silence and discretion, the so-called *dark virtues*, it's no surprise that neither ever quite managed to open up to the other, is it?) So, the trip from Montréal to Kingston was as mournful as the previous day's had been.

In Kingston, Franklin's aunt suggested they visit the penitentiary where her husband worked. And from his first sight of the pen, Franklin was intimidated. It wasn't only that the main building was physically impressive. It had a psychological density as well. The building was a disturbing mélange of regal grandeur and near-religious menace.

If the forecourt was intimidating, the interior of the prison was mystifying. The smoothness of the walls and the place's institutional smell filled Franklin with such deep discomfort he felt a kinship with the prisoners, one of whom, for months, haunted his dreams of the penitentiary: a tall black man in prison garb, his hair greying, who walked with a limp. This was the first black man Franklin had seen and the sight puzzled him, because although the man was a prisoner, was being led by two officers, he carried himself with the kind of dignity Franklin associated with pastors or politicians, with men for whom one felt friendship as a matter of course.

As he passed, the prisoner smiled at Franklin and winked. The man's teeth were missing on one side of his mouth, so that Franklin saw, or imagined he saw, the man's tongue. It seemed dreadful that anyone should be so vulnerable.

– Why is he here? Franklin asked his uncle.

– Because he killed his children, was the answer.

Whether this was true or not, Franklin never discovered. It is difficult to tell by a look if a man is murderous, and his uncle, a practical joker, may have been trying to frighten him. If so, he succeeded. Franklin was frightened by the idea of a child killer. And yet, he was also fascinated. Something in his young psyche responded to the suffering he imagined at the heart of the man's being, was attracted to the suffering. And when, in the months that followed, he dreamed recurrently of the prisoner, he dreamed of him as a good man who became evil only when he spoke. This made for unpredictable dreams: Franklin could never tell if the prisoner were going to speak or not, though he himself was always, for some reason, compelled to talk to the man.

The dream stopped as suddenly as it had begun and, for a time, Franklin was not disappointed exactly but dismayed that the dream he anticipated (and feared) no longer came.

So . . . his mother died. He and his father lived on opposite sides of a silence. He did not feel part of Anse Bleu, and he was born with a premonition of his destiny, with the conviction he was meant for more than his hometown could provide. He was, as they say, sleepless in the bed of Being, saved from raw unhappiness by a vivid and distracting imagination and by his ability to keep himself entertained.

––––––––––

Naturally, Franklin fled Anse Bleu as soon as he could, attending Acadia for his first degree (a B.A. in history). But despite the charm of Nova Scotia, despite his repeated and uninhibited exploration of a young woman of Russian descent (Alexandra Byeli, his first love), despite the small, sea-blue beauty of Halifax, a city he visited often, despite his first friendships and his first steps taken in Politics (Conservative), Franklin was not at home in Wolfville. He was in flux, returning to Anse Bleu for the endless and lonely summers spent working at his father's office. It wasn't until 1959, when he went to McGill, that Franklin left Anse Bleu for good. His final impression of the town was of grey sky, grey water, and white houses.

His father paid for his education. His family visited him, from time to time, first in Montréal, where he studied law, and then in Ottawa, where he worked as secretary to Mr. Diefenbaker. But Franklin never set foot in Anse Bleu again, not for his father's funeral, when it came, not for the weddings of his half-sisters, not for any reason, sentimental or otherwise.

———————

Franklin's Montréal was all pavement, noise, and a peculiar impermanence. It was a sense of possibility, a vantage on the wide world. It was a place on which one might impose a vision, if one had the will, but, at McGill, Franklin spent much of his time carousing. There were reasons for this, of course. First, there was something "exotic" about Montreal. Meaning: Franklin did not feel part of the city, though he didn't resent his alienation. Also, he had little sympathy for the new politics; the Catholic mysticism of *Cité Libre* was more appealing than the *Maître chez nous*–ism of Jean Lesage, but they were both "vague." (It seemed to him that Lesage was speaking of a Québec that was not credible. Christmas fiddles, tourtière, endless coffee on Ste-Catherine . . . It was ridiculous to call a collection of bad habits home.) And then again, though he knew in his heart Montréal was not *his* city, it was at McGill that he discovered he had charm, that he could be charming when he wished, and that charm was a perfect counterweight to the solitude he often needed. That is, when he smiled and spoke and put others at ease, they seemed to forgive him his absences, the time spent alone reading Turgeniev's *Spring Thaw* (an inexhaustible gift from Ms. Byeli) and contemplating the painting of Antonio Pollaiuolo, which, even in reproduction, brought him solace.

(When Franklin told me of his admiration for Pollaiuolo, whose paintings he first saw at the Musée des beaux-arts de Montréal, I was a little surprised. I mean, I know of few paintings more brutal than those of Antonio Pollaiuolo, but on reflection,

I think I understand. Franklin was sensitive to suffering. He felt great empathy for those he imagined in physical or mental distress. So it's possible that, in the paintings of Pollaiuolo, he constantly encountered his deepest, most empathetic self, something that would bring solace to most of us, I imagine. On the other hand, though Pollaiuolo's paintings of men are almost unbearably brutal, his portraits of women are inexpressibly graceful. The contrast is striking and I don't know which of Pollaiuolo's paintings he dwelt on, the women or the men. In the end, Franklin's solace in the paintings is, like so many of the details one knows about others, only fleetingly meaningful.)

He did manage to study at McGill, assiduously even, but he was never more than a mediocre student, a bright man with only a middling interest in law. During his years in Montréal, his attention was given to drink, camaraderie, and friendly argument: good-natured naysaying that usually ended, at the end of an evening, with a dismissal of God or any position that smacked of intemperate belief. Of course, Franklin's nihilism was largely conversational, the product of his desire to please. He believed, lightly, in God, but his secular beliefs were unshakeable. At McGill, he was president of the Young Conservatives Club for three terms, and when he earned his degree, he moved to Ottawa to work for the prime minister.

Not a nihilist at all, then; a believer, rather.

———————

From the beginning, Ottawa was a disappointment. Franklin walked into a dull city that smelled faintly of a pulp and paper works. The train station, at the centre of town, was squalid, despite its high ceiling and high windows. It's true that his first view of Centretown, when he stepped from the terminal, was of the Château Laurier in its copper-roofed glory, but right beside the Château was the Daly Building, a soulless box, and the city streets were empty, though it was midday.

Ottawa was a contradiction: a city on the surface, a town in essence, as if Cornwall had conquered Montréal. Nothing of importance was far away; no one lived south of Riverside, no one west of Bronson. You could not be anonymous, as you could in a real city. Instead, you lived on the *verge* of anonymity. It was not a capital in the manner of Rome, Paris, or St. Petersburg. It was an industry town on which the instruments of state (office buildings, politicians, bureaucrats) were imposed. It was a place that drank itself, politely but determinedly, insensate every Friday, and Franklin did not imagine he would stay long.

And yet . . .

In 1962, the presiding spirit, the heart of the city, belonged to Mr. Diefenbaker. Mr. Diefenbaker, owl-faced and tall, genuinely kind and sweetly uxorious, possessed a vision not of himself but of a country like his better self: generous and plain speaking. A smidgen of his charm adhered to the city itself, so it was possible, from the proper angle, to see in Ottawa more than its drab exterior, more than its pasty soul. Of course, some aspect of a prime minister *inevitably* rubbed off on the city. With MacKenzie King, Ottawa was paranoid and grey; with Bennett, poor and resentful. With St. Laurent, the city was optimistic; with Pearson, it would be fresh scrubbed and outward-looking, and with Trudeau, it would become its most splendid self: proud, flamboyant, wilful, and secretive. But when Franklin came to Ottawa, the city held something of Diefenbaker, a man he admired, and that small fact would have great influence on his life.

Not that the Chief was flawless. Franklin, who worked in his office as a clerk or, more accurately, *un homme à tout faire*, was not quite certain what to make of the man. Every morning, Mr. Diefenbaker would greet him in execrable French

– Bong djoor, Mawnseer Dupwiss

and Franklin would answer

– 'morning, John

in what he thought of as Saskatchewanese.

Mr. Diefenbaker could be stubborn, narrow-minded, and thoughtless. He could be distant, preoccupied, a stickler for details that mattered to him alone or to his wife (the annual Christmas dinner for foreign students, for instance). And when he was annoyed, his remarks could be genuinely cruel. He was not flawless, but he hid his flaws from the public so well that there seemed to be two Diefenbakers. And those nearest him, the men and women who worked in his office, were more faithful to the public "Chief" than they were to the Diefenbaker for whom they actually worked.

Though Dief had often called him "witless," "careless," or "inane," Franklin's persistent memories of Mr. Diefenbaker were mostly agreeable. There was, for instance, an afternoon in summer when they walked together by the river. They'd taken egg salad sandwiches from the cafeteria and gone outside to eat. The sky was blue, the city almost white in sunlight, the river greenish and noisy. They stood wordlessly, uncomfortably proximate, regarding the modest sprawl of Hull, and then, when they'd finished eating, when Dief had rubbed a spot of mayonnaise from his lip, they walked along Wellington, the river on their right.

– And what are you going to do with yourself, Mr. Dupuis?

– I don't know, said Franklin.

Mr. Diefenbaker looked at him as if he were suddenly interesting and asked, with faintly sulphureous breath

– Aren't you a lawyer, Mr. Dupuis?

– Almost, sir.

– Then you're halfway hanged already, Mr. Dupuis. You might as well finish the thing and take up politics.

The Diefenbaker who spoke these sweetly bitter words was, for Franklin, the Diefenbaker of Diefenbakers: a little gangly, square-faced, much of his curly hair still dark, with a shock of white, his voice a trifle shaky, his manner casual, but casual for the ages, as if historians lurked wherever he went. They spoke of other things that day, but Franklin particularly remembered the Chief's kind advice, his mildly mocking tone, and sunlight that covered the city like quicklime.

Years later, Franklin took Dief's advice.

He worked with Boluo and Associates in Ottawa, articling with the firm before becoming one of their junior corporate lawyers and, finally, deciding to run for office. He was a "junior" corporate lawyer, yes, but he had mentors from the business world as well as the political. Mr. Diefenbaker, for instance, allowed himself to be seen, smiling, in his vicinity, and Mr. Stanfield, leader of the Conservatives, had confidence in Franklin's youth and his charisma. Franklin was restrained and thoughtful, personable and charming. He believed the Liberals were a nuisance, and he said so with conviction. He was, in other words, a flawless candidate and he should have won his riding (Ottawa West).

In fact, if he'd avoided Ottawa West, if he'd allowed his constituents to use their imagination, he might have won. Instead, inexperienced as he was, he chose to campaign among "his people," without being certain who "his people" were. He went door to door, from Mechanicsville to Nepean, from the Ottawa River to Somerset, stepping into a host of foyers, smiling warmly, unable to disguise his own confidence, pleasing those who liked their politicians smug, alienating most others.

It was the year of Trudeau, it's true, and Trudeau was at least as haughty as Franklin, but Franklin had no talent for the prickly phrase, words that would lodge in the minds and hopes of his constituents. His constituents: doughy faces in darkened interiors, moist hands, simple dresses, ruddy cheeks, hopeful smiles, worried frowns; homes smelling of onions, cabbage, wet shoes; filthy carpets and pebbled plastic doormats, lace doilies and low tables.

On Somerset, an old man, the front of his shirt soaked with the cocoa he drank from a proper porcelain teacup:

– *I'm for you, boy. We haven't voted anything but blue for forty years.*

Off Carling, a black woman with bandages on her head, the fingers on one hand swollen to twice their size:

– *Allayuh cyar come in.*

On Nepean, a young couple, well dressed, living room in amber, smelling of pears, invited him in to speak of their money, their children's education, their mortgage, their old age, smiling kindly:

– *Du thé Monsieur Dupuis? Nous admirons tant notre Trudeau.*

because they mistook him for a Liberal, and were aghast to discover their mistake:

– *Excusez-nous monsieur . . . Mais, quand même, les Conservateurs parlent pas français d'habitude.*

Not all of his encounters were futile or mysterious or bitter, but they were all slightly unreal. Even those whose votes were assured seemed to be voting not for him, nor for his vision of the country. They were voting for the Great Mother, the dignified party, the one that had lifted Franklin up, brushed the lint from his clothes, and proudly sent him out. Of course, Franklin did not have a particularly personal vision of the country. He held to the party's version of Canada, but what was this collection of faces, hands, and accents, of thresholds, doorways, and kitchens? What to make of the country that lurked behind this encounter with its citizens?

What was Canada?

On the evidence, it was a baggy and harmless hydra, a grey beast pulled from its wood-panelled lair by Trudeau, a man who dressed like a dandy and prattled like an academic, by Trudeau who, to his credit, wished the place were nobler than it was, nobler than it wished to be. Yes, that was the insight: a country like Canada, self-blind and addled by the cold, needed a visionary, a man to lead it from nothingness to nobility. Franklin had had no specific vision of the country or, if it comes to that, of his own riding, but he'd campaigned with the arrogance of one who did.

Ambition had so clouded his mind, he had forgotten the basics: an identifiable position, relentless optimism, and good cheer.

He lost Ottawa West by five thousand votes to a Liberal drudge who feigned modesty, in victory, as gracelessly as Franklin, in defeat, feigned pride.

The painful truth was that, at the time, Franklin Dupuis had had nothing to offer save a vision of his own destiny. And what was this "vision," exactly? Well, to begin with, it wasn't quite a vision. It was a sense (one he'd had from childhood) that he was destined to leave an impression, to change the world. He was destined for "something" and this "something" had guided him until, the day after the election, he began to doubt the weight of his destiny and to question his own worth. Was he a great man? Was he the kind of man to whom vision came? Or was he dross? More confounding still was the fact of Pierre Elliott Trudeau. It seemed to Franklin that Trudeau had neither sought nor needed external proof of his own worth. Men like Trudeau drew strength from within, needing no one to feed them. That is, Franklin could not imagine Trudeau devastated (as Franklin had been) by his encounters with his constituents. And, if it came to "vision," well, it seemed Trudeau did not *have* a vision but, rather, embodied a version of the world one could admire or disdain. He *was* his own vision. This idea, banal and, by Franklin, irrefutable, was so troubling it brought out the real abyss that had hidden behind his youthful nihilism. In the face of this, to save his soul, Franklin clung to the idea of his destiny and purpose.

If he had been an unexceptional man, a man with no sense of his own fate, Franklin might have taken heart in defeat. He might have renewed his attempts to win an election, butted his head against the door until he opened it. But, like many who feel "destined," Franklin chose a form of exile. The next fifteen years were a wandering in the wilderness. He abandoned law, studied

Russian, translated (for himself alone) the *Life of Avvakum*, and worked as a parliamentary secretary, working tirelessly, menially, for several Members of Parliament. His exile was lived beside the life he wanted, as a lackey to men who were what he thought he should have been.

Then a new age (or its possibility) glimmered.

Brian Mulroney was chosen to lead the Conservatives and, as if it had been waiting for Brian's advent, something in Franklin came to life. Mulroney seemed wholly admirable and shared Franklin's longing for a united party that acknowledged the differences among people but favoured those who had talent, integrity, destiny, regardless of class or station. With such a leader, if they won an election, the Conservatives might bring something of lasting value to the country: profitable co-existence.

In the months following Mulroney's ascent to the head of the Conservative Party, optimism stole into Franklin's soul, along with an inkling that his time and the party's were twinned. They would rise together.

That is: if he did not yet know what his destiny looked like, he could at least hear its footsteps approaching.

So . . .

It was November 1983, and it was cold and Franklin was on Elgin, walking south, away from the Parliament Buildings. He was going to the studio of an acquaintance, Reinhart Mauer, to meet his friend, Edward. Perseus was well above the horizon and east of Perseus was Andromeda, swimming away from him and away from Cetus, who rose beneath them, as befits a sea monster.

Franklin was wearing a plain black coat, beneath which: a kangaroo jacket that gave him a bohemian allure. The hood of the jacket covered much of his forehead and his ears. (Franklin is a short man, but he has presence. His eyebrows are thick and dark; his nose large and hooked. His bottom lip is fleshy and makes for a slight pout. His cheekbones protrude; he is gaunt. His eyes are slightly sunken, but they are a beautiful brown.)

And what else?

The city smelled, faintly, of smoke.

{ 5 }

IN REINHART'S STUDIO

— Sit still, Eddy, for the love of God.

Edward, dressed like a Venetian doge, stopped fidgeting, though the ermine cap made him itch and he was thoroughly bored. He was relieved Reinhart hadn't asked him to pose nude, and grateful that Reinhart had tired of ecclesiastical subjects and crucifixions.

For some time now, he'd entered his friend's studio with trepidation. In the service of Art, he'd spent hours naked, lashed to bicycles, burnt doors, or chicken wire while Reinhart painted. It was no longer amusing to see himself as Thief, Christ, or Pharisee. The thrill of being painted, if it had ever been thrilling, was long gone, but he sat still for friendship's sake.

Ed Muir and Rein Mauer were as close as close siblings. Reinhart was a year older, but they'd met when he was three and Edward two, so the difference was only a slight impediment. Their parents, Muirs and Mauers, were friends, owned adjoining houses in Manor Park, and so abetted their sons' friendship that Reinhart, who was taller and stronger, spent much of his early childhood protecting the slighter and more fractious Edward.

Edward had been born fractious. It seemed to his parents, who loved him, that he was also born cantankerous or that he became cantankerous moments after the doctor held him by the ankles and let him have it. You wouldn't have called him an evil child, exactly. His parents called him "special" or "difficult," though his difficulty lay less in what he did than what he did not: he rarely smiled, he did not like to be held, and he did not like toys (with the single exception of a wooden squirrel – ancient, its paint rubbed off long before it was given to him, not at all lovely).

Edward's gloom permeated what had been a joyful home and dampened the mood, until the birth of his sister, Anne, and the beginning of his friendship with Reinhart, events that took place within months of each other. It wasn't that Edward suddenly became outgoing or friendly, but he was both of those things, some of the time, with Reinhart, and he was both of those things, much of the time, around his little sister, whom, despite his temper, he adored. In fact, from the age of three to eighteen, when he first met Franklin Dupuis, Edward was somewhat spiteful, mean at times, but also thoughtful, optimistic, and, above all, loyal. He was fiercely devoted to his sister and to Reinhart, blindly loyal, unable to think anything but the best of those he loved. To Edward, Reinhart was, simply, a talented and generous man. Not that he was unaware of Reinhart's peculiarities: Reinhart was pre-emptory. When he was on about something, when he was inspired, you couldn't have a conversation with him. Reinhart was tireless. When he was inspired, Reinhart could go for days without bathing, eating, talking – not that unusual, save that he expected the same passion of Edward, Edward whose passions were more restrained. And, really, it was no picnic sitting for hours beneath a moth-eaten cape. Reinhart was homosexual. But Reinhart himself made so little of it, Edward imagined his homosexuality as a kind of drastic horsing around. Besides, Edward himself had ambivalent feelings for women. He was heterosexual, and loved the smell of women, but something in him could not stand the emotional clutter sex brought, the gratitude (his, hers), the exhausting late-night condolences, the "when next?" and "is this it?" He had not found the woman with whom he could build a nest, with whom he could live forever and ever, amen, and he often wondered if she mightn't be easier to find if she were male. This being the case, he saw his friend's proclivities in a flattering light: Reinhart chose his sexual partners rationally. That is, he slept with men because they were easier to get along with.

Reinhart was almost as devoted to Edward, devotion springing from similarity. For instance, both had been dour, inward children. They'd spent hours together doing nothing at all, at ease with talk or silence, and this habit of ease never left them. That's not to say their affection for each other was untested. Painting divided them.

Reinhart had always loved to draw and had, from the time he could hold a pencil, scribbled on the paper his parents gave him. At first he drew without meaning to draw, mindlessly tracing the horses in racing forms or the faces in *Redbook* and *Chatelaine*. You wouldn't have said he was interested in Art. He was unimpressed by the books his parents bought him, flipping through the monographs on van Gogh, Monet, and Seurat as if they didn't concern him. And then, at eleven, without prompting, Reinhart began to read about Art, to drag his parents to the National Gallery. Everything changed. Over the next ten years, he spent hours in the National Gallery, studying the early work: El Greco, Rubens, Hals. At fifteen, he began to dress in his own version of finery: dark capes, frilled shirt fronts, narrow pants, bowler hats, anything his indulgent parents allowed, anything that caught Reinhart's eye on their rare visits to a costume shop in Toronto. For a time, he even affected an Italian accent, in honour of Masaccio, Giotto, Spinello Aretino . . . names read in books on the Renaissance, their works poorly reproduced in old monographs about old churches.

What inspired this mania for painting, Reinhart himself couldn't have said. The blue of a Poussin sky (in reproduction), the trees in a Fra Angelico (in reproduction), the curve of a shoulder in an otherwise dull Pontormo (yes, ditto)? Or was it the sky itself, or a colour wheel from Lefranc & Bourgeois, or the soapy smell of a boy he'd decimated? Whatever it was, his devotion was happy, slightly obsessive, and it pushed his gloom aside. By the time he finished high school, Rein Mauer lived more comfortably with the dead, with Brunelleschi and Dürer, Holbein and Alberti, than with the living. His contemporaries and their concerns were an unwanted distraction.

He studied architecture at Carleton, but only to please his parents, who worried that painting would not help him to pay the rent. He was not an architect. He didn't care for the fashionable modernism of Le Corbusier or Sullivan. His taste ran to things older. Yes, his knowledge of materials, physics, math, and design was impeccable, but what architect could take Reinhart's world of domes, towers, marble, and wood seriously? He was, perhaps, sadly, a little out of step with the times? Yes. He was, to his own detriment, obstinate? Yes. But what of it? It was painting that moved him, not architecture, and no one who heard him speak of this or that painter (Max Beckman, say, or Franz Marc), of this or that technique (egg tempera on stone or paraffin encaustic with northern umber), could doubt the depth of his passion.

Reinhart had given his soul to painting.

From early on, Edward was Reinhart's preferred model. For Edward, the "privilege" was, at first, flattering and sometimes tiring. He did not begrudge Reinhart the hours, but the nudity, stillness, and contortions of modelling were made bearable only by his admiration and respect for Reinhart. He did not think Art worth the suffering, though he would have said he did, if Reinhart had asked. It would have felt disloyal, otherwise. On the other hand, it occurred to him, every now and then, that in being dishonest he was also being disloyal. How to resolve the matter?

– What's wrong, Eddy? I can see you thinking.

– Can we call it a night? This hat's itching. Besides, Franklin should be here any time.

They had been at it for an hour. The sky was black and from his window Reinhart could see the three-quarter moon.

– Why don't we go on 'til Franklin gets here? he asked.

6

ARS LONGA VITA BREVIS

— Why don't we go on 'til Franklin gets here?
The sky was black and from the window of the studio you could see the moon. Reinhart's studio was in a square, decrepit building on Argyle, near Elgin. On the ground floor, the Spanish ambassador kept a modest suite of offices whose purpose was obscure: no one ever entered, no one left. The rest of the building, whose elevator worked only in winter, was given over to studios, storage, and lofts.

As it was not quite winter, Franklin walked up to Reinhart's studio and knocked on the metal door. He heard a muffled phrase, then nothing. He was about to knock again when the door swung out and open.

– Yes? asked Reinhart.

Franklin looked up and smiled.

– How are you, Reinhart? he said

and put out his hand.

Reinhart, whose hands were dirty, put his elbow forward and said

– Wonderful. Come in. How are you, Frank?

And, walking away from the door:

– Okay, Eddy, your saviour's here.

The studio was a thousand square feet of not much. The wooden floor was cracked and squeaky, its crevices black with dirt. The grimy panes of five tall windows took up most of one wall. The other walls were white. Against two of them: innumerable paintings, faces turned from view. Along the third: a small fridge, a sink, a door, a metal cabinet, a folding screen, folding chairs, a roll of canvas.

In the middle of all this stood Reinhart, dressed in honey-coloured pants and a green-and-white smock. A few feet from him, Edward stood beside a high-backed, velvet-cushioned chair. He was in a royal blue gown, white leopard-skin shawl, and a blue-and-gold Venetian hat that rose to a soft peak at the back.

– Franklin . . . , he said.

– I hope I'm not interrupting your sitting, said Franklin.

Reinhart said

– Not at all. We had to finish sometime, I guess.

– I'm getting out of these things then, okay? asked Edward.

– Hmm . . ., answered Reinhart.

Edward moved behind the folding screen to change his clothes. Franklin approached the canvas to look at Reinhart's work. For some time now he had been fascinated by it. Something in the work touched the depths of him: bold lines, light colours, more drawing than painting, with the particular charm of a work in progress, direction without a clear terminus.

– A lovely painting, said Franklin.

Without turning to him, Reinhart mildly said

– You know it's still the underpainting.

– Yes, I know, but I was going to say it looks like you're working in the old way, from the underdrawing up, light colours first, dark colours last, so external light goes from the surface of the painting to the depth. It gives the painting something like internal illumination, doesn't it?

Reinhart turned to Franklin.

– I'm sorry, Frank. I didn't know you knew about all this.

And despite his mistrust of people who talked about painting, Reinhart generously gave Franklin a short tour of the underpainting, pointing out how and where his own technique diverged from that of the Old Masters.

The truth is, Franklin was not familiar with the techniques of painting. Rather, he'd been reading Meyer's *Handbook*, inspired by his fascination with Reinhart's work. The *Artist's Handbook* was dry as dust, but every once in a while it illuminated some aspect of painting, illuminated both Reinhart and Pollaiuolo at once.

What's more, Franklin did not usually admire "modern art." There were at least two aspects of it he found off-putting: the work itself (it meant nothing to him) and the people who produced it. The work was a simple matter. It seemed a morass of splatters or barber poles on canvas. That which wasn't on canvas seemed, most of it, an excuse to repeat the same tired question: what is Art? In fact, there was for Franklin something like a line in history, a moment somewhere around 1400. Before 1400, Art had been an expression of Man, Nature, and God. After 1400, it was a remembering, and by 1900, it was all a forgetting. Really, a world that did not know what Art was could not be expected to produce it, and one might as well admit that, in our time, with few exceptions, Art expressed nothing. It was a make-work program for the sensitive, or a longing for itself. There were still artists, of course, and, in his way, Franklin pitied them: the good and the bad, the ones who knew they were lost and the ones who didn't. He pitied them because he thought he understood their dilemma. They were worshippers of an eclipsed god, with nothing left but plain rituals and old rites.

Reinhart and Reinhart's work were different, however. You could see (or Franklin could see) Reinhart was one of those for whom Art was a communion with all that was best in the human psyche: God, the land, the minutiae of the day to day, which, on canvas, was not minutiae at all but the sacred in its day-to-day disguise. This "communal communion" is what touched him, and it was why Franklin occasionally opened Meyer's *Handbook* in the hope he would some day understand the force of work like Reinhart's.

When Reinhart finished his short talk on underpainting, he wiped a stroke from his painting, as if he were wiping the mouth of a toddler.

Franklin nodded wisely and, when Edward joined them, said

– Reinhart, why don't you join us for a drink? It's on me.

They drank at the Metropolitan. It was more restaurant than bar. The ceiling was low. The interior was dark. The fare was expensive and you couldn't see what you were eating, but it had a good reputation. A waiter approached, filled their glasses with ice water, and waited for their order.

– Something to eat? Franklin asked Reinhart.

– I'm not hungry, said Edward.

– How is the couscous and merguez? asked Reinhart.

– Ahh, said the waiter. Our chef, Mr. Sinna, is from el-Andalus.

Reinhart looked the waiter over, smiled, and gently touched his forearm.

– El-Andalus, eh? Then, I'll have to have the merguez and a Pilsner Urquell.

– Two Pilsners, said Franklin.

– Three, said Edward.

– Three in all, added Franklin.

– Very good, said the waiter.

The waiter was short, broad-shouldered, and handsome by candlelight. His hair was thick, black, recently combed, and Reinhart felt an almost irresistible desire to pull his head back by the hair.

– What would it take to build the perfect city? asked Franklin.

– What? said Reinhart. That's a strange question.

– Well, what would it take to build a cathedral, then? Theoretically.

– Money, said Reinhart. Much money. But why are you asking me?

– You're an architect, aren't you, Reinhart?

– And you're building a cathedral?

– No, no, said Franklin. It's just something that interests me: cities and buildings.

– Interesting interest, Reinhart said. So, what's the point of this cathedral?

– It's a place of worship, answered Franklin, but it should instill . . . what's the word? Reverence. We live in such decrepit times.

– And you want to improve them? That's wonderful, but it's not like there aren't enough cathedrals in this city already, you know.

Edward, who, to this point, had kept quiet, basking in the presence of his closest friends, happy to sit by as they exchanged ideas, said

– A cathedral that could instill reverence *would* be pretty interesting, though, wouldn't it?

– Sure, said Reinhart

though his mind was squarely on the waiter, the waiter who, when he'd brought their beer, had looked him in the eyes and smiled.

– Sure, Reinhart repeated, but I'm not really an architect. I studied architecture and I work for Kessler and McAdams, a firm of architects, but my real love is painting.

– You're an artist, said Franklin.

Reinhart squinted to look at the man: Franklin's nose looked longer by candlelight, his eyes black, his lips dark. One of Franklin's eyebrows was raised and there was something like mistrust to his posture, but his manner was polite and encouraging.

He's not a bureaucrat at all, thought Reinhart. He's a politician. In Reinhart's experience, politicians were the only beings who could say so many contradictory things without speaking.

The waiter brought the couscous and merguez from the kitchen and put his hand on Reinhart's shoulder.

– Would you care for hot sauce? he asked. It's our own.

– Yes, please, answered Reinhart.

The merguez was marvellous, but the red paste was hot. Reinhart felt as if it were tormenting him, but he couldn't stop and he invited Franklin and Edward to share it with him. Franklin took a little of the paste with a mouthful of couscous.

– It's good, he said. (Without flinching.)

– I don't know how you can eat it, said Edward.

The rest of the evening passed agreeably.

They drank until they were just beyond comfortable, and Edward, though still thrilled at the company of two interesting men, allowed himself to speak about the state of the world, by which point Franklin suggested it was time to call it a night. It was only eleven, early by certain standards, but there was work the next day.

The waiter brought Reinhart a plate of green and yellow peppers and a generous shot of raki.

– I think I'll stay a little longer, said Reinhart.

– Oh, said Franklin. Okay. But listen . . . I honestly love your work.

– Thanks, said Reinhart. I really appreciate it.

They shook hands and Reinhart raised his eyebrows in farewell as Edward and Franklin left the Metropolitan, but Reinhart's mind was on other things the moment they were out of sight: the warmth of the raki, the meaning of the word *haunches*, the way the waiter's little finger was at an eccentric (and erotic) angle to his hand. He forgot Franklin, Edward, buildings, and cities as soon as the waiter brought him another drink.

7

IN WHICH: RUNDSTEDT

I t wasn't Franklin alone who took the coming of Brian Mulroney for a bright portent. The Progressive Conserva-tives, led by the Right Honourable Brian, were all of them full of hope for the future. It's true, conservatism's future is usually a version of the past, and Mulroney's conservatism was no excep-tion. It took its cues from the recently successful, backward-leaning Grand Old Party (U.S.A.), which was as it should be, because it is a conservative's moral duty to hold to a time in which the world was good, to hold to the past, in other words. So, the last half of 1983 was an exciting time, a time of ideas, expectations, and hope. Mulroney was a godsend: a man from Quebec who would keep the French in line, soothe the West, and bring prosperity to all, a prosperity Canada had not seen since days long gone.

Of course, Franklin was well placed to share in the prevailing optimism. Though he'd sworn off campaigning, he had not aban-doned the party. Yes, there was lingering suspicion that a man who could so easily leave a career in law was, to put it kindly, unstable. But, in the new Conservative mood, anything might be forgiven. Besides, Franklin had worked with Stanfield and toiled for Clark and, before the leadership convention that brought Mulroney to power, he'd let anyone who'd listen know of his deep respect for his compatriot, Brian Mulroney. What's more, Franklin was now a secretary to the Right Honourable Pierre Boudreau, of Rouyn-Noranda, and Pierre Boudreau was a close friend of the Right Honourable Brian.

If there was a cloud on Franklin's horizon, it was his continued devotion to (and fondness for) Diefenbaker. How quickly the Chief had changed from a respected leader to an embittered and poisonous relic, a blind but vicious mastiff in a corner of the house. In 1976, Diefenbaker had attacked the young Brian, whom he thought a treacherous pup, and helped sink his first leadership campaign. By that time Diefenbaker thought everyone treacherous, the universe in a conspiracy against him, but young Brian had taken his rebuff personally and, in 1983, the newly honourable Brian was not fond of Dief's partisans. And, yes, there were still Dief partisans on the Hill. They reminisced about the old man, about the old Conservative Party, about the funeral of 1979 when John's corpse was paraded before the public, like an owl in a box, before being shipped to Saskatchewan.

Franklin himself did not reminisce often, but his admiration for Diefenbaker was no secret. If pressed, he would admit that he had not known the man in his best days, that he'd been saddened by Dief's bitter pontifications (*"towards the end . . ."*), and he would add that, it seemed to him, Mulroney was all that the young Diefenbaker had been and, perhaps, more. Franklin was proud of his association with Dief and, naturally, he had the respect of those who still had affection for the old curmudgeon, but he easily sided with Mulroney and the bright, new Progressive Conservative Party.

Boudreau's offices were in the Centre Block. He had two suites, 642S and 641S, one on either side of the hallway, both modest. Boudreau's own (642) had space for two desks, several filing cabinets, and four bookcases. He shared this one with Mary Stanley, his secretary. The other (641) was for Franklin, his research assistant.

It was small and windowless, with room for a desk, a bookcase, and little else.

There was something paperish about Franklin's office. The bookshelves were congested with bound Hansards, full binders, and office supplies, but that wasn't it. The office wasn't so much desiccated as desiccating. The room itself was like yellowing paper. Franklin was happiest in the library or the cafeteria or even the offices of other assistants and other Members, but when he had time to socialize, Franklin's favourite refuge was the office of Albert Rundstedt (644S), the Member from Calgary West. The office was as uninteresting as any in Centre Block, but Rundstedt's company was diverting. To put it plainly: Rundstedt was the kind of man who would not have believed you if you told him he was *not* universally admired. He would have put his arm around your shoulders and offered solace for your delusional state. He wasn't simply a "good guy" from out west. He was a true believer in his own irresistibility, and, though he could be annoying, the heat of his self-confidence was, more often than not, like an invitation to bask and unwind, agreeable.

For Franklin, who liked the man, Rundstedt was, in many ways, the opposite of the usual politician. He was less restricted intellectually, more attentive to his constituents than to systematic (that is, Conservative) thought. He was also slightly peculiar. He was "peculiar" in the usual ways, of course: his friendliness was (perhaps) a mask, he was (often, almost certainly) devious, and he was not unwilling to blame his own failures on his hirelings. These particular failings were common and only mildly disturbing to Franklin, who had come to accept that there is no political achievement without self-regard or ruthlessness, or self-regard and ruthlessness or, for that matter, ruthless self-regard.

However, Rundstedt was peculiar in his own way as well. He seemed, at times, possessed by the idea of incarceration. Now, Conservatives of every stripe had faith in prisons the way Liberals had faith in "tolerance," but Rundstedt had actually read a few things about prisons and prisoners: articles and such, mostly. He had paid attention to the lectures on deviance when he'd taken first-year sociology, so he recognized the names of Sade and Solzhenitsyn, Villon and Verlaine, without being certain who they were or what they had done. He'd even thought about studying games theory in order to fathom the Prisoner's Dilemma but had been mystified by the calculation involved.

For all that, Rundstedt was not an intellectual. He believed prison was the best resource of a careful society, and that proposition was the full extent of his "philosophy," a philosophy that certainly didn't alienate him from Franklin, though Franklin was sometimes dismayed by the manner in which the subject overtook Rundstedt, from time to time. One moment they'd be speaking of something banal and unprovocative (the weather, say) and the next Rundstedt would be off on one of his tangents: *Why, oh why, don't people understand that prison is a golden resource for all concerned, for society, for lawmakers, for the prisoners themselves? What is it that keeps the citizen from his own good?*

Perhaps because he was unaccustomed to voicing ideas that might be thought controversial, Rundstedt's face would turn a light pink and his voice would rise. Staring at Franklin's forehead, he would speak at him or through him, and Franklin would feel himself disappear. Rundstedt's thoughts never took long to express and, as if embarrassed at having voiced an opinion, he would return, mildly, to the subject at hand – the weather, say.

Though Franklin was unsettled by these sudden shifts in conversation, he admired Rundstedt's passion, its stimulating chaos. More than that, he felt kinship with a man who shared his fascination with prisons and the process of punishment, a fascination that had been, until he met Rundstedt, long unexpressed. And once Mulroney came to power, Franklin even began to encourage Rundstedt's diatribes, encouraging Rundstedt to take his own convictions seriously. The two of them would spend hours fancifully considering unusual details: the layout of the Bastille, the sense (or not) of Scandinavian blood guilt, the idea of "justice," its relative value . . .

Franklin had no political power to speak of and, before the election, Rundstedt had not much more. But Rundstedt had two things going for him, where influence was concerned. First, he was acquainted with Mulroney. Second, and more importantly, there were some mucky-mucks who found his passion for "law and order" appealing. A correctional institute, whatever its raison d'être, provided employment for a host of constituents, from architects and contractors to guards and administrators. In practical terms, an institute of correction was as useful as a museum, a gallery, or a church. In practical terms, there was little difference among them. So when Rundstedt began to make serious, preelectoral noise about a new federal prison, though it was a noise he (and any number of others) habitually made before every election, he had the attention of his peers.

8

A PROPOSITION AND A LETTER

Mary Stanley was on her way to the restaurant when she heard a Member of Parliament say
– I speak what appears to me the general opinion, and where an opinion is general it is usually correct.

And she thought, How pompous the men from small towns can be. They came from towns of "youse," "boughten," and "pogey," but it was rare to hear them speak their own dialects. They stepped into Ottawa as if they'd stepped from Westminster Abbey. The man who'd spoken was from Moosonee. He'd raised his voice to give his opinion on opinions, but it was as if he were not from Canada at all.

Perhaps he was rehearsing for the election.

Moosonee and his assistant brushed past her on their way to the restaurant, leaving a whiff of toothpaste, the rumps of their grey suits rumpled. No, it was the attitude she disliked. It was not the accent. Franklin, whose office was across the hall from hers, spoke with an unplaceable accent and she was not put off; but then, Franklin never raised his voice. He looked at you, not through you, and he listened. It was rare that anyone listened, and listening itself was an intimacy. There was something feminine about him, and gentle. She could speak to Franklin about anything,

about her grandmother, her family, her thoughts on this and that
. . . and always: he listened and asked thoughtful questions, and
although he was not at all her type, much older, she found him
appealing.

Older . . . a little older? How old was he? He rarely spoke about
himself, but he was older than she was: twenty-one, her light
brown skin unblemished, her figure slight and beautiful. Not too
young and besides, the years between any two people are insignificant if there is understanding, yes?

It was two o'clock. She'd been invited to lunch by the Member
from Athabasca, but he and his secretary had, at virtually the
same instant, remembered a call they could not miss and they
had rushed back to their offices, leaving Mary to dine alone but
on Athabasca's card. On offer was something called Lobster
Newburg.

– Le homard s'il vous plaît.

– Okay, d'abord, mais j'sais pas s'il me reste du pain.

Unfortunately, "il en restait" and it was toasted, or had been
toasted. It was now chewy, with blackened edges. Beneath its
Newburg glue, the lobster had the consistency of soft plastic. Yet
it was good, or good enough, because Mary was, after a year, still
captivated by the restaurant itself, an inner sanctum where, occasionally, you found yourself sitting beside men and women who
mattered. She knew that habitués found the fare uninteresting,
and she herself had taken to complaining about the meals,
though she seldom dined there and, really, she was captivated.

She ate the lobster in silence, leaning over her plate, one hand
in her lap. She did not notice the entrance of Franklin and
Rundstedt. They sat by a pillar on the other side of the restaurant.
It was not until she got up to leave that she saw them. She
approached their table.

– Franklin, she said. Do you know if Mr. Boudreau is going to
be in the office this afternoon?

– I don't think so, Franklin answered.

– Busy, busy, and darned busy, said Rundstedt.

– He decided to meet Mr. Simard at the Château, Franklin continued. He didn't know when he'd be back.

– Oh, said Mary. That's what I thought. Okay. See you in the office.

Looking down, she saw that the side of her skirt had brushed the table as she spoke. There was dust on it and as she walked away from them she distractedly hit at the skirt, to the side and behind her.

As if he were a ladies' man, Rundstedt said

– Now that is admirable.

– What is? asked Franklin.

– Oh, the skirt, the skirt, said Rundstedt. I'm a married man. I didn't notice the woman in it.

– Is it a sin to notice? asked Franklin.

– Only if you're Catholic, son.

– Yes, that's great, said Franklin. But you were saying?

They'd been talking about prisons, about the upcoming elections, about the solitude of electoral campaigns, and, most important, about Rundstedt's chances for re-election, a subject of interest to Franklin.

– Hard to lose when there's no opposition, said Rundstedt.

– No one's running against you?

– Not unless you count the Liberal.

He would have his fourth term, then, no doubt about it. He was, by his own reckoning, a wonderful Member of Parliament: balm for his constituents, balm for Calgary. The only cloud, as far as he could see, might be Mulroney himself, because Rundstedt had, as did most Westerners, an almost inbred mistrust of all Québécois. Perhaps Brian was the exception, but it would take some convincing and it was possible Rundstedt's constituents would resent the Conservatives' turn to Quebec. Then again, the Liberals were saddled with John Turner, the Bay Street nudist.

– He's a nudist?

Rumours were a dime a dozen, these days. What hadn't people said about Turner? Still, what one wouldn't give for a clear photograph of the man and his shortcomings. The very idea filled Rundstedt with glee, not that he wanted to see Turner's short arm, you understand.

– Of course not, said Franklin.

Really, there was something immaturely carnal about Rundstedt.

– Anyways, said Rundstedt, what about Boudreau? Harder for a Conservative to win in Qweebec than Alberta. Course, Boudreau's not a real Conservative. I don't think they make 'em in Qweebec. They're all busy sucking federal tit, doesn't matter what party. No offence.

– None taken, said Franklin.

For a time, they ate in silence. Rundstedt dipped pieces of crust into the Lobster Newburg, as if he were eating the yolk of a soft-boiled egg. Franklin nudged the Newburg with his fork, risking a mouthful only after due consideration. He didn't care for food doused in cream.

– You ran for election a while back, didn't you, Frank? Ever think of running again?

– Not really.

– Why not?

– Gun shy, said Franklin.

Rundstedt was about to deliver his speech on courage, hard knocks, and the remounting of horses when, reaching for a glass of water, he noticed the time. He rose from the table, put a hand on Franklin's shoulder, and said

– You know, if Boudreau doesn't make it, you can come work for me. I can use a good assistant.

– Thank you, Franklin said.

– Even if Boudreau *does* make it, come work for me. It'd be good for you, Frank. Gotta go.

Then, he left.

Despite his brave words, Rundstedt was worried about the election, and Franklin knew it. Rundstedt was worried about the slip-ups that marred the best campaign: an uninspired platform, a sullen wife, unmanageable children, unintended revelations of private matters. No election is won before votes are counted. Still, Rundstedt was as secure as a politician could be. He was a conservative in Alberta, than which, none is more secure.

Franklin sat at the table alone, distractedly pushing pieces of lobster to one side of his plate. This was a fateful moment, for him. Or so it felt. Here was a chance to re-enter politics through a different door than the first he'd taken, with someone who understood and appreciated Franklin's opinions and ideas.

A man touched Franklin's arm.

– Je regrette, monsieur, mais nous fermons.

– Comment?

– Le restaurant est fermé.

It was the chef himself, or perhaps one of his assistants. The man's whites were dirty and the cap on his head tilted to one side, rakishly, you might have said if it were possible to be rakish in kitchen whites and a toque.

– Monsieur n'a pas aimé le homard?

– Si, mais j'avais moins faim que je n'pensais.

As he walked back to his office, Franklin found himself thinking of Mary Stanley. It struck him, not for the first time, that the young woman had an "interest" in him. He felt about her "interest" a kind of confusion. He was not handsome, and he knew it. He did not think himself particularly witty and he was not physically prepossessing. So what was there in him to attract the interest of a young woman? The thought made him smile, as at some subtle humour he couldn't really grasp. Himself, attractive? How strange. And yet, her "interest" made her more interesting to him as well. For instance, he found he could listen to the particulars of her life – her conflicts with her mother, her strange grandmother – without boredom. Given how few women had attracted his attention since Alexandra had abandoned him, it sometimes felt as if he were, again, in Mary's company, awakening, again, to the world of sentiment.

And it was with this thought in mind, as he walked back to his paper-filled office, that Franklin resolved to accept Rundstedt's proposition. He would work for the man, if, that is, Boudreau allowed it, and perhaps bring something of himself to bear on the work they hoped to do: prisons, prisoners, law and order . . .

– Franklin?

On hearing his footsteps (and then his key jiggling in the lock of 641), Mary had got up to show Franklin a letter they'd received from one of Mr. Boudreau's constituents. She had called his name from within her own office, but when she reached the door, she saw that Franklin hadn't heard. He was bent over the doorknob, keys in hand, a look of intense concentration on his face.

– F . . . , she began again

but changed her mind, not wishing to disturb his thoughts. She withdrew from the hallway, returning to the letter she'd left on her desk:

Cher Monsieur le très honorable,

Je ne sais pas écrire et je suis aveugle. C'est ma fille Micheline qui écrit pour moi. Aussi j'ai perdu les doigts de ma main droite lors d'un accident de chasse. Comme vous voyez, ma vie n'est pas facile ces jours-ci et mon mari est en prison.

Je n'aime pas me plaindre parce que je sais que Dieu va s'occuper de moi. Mais j'ai des enfants. J'en ai quatre. J'avais six mais deux son morts pendant l'hiver, dont Roger et Georges, mes plus jeunes, et il n'est pas facile de voir ses enfants mourir même quand on ne voit plus.

Malgré ma mauvaise fortune, je ne vous aurais pas écrit si ce n'était pas pour mes enfants. Étant aveugle, je ne peux plus travailler à l'usine, et on menace de m'enlever les petits.

Alors, Monsieur le très honorable, vous voyez que ce n'est pas pour moi-même que je vous demande un peu d'argent.

Nous n'avons pas besoin de beaucoup. Si vous pouvez trouver en votre honorable soi un peu de pitié pour une aveugle et les quelques enfants qui lui restent, cinq mille dollars (5 000) nous protégeraient surement du loup à notre porte.

Bien à vous,

Nicole Lévesque[1]

---

[1] Dear Honourable Sir,

I do not know how to write and I am blind. My daughter Micheline is writing this for me. Also, I lost all the fingers on my right hand in a hunting accident. As you can see, my life is not easy these days and my husband is in prison.

I do not like to complain, because I know the good Lord will take care of me. But I have children. I have four of them. I used to have six, but my youngests, Roger and George, died this winter, and it's not easy to see your children die, even when you're blind.

Despite my misfortune, I would not have written you if it weren't for my children. Being blind, I can no longer work at the factory, and they're threatening to take my children away.

And so, Your Honour, you can see that it is not for myself that I'm asking for money.

We do not need much. If you could find it in your Honourable Self to take pity on a poor blind woman and the children still left to her, $5,000 would surely keep the wolf from our door.

Yours truly,

Nicole Lévesque

It was this letter she had meant to show Franklin. It was a hoax. There was no Nicole Lévesque, no blindness, no children. And although someone had taken the trouble to write the letter by hand, it was accompanied by a folded, stamped manila envelope whose address was typed: *Nicole Lévesque c/o Merci Des P'tits* in Chicoutimi.

It wasn't the address that gave it away, however. Mary had read it in good faith, rather moved by the thought of a fingerless woman and her daughter, until she came to the "cinq mille dollars" and the "loup à la porte." Five thousand bucks and a wolf at the door? She had heard that before. This same letter, in English, had only recently made the rounds of Parliament. It may even have elicited contributions, until a secretary had actually looked for Mrs. Lévesque and discovered that Nicole did not exist, that "Nicole" was, in reality, an Algerian national who was not of sound mind.

Although Mary had not been gulled, it was infuriating that a thing she'd taken for naive and ill bred (the handwriting) was *meant* to look naive and ill bred, its naiveté part of a design. Someone had practised that hand, had practised it with her, or someone like her, in mind. But the most disturbing thing was that, despite herself, she *had* been moved, moved by what she assumed was the desperation at the root of the letter, moved by the idea of a family in crisis.

Of course, the tensions in her own family were much on her mind at the time, and something in the letter's tone (aggrieved, threatening, touching) reminded her of her grandmother, Eleanor. Eleanor, old and lonely, had begun to lose herself, and it upset Mary deeply to think about her grandmother's mortality.

Not that Eleanor was what you'd call a grandmotherly grand-mother. No, she was intricate in ways Mary could not fathom and she could be prickly. For instance, she seemed to dislike her son, Stanley. No, not "seemed." Eleanor clearly disliked her son; though, whenever Mary was with them, Eleanor tried to disguise her feelings. (At such moments, it seemed to Mary her grand-mother was like a dog that growls at a stranger until someone from the house comes in.) What made the situation even more difficult to understand was the love Mary felt for both of them, her father *and* her grandmother.

The love she felt for her father was uncomplicated. It was love for one of the most agreeable men she had ever met. He was so easygoing, it hadn't always been clear her love was reciprocated, wasn't clear until she was old enough to understand and appreci-ate his unflappable good nature. And this understanding deep-ened the mystery of Eleanor's animosity. How could she dislike such a loving man? There was no obvious answer, so, after years of wondering, Mary had finally got up the nerve to ask her grand-mother if she loved Stanley.

She hadn't asked directly. Though she and her grandmother were very close, Mary chose to come at the matter from the side. She'd asked

– Gran, do you love Dad as much as you love me?

Eleanor had looked at her coldly, as if exactly sizing the degree of her offence and then, offended, had answered

– Of course

and refused to speak to her for a week.

It had been a sad, guilt-addled week for Mary. She'd felt ashamed at having broached a subject she'd suspected was sensi-tive, but the week's dénouement was disturbing. After seven days, her grandmother had called her to her bedroom and had chided her for being an unworthy grandchild, *not* because Mary had ques-tioned her affection for Stanley, but, rather, because Mary had been "avoiding her." For some reason, Eleanor had mistaken her own unwillingness to speak to Mary for Mary's indifference. It seemed uncalculated, as if her grandmother had genuinely forgot-ten both their contretemps *and* her refusal to speak.

To Mary, this was mystifying. Her grandmother had always been a woman in control of her faculties. Eleanor often insisted on her own frailty, but, in all the time her grandmother had lived with them, Mary had seen little sign of it. She'd wondered if, in chiding her for her "absence," Eleanor were being unfair as well as unkind and then, after reflection, put the whole thing down to "age" (such a small word to hide so many cataclysms) and that had saddened her even more. The time would come, wouldn't it, when Eleanor needed her as much as this fictitious "Nicole" needed her "Micheline"? Yes, it would. And that is why, when she discovered the letter's dark intent, the hoax at the heart of it, Mary took it personally, as if she herself had been betrayed. She had thought to tell Franklin of her distress when, seeing him hard at work, or just about, she suddenly felt abashed at the thought of sharing so much; and so, she buried her feelings and got on with the business of the day.

9

A FAMILY DIVIDED

Mary's family was divided against itself. Mary's mother, Beatrice, disliked and resented her mother-in-law because of the way Eleanor treated her (with indifference) and because of the way she treated Stanley (with barely hidden contempt). Mary's father had feelings for his mother that were complex. They were a constant sifting of love and wariness. And then, finally, there was Mary's younger brother, Gilbert, whose feelings for his grandmother consisted of dislike and affection. He disliked Eleanor but remembered a time when she was fond of him and, for this, he could not entirely dismiss what love he felt.

And Eleanor's feelings?

Eleanor had been living with her son's family for three years. She had convinced her son to take her in because, she said at the time, she feared the onset of senility and death. It had not taken much convincing. Though she had never been a loving mother, her son was a dutiful and kind man. He would have taken her in whatever her condition.

Mind you, he could not afford her. The house on Spadina was too small. There had been just enough room for himself, his wife, their daughter, and their son, so Eleanor's intrusion had caused hardship. To begin with, Beatrice was not pleased to have Eleanor live with them. Throughout the years, Eleanor had treated her and Stanley with unsheathed scorn. Because she loved her husband, Beatrice reluctantly allowed the arrangement, but there were times you could almost hear her grinding teeth. And then, their son, Gil, had had to give up his room outright and now slept in the basement. But what was hardship, weighed against duty?

Yes, but there were things the family did not know about Eleanor. For instance, they did not know she actually owned the beautiful house on MacLaren that overlooked Dundonald Park, a house with five bedrooms, a sitting room, an accommodating kitchen, a library. When she moved in with her son, she rented out the rooms she had occupied in this house, a house that would have suited them all much better than Spadina Avenue did. But she'd kept her ownership secret from everyone save her lawyer, Mr. Bax, pretending to be a mere occupant, a poor woman dependent on her late husband's army pension.

Nor was the house on MacLaren her only asset. Though she'd spent most of her life crying poor, living in her own house as if she were a tenant among tenants, Eleanor Stanley was a wealthy woman. She held bank accounts in Paris, Indianapolis, Naples, and Edinburgh. (She had also, at one time, owned property in Athens, Potsdam, Princeton, London, and Evora.) That is to say, her net worth was in the millions, a fact she kept to herself. This was certainly mean of her, but because she intended to leave her money and her estate to her granddaughter, this pettiness did not trouble her conscience. She would end her life with an act of generosity that would, to her mind, absolve her of any sins she might have committed.

Still, why leave everything to her granddaughter, when Stanley, her son, was the rightful heir? That was a question that caused Eleanor a curious distress. She did not feel it unjust to cut Stanley out of her will. The choice of a beneficiary was her business, hers alone, but there was something inadmissible behind her choice: she did not love her son, had never managed to love him. She might not have minded these feelings, if she'd been incapable of love, but this she was not. She loved her granddaughter. She even felt (diminishing) affection for her grandson, but for her own son there had never been anything but a kind of repugnance. It had little to do with Stanley per se. She could see he was what is called a "good man." No, her dislike had to do with things per accidens. First, there was Stanley's father. Eleanor's relationship to Stanley's father had been, well, tender but intricate. Her husband was related to the Marquess of Exeter or the Earl of Devon or some such. A young man of great wealth, he had, inexplicably, fallen in love with Eleanor and, "going unaccountably native," married her. Though it offended and appalled his family, though he was cut off from the even greater wealth that would have been his had he married sensibly, Robert Stanley married a woman he loved, a black Trinidadian, and lived in the colonies until he was drafted into the war and died overseas, in Italy, in 1943. You'd think Eleanor and her son would have been, at Robert's death, shunned by his family, but she did not give them the chance. She refused to have anything to do with any of them. Instead, she (and her lawyer), after many bitter (and, for Eleanor, frugal) years, took stewardship of Robert's estate (two million pounds, with property in London, Dawlish, and Lans-en-Vercors), and cut his family dead.

It was a strange kind of cutting, though, because there was something frankly self-lacerating about it. Somewhere in her consciousness she must have believed her husband's relatives were superior to her, believed their culture superior to her own, their holdings greater than the place from which she'd come. That is, she must have believed in her own unworthiness because she abandoned Trinidad not long after her husband died and, from then on, would no more speak of her own family and culture than she would of her husband's. At her husband's death, she found she could move neither forward (to England) nor back (to Trinidad) and so was left stateless as well as bereft.

Had Eleanor felt any love at all for Robert Stanley? Yes, she had. (He was, in fact, the only man she would ever love.) But she was young and her feelings, deep as they were, were an erotic confusion. She was flattered and moved by Robert Stanley's affection, impressed by his social standing, overcome by his choice of her above all the eligible women he might have had. At the same time, she doubted his motives, suspected she was being used to hurt his family, and could not quite believe his liltingly mumbled avowals of devotion. And yet, in the end, something within her was broken by his demise.

By the time her granddaughter was born, she remembered her own emotions more than she did the man himself. He'd smelled of lilac soap, he'd had a slight stutter, and it was he who'd named the boy Stanley Stanley, insisting that "Lord Stanley Stanley" had an aristocratic ring to it. Very little left of him, really . . . except, well, Stanley himself, who so resembled his father he was a constant reminder of Robert: a living memento mori, a keepsake of worlds gone and worlds abandoned. (All of this would, of course, have interested her son, who knew nothing of his father or his father's family because Eleanor pugnaciously discouraged his curiosity, just as he, more gently but with as little yield, discouraged his children's curiosity about all that had been kept from him.)

There was another, more particular reason for her dislike of her son: she had been told, before his birth, that she would love her child. Love, they said, would overcome her, and she had looked for it, only to discover the great lie. She'd felt distaste at first sight of the boy, as if she'd given birth to her own ambivalence. Every now and then, a tide of maternal sympathy would wash over her and, briefly, she would look down at Stanley and think herself favoured, but these feelings did not last long and, in the end, she came to resent her own "instincts."

So, she disliked him, but why could she not love her son? People often love those they dislike, don't they, especially when it comes to family? She'd given this some thought, desultorily, over the years. She first assumed it was because he was a "trying" child, but even she could not keep up that pretense for long. Stanley had been a quiet and affectionate boy. Then she supposed it was this very quiescence and affection that put her off. Yes, perhaps, but . . . in the end, it seemed it simply was not in her nature to love her child, as it was not in her nature to do *anything* expected of her.

Why, then, had she chosen to live with Stanley? Well, whatever her instincts and whatever her emotions, she was a frugal woman and, as she got older, she felt increasing worry at the thought of expenses and spending. As living with Stanley would cut her expenses down, it was an attractive idea; more attractive still, given her recent, nagging sense that all was not right with her. There wasn't anything she could put her finger on, but there you are. If something *were* wrong, she would need whatever family she had. Her feelings for her son had nothing to do with it or, if they did, they were trumped by practical considerations.

So, she had come to live with Stanley and his family in 1981, still vigorous at sixty-eight. Still vigorous? Yes, but she kept this to herself. It did not seem to her "helpful" to appear too healthy, so she'd insisted on imaginary ailments, leaning on Stanley's arm whenever they walked about, moderating her temper, making herself mild, or almost mild. She had done so well that it was now, three years later, difficult to do things she should have had no trouble doing: walking alone, getting up from bed, and, most important, keeping her affairs in order. It was bewildering reading a bank statement or letter, like staring at a face or landscape that one knew well and having it become suddenly strange. It was as if memory itself suffered a defeat, though she didn't quite understand it was memory that had been defeated. Rather, she sensed something was wrong or something was missing, and she was sometimes convinced that someone was out to get her.

Before coming to Stanley's house, she'd had a routine, places to go. She had, or thought she had, a reasonably firm hand on the rudder. But since coming, she had abandoned her schedule and she'd begun to lose track of her own life. For some time now (a year was it?), the details had become simply unmanageable. The worst of it was the being lost. There were times she couldn't remember where she was or what she was doing and even the city landmarks didn't help. How could they, in April, when the city was just warm enough to be a somewhere else, like Port of Spain, the city of her birth, and the War Memorial a strange distortion of Cipriani, his statue on Frederick Street, as if the world itself wished to see her by the wharf with her Gra'ma Ada, the sky above the sea an indescribable blue and her grandmother smelling of cocoa butter?

Until now, Ottawa had always refused to be anywhere else, even when she wished it were. It was dull, cold, and homely, but she had come to feel for Ottawa as she'd felt for her grandfather, a man of tweed whose feelings for her were scarcely perceptible, save that he was the only one to speak to her as an equal and he always managed to pass her a dollar note, even later when he had to be helped to sit up and he smelled of creosote, because he insisted on shaving himself, though his hands shook and he cut himself horribly . . .

And where was he, now? Dead and buried in Trinidad.

And what if Ottawa died within her? Where would that leave her?

– Stanley! she cried.

She had moved in with Stanley, pleading frailty to justify the intrusion. But perhaps she had outsmarted herself. The pretense of frailty seemed to have led to frailty, and she was something of a prisoner in her son's house. She managed to be on her own no more than once or twice a week, her family being loath to allow her out without company. And now, it seems, they were right. She got lost in the city, forgot her son's address, forgot what his house looked like, wrote letters that she'd discover in her purse weeks later, unposted, there in her purse along with packets and packets of sugar. The only bright side was that these episodes were, as far as she could tell, infrequent, and she had always returned to herself, posted her letters, threw out the sugar, found her way home.

But for how long? And what could she do about it? She would have to consider doing the thing she'd so far avoided: she would have to confide in someone, because it was now clear that, one day, she might not return to herself, and what would happen to her then? How bleak it was even to think about these matters.

At least it was clear in whom she would confide: Mary, her own granddaughter, her best hope in all of this.

– Stanley!

Stanley and his daughter were in the kitchen when they heard Eleanor's call. They'd been discussing politics, as they often did together. Though Mary was Liberal, she could not stand John Turner: white-haired, falsely jovial. She was actually thinking of voting Conservative in the next election.

– Really? Stanley asked. You like Mulroney, then?

Stanley himself belonged to no party. He voted based on what he could make of the candidate. He agreed with his daughter that this wasn't the best way to go about voting, but if it's true good men could be brought down by rotten parties, it was also true they sometimes brought the party up with them, wasn't it? He had voted for Diefenbaker, and then he had voted for Trudeau. Hard to say whom he would vote for next, but, these days, his chief political pleasure came in talking politics with his daughter.

They heard Eleanor's muffled call and Mary stood up.

– I'll go, she said.

– No, no, said Stanley. She's calling me.

And he went unhurriedly up to the second floor, preparing himself for whatever Eleanor had in mind or whatever mood she was in.

As it happened, Eleanor wanted to use the bedpan, and this was a complicated matter, not biologically, but emotionally, because she did not, in fact, need help to use the bedpan. When she first moved in, she had asked for help and, to her chagrin, had found the experience humiliating. But, as she could not admit that asking for help with the "po" had been a ploy, she went on asking, though it never ceased to be an embarrassment.

Of course, Stanley understood that when his mother hesitated or began to speak about the weather, say, what she really wanted was the bedpan, but he felt it would be rude to simply hand it to her. So he always waited until she asked for the pan. As a result, although they never spoke of important things, the moments before Eleanor asked for the bedpan were among the closest they shared.

Eleanor: (pause) Stanley. I wonder if you would . . . open the window for me?

Stanley: The window? It's pretty cold out, Mom. Are you sure?

Eleanor: Stanley. I find it insufferable.

Stanley: (sighs) Okay, Mom.

He opens the window.

Stanley: Is that all?

Eleanor: No, no. (pause) I was also wondering if you might (pause) bring up the newspaper? It's intolerable to be bedridden and ignorant. It's really

	too much, on top of all the other indignities.
Stanley:	What indignities?
Eleanor:	Well, having to ask for the po, for instance.
Stanley:	You need to use the po, Mom? Why don't you just ask me?
Eleanor:	You simply *will* not understand the humiliation.

Stanley reaches under the bed for the bedpan, then hands it to her.

Eleanor:	Thank you. I wonder if you would step out while I use it?

When it was over and he had emptied the pan and replaced it beneath his mother's bed, Stanley made sure she was comfortable and then returned to talk with his daughter, whom he loved without a hint of complication.

– Is Gran okay? asked Mary.

– Oh, yeah, said Stanley. She's just getting older. Like all of us.

10

A FACT ABOUT WALTER BARNES

It was around the time Eleanor began to die, a year or so *after* Walter had ended his relationship with Louise, that Louise's husband, Paul Dylan, began to suspect his wife and Walter were having an affair. He was a jealous man, so suspicion of his wife's fidelity was almost second nature, but this was the first time he imagined that Walter had betrayed him.

His suspicion of Walter was well founded, of course. What was unusual was that it took Paul so long to suspect Walter. Most of the other Fortnightly Club members, had they been as uxorious or jealous as Paul, would have been wary of Walter from the beginning.

The Fortnightly Club had begun with a kind of nostalgia. Paul Dylan, Robert van Leuwen, and François Ricard had been drinking at the Royal Oak. They'd been drinking for hours when François made a disparaging comment about the civil service. Van Leuwen then suggested that civil servants hadn't always been so ignorant, that at the turn of the century there had been standards that today's bureaucrats would not meet. Bureaucrats had been expected to be morally irreproachable and to know Latin, Greek, algebra, history . . .

Yes, but in those days the general public was better educated. Besides, there was a long tradition of intellectual intercourse in the capital. People would meet to exchange ideas, to debate the significance of this and that.

Was the tradition dead?

Yes, because there was no one to revive it.

Messrs. Dylan, van Leuwen, and Ricard did not imagine they could revive a lost tradition, but the idea was amusing. The three of them already formed a group of sorts. They met often, and spoke of ideas until late at night. They were undisciplined, however, and though ideas were exchanged, it was like an exchange of fog. The presence of others, a community, they felt, would raise the stakes, provide a real challenge to their shared beliefs.

For the first gathering, van Leuwen invited Henry Wing; Mr. Ricard invited his wife, Michelle, and Mr. Dylan invited his wife, Louise, Perry Newman (his lawyer), and Richard Nevins (his dentist). There was no agenda. Amateurs all, they talked about nothing much, but they did so with emotion, and it was this emotion that enticed them to the next gathering and the one after that. A small community was formed: unstable, not quite compatible with its own ideals, more practical than metaphysical, because Canadian. No one could remember who brought Professor Barnes, but by the time Walter attended his first gathering, the salon had existed for a year and things had already changed, becoming more casual but, also, a little more obscure.

Walter was liked, especially by Paul, who thought him a dry, ascetic academic with a meticulous memory for detail. For Paul, head of his own company of computer programmers, Walter was exotic without being a threat, and he was more interesting than most programmers, solid and good men who stared off into space if asked about anything other than computing. And then there was Walter's voice: deep, muted but distinctly attractive, alluring, even.

Now, like Paul Dylan, a number of those who knew Walter thought him shy, not given to physical expression of his emotions. The impression came, perhaps, from Walter's reserve and discretion that could be misinterpreted as disinclination to physical intimacy. This was not at all the case. In fact, Walter's chief respite from the *vita contemplativa* came through sexual intercourse, through banter, foreplay, intercourse, and brief post-coital familiarity. When his own company was too much to bear, which it often was, he put on his coat and went out and petitioned the first woman he happened to see.

What kind of man was he, at those moments?

He was calm and reassuring, his persona that of a man who is lonely but not desperate, a lyric poet, say, his loneliness a wound but also the origin of his attraction. (It didn't hurt that he was tall, patrician in looks, with a slightly hawkish nose and lively blue eyes.) His approach, though abrupt, was playful and deeply confident. (He was almost certainly aware of his talent to seduce, but this, for those who found him charming, was part of the charm.) From the first moment, before he spoke a word, Walter's presence suggested something like a pleasant conspiracy, and an attentiveness, though his attention was not such as to make one too self-conscious. All in all, there was to Walter a melancholy charm, an obvious intelligence, and a frank sexual appeal. He was sometimes slapped and occasionally insulted, but he inevitably found someone in the same mood as he was, with similar desires. (Perhaps it says something about Ottawa that his average was much better than one in ten, though there were evenings when he would petition ten or twenty women before succeeding.) It wasn't that Walter didn't mind rejection, but rejection was as intimate, in its way, as what followed acceptance, and he had learned to appreciate its fascinating range.

In his pursuit of women, however, a kind of pedantry plagued him. Walter actually had personal preferences. He preferred to sleep with young women of Malaysian descent. He found pageboy haircuts and plucked eyebrows positively arousing, but he had long discovered how hopeless it was to seek those things out. By the time you found a woman with a pageboy do, hours might have passed and there was no guarantee she'd be willing to sleep with you. It was, quite simply, inefficient. Besides, in the end, it didn't matter about the woman's hair and eyebrows. It didn't matter what she looked like at all. A singular appearance or beauty only made it harder for him to forget the woman afterwards. So he had resolved to systematically accost: whichever woman he encountered, he propositioned. In this way, he slept with a fair cross-section of the female population.

There were other "rules." He did not knowingly sleep with women younger than sixteen or older than seventy, and he tried very hard to avoid the beds of his colleagues and acquaintances. These were not moral limits as such. They were practical:

1) Sex with young girls was unappealing.
2) Sex with older women was sometimes physically awkward and took a great deal of foreplay.
3) Sex with colleagues was a fouling of the workplace (though, curiously, sex with his students was not).
4) Sex with acquaintances created emotional expectations he would not (or could not) satisfy. (Or, as with Louise, depths of feeling he could not deal with.)

One might have expected joy or at least gratitude in all this philandering, and there was some, but there was mostly release. The small variations (women who wanted to be kissed and women who did not, who liked to be bound or bitten, who took pains to give him pleasure, who kicked him out when they came, who enjoyed cunnilingus, who did not, who wished to have their breasts fondled, who did not, who closed their eyes, who kept them open, who invited him home, who insisted he pay for a room, who had birthmarks, who had scars, who limped, who stuttered), the details that might have brought pleasure or, at least, wonder, were not significant to him.

In his heart of hearts, Walter believed the world was a sad place, a place whose sadness would not wear off, a place so profoundly sad that one could say "the world is joyous" and mean the opposite: it was sad, given how pallid its supposed joys actually were. That he added to its sadness was a thought that did not occur to him.

You can't salt an ocean, after all.

Paul Dylan's first impression of Professor Barnes was of a likable academic. Although he was an intensely jealous man, Paul had convinced himself of Walter's asceticism. To his mind, it was easier to imagine, say, Elwy Yost as a cocksman than it was Professor Barnes (Elwy being, for Paul, perennially avuncular and soft as dumplings). And yet, there is, in a relentlessly sexual being, something like a particular light that is bright to those with experience and cloudedly perceptible to those without. Though none of the other members of the Fortnightly Club had anything like Walter's libido or experience, he was an unacknowledged object of fascination to them (to me, certainly) and, despite his discretion, most suspected his philandering without being certain of it. The same "light" was perceptible to Paul as it was to the others, but he interpreted it as a kind of saintliness, an almost religious aura that made Walter interesting, yes, but not ("Oh, please . . .") sexually suave.

So it was that Paul's first impression provided a screen for Walter and Louise. And then, in the months following Walter's affair with Louise, there was little sign that anything had happened between them. Though it hurt to be in each other's presence, neither stopped attending meetings of the Fortnightly Club. They greeted each other as acquaintances do and tried to ignore each other in the same way, as if their acquaintance were valuable but well within the bounds of decorum.

This was difficult for both of them and, in retrospect, there were a number of signs the two had been intimate. For one thing, Louise *was* somewhat uneasy around Walter. It was as if she were trying to behave as she had behaved but, because she had been unselfconscious before sleeping with Walter, she was not quite certain she managed to behave unselfconsciously. With Walter, the signs were subtler. Immediately after their breakup, he was fine, his old self even, as he was a man used to moving on. Besides, he had resources to help him through: books, drink, and the company of women. Gradually, however, his resources failed him. The women he slept with all began to remind him of Louise, the only one whose features, body, and voice would not fade. Drink, too much drink, was a ticket to his own childhood, to his memories, and this was as painful as being without Louise. So, drink was not helpful. And, finally, books. The week after leaving Louise, Walter happily read a novel called *Lanark*. After that, however, the desire to read abandoned him. He picked up any number of books and put them down again, unable to read much beyond titles and the distant promises the titles held: Boethius' *Consolation*, Rolle's *Fire of Love*, Abelard's *Historia Calamitatum* . . . With the failure of his usual resources, Walter grew progressively helpless before his own longing. It became a struggle to find solace in justification. It had been honourable to stop seeing her, hadn't it? Well, so much for honour. He had been right to consider Paul's feelings, hadn't he? He would do the same again, given the chance, wouldn't he? So much for right. So much for calculation. None of it eased his longing. And then, worst of all, there were the memories that overcame him at the most unpredictable moments, memories so intensely erotic, it's a wonder they weren't perceived by everyone around him: Louise's hand reaching down to guide him inside her, a trace of her lipstick on his penis that they discovered while washing under warm water, the first time he had looked into her eyes (hazel: light green, golden brown), which was the first time he was conscious of looking into anyone's eyes. And so, months after his affair with Louise, months after Louise herself had recovered a certain ease in his company, the signs of their relationship were perceptible in Walter's behaviour: his sudden "hot flashes," his occasional discomfort while standing, his distraction. All signs that, at first, Paul Dylan completely ignored.

11

SAINT MICHAEL

A year after Paul's trip to Amarillo, his wife had been unfaithful to him, or so he suspected, without knowing the why, the when, or the how often. Of course, being jealous by nature, his suspicions were an aspect of his love for her. He was inevitably jealous, had always been, but jealousy wasn't the dragon in their relationship, it was the sword. The real problem lay deeper, and the worst of it was that he could figure her in the most compromising scenes, could not keep from figuring her. He could clearly imagine the men to whom she gave herself. They were younger, taller, and they had tousled hair.

He still loved her, but his jealousy was a torment, and its manifestations were in

- the look of him looking at her when she wasn't looking
- the questions that couldn't be formulated because the right tone eluded him:

    Wouldn't you . . . *like to sleep with x?* Don't you think you'd be . . . *happier with x?*

- the evening inspection of the bedsheets (that he changed every morning, even when she wanted to stay abed):

palpating the covers, burying his head in the pillows.
(Louise thought him fastidious)
- the random homecomings, midafternoon, to collect
  some thing he'd purposely forgotten (a chart, a graph, a
  credit card, always left on the dresser or atop the fridge)
  (She thought him forgetful)
- the insistence that he alone should do the laundry. (She
  thought him eccentric but, on the other hand, her clothes
  were always clean)

But there were no satisfying answers to the questions he
wished to ask; the sheets always smelled as fresh in the evening as
they had in the morning; and, though she was sometimes absent
during his midafternoon homecomings, there was always good
reason and, often, witnesses to her excursions. That is, nothing he
did helped, if the object were to catch his wife in flagrante delicto.
However, it was not as clear as that. He didn't actually wish to discover proof of Louise's infidelity. That would have been unbearable. But if he couldn't stop himself from looking for proof, it was
because looking had also become a dimension of his feelings for
her. Not that it wasn't painful each time he inspected their bedsheets or washed her underwear. There was, inevitably, an instant
of panic, a fear of finding out and confusion about the consequences. What *would* he do if the bedsheets were damp or their
room smelled faintly of ejaculate? No idea. He would cross that
bridge when he came to it.

Strangely, given the torment his doubt occasioned, there was
little relief in the proof of Louise's fidelity. Then again, there was
no proof. There was never proof. A spotless bed meant only that
he'd been negligent. If he'd come home sooner, spent a few
more minutes looking, palpating, asking. If only he knew exactly
where or how to look. If he could only discover the irresistible
question, the one whose answer would cure him.

In the end, all of this, which might at least have drawn his attention to Louise, drew attention only to himself, to his (possible) incompetence where proof was concerned. It was tiresome and shameful. He knew himself to be thoughtful, sensitive, and kind, but it was difficult to reconcile his love with his moments of abandon. And that is what they were: moments during which the strange pleasure his rituals afforded him was all that mattered.

Could you really call what he felt for Louise "Love," given his routine betrayal of her trust? Yes, of course you could. Nothing mortal is flawless, and Love doesn't need a perfect vessel. (If it did, we would all be loveless and unloving, being imperfect.) Because Love itself is an imperfection. (Technically speaking, it could not be otherwise, what with the imperfect vessel and all.) Because Love is mortal. (Really, if Divine Love were anything like what humans feel for one another, we should have to accept a God who is jealous, unstable, and often delirious – an idea that makes sense of our world, it's true, but Paul Dylan did not then believe in "God," except as a rhetorical foil to "humanity" or as the embodiment of Chance.) Because Love is what kept him from doing violence to his wife when he finally "discovered" her affair with Walter Barnes.

He was in the glass-enclosed porch they'd built in 1980. Louise was with friends at the Towne Cinema, or so she'd said.
– *I'm going out with Marthe, Fred, and Vé.*
– *Oh?*
– *We're going to* Fanny and Alexander. *Want to come?*
– *Not really.*
– *Okay, then . . . (kiss on the neck)*
When she came home, he would ask about the film.

It was a warm night and cloudy. Through the panes, he could see the clouds and a moon that flickered as the clouds passed. Beyond the clouds, as unaware of his misery as he was unaware of them, stars and constellations took up their places: Virgo and Libra in the sky, Lupus on the horizon.

He sat in the old chesterfield. On the wall behind him was the framed reproduction of a Renaissance painting:

the sky is blue and Saint Michael's wings are white
in one hand he holds the head of a black serpent
in one hand he holds a sword whose blade is sullied
Saint Michael is impassive
the serpent's mouth is agape

It was not Paul's favourite painting. He preferred the work of Raphael or Il Rosso, but this Saint Michael was a memento of time in London: with Louise, on their honeymoon. They'd spent two marvellous weeks in a city filled with lovers. He could not imagine a better time or place, though the pleasure had less to do with London per se than with the sense of wonder the two of them brought to the city. Everything was new, even bridges and bars that were hundreds of years old.

How did he discover Walter had slept with his wife? Through a strange, but irrefutable, chain of moments and logic. The first moment, from some time ago now, was just peculiar enough to have stayed with him. Walter had lent his wife a copy of the *Summa Contra Gentiles, Volume 1*. She'd asked for it, to prepare for an evening on Aquinas. She'd read quite a bit of it, bringing the book to bed with them for weeks. He'd been surprised that she could keep herself amused with such twaddle, but she'd persisted with the *Summa*, even reading aloud the objections to water in Heaven, the idea that God can make the Past not to have been, and the proof that God is mercy.

On his return from Amarillo, however, Paul discovered the book in their garbage pail. Some of the *Summa*'s pages were torn; others appeared to have been ripped out. When he asked Louise

– What happened?

She answered

– It fell under a bus. I've got to get Walter a new copy.

– Did you tell him?

– Yes, I did.

And that was that until, speaking to Walter at an evening devoted to Hegel, Paul mentioned the sad ruin of the *Summa* and Walter blanched. Paul said

– Didn't you know?

and Walter answered

– Oh yes, of course. Now I remember.

before expatiating on the burnt library at Alexandria.

This encounter was more meaningful in retrospect than it was at the time, but there it is, *moment one*: proof his wife and Walter were or had been intimate.

Moment two took place on an evening devoted to Nietzsche. They had all been invited to Walter's house. They had eaten and they were sitting in the living room when Walter brought out a decanter of Newman's and poured a quantity of port into each of six six-ounce snifters. Nothing unusual about that. Walter was proud of his vessels. He had a cabinet full of them, from snifters and flutes to tumblers, tazzas, noggins, and patellas. As he held out a snifter for Louise, Walter's hands shook. Paul was thinking about Nietzsche, but he noticed the tremor and smiled to himself. How amusing for a man to be so awkward with women.

– Careful, Wally, he'd said.

Walter, flustered, answered with a disquisition on Machiavelli and *virtù*. Nothing unusual about that, either. It only confirmed Paul's view of Walter as a gawky man in desperate need of female companionship. In fact, this might not have been *moment two* at all, were it not for *moment three*, which took place later the same night.

As they were all getting ready to leave, and Walter had gone off to get something from somewhere, Paul happened to overhear van Leuwen say

– I'm not like Wally, you know. I don't have any talent for seduction.

– Hmm, answered François Ricard.

Then, noticing Dylan, van Leuwen said

– How are you, Paul?

– Fine, said Paul.

But he was caught off guard by the (most peculiar) thought of Barnes as a seducer. And, yet, van Leuwen had sounded serious in his suggestion that Walter had talent for seduction.

– Were you just talking about Walter? he asked.

– Yes, I'm afraid I was gossiping, said van Leuwen. Wally's –

But they were interrupted by the return of the man himself, and Walter looked every inch the retiring academic Paul assumed him to be. No, it was not possible. It was all rumour and . . . what is the opposite of character assassination? This gossip made Walter seem more interesting than he was in reality. And yet, though Paul could not credit Barnes as Don Juan, something about the idea must have remained with him because . . .

Moment four, the irrefutable moment, the moment that made all other moments momentous, came months later at his own instigation. He was conducting interviews for a new secretary. He had seen a host of men and women when, finally, he spoke to a young woman who seemed ideally suited to the position: previous experience, good references, a knowledge of computing, personable, and quite elegant. He had decided to offer her the position when, glancing at her curriculum vitae, he noticed she had studied sociology at Carleton.

– So you know Professor Barnes? he asked.

She hesitated, uncertain if it were an advantage to admit the acquaintance.

– Uhm, yes . . ., she said.

Something in her hesitation aroused his curiosity.

– You studied with him?

– First year, she answered. Is Professor Barnes a friend of yours?

– Not really. An acquaintance. Was he a good teacher?

– Oh, well . . . Yes, I guess so.

– And?

She looked up at him, and then decided to tell the truth as she herself had heard it.

– He was a little, you know, indiscreet.

– Ahh . . . , said Mr. Dylan.

And hired her.

And, in the weeks that followed, avoided the matter, though he was unable to get it out of his mind, as if Walter were a word on the tip of his tongue, an obvious answer to a convoluted question, one down in the daily cryptic: a seven-letter word for one who is hornèd.

Sharon Oswald, the new secretary, had been surprised when Professor Barnes' name came up during her interview. She hadn't suspected the man would figure in her life after Carleton, and, following the interview, she'd felt a certain pettiness. After all, she was one of the women Professor Barnes had not propositioned. She did not actually know what kind of man he was, but his reputation . . . *that* was well known and she *did* know one of the women who'd succumbed to him, a woman who'd described Professor Barnes as a night on a broken Ferris wheel: pleasurable but unending. The image of an endless ride had struck Sharon as vivid and not unenticing and, thereafter, she'd found it difficult to look Professor Barnes in the face and had come to think of him with something like disapproval. It was this disapproval she'd expressed at her interview and she regretted it, but when, a few weeks after that, Mr. Dylan returned to the subject, she felt constrained by her initial tack and, of course, the need to please her employer.

– So, he said, Professor Barnes was indiscreet, eh? You don't mean he slept with his students?

– Yes, he did. He slept with a lot of women.

Ms. Oswald nodded her head and then shook it.

– He's not my type, she said, but some people aren't picky.

– Did *you* ever see him with any women?

Ms. Oswald, uncertain where the conversation was leading, lied.

– Oh yes . . . Lots.

Then Mr. Dylan lied.

– The only woman I ever saw him with was . . .

(Here, in a fit of inspiration, he precisely described his own wife.)

– Did you ever see him with her?

Ms. Oswald said

– Yes, I do remember someone like that. Now that you mention it.

– I don't remember her name. Do you?

Ms. Oswald said

– Lucy?

the name of a woman she knew had slept with Professor Barnes. Nothing to do with Louise at all, and yet . . . *Lucy?*

Paul sat at his desk, flustered, as if he'd misheard.

– Louise, you mean?

– Oh yes, said Ms. Oswald, Louise. Definitely.

And anger descended on Paul Dylan, like nightfall at noon.

– Walter's quite a character, he said.

– Isn't he, though.

After a bit of feigned commiseration, as if he agreed the world were too mysterious to fathom, they returned to the work at hand: correspondence. Actually, Paul Dylan did *not* return to it. This "proof" of Louise's infidelity was something that gave new meaning to everything. It was now possible to see his world in a different light: his wife was not his wife, he was not her husband, their home was not a home. An emotion very like ecstasy accompanied all this. As if his house had burned down, Paul felt unburdened: to think that the worst had happened, that he was living through moments he'd spent so much time living through in his imagination. Yet he was fine.

There was a curiously metaphysical satisfaction as well. The truth had liberated him, it seemed (though his was a truth that was both the truth and not the truth). It was good, finally, to know this about his wife, to know this about Walter. He wasn't even angry. He *was* angry, but he was so lucid, he didn't take it for anger. He made calls. He signed letters. He attended a meeting at which he was calm and composed. The only hint there was something darker on his mind was the irritation provoked by trivial things:

- the pattern on one of the programmer's shirt was too busy
- the treasurer's makeup was pasty
- someone was wearing an earring that looked as if it would fall off

Did he think about his wife through all this? Yes, but very little. It was rather that he thought about himself through her: his feelings for her (betrayed), his sacrifices (useless), the unveiling of his deepest self (humiliating). Louise was obscured in him by his own emotions. The one he couldn't stop thinking about was Walter.

That night, for the first time in their years of marriage, he returned from work late, did not touch the bedsheets, could not speak to her, except to say that he'd brought vital work home, and locked himself in his basement office where he wrote letters to people he hadn't seen for years. It was, as they say, a dark night of the soul. He slept very little, sinking only briefly into a dream

in which, inexplicably, Walter Barnes was the sous-chef in a
Carthaginian restaurant that served nothing but salted eel.

Weeks had passed since then. Sitting in the glass porch, staring
up at the clouds, it was still as if he were enduring the after-effects
of a strong drug. The weeks since Ms. Oswald's revelation were
cloudy. How had he managed to keep from destroying his house?
How had he managed to sleep with his wife? Why was Walter
Barnes, the man who'd stolen his life, still alive? The answer to the
first two questions was simple: Paul Dylan was not a man to act
without deliberation. It wasn't in his nature. He *might* burn down
the house. He *might* kill himself, but it would take more than a
few weeks to bring himself to the act. He was indignant and he
was certainly capable of violence, but the time had not yet come.
For that reason, he continued to sleep with his wife. To do otherwise would have so changed his environment he might have done
something unpredictable. As it was, he slept beside Louise, but he
did not kiss her while they were abed. When he had to kiss her at
all, which he did, for appearance's sake, he kissed the back of her
head or her hair or the side of her face. Besides, in the weeks he'd
had to think all this through, Paul had discovered in himself a
genuine, helpless devotion to his wife. It was not his fault and
there was nothing he could do: the woman was as important to
him now as she'd been on the day they met. It wasn't as difficult
to sleep beside her as he'd first imagined. It was more difficult to
avoid her kiss.

There was no suitable answer to the question of Barnes.
Walter Barnes was in need of correction. If only to protect other
men (and other wives), Paul would have to teach him a lesson. It
wasn't even personal now. It was a sad duty.

12

SEPTEMBER

It was a beautiful Saturday in September. In the Glebe, citizens were out in shirtsleeves, tending to their lawns and gardens. There was a light breeze, but it was as warm as calf's breath.

Paul had risen early. It had been months since he'd discovered his wife's infidelity. (In that time, he had managed to forgive her, or so he believed. But it was, in any case, an act of secret generosity, since he did not (could not) speak to her of her sins or his forgiveness.) He'd risen early and, after telling Louise he'd forgotten important papers at the office, he'd gone out for breakfast: eggs and bacon in a diner where the patrons looked as if they hadn't slept in decades.

It was a weekend, so he was at leisure. He left the restaurant at ten o'clock and it was around ten thirty that Paul, angry but self-possessed, knocked at Walter's door.

And knocked again.

And knocked a third time.

It may have been his intention merely to talk to Walter, to tongue-lash him. He himself might have said it was. Then again, whatever his intentions may have been, this knocking at the door was irritating. It felt undignified, standing on Barnes' threshold in full view of the neighbours. He would knock a final time and then wait, but he became angrier each moment he waited.

Walter had also risen early. He'd had coffee and toast in his kitchen and then begun an article for the *Queen's Quarterly*: a re-evaluation of Seymour Martin Lipset. His dissatisfaction with sociology had become a dissatisfaction with its American proponents, but he was respectful and scrupulous and struggled to write a nuanced critique. At ten thirty, he was washing his hands and he didn't hear the knocking at his door. Walter did not often reflect on little rituals, but something about the water this morning, as it ran over his palms and fingers, attracted his attention: such a common element, but the sound of it as it sputtered from the spigot and circled the drain . . . He had shut off the tap and wiped his fingers on a worn hand towel when he heard the third of Mr. Dylan's forays at his front door.

– Just a minute . . . , he said
the fingernail on his left thumb having caught a loop of cotton in the towel's weave.

– Just a minute . . . , he said
beneath his breath, trying to disengage his thumb without tearing the fabric, going slowly downstairs with the towel hanging, as if by magic, from his left hand.

Walter opened his door, and he was about to express his surprise when Paul Dylan took him by the front of his shirt, pulled him out, and head-butted him, breaking his nose immediately or, rather, rebreaking it.

After that, there wasn't time to say anything; although, before he lost consciousness, Walter had the strange feeling he and Paul were actually conversing. Among other things, he thought he said

– What are you doing, Paul?
but he said nothing, because his nose was broken and, thereafter, he had difficulty thinking and breathing.

Paul then managed to punch him on the cheek, the neck, and the back of the head before he paused for breath. He fractured

Walter's cheekbone and bruised his neck, but the annoying damage (annoying to Paul) was done to Walter's shirt, the buttons of which hit the concrete like pebbles, and Walter's glasses, which broke neatly in two but hung from his ears before falling to the ground. Everything about Walter was annoying and fed Paul's anger: the towel he'd brought to the door, the sound of his buttons falling, the way his glasses had broken, the fact he wouldn't stand up, the dead weight of him. None of this inspired anything but rage. He hurt his hand when he struck the back of Walter's head so, when Walter fell to the concrete, Paul began to kick at Walter's head and ribs.

(Walter's head hit the pavement at an awkward angle, but it was not until the kick to his ribs that he, temporarily, lost consciousness.)

Though Walter didn't speak, while imagining he did, Paul spoke without realizing he was speaking, and it was Paul's loud imprecations that first attracted the attention of Walter's neighbours. He was using vile language, and this was, initially, as disturbing to the neighbours as the sight of Walter's agony or the sounds of the beating. By the time Paul began kicking at Walter's ribs, a half-dozen spectators had timidly approached to see what was going on. They were, of course, horrified by the spectacle. Should they intervene? Yes. A woman went in to call the police. No, it looked to be over. Yes, it would soon be over. But, no, Paul had simply paused, again, for breath and he was kicking again.

All of them were disarmed by the violence. It was astonishing, on such a lovely day. Minutes passed, minutes that would stretch out in their imaginations, before a young woman pushed her husband forward, entreating him to separate the antagonists, if you could call them that, there being so little antagonism: Paul kicked out and his foot was accommodated by Walter's body. The young husband, a tall, muscular man, was almost certainly stronger than Paul or Walter. He could have picked Paul up by the scruff of the neck, but one never knew when a smaller man,

charged with adrenalin, would present more problems than anticipated, and the last thing he wanted was to join the fray, though
he felt his own adrenalin rise as he approached.

– Hey you

he said, tapping at Paul's left shoulder as if it were hot, then stepping back.

– Mister

he said, tapping again.

– What're you doing?

Paul ignored him, kicking Walter again, though there was no
longer any satisfaction in it. The young man, somewhat aggrieved
at being ignored, pulled him away from Professor Barnes.

– Listen, buddy, you shouldn't be doing this. It isn't right.

It occurred to Paul that this was true. What was he doing?
What did all of this mean?

– He slept with my wife, said Paul.

It was a straightforward reply, but the emotion of years came
out with the words, and the young husband was unexpectedly
moved. He understood entirely.

– Oh, he said.

And, feeling remorse at his untimely intrusion, not knowing
what else to do, the man kicked at Walter's chest, as if to express
solidarity for the cuckold, a solidarity that, to his mind, any
honest man would admit.

This last assault brought great dismay to the onlookers, dismay
and consternation.

The young husband returned to them, thoughtful and contrite
at his intrusion.

– Mr. Barnes slept with the man's wife, he said.

– So what? someone shouted.

– So he deserves what he's getting, that's what.

There was a brief, reflective silence before someone else said

– Wait a minute. How do you *know* he slept with his wife?

A good question.

– Well, he wouldn't kick him for nothing, said the young husband.

And, from someone else:

– Sleeping with his wife isn't even a reason.

– It is as far as *I'm* concerned, said the husband.

And, at that, Walter's neighbours began to argue with the young man. Most of them were outraged, but a few of the men were unsure just what the "proper" punishment for adultery should be and their respect for Professor Barnes was not unaffected by the thought that he had slept with another man's wife. That is, from the moment his neighbours saw him beaten and unconscious, Walter Barnes lost much of the standing he'd had on his street.

The young man had added to Walter's agony, but he had also broken Paul's resolve. The thrashing had ended. Paul, tired and numb, the little finger of his right hand fractured, wandered away from the scene, spent. Such a futile campaign, and no real battle. He had taken Walter by surprise; so little satisfaction. He did not know how badly he had hurt him, but Walter no longer mattered.

A woman, indignant, said

– Don't let him get away. The police are coming.

Someone called out

– Hey you! Mister! Come back here.

Though Paul was not a big man, they had all witnessed his frenzy. No one was eager to restrain him, and he was at Bank Street before someone felt, really, that it would be good to go after him, by which point . . .

– What was he wearing, again?

it seemed best to leave the matter to the police.

Still irritated by her husband's insensitivity and upset by what she'd seen, the young wife had turned away from her neighbours, unpleasantly surprised by their bickering. She approached Professor Barnes and, kneeling beside him, asked

– Are you all right?

– Thank you, he said.

But he thought he was speaking to someone else entirely, to his father, in fact, and he said again

– Thank you

imagining he'd been asked, as he had always been asked after a caning, what one said to someone who'd done one a favour.

{ 13 }

MR. RUNDSTEDT IN HIS GLORY

The election had gone very well indeed. Not only were the Conservatives elected, but the Liberals, the corrupt machine, were pushed aside. Martin Brian Mulroney had moved them aside as one moves a dead rat: with the tip of one's shoe. What a man he was: "A runnable Tory, Mr. 'I'm In,'" according to the *Calgary Herald*, and he was that and more: not tall, but statesmanlike, his light brown hair slicked and neatly parted, his mouth slashed into the noble half-moon of his long face, his ears akimbo.

The Conservatives had won in Quebec, had taken Ontario, and they ruled the West: 211 seats, the largest majority in history, a resounding vote of confidence for the man from Baie-Comeau, Baie-Comeau the beautifully blushing.

The celebrations begun in each riding continued in Ottawa.

The celebration continued for months, it seemed; months of formal wear and alcohol, evening clothes, blue serge, loosened ties, floor-sweeping gowns, lifted skirts, hastily lowered stockings, flimsy panties, and the midnight rummage for a carelessly discarded shoe.

There was a cloud on the horizon, of course. There is always a cloud. Having won in Quebec, where the party was not wont to win, there was some fear Quebec would drive the new agenda. Wonderful though he was, Martin Brian was from Baie-Comeau, splendid though it was. He spoke French and was surrounded by Quebecers. What were the chances of him *hearing* of Western desires, let alone working to satisfy them?

As it turned out, Martin Brian was shrewd enough to understand he could not be successful without the West. There was, in him, something of the Khan: desire for an epic reunification, a country-binding harmony. He, Martin Brian, would soothe the Trudeau-troubled civic breast, and although he could not do this without Quebec, neither could he do it without the West: the great star-flooded prairies, the dark mountains, the islands looking back on a pine-dense coast. Very poetic, to be sure, but what it meant, in hard terms, was the anointing of a few Westerners; enough of them, so he might be seen to have their interests at heart. That meant, for the anointed, a special status: not close to the prime minister, necessarily, but necessary to him and, necessity being the political equivalent of intimacy, intimate as well.

For his first Cabinet, the largest in our brief history, the Right Honourable Himself chose thirteen Westerners.

Harvie Andre	(*Alberta*)	Supply and Services
Pat Carney	(*British Columbia*)	Energy, Mines, Resources
Joe Clark	(*Alberta*)	External Affairs
Jake Epp	(*Manitoba*)	Health and Welfare
John Fraser	(*British Columbia*)	Fisheries and Oceans
Ramon Hnatyshyn	(*Saskatchewan*)	Government House Leader
Don Mazankowski	(*Alberta*)	Transport
Bill McKnight	(*Saskatchewan*)	Labour
Jack Murta	(*Manitoba*)	Multiculturalism
Erik Nielsen	(*Yukon*)	Deputy Prime Minister

Duff Roblin	(*Manitoba*)	Government Leader in the Senate
Albert Rundstedt	(*Alberta*)	Prisons and Correction
Thomas Siddon	(*British Columbia*)	Science and Technology

(What curious annals are hidden behind each of those names: handshakes and broad smiles, Jake Epp's hair, Pat Carney's teeth, Joe Clark's shoulders, Ray Hnatyshyn's eyebrows, Erik Nielsen's sneer . . .)

Though it was wonderful to see so many Westerners in Cabinet, most of them were aware of being not quite there. Martin Brian had run on the promise of reconciliation. He'd pledged to unify a Conservative Party that was prone to bickering, that had grown scruffy in exile. To that end, he'd filled his Cabinet with women, Albertans, George Hees . . . all of whom were as important for what they represented as for who they were. It's in this sense that they were there and not there.

Albert Rundstedt, for instance, was insignificant. There was very little about Rundstedt (as Rundstedt) that made him more valuable than any other Westerner. He was reliable, a long-time Conservative, fond of Joe Clark, but you could say the same of any number of them. He was clever, which was a liability, but he was also practical, experienced in electoral matters, and capable of being led. *L'homme moyen conservateur*, in other words. What Rundstedt had in his favour, the thing that made Rundstedt valuable (as Rundstedt), was his chief interest: prison, a subject of universal interest, a good idea in both the best and worst of times. One could always count on the public's fear. So, prison was, to the political sphere, immaculate?

Well, no, not exactly.

A prison was nothing (in itself). It was not an edifice meant to please aesthetically. In fact, a prison is always best when somewhere else, best when invisible, though behind the walls and beneath the searchlights there is Law and Right and the assertion of a Moral Order, and that is what's needed and what is repre-sented: a return to morality, a halt to the decay that looked indif-ferently on crime and churchlessness. Still, though prisons were wonderfully significant, they were much *less* important than taxes, say, or education or health care. They were also a partial preserve of the provinces. And so . . . a real politician (Rundstedt) with highly symbolic concerns (prisons and houses of deten-tion) was assigned a symbolic portfolio (Cabinet Council to the Secretary of State on Prisons and Penal Reform) in a symbolic Cabinet; though, because the symbolic carries real weight in pol-itics, Rundstedt was given an actual budget and that, of course, meant he had real, if circumscribed, power.

It was, for Rundstedt, a moment of pure pleasure. For the offi-cial photograph, he stood beside Duff Roblin, smiling broadly, showing his teeth. He was given three offices in Centre Block: for himself, for his policy adviser (Franklin Dupuis), and for three assistants: his personal secretary, Ms. Rees; the ministry's secretary, Mary Stanley; and a research assistant, Edward Muir. Though these offices were smaller than what he might have had in either wing, he basked in the prestige of Centre Block, basked in its history. It was as if you could smell the foul breath of John A. Macdonald or kick MacKenzie King's dog. And along with history, there came an inkling of the "historical," a desire to belong to the story of nationhood. This was like a wonderful civic mirage in which all he could accomplish shone before him as if to light his way.

Then there was the respect, the sheer *Excuse me, sir. Yes, Mr. Rundstedt*, slightly bowed greetings of pages, underlings, and hon-eymoon journalists. You could see the *Who knew?* in them, the *What was that? What did he say?* attentiveness, as if his every *hem* and *haw* now had potential. A more self-conscious man might have found some of this attention difficult, but Rundstedt was not particularly self-conscious. It did not disturb him to find matter trapped among his teeth, and, though he was reasonably careful to avoid them, stains to his clothing did not concern him. He was confident his inner being, now that he was a member of Cabinet, was worthy of presentation, whatever the circumstances.

This was a remarkably wrongheaded attitude for one so experienced in politics. There was, of course, precedence for such seeming guilelessness. Eugene Whelan had traipsed about in a green Stetson for years, but Whelan had craftily evolved into a parody of the good old Western guy, had hidden behind the Prairies, much as John Crosbie hid behind the Grand Banks. (Also, Whelan was Liberal, and a Liberal from Alberta might do the strangest things without raising eyebrows: a talking dog that does math gets little attention for its sums.)

A remarkable attitude indeed, because Rundstedt's *inner being* was inimical to Politics. It might even be fair to say that any *inner being* is (by degrees) toxic to the body politic, or that Politics is that aspect of the imagination that begins with a partial occlusion of the *inner*. The more particular the individual, the less likely is election. It is a failing, in *Homo politicus*, to allow glimpses of a private agenda, unless, of course, the private agenda is so innocuous that it is, in its wide appeal, as close to *public* as the *private* can be. Yes, of course, the particular sometimes meets with public approval, but the fortunate politicians who embody a particularity are not so much individuals as personae. That is, once it's established that Trudeau is the "intellectual," Trudeau can wear buckskin breeches and Hawaiian shirts without ruffling the public's feathers. One simply says

– *Ahh, there goes a university education . . .*

and turns to the Sports page. For the average politician, however, for one not blessed with a vivid persona, a white smile, a clean suit, and an inoffensive demeanour are not simply a curtain on the *inner being*, they are a tithe paid to the public, a way of saying "my own concerns are insignificant compared to my devotion to you, to your standards, to your interests . . ." No one believes this, of course. The jack-in-the-box has sprung so often one waits almost impatiently for the appearance of raw self-interest, but one objects when the tithe is not paid. The box must be closed for the music to sound.

All of this was standard fare to Rundstedt. He knew better than to allow the public an unobstructed view of his inner self or his sartorial indifference. But in the excitement of victory, he permitted himself a *je m'en foutisme* that he came to regret. It's true that journalists listened to what he said, but they *wrote* about his appearance and his manner. In the first two months, reading through his press clippings, Rundstedt saw the words

> *rumpled, careless, arrogant, unprepared, not serious,*
> *eccentric, obsessed, clownish, clownlike, motley, buffoon*

used to describe him. They were used so often, he began to wonder if he had not, now that he thought of it, always had something of the buffoon about him. Perhaps he could make motley work for him? No, he could not. No one was impressed by his sense of humour. His witticisms were abysmal: stilted, obviously rehearsed, and beside the point when the discussions were serious, as they sometimes were when prison was at issue. His witticisms were early Churchill by way of Diefenbaker:

– *Madam, in the morning I shall be sober, but you will still be ugly.*

and so on. Hard biscuits, even for the committed conservative. So, for two months, Rundstedt floundered. He floundered until his secretary, an experienced parliamentarian, tactfully suggested they shop together for "a few things." They were, at the outset, looking for women's shoes, but, mysteriously it seemed to Rundstedt, they ended up in a peculiar boutique on Rideau (by King Edward): Les Cheveux Rouge du Forgeron.

Les Cheveux Rouge was unusual for a number of reasons. First, it was almost as anonymous as a store could be. It was on Rideau, yes, but its name was nowhere to be seen on the storefront. There were no picture windows and its single metal door was platinum, opaque and intimidating. It was almost as anonymous on the inside: long, narrow, bereft of merchandise. Its walls were white, recently plastered; on one, there was the print of a woman: glance askance, head bound in a white scarf, holding a small child, its face in shadow, its plump hand nestled at her throat. Towards the back of the shop, there was a silver counter, waist high. On the countertop there was nothing at all. The counter looked like a rectangle of polished silver; behind it, there stood an impeccably dressed young man: square-jawed, smooth-faced, his nose descending classically from between his eyebrows, his blond hair falling liturgically in ringlets.

– Please? he asked.

– Is Rossastro in? asked Ms. Rees.

– No, that he is not, said the young man.

– Eh bien, said Mr. Rundstedt

who thought he'd detected a French accent from the young man.

– Are you expecting him soon?

The young man considered the question carefully.

– Perhaps, he said.

– Perhaps?

– Lately, his hours are most unpredictable.

– Eh bien, repeated Rundstedt

in an effort to be friendly.

The young man considered Rundstedt.

– A politician? he asked.

– Yes, answered Ms. Rees.

– Liberal or Conservative?

– Conservative.

– Ahh . . . May I?

– I guess it's all right.

– What's he doing? asked Rundstedt.

From beneath the countertop, the young man took a square of coarse white paper and a tape measure.

– Allow me, he said

coming out from behind the counter. And, before Rundstedt knew it, he was being measured for a suit.

– I thought we were looking for shoes, he said to Ms. Rees.

– You certainly need them, said the young man.

Rundstedt was too much the politician to take offence. He watched as the young man wrote figures on the square of paper, and then he was astonished when the young man handed the square to his secretary.

– Won't you need that? Rundstedt asked.

– It is for you, sir. I have good memory. Your clothes will be ready in two weeks.

– What clothes?

The young man was momentarily puzzled. He looked to Ms. Rees, who discreetly nodded, before turning to Rundstedt.

– Do you also need undergarments?

Fifteen days later, Rundstedt received two Brioni suits (double-breasted, blue and navy blue), two white shirts, silk ties from Gianfranco Ferri (red), Gucci shoes (ox blood), (black) Stanfield's, and a receipt for $5715.70, a considerable amount for Rundstedt, who had never really considered the value of clothes.

Their effect was immediate and not unsubtle. To begin with, journalists stopped writing about his clothes, but they did not mention his new elegance. Rather, it was as if his clothes did not signify, though Rundstedt himself was treated with restraint and there was new respect for his humour, which hadn't changed but which now seemed subtler, somehow. He was still a Westerner but, in Italian clothes, this was more acceptable, even to Western journalists who, perhaps unconsciously, took pride in him. Here was a man to represent their interests, a jocular but important politician, a man who quoted Churchill and one who knew all one could know about his own portfolio.

– I am not sure importance is important . . .
said Rundstedt when it was suggested that his position in Cabinet
was quite important

– Truth is.

An answer that, though stolen from a philosopher, pleased
everyone.

And so, after a fall from grace, Rundstedt regained some of the
esteem he'd lost, regained enough esteem to recover a measure of
self-confidence and that was most helpful, to himself, above all,
but also to the prime minister and those in caucus who kept close
watch on who had and did not have the confidence of the public.

Rundstedt's real victory, then, came not immediately after the
election but some two months later. He had erred in disregarding
the importance of dress, but there must be a fall if one is to rise
and Rundstedt was fortunate in his fall. By placing his faith in
Rossastro's boutique, he had solved a minor but potentially fatal
difficulty with his image.

Rundstedt was gratified.

14

WHAT IS NIGHT, ANYWAY?

Franklin's first months as Rundstedt's policy adviser were bewildering and unproductive. Rundstedt seemed unsure of what to do, unclear what was expected of him, and uncomfortable in power. He floundered until, miraculously, he found his footing and assumed his stature, *becoming* a Cabinet minister almost overnight. After an interval of doubt and uncertainty, Rundstedt managed to restore Franklin's faith in him. This was good, in itself, but it preceded and, perhaps, influenced the most important moment in Franklin's life. Shortly after he and Rundstedt found their bearings in office, once he regained confidence in Rundstedt, his life's purpose was revealed to him and, finally at ease in his work, Franklin took it for what it was: his long-attended inspiration.

It happened like this: Franklin was by Dow's Lake, happily strolling. It was evening on a Friday and he was thinking of winter and windows when he suddenly recalled the words of a poet, words he had first heard in university: "I call architecture frozen music." The words were Goethe's, and they had, perhaps, been meant lightly, but there was, suddenly, something about them that made him stop and think: a little something at the edge of Franklin's mind, like a moth trapped in a light fixture.

As he looked across the water towards the experimental farm, its bare trees, more words came to him, along with a thrilling question. The other words were mine, spoken the night Franklin and I met:

– Prisons aren't civilized . . .

The question, though, was his own and, as if he'd finally managed to ask it so that it sounded in his depths, the thing made him reel:

– Why *shouldn't* they be?

As the shepherd (or the wolf) makes the flock stronger by culling, so does the politician make his community stronger by taking certain men and women from the throng and shutting them away. Not so? But politicians can do what wolves and shepherds cannot. They can improve those they take away and return them (stronger) to the flock. That, at least, was the theory, but the words "prisons aren't civilized" had astounded Franklin by their obvious truth. Prisons are *not* civilized.

But why *shouldn't* prisons be civilized? That was the question, and it brought with it a vision, not of a penitentiary but of a place created as art, an institution that helped strengthen community while instilling community at its noblest. Not simply a good-looking prison but one whose effect was ennobling on a number of levels: aesthetic, social, political, perhaps even religious. A building, that is, to civilize those who passed though it or lived within. A building that would do what great art does: enrich the soul.

For the first time in years, Franklin remembered the black man he'd seen in prison: golden brown pants, blue-and-white-striped shirt, black shoes, missing teeth, pink tongue. He felt a rush of warmth, of fellow feeling, of emotion that turned the bare trees beautiful. *This* was his mission: to civilize those who had been cast aside, to find or create a building that would inspire in its inmates not fear or disdain, as most prisons did, but nobility, civility, and awe before the creations of man and God. It's true, he'd had versions of this very idea before, but those had been the imaginings of a man wandering in wilderness. The man who stood by Dow's Lake contemplating the autumn trees was in a position to bring his vision into being: he worked for a minister as interested in prisons as he was, he knew an artist, Reinhart, who might be persuaded to design the very building, and he himself was familiar with the ways of bureaucracy and government. In other words, Franklin was now an ideal steward for his own imagination.

Besides turning the dull landscape bright, the discovery of a purpose filled him with a joy he had not known since childhood and reconciled him to Ottawa, the city in which his purpose was, finally, revealed and in which it would be (he would see to it with all that was in him) accomplished.

It was quite a moment, but Franklin kept it to himself for weeks, turning the idea about, thinking it through. Was Art really ennobling? Yes, if it was truly Art rather than, say, a record of some suffering or another. Was it possible to create a building as great as *La Giaconda* or *The Ninth Symphony?* Yes, he was sure of it, but only if "Alba" – the "white one," a name he imagined for the prison of his imagining – were designed by an artist and he was certain Reinhart was at least that. And what were the arguments against Alba? That it would be expensive, that it was an experiment, that it would mean housing criminals in a place more beautiful than the average citizen's. Yes, okay, but, to begin with, crime itself cost society more than Alba would, and then again, we have had centuries of horrid and ugly prisons that killed the spirit. Wasn't it time for something else? And as for Alba's beauty surpassing that of the average habitat . . . it was Dostoevsky who'd said, "A civilization is best judged by how it treats its prisoners." (A sentence that came to Franklin in Alexandra's voice.) Though it might be counter-intuitive, it was perhaps time to treat prisoners better, wasn't it, time to bring them into the noblest fold? Questions, questions, answers, answers . . . they took over Franklin's thoughts, plagued him, one might have said, but, far from defeating him, they gave him countless occasions for little victories that, in the end, amounted to a successful campaign.

Though he was by nature cautious, he allowed himself, in the months following his revelation at Dow's Lake, a hopeful thought for this endeavour that sought to achieve, on such a grand scale, a sense of belonging that usually existed only on a small scale, at home, say, home itself being the greatest human accomplishment. He even permitted himself kind words for his own family, though he did not go so far as to visit any of them. Instead, he embraced friendship. That is, he was happy in Edward's company and he was less guarded with others.

Myself, for instance. It was almost certainly around this time that, meeting by accident on the Laurier Bridge, Franklin invited me to his apartment, a modest, not quite austere collection of white rooms, with two bookcases, a striking, hand-sewn rug (crimson, cream, orange, with the figures of men, birds, turtles and horses, woven into it), and a dining-room table that looked as if it had come from a poor farmhouse.

This sense of purpose was good for Franklin, in general, but it also made things easier for him, as head of the Commission for the Investigation of Penal Reform (CIPR). Appointed in late November, by the Right Honourable Rundstedt, Franklin had, by early December, assembled a committee of lawyers and sociologists, none of whom was experienced enough to offer resistance to his directions, or to fend off his enthusiasm. They all did as they were guided to do and, on top of that, they did it for very little money, the CIPR being, for most of them, a first government commission. The lone exception was Jackson Tate, a highly regarded intellectual who had, in his day, written a controversial and widely respected study of Antonio Gramsci (*Greece and Gramsci*, Carleton University Press, 1957).

It was clear, from the outset, that the Canadian penal system would be found wanting, that it would need additional and different prisons. Franklin and Rundstedt believed this to be the case, before the first penny was spent on airline tickets, personal assistants, or office supplies. Not that the commission was a cakewalk for Franklin. There were a few small hedges to jump. For instance, Professor Tate, whom Franklin took on for his reputation and prestige, was not unequivocally *for* penal reform. He was, in fact, against it, or against the Conservative version of it, which, it seemed to him, was a matter of locking more people up for longer. But he was now, at eighty-three, too preoccupied with his own mortality to care one way or the other. He was only a temporary public face for the CIPR, and that suited them all. Then there was the matter of Franklin himself. In what way was he qualified to head an investigation into the penal system? This was the question at the commission's initial press conference.

– Well, Franklin answered, rubbing his hands together, though I'm co-chair of the commission, my role is administrative. I'm a handmaiden to Professor Tate. I'll see to the small details, organization, and so on. And Professor Tate will sift the evidence and oversee the commission's final report to Minister Rundstedt.

– Do *you* have any views on prison reform? a reporter asked.

– None, said Franklin. I'll wait until we finish our report. The minister would like this to be as objective an investigation as possible, and so would I.

– I see . . . , said the reporter before turning his depleted attention span to Professor Tate.

Finally, there was the matter of budget and timetable. These things Franklin managed with relative ease. The CIPR would cost the public hundreds of thousands of dollars, a million actually, but Franklin was efficient. He assured Minister Rundstedt that it would take no more than six months to collect the (appropriate) statistics and (appropriately) interpret the data. And it took no more than six months, months during which Franklin demonstrated his ability to think of one thing to the exclusion of everything else. He worked unstintingly, to the credit of Minister Rundstedt, whose judgment came to be admired in those circles where admiration was useful.

And it was all to Franklin's credit as well.

On a winter evening, after much of the commission's work had been accomplished but before its report was published, Franklin went to Reinhart's studio, as he'd been doing regularly over the preceding months. As if he had been waiting for him, Reinhart opened the door and gave Franklin a friendly, sideways hug.

– Frank, what's the story? he asked.

– I just wanted to have a word, said Franklin.

– Come into my office, why don't you? said Reinhart.

He put his arm around Franklin's shoulder and shepherded him in. When Reinhart had taken his coat and draped it over a stool, Franklin said

– I wonder if we could talk about a commission?

– A commission?

– For a prison, answered Franklin.

– You want me to paint a prison?

– No, no. I'd like you to design one.

Reinhart smiled. He had just finished a painting he was proud of and he was grateful for company and diversion. He stared at Franklin as if the man were a new subject . . . an interesting face he had, and familiar too.

– Edward mentioned something about prisons, a while ago. So did you, now that I think about it, but, you know, I *work* for architects. I get enough architecture at Kessler and McAdams and I'm not really interested in buildings.

Franklin looked disappointed. Reinhart smiled, handed him a shot glass of rye, and said

– Drink.

while he, too, downed a mouthful of whisky.

– I have my own work to do, said Reinhart, and, besides, I haven't designed a building since university. I mostly do modelling these days.

– Well, answered Franklin, it wouldn't be a building, exactly. It wouldn't be the usual thing. I had something else in mind, a work of art, something great and deep and noble, the equivalent of . . .

On hearing the words "great and deep and noble," Reinhart stopped paying attention. These were the kinds of words people who knew nothing about art commonly used to describe it, but "greatness," "depth," and "nobility" inevitably meant something ancient, something known, something dead. "Greatness," "depth," and "nobility" were what happened to works of art over time, like rust or tarnish. No serious artist ever strove for them.

– You know, I don't think so, Reinhart said, but thanks for the offer, Frank.

– I'm disappointed, said Franklin. There can't be many artists out there who could create something deeper than the usual lines and planes.

– It's a wonderful idea, said Reinhart, and I suspect it *will* be difficult to find someone like that, but, you know, me and architecture . . .

He took Franklin's empty shot glass, filled it with rye, then said in an atrocious accent

– Und jetz mussen wir trinken, Herr Dupuis.

Both of them downed their ounce of rye. And, after this second round, Franklin felt as if he'd missed the right words, because there were surely words to convince an artist like Reinhart of the significance of what he, Franklin, wanted. He would try again, another evening. It made no sense to harass the man in his own studio. He wandered around, quietly looking at paintings, as Reinhart puttered about the studio cleaning up.

– It's a beautiful night, Franklin said, finally.

– So it is, said Reinhart.

Franklin turned his back and looked out the windows, up at the sky. After a while, he said, more to himself than to Reinhart:

– And yet, there's no such thing as night.

Meaning: it had occurred to him, just then, how arbitrary it was to give such weight to the distinction between light and darkness. It's true there were times when you bumped your head going in or stumbled going out but, really, the bright blessed day and the dark sacred night were one and the same. Or so they must be for the stars or the gods. It was only man who needed the distinction. *There* was a melancholic thought.

But it was as if Reinhart had been stung.

– What did you say? he asked.

– Nothing, Franklin answered. Nothing.

– You said there was no such thing as night.

– Yes, I guess I did.

– What a thing to say.

– I didn't mean anything by it, said Franklin.

– No, you don't understand, said Reinhart.

Which was true because Reinhart himself didn't understand. Franklin's words had entered his consciousness at an odd angle. They'd clicked against a hidden and vague inspiration and knocked it momentarily into the light. On hearing Franklin's words, Reinhart had felt elated and then unsure why he'd felt anything at all.

– Here, he said

pouring Franklin another shot.

– What were we talking about, again?

– A prison? answered Franklin.

– Hmm, said Reinhart, maybe that's got something to do with it. Why are you so interested in prisons?

For the next few hours, during which they finished the Crown Royal ounce by ounce and Reinhart listened closely, rarely speaking, Franklin gave rein to his enthusiasm for this grand penitentiary, for the prospect of building something of lasting value and ongoing effect, a prison that, in itself, might soothe the savage breast. By the end of the evening, you wouldn't have said Reinhart had been impressed by anything Franklin said. Reinhart wasn't easily impressed by ideas. He could be moved by the slightest display of genuine emotion, though, and as Franklin's emotions had all been genuine, Reinhart had been moved.

But then, though he'd been moved by Franklin's passion, he

couldn't see its connection to him. Why should he, Reinhart, care about Franklin's concerns about penitentiaries and penitents? Then again, something in Franklin's words had struck him and gone deep.

– There's no such thing as night?

Long after Franklin had wobbled out of his studio, Reinhart grappled with the idea of nightlessness, intrigued and, as it happened, taken.

– What an idea, he thought.

––––––––––

Once the commission's report was printed and sent out to interested parties, Rundstedt liked to call Franklin his "author," a true compliment because, although Rundstedt was intimidated to the point of dislike by "real" authors (he had once been introduced to Robertson Davies and had perspired for hours afterwards), he did, in fact, have deep respect for them. He was not intimidated by Franklin. Au contraire, it was as if he could relax in the company of a talented collaborator. More than that: the commission was a Rubicon of sorts for both Franklin and Rundstedt. Once it was forded, their acquaintance became a friendship. The feeling *both* had was of mutual understanding. Rundstedt allowed himself to speak of his personal life and of the concerns he had for his family. This was something he shared with few people in Ottawa. Franklin reciprocated by listening to Rundstedt and offering mild advice, when it was solicited, and commiseration, when advice was not wanted. Also, Franklin openly voiced his (rather good, thought Rundstedt) ideas about a new penitentiary, going so far (too far, in fact) as to admit that he had already spoken with an artist (Reinhart Mauer), a true artist, one with a degree in architecture.

Something bristled in Rundstedt at mention of this "true artist." Who was Franklin to speak to outsiders about a project that did not as yet exist? Should he, Rundstedt, not have been told of this collusion *before* it was begun? He chided Franklin for his lack of discretion, but once Franklin apologized and assured him his talk with Reinhart had been vague and theoretical, it occurred to Rundstedt that Franklin's mistake had been made through exuberance. And though exuberance is political poison, it is a desirable quality in one's collaborators, yes? At least it was desirable to Rundstedt. So, in the end, he did not hold Franklin's little "transgression" against him.

For his part, Franklin was exasperated, believing he should have known better than to mention Reinhart when he did. It was the kind of mistake a neophyte might have made, and he resolved not to make it again. So, though his friendship with Rundstedt was not damaged by his indiscretion, he became a little less open, with everyone, not just Rundstedt.

Despite their misunderstanding, Franklin and Rundstedt spent the months following the release of the commission's findings in intense collaboration. Edward did not really understand what Rundstedt and Franklin were going on about. It seemed to him that, if great Art could tame vicious men, it would have done so by now. (It was either that or admit that no Art had, as yet, been great enough, an idea he found easier to accept than the one at the heart of this new prison.) Still, he was swept up in the enthusiasms of Rundstedt and Dupuis and flattered to be let in on their plans, to be a junior member in a society of three, an underling, yes, a mere research assistant, but one who had the consideration of his superiors. He hid his doubts about MacKenzie Bowell Federal Penitentiary (as Rundstedt believed it should be called). In fact, after a while, Edward even came to agree that the worst criminals, being uncouth, were helplessly criminal-minded, and that MacKenzie Bowell penitentiary was, in so far as it could change those minds, a step in the right direction.

The three of them met, now and then, at one of the bars in the Market and, after discussing some point of theory (for instance, the idea that criminals can be identified from the shapes of their skulls) or some point of procedure (for example, Rundstedt had begun to solicit the opinions of other Conservatives and was pleased to discover the amount of support there was for a MacKenzie Bowell penitentiary, Sir MacKenzie Bowell being a Conservative prime minister whose name was on very few federal buildings), they would drink (modestly), and then go home warmed by the company and by the thought they were working for good.

The problem with this camaraderie was that it hid their differences. Edward, of course, did not share either Rundstedt's or Franklin's belief in MacKenzie Bowell. But there were differences between Franklin's belief and Rundstedt's as well. For Rundstedt, a house of correction was simply an appendage of the Ministry of Justice. A prison was a building whose primary function was to keep those who were a menace to their fellow citizens apart from the law-abiding majority. It was wonderful to imagine MacKenzie Bowell pen as a civilizing influence, but one had to see to its practical function first.

For Franklin, the "practical" prison simply did not figure. The place where men and women suffered, deservedly or not, for their crimes was a detail, trivial the way all details are. Moral significance is what gave meaning to any building, especially a prison. So, a prison was important only in what it represented: the idea of order, the force of law, the way to community. In so far as the idea of order is metaphysical or sacred, so, too, was Alba, and Franklin thought of himself (and Rundstedt and Edward) as the prison's acolyte. Alba meant more to Franklin, of course, in that it provided him with purpose, but prisons had not, since his childhood visit to Kingston pen, been the simple bricks and mortar they were to Rundstedt.

Despite their differences, or because their differences were hidden, Rundstedt agreed when Franklin proposed he speak again to

Reinhart Mauer. Nothing official was to be put on offer. It was, rather, a delicate exploration, a gentle probing, a feeling out. Franklin should be cautious in his approach to Reinhart: lead the man gently, until you were certain he was the one.

And, in fact, Rundstedt's caution was well placed, because, where Reinhart was concerned, Franklin was somewhat naive. Franklin admired and respected Reinhart's talent, but he did not understand that Reinhart was not, ultimately, master of his own artistry. Once in the grip of an idea or a vision, Reinhart was lost. He entered a place where success, failure, money, attention, and affection ceased to matter. In this state, Reinhart could not be made to do what was wanted, in part because Reinhart himself, try as he might, had no idea how to get to the place or, again, how to leave it; no way to rise above himself, or away from himself, no way to do anything but what the vision demanded. He was, indeed, an artist and, as such, faithful to the chaos from which all Art springs. So, he was not, strictly speaking, an ideal government appointee.

15

A SENSE OF PURPOSE AND A CLOUDY MIND

I t seemed to Mary that Franklin had become more focused. You could see he was pleased to be in the office of the Right Honourable Councillor to the Secretary of State, but his focus narrowed as he dealt with the tasks Rundstedt assigned him.

The election had, to varying degrees, changed all the Conservatives. During the early months, some of them had grown giddy and overassertive. Not Franklin. Franklin became something like an idealist, not confident in the rightness of power, exactly, but willing to believe in its rightness. Things had worked out well for Franklin but there wasn't an arrogant bone in his body. Franklin was loyal to Rundstedt and loyal to those he trusted. (The cloud on this silver lining was named Edward Muir. Because the department had the funds, Franklin also found place for the morose and unappealing Muir.)

Rundstedt also became, unexpectedly, in Mary's eyes, a man to respect. You couldn't exactly say why but, suddenly, there he was: upright in demeanour, serious in intent, forthright, and impressive. Wasn't it odd how some men rose to the dignity of power, as if their better selves had only been lurking, lying in wait for elevation? Mary had never suspected Rundstedt of dignity. She'd always thought him a man on the verge of fondling someone, although, to be honest, in prurience he was so like his peers (Franklin excepted) you couldn't have called him exceptional. No, what was exceptional was his rise to propriety. And how was Rundstedt's propriety expressed? As Mary saw it, it, too, was expressed as loyalty. When Rundstedt took over his portfolio, he immediately set aside a part of his budget for the creation of an independent commission that would look into the prospects for new prisons, and the man he chose to head the commission was Franklin himself, his own policy adviser. Franklin had told her all of this himself, in confidence, and Mary, instinctively protective of him, imagined the worst: that the commission was a make-work program for Rundstedt's department, that it was only for show, that, in the event its findings proved controversial, Franklin was there to take the blame. It did not take much presence of mind to question Rundstedt's motives. For Mary, there were two possibilities: either Rundstedt was conniving when he chose Franklin to head his commission or Rundstedt was loyal and generous. (It did not occur to her that these were not mutually exclusive.) But here was the post-electoral Rundstedt: well spoken, well dressed, and smelling of vanilla. Gradually, after a few months, Mary began to accept that, whatever her initial doubts, this plum appointment was, in the end, good for Franklin. It was a small honour, a recompense for his time in the trenches of the Conservative Party. Perhaps, after all, politics remade men in its own, mysterious ways, leaving some hollow while renewing others.

Franklin's strong sense of purpose was all to the good but, through no fault of his, Mary began to feel as if it would be wrong to speak with him as they used to. He listened to whatever she had to say, fully *there* in their conversations, interested in the details of her life, but she felt, now, as if her life were petty compared to the business of state, that it was wrong to divert him from his work.

She hadn't realized how important it had been to have his sympathetic ear. And it was painful, now that her grandmother had begun to behave strangely, to be without his kindness and his ear. Painful? Was there, perhaps, more to her feelings for Franklin? No, no . . . he was not her type. They were friendly, nothing more, and yet she missed his company (his real attentiveness) more than she expected, and she felt the change in him as a rebuff, despite herself.

For entirely different reasons, for reasons other than politics or power, her grandmother, too, had changed. Eleanor was obviously waning, and it was distressing to watch the onset of frailty in a woman who had been so strong.

One day, some time before the election, she had handed Mary a note on which was written, in pencil:

> You must see me on Monday.
> Show no one.
> Eleanor Stanley
> (your grandmother)

and, odd though the note was, its delivery was stranger still.

It had been some time since Eleanor had come downstairs for supper, but on this particular evening she'd descended as the family sat at the table. She had smiled, or seemed to smile, and then slowly approached. When she was beside the table, she took the note from her brassiere and, with something like rehearsed indifference, pushed it into Mary's hand.

Her father asked

– Everything okay, Mom? You want to eat with us?

and she answered in a strange accent:

– Is how long since yuh see de Kwayzay?

– The what?

– How yuh mean?

and, with that, Eleanor had sucked her teeth and retraced her steps, going up the stairs as slowly as she'd descended. To say that they'd all been mystified, well . . . To Mary's knowledge, her grandmother had never spoken with any but a slight British accent. This was as if a strange woman had entered their home, spoken in code, and left before anyone could ask what she meant.

– The quay what? Mary had asked.

– Search me, her father answered. What's the note say?

Mary had shown it to them.

– Gran's definitely losing it, said Gil.

That had precipitated an argument: her father on one side, the rest of them on the other. It seemed clear to Mary that Eleanor was indeed coming unglued, but she loved her grandmother and, however mysterious the details, however unclear it was as to when or on what Monday Eleanor wished to see her, she tried to keep their appointment.

It was not an easy thing to do. For a month of Mondays she went up to Eleanor's room, but although her grandmother was invariably happy to see her, and though they spoke of this and that, Eleanor simply *could* not recall requesting Mary's attendance. Mary tried to prompt her grandmother by showing her the note, by explaining that, yes, she (Eleanor) had herself passed the note along. But Eleanor recognized neither the note nor her own handwriting. She could not think why she should want to see her granddaughter so urgently, unless of course it was simply to have her company. Yes, that must have been it. She very much enjoyed Mary's society, you see?

Then, on the fifth Monday, she'd gone up, and Eleanor said

– You didn't tell the others, did you, dear?

– Tell them what? Mary asked.

– Forgetful girl! About my little note.

– Oh, that . . . No.

– Are you sure?

Her grandmother sat up in the bed, looking at her closely, listening intently, speaking with her familiar, slightly clipped British accent, as if her old self had decided to revisit its confines.

– Yes, said Mary.

– Good, said Eleanor. Come sit here.

She indicated the place at the end of the bed.

– Would you mind, dear? she asked

and pushed her feet out from beneath the blanket so Mary could massage them.

– It's doubtful that in all Canada you'll find three pairs of shapely feminine feet, don't you think?

It was their own little joke, a question asked by one or the other whenever Mary massaged her grandmother's feet. Her feet must indeed have been beautiful when Eleanor was younger, though. They were still elegant and smooth, and it pleased Mary to hold them in her palms.

– Now, Mary . . .

Eleanor said as her granddaughter rubbed the sole of her right foot

– I know you think I am your poor grandmother, and you've been good to me all the same. You've been like a daughter to me. You *have* been a daughter to me. It's no fault of yours if others haven't been so loyal.

– Dad's been just as loyal, Gran.

– Never mind, child. You've been good to me, but I must ask you a favour.

– What is it, Gran?

– I want you to keep a secret, but really keep it.

– Of course.

– Will you swear?

– Of course I will.

– Good, good. I trust you. Mary . . . I want you to know I am not without means . . . I am the opposite of penniless.

– Oh?

– Yes, my dear, it's quite true.

It was a peculiar moment for both of them. Eleanor blushed. She had revealed a long-kept secret, a source of satisfaction in its secrecy, and though she did feel a kind of relief, she also felt humiliated, because it suddenly seemed mean not to have told Mary before now. For her part, Mary found the moment surreal. Though her grandmother was lucid, it was as if she were lucid in an obscure language. What was the opposite of penniless?

– After all, Eleanor continued, I don't see why I should be ashamed of my money. I've worked all my life, and I would certainly have lost everything if I'd told your father. You won't tell him, will you?

– I won't if you don't want me to.

– Good. I don't mind if Stanley has means, once I'm gone. Once I'm gone, I don't suppose it matters, but . . . Look, let's go to the heart of it, Mary. I'd like you to take care of things for me.

– You'd like me to take care of things?

Her grandmother was, it seemed to Mary, in the midst of a vivid dream she was trying to recount: she was (she said) worth millions, she had once owned houses in cities all over the world, she had managed the wealth on her own for years and years. No, that's not quite true. In the past, there had been two or three men, faithful employees. Now there was only one.

– Here is his card, Mary. Honestly, it gives me fits trying to remember names. It never used to.

She pressed a bone white card into Mary's hand.

– Can you read it? she asked.

– Yes, Mary answered.

– Now go into the closet . . . Go ahead. There is a blue purse on the floor at the back.

Mary did as she was told, but it now felt as if *she* were dreaming. Yet, there it was: an oversized, baby blue purse, something she vaguely remembered having seen in her grandmother's hand. As she picked the purse from the floor, she had a precise memory of the thing. She'd seen her grandmother carry it into her room. Now when was that?

– Bring it here, said Eleanor.

From the bag Eleanor drew countless envelopes, envelopes of varying size, colour, and age; some of them were ancient and brittle, some were cream-coloured, some yellow, some blue; most had strange stamps on them and these were as fascinating as the envelopes themselves.

– Don't paw them, Mary.

From the envelopes, Eleanor drew more particular documents: copies of deeds from before the turn of the century, elaborately embossed contracts, a black bank book whose first entry was from 1915, maps of various cities in various times, receipts, business cards, and a photograph of "Robert Stanley."

Really, it was all absurd. Her grandmother's revelation and unveiling did not seem so much truthful as elaborate, and Mary's first coherent thoughts were questions: Why would anyone go through such trouble trying to prove the fantastic? What must it have cost, in time and money, to gather so many strange documents? And then, as if the documents weren't enough, Eleanor spoke of the one thing she had never, ever mentioned: her marriage to Robert Stanley.

An English aristocrat marrying a Trinidadian schoolgirl? Not likely, thought Mary, not even in Grimm's, and the old photograph Eleanor showed her (pale man before chapel, his name – Robert Stanley – written on the back) did little to persuade. Detail on detail contributed not to a feeling of truth but to a sense of delusion. That is, when she heard about her "grandfather," Mary was convinced her grandmother was lost in some orphan's fantasy, where one is secretly related to Sir Such-and-Such who is wealthy and kind and, besides, a close friend to the king of Spain. On hearing about Robert Stanley's estate, Mary couldn't help smiling. Eleanor caught it immediately. Most perceptive when she was perceptive at all, Eleanor sensed Mary's disbelief and, perhaps thinking disbelief would lead to betrayal, suddenly said

– That's enough for today

and collected her envelopes and documents, put them back in the purse, and dismissed her granddaughter with the words:

– Now remember: you promised not to tell anyone, Mary. Not a word. You swore it. I hope you won't make me regret what I've told you.

That was months ago now, and Mary had kept her word. She'd told nobody. But what did it mean to give your word to someone who was unstable? Eleanor's delusions of wealth, her tale of marriage to an aristocrat, her collection of arcane documents, sepia photographs, brittle envelopes, and exotic postmarks were not dangerous in themselves, but they were proof of her mental decline. Though Mary had sworn to keep everything secret, she worried that, in keeping them secret, she was hiding information that, revealed, would benefit Eleanor herself because, if Eleanor needed the kind of care needed by the delusional, she should get it as soon as possible. Shouldn't she?

On the other hand, she had given her word and one had to be faithful to that, at least. She couldn't break her word simply because her grandmother was not who she seemed, or because she had changed. People always changed. They were themselves for such a short time, it was impossible to keep your word to the person to whom you'd given it. Your friendship, your love, your respect are given to loved ones but kept for the strangers they soon become. Take Franklin, for instance. He was no longer the man he had been before the election, but she would not think of turning her back on him, would she?

How she would have liked to talk to Franklin about all this, to see him nod sagely and smile, but two fidelities stood between them: his fidelity to Rundstedt (to his work) and hers to her own word. She would have to keep watch on Eleanor, alone, and keep her own counsel. There was nothing else for it.

16

ELEANOR GOES GENTLE, MORE OR LESS . . .

D ecember 4 began early for Eleanor Stanley.
She woke at two in the morning from a peculiar dream
in which her house in London was huge and ran for
blocks. In fact, it ran through countries, because at the far end of
it the Palestinians were street fighting. Her father was in it, trying
to hurry his death along, because he hated the painful slowness of
it. Her mother was living in a tiny cubbyhole, on a bed, a slat
really, between walls that looked too small for the smallest child,
and when Eleanor asked her why she hadn't moved (there were
many rooms), her mother said she didn't want to. One of her
uncles was writing a book about the house's mazes and back stair-
ways (numerous and tiny). And Eleanor herself was pleased to be
there, moved by the sight of her parents, whom she hadn't seen
in years. They looked lovingly at her, and she was happy, until she
remembered she was an old woman, that she couldn't possibly
climb so many stairs, and her heart began to race, and she grew
short of breath, and woke from sleep with the sound of the ocean
in her ears.

As it happens, she was lucid when she woke. That is, for the first
time in a while, the place where she thought she was coincided
with the place she actually was in: her son's home in Ottawa. The

time coincided as well, though she thought it closer to dawn than it was. None of this brought her comfort. Her bed was wet. She was worried her incontinence would be discovered. It took her some time to catch her breath, and though she eventually did, the sound of the ocean would not fade and she grew anxious.

Of course, she had no idea she was lucid, no idea she had ever been anything but lucid. It's true that, at times, she could not quite place a face, and that was frustrating, but, for the most part, she either knew the people around her or she did not. It *was* embarrassing to have strangers looking down at you, but she was too proud to give anyone the satisfaction of seeing her flustered.

There were also those peculiar moments when she recognized a face but could not place it in the place she found herself. It had happened, for instance, that Stanley had entered the Port of Spain of her youth. She knew that was impossible, so she had called him father (and felt, briefly, the thrill that it really was her father), but she'd known him for Stanley all along or, at least, some part of her had known him for Stanley. But, thankfully, the memories of her derangement were fleeting.

On December 4, she woke early from a dream and she was in Stanley's house.

It seemed to take hours to return to sleep, once she realized it was too early to call out for Stanley, too early even for him, but, then, perhaps it was not too late for her sheets to dry before anyone came in to see her. She slept, and then she woke, and her sheets were clean and there was a tray of food on the chair beside her bed: oatmeal (cold), which she couldn't abide, toast (cold), which Stanley knew she couldn't abide cold, orange juice (warm), which she drank, resentful, because there was nothing to eat. She thought of calling out, because it wasn't right to starve, and she did call out, but no one came, which agitated her, and she resigned herself to hunger, though what was the point of resignation if no one knew you were hungry?

This was the kind of indignity that had forced her to strike her family from her will, but then she remembered her granddaughter and wondered if she'd given Mary all she needed. She would have to talk to Mary. She would have to get out of bed. Perhaps, while she was up, she could make herself a proper meal. But she was tired and agitated and short of breath. She would have to calm down a little. Which she did not do. Instead, she sank into a troubled and breathless sleep. She returned to the house in London, but she could find neither of her parents and, frustrated and angry, she took a map of the house from a drawer beneath the kitchen table and spent hours, or perhaps it was days, following its obscure symbols, going up and down the endless stairs until she realized her map wasn't a map at all, it was the coiled and flattened body of a *Mapepire balsain*, a viper, and it led nowhere.

When she awakened she was anxious. The food on the chair beside her was something like dinner: a cold veal cutlet (breading curled), a mound of corn, a scoop of mashed potatoes, a kaiser roll, and a glass of pink lemonade. Had they even tried to wake her? Was there a reason she should have her food cold? It didn't matter. It didn't matter because she suddenly remembered the morning's oatmeal and she was not hungry. Though she hadn't actually touched the oatmeal, she remembered it so vividly it was as if she'd just eaten.

She could afford to leave the cutlet and potatoes untouched: a reproach to her careless kin, none of whom, save Mary, knew how easily she could cut them off, how much they stood to lose. She could leave her estate to Mr. Bax, for instance. Dear Mr. Bax, her own lawyer. Now, there was a man who put her concerns squarely before his own. He was paid to do so, it's true, but he was conscientious and indefatigable, and no amount of money could buy those qualities if they weren't there to begin with.

No, of her family, Mary was the only one who had the kind of backbone that made money bearable, the only one with a sense of responsibility. Yes, she would certainly leave everything to Mary. Or had she already done so? Annoyed, she called out:

– Stanley!

She called her son's name half a dozen times until, to her own surprise, she was too exhausted to call out any more, her voice sounding faint even to herself. There was no profit in getting old, no point, no saving grace.

And, again, she fell asleep. Or, rather, it was not sleep, though it was very like it. She was light-headed and she could hear the ocean, but she could also feel the coming of night, see the darkening shadows, mark the passage of light, and hear footsteps outside her door. At some point, her cutlets were taken away and macaroni was left behind. The curtains in her room were closed. The light in her room was turned on. But these things happened while she was talking to her father, and she couldn't decide which was the real room, which the real night: the one in which she was an old woman or the one in which she was a child.

And then, for the last time in her life, she fell asleep. And it really was sleep this time. She returned to the house in London, walking up and down the stairs, looking for a manila envelope in which she'd left an old picture of the house, a marvellous photograph, so sharply in focus that although it had been taken from the exterior, you could see in it every inch of the house's interior.

She found it in a kitchen cupboard, and the sight of it filled her, unexpectedly, with joy. It wasn't simply the photograph or the miraculous expanse of the house. It was a thought or, rather, not a thought at all but a feeling of such depth it was a conviction, a conviction so bright and irresistible it was indistinguishable from truth. That is, she felt, for the first time in her life, as far as she could remember, the profound insignificance of the physical "where." All places existed within her, as they existed within this house. It was only a trick of the light that separated Ireland, say, from Nigeria. They were cradled within her, every point on Earth was cradled, as memory or as possibility.

Time and space collapsed on themselves and left only the sound of the sea, her heart beating. And to think she'd spent her life acquiring what she already possessed. To think she had spent so much time trying to keep from others what they also possessed. And, if it came to that, was she not all people, and all people her? Yes, even Stanley. How had she ever believed otherwise? She had believed otherwise, had believed in her difference, but in a world so full of false corridors and empty rooms, it was easy to get lost. Now, however, she knew where she was, and a feeling of harmony overcame her. For the first time in her life, as far as she could remember, she possessed a truth that did not begin and end with her own needs. And she was certain that, when she awakened, she could hold to this joy.

And she did wake.

And she was as ecstatic as she had been while dreaming. It was night, and the world was One. There was no reason to hold on to her pride, her anger, her shame, her wounds, her place, her desires, her wants, her needs. She had discovered what she should have known long ago, but there was not even a hint of disappointment that this had not come sooner. It had come, and she was grateful she had been allowed to see the world for what it is: One, singular, forever whole, an endless bliss.

Her heart beat strangely, like a butterfly's wings, and then stopped.

17

WANDERING

It was February, five months after Walter's contretemps with Paul Dylan.

Walter had spent much of that time recovering from the damage to his nose, cheek, and ribs. At first, there had been blood in his urine and he could not comfortably lie on his left side. A concussion had wiped his memory clean for a few days, and that was bewildering, but his memory's return was accompanied by violent headaches and that was worse. At first, he had no memory of the fray. He remembered washing his hands and walking about with a white towel fixed to his thumb, but after that there was nothing until his awakening in a room with thick white curtains, a woman's face looking into his. After a day or two, he remembered Paul's face. He could not remember who Paul was exactly, and then when he did, he remembered all that had happened, though he couldn't think why Paul would attack him . . . except for . . . a little something at the edge of memory, something he preferred not to remember, something about a woman, a woman whose face returned to him, eyes first, along with a handful of names: Lucy, Luba, Louise . . . Laura, Lena, Lara . . . No, it *was* Louise, and Louise was married to Paul.

With Louise's name, there came a sharp image of the Dylans sitting beside each other, Paul looking up, Louise looking down at the floor of someone's living room. Then Walter remembered that he had slept with the woman. But he hadn't felt anything for her, had he? The occasional wave of desire. You couldn't call that betrayal. No, wait . . . that wasn't true. He had felt, for Louise, something deeper. Yes, but it had all been an accident. He hadn't meant to allow himself anything like deep feeling. It had all been a mistake, and he had broken it off. He'd stopped seeing Louise. To think you could be kicked to death for that . . .

If that was the reason. *If.* After all, it was hard to credit. Paul was such a reasonable man: even tempered, a gentleman. It was difficult to know what to think.

During his first weeks in hospital, Walter had been visited by a number of people: his fellows at the Department of Sociology, his teaching assistants, even the dean. There had also been his friends from other faculties, and a number of women with whom he'd once slept and with whom he was still on friendly terms. Henry Wing, François Ricard, and I all visited. And, in the end, so did Louise, though not Paul.

It seemed mysterious to Walter that so many people knew of his "accident," as if there were a secret channel over which news of one's misfortune came. But, of course, it was not really mysterious. Someone told someone who told someone else, and on it went until, after a time, anyone who knew his name had heard some version of events: he'd had his arms broken by loan sharks, the father of a student had broken his nose, he'd been roughed up by the police, he'd had a heart attack and fallen from the ambulance carrying him . . .

Walter treated all who visited with gratitude and silence. He did not want to talk about the beating or his "guilt," so he kept quiet. He told no one who had done the damage. And in the end, all were convinced he'd been attacked by a lunatic, perhaps a lunatic on angel dust. And, come to think of it, he'd been fortunate to escape with as little damage as he had.

Louise Dylan had come on a weeknight, but she came as visiting hours were ending, and Walter was going under from the Seconal he'd asked for. He could barely speak. He held one of her hands in his and squeezed it convulsively while mumbling something that sounded like

– Leave me . . . leave me . . .

Louise was distraught to see Walter helpless and she was impatient to know what had happened to him. She would have stayed with him until he awakened, but he had asked her to leave and then the night nurse had done the same. So, there'd been no reason to stay. No reason but her own longing. In the months following their breakup, Walter had not even hinted at their feelings for each other. He had given her no hope that they might ever recover the intimacy they'd had. Seeing him like this, alone, brought out her feelings for him, but also her resolve. It made no sense to suffer by his bedside when, though he could barely speak he'd still managed to reject her. So, she left, and she put him out of her mind as best she could.

Walter's (fleeting) impression of their encounter was entirely different. It was of a miraculous breakthrough, an awakening. He had, in his own mind, finally confessed his feelings. The Seconal had given him the courage to say

– Don't leave me . . . don't leave me . . .

but when he woke from his chemical sleep, he was not certain she'd been with him, not certain he'd spoken at all, and he could not bring himself to call her because of her husband (the embarrassment it would cause them all to talk of what Paul had done) and, oddly, because of his emotions, or his strange distaste for emotion, rather. He did not want the intimacy that contact would bring. From the moment he woke from unconsciousness, Walter felt no anger, no shame, no consternation: nothing of depth, not even desire for revenge. And that is how he wanted it.

In the weeks that followed, there were times he wept, but you wouldn't have called that deep feeling. It was something his body did when he wasn't looking. It was like rain on a sunny day. He was grateful to have escaped with the injuries he had, grateful when his memory returned, and grateful there were, after the first weeks, fewer and fewer visitors to see his agony.

But was he really grateful for his memory?

Yes, in a way; though the more he thought about it, the more disappointed he was that *his* were the memories that returned to him. It was absurd, but he felt he'd missed an occasion to become someone other than Walter Barnes. The thought wasn't as amusing as it should have been. So, along with the weeping, the pain in his ribs, the difficulty eating, the blood in his urine, and the headaches, there was now the insufferable question of who he was, given the memories that persisted: his mother's robe falling open at the dinner table, the sound of his father's car coming up the gravel driveway, his fingernails cut so close to the quick it hurt to pick things up. Who was there in all that? The question was not at all amusing and there was, finally, no release from it.

Then, after three weeks in hospital, drifting in and out of speculations and sleep, Walter was set mercifully, unexpectedly free. On the night of October 17, 1984, days before he was to go home, Walter woke suddenly and opened his eyes. He had no idea where he was or when, but in the light of his semi-private room he saw, in profile against the indigo of a curtain that had been partially drawn around his bed, the head, neck, and shoulders of a young woman: a nurse most likely, but out of uniform, in street clothes, if you could call them that. She wore a dark yellow dress with billowing sleeves on which three dark palm leaves were embroidered. Around her neck there was a necklace of amber beads, from which a single pearl depended, nested in the hollow of her throat. The back of her neck was accentuated by the way she wore her reddish-blonde hair: held up in a white kerchief that covered her ears and emphasized the curve of her forehead.

Like all visions of beauty, there was something unpleasant about her. Not the slight bump at the bridge of her nose, nor her thin lips. No, it was something to do with the woman herself, an uninflected presence, as if she were simply there, at the foot of his bed, reading his chart before going off to a place where she was expected, or perhaps wanted. She was gracefully unselfconscious, perfectly unaware of him, and though this added immeasurably to her beauty, it annihilated him. For the first time in his life, briefly, for as long as it takes, say, flame to rise on a wick, Walter Barnes was aware of a woman as a woman, distinct from anything he may have wanted of her, with her, from her.

He was not freed by a woman or a vision or love. Rather, the idea of "woman" distracted him from the thorny idea of "self." Why had it taken him so long to see a woman in this way? There was something in the purity of his vision that suggested an exile, an exile not from "woman" exactly, but from something deeper, from the "Feminine," let's say. That was the idea that took hold of him. How had he lived so long without realizing he was in exile, so long without realizing there was a world beside his own, a world to which he must once have belonged?

Exile from the Feminine? Now what could that mean (if, in fact, it meant anything at all)?

First, it did not mean that he wished to be a woman. He was depressed, it's true, and if he could have chosen *which* woman he would become, he might have agreed to the transformation. But, for the most part, he was resigned to his masculinity. Second, he felt no pressing need to return to the womb. Well, not to the womb from which he'd come, in any case. That would have meant a return to his mother's care, and that was worse than the exile that now fascinated him. Still, if he was now in exile, he must once have lived in the realm. It was, perhaps, a home on the shore from which he'd set out, and, despite himself, he did remember a beatitude that had his mother's face to it. No, not her face, her being, a being almost indistinguishable from his own; a time before he was himself and knew his mother for the woman she was, a time that followed the womb but preceded his earliest memory.

Finally, he did not suddenly believe women superior. It simply didn't follow. They had all of them set out from the same place, men and women. And though it was true women might hold a key to the place, that made no difference. They could not return to it themselves. The realm was beyond them as well. Had to be, didn't it?

But what did he know about women, exactly?

Now there was a question. He had slept with a community of them. With, beside, atop, among, beneath. On average, four a week for twenty years (Thursday, Friday, Saturday, Sunday): four thousand, one hundred, and sixty. Greater than the population of Lobo but somewhat less than Chatham. He had been industrious but unmindful. He could remember few faces, fewer names, and even fewer of the other details: voices, hair, smell, and taste. When you came right down to it, he knew as little about women now, after twenty years of fornication, as he had when he lost his virginity to a woman whose name was . . . Erica?

Erica, if it was Erica and not Ruth, had rubbed against his late-blooming self in a bar off Metcalfe. She had paid for his drinks, walked him up and down the canal, and taken him to her apartment on Cooper. Despite the alcohol, pleasure had been intense (almost mystical) and, when it was done, and done again, she had yawned and shown him the door. It was, when you thought of it, miraculous he remembered that much about her. He had tried to find her again, to express his gratitude and his willingness to repeat the procedure as often as she wished. He had haunted the streets and taverns, trawling in a two-mile circle whose centre was the public library, but he never saw her again. Now that he thought of it, in fact, she was, aside from Louise, the woman to whom he was faithful longest. Weeks passed before he had intercourse again, this time with a woman of whom no trace remained in memory.

He knew nothing about women, then. But his search wasn't about women, was it? It was about a place no one possessed and none occupied: the Feminine. Better to call it a country, a land, an ocean; a place outside the cave, if you were Greek; the unsayable, if you were Austrian. Oh, but you could say as much about the Masculine, couldn't you? Yes, but that was the shore towards which he'd been made to swim. It had a profile he could recognize. The other shore, the other land had long since disappeared, and he had not thought to look back.

So, it did have something to do with men and women?

Why, yes . . . But how would *he* get to the place that was an absence in himself? There were, it seemed to Walter, two ways to proceed. First, he might, through prolonged introspection, discover what he was, exactly, and then, subtracting what he discovered, discover what he was not. This road, though it looked straight and clear, was not the one he chose, as he was not inclined to look closely at himself or his life. The second way, more agreeable to Walter, was more complicated. If, as he reluctantly accepted, women did have something to do with the Feminine, mightn't it be possible to observe *them* closely, to catch in their common trajectory a hint of the place that he had left? Observation? Yes, and this he could do methodically, with a degree of objectivity, of attentiveness, but only on condition that he learn to suppress desire, desire that would confuse matters. And, aye, there was the rub, because desire was a habit with him. It was a habit more than it was an instinct or even a reaction. That is, it was possible for Walter to desire a woman *before* he met her: any woman, any time. In a sense, he did not desire women at all. They were, rather, the accidental objects of a want, and it was suddenly clear to him that this very want was what had hidden women for so long. It was this that obscured the metaphysical texture women had in common.

Was it possible to unlearn promiscuity? That was the question at the heart of his *vita nuova*. He left the hospital on a Saturday. He prepared for a return to teaching, resuming his courses after a month's absence. He cleaned the dust from his floors, counters, sills, rugs, and glasses. He returned to the world he'd known for some twenty years. True, he now avoided his friends, seeing no one. He was humiliated by the thought of community, embarrassed by his (secret) intimacy with Paul Dylan and his association with the rest of the Fortnightly. Thanks to his new pursuits, however, he did not miss them. It was his purpose to become chaste and to discover the Feminine.

After a week out of hospital, however, he felt as if he were mysteriously "off." It was a chore to read, to teach, to cook, to go out. There was little pleasure in his return to the world. He did not sleep with a woman from October 20 to 27, but neither did he succeed in paying more than cursory attention to this woman or that: a waitress with a nose ring, a woman at a Becker's whose knees were skinned, a student above whose left shoulder blade was the tattoo of a blue plant . . . meagre returns, despite having given a great deal of time and thought to his new pursuit.

Around the same time, he realized two things. First, he had never been quite so unobservant before. He had never actually been incapable of telling one woman from another. The particular details had not stayed long in his memory, but they had been there more vividly than they were now. So, he was, in fact, regressing, where observation was concerned. Second, now that he was at home, the idea of the Feminine began to seem, well, faintly ridiculous, an idea born of too much time. Moreover, he was almost certainly going about its discovery the wrong way, whether the Feminine existed or not. A collection of distinguishing physical particulars was, perhaps, interesting, but even if it were done well, that is exhaustively, it would bring him no closer to any essence. Deeper details, more personal revelations called for intimacy. He would have to talk to women and, surprisingly, this was something he now found intimidating. He could speak with female colleagues or female students about sociology, of course, but a woman speaking of Gregory Bateson or Paul Watzlawick was not a woman so much as an intellectual position with secondary sexual characteristics different from his own, or so he believed.

No, if he was going to pursue the Feminine, he would have to rethink his approach. Not only would he have to speak to a woman without mentioning the thing uppermost on his mind (sex), but he would have to discover a subject that led naturally to the most candid revelations, on their part. And was this possible? Yes, perhaps. And was it worth the deprivation? Yes, it might be. And would he stay the course? Yes, because something in him had changed. Yes, because his old life was unpalatable to him because, when he thought of it, which he did despite himself, he could think of little in his old life that had made him happy. So, he would, yes.

If he was despondent after the first week, he was near despair after the second and the third. During these weeks, a typical excursion went like this:

We are in a tavern, on Elgin. The lights are dim, but not enough to disguise one's identity. Walter sits at the bar. Beside him, a woman, unaccompanied.

Walter:	Some weather we're having.
Woman:	(turning, briefly, to face him) What?
Walter:	Some weather, eh?
Woman:	(turning away) Yeah.
Walter:	(pause) Can I buy you a drink?
Woman:	I've already got one.
Walter:	(pause) Maybe after that one?
Woman:	(unenthusiastic) Sure. We'll see.

Walter: (pause) So . . . have you lived in
Ottawa long?

or

Walter: (pause) So . . . do you like this bar?

or

Walter: (pause) So . . . are you interested in
philosophy?

or

Walter: (pause) So . . . what do you do?

*Woman drinks up, politely declines more alcohol, and moves on. There
is the sound of laughter, conversation, music, and the cheerful clink of
glass. It is early. Through a window, the sky in the distance is pink and
orange beneath its blue hood.*

Curtain.

Some of the conversations went on beyond this point, but not
many, and their chief parasites were boredom and inattention.
The woman would look away, and Walter would look away, and
closeness would come only with the unstated, but mutually felt,
desire for flight.

Walter had wide experience with rejection. He had heard
everything from the horrified "No!" to the more restrained "No,
thank you," but nothing had disturbed him as much as did this
trailing off of conversation. It made him feel dishonest, sidewind-
ing, and foolish.

In November, a woman at the Penguin Café asked

– Are you trying to pick me up?

– No, not at all, he said.

– Then, fuck off.

Which he did. He got up and left, convinced she was right, that
he was no longer fit company for a woman, that if it came to
loathing, it was just as well to loathe the old version of himself, a
version lacking all virtue save concupiscence and honesty. So, that

very evening, November 10, he had abandoned his search for the so-called Feminine. Wherever it was, if it was, it was unattainable by Walter Barnes. He had given three weeks of his life to a diverting idea. No one could say he hadn't looked. He had been faithful to the idea, but there was nothing to show for it. So, he returned to his old ways. Beginning at the bottom of Elgin Street, walking up the east side to the National Arts Centre, he solicited every unaccompanied woman he saw. When this proved unproductive, he crossed to the west side of Elgin and, going south, propositioned the women in that sector. And, when this was equally unsuccessful, he walked to Bank, along Gladstone, and, from Gladstone to Rideau, east side, west side, north and south, he did the same. Three hours and some forty propositions later, Walter was as alone as when he'd started. It had been an unsatisfying evening, but he'd had such evenings before, hadn't he? He returned home, exhausted by the pilgrimage, ribs aching, but satisfied that he had returned to a life he knew, to a purpose whose point was a known pleasure.

On the following night, the end was the same: solitude.

For four weeks, every Thursday, Friday, Saturday, and Sunday, he had gone out and come home, and there had been not one woman to accept his proposition. Not even close. None bothered to look at him twice and, worse, none had even bothered to insult him. He had, apparently, in some mysterious way, ceased to exist. How had that happened? It wasn't as if he'd lost his technique. He'd had no technique to speak of, or none he could recall. A proposition was advanced, an answer given. It was as simple as that. It had been simple. It would be simple again. It was a matter of time.

Ah, but it wasn't simple.

Whereas, previously, he had been unselfconscious in his propositions, a charming presence, amusing, the kind of man you couldn't imagine suffering from rejection, there was now a vulnerability to him, the kind of desperation that might have worked if he were twenty but which, in a forty-year-old, suggested a complicated history and, really, if all you wanted was sex, it was the kind of vulnerability that put a damper on the whole thing.

Nor was there comfort in the idea that his bad luck would pass, in time. In fact, it didn't help to think about time at all. Years, moments, months ago, he had been a dissolute and unhappy man. He himself had hoped for change, but now that change had come, he looked desperately for a way back. He modified his approach. He said "please" and "would you mind." He bowed. He smiled. He spoke louder. He spoke more softly. But even he could see there was no dignity in his approach. It all meant too much to him. The women walked on, pulling their coats closer about them.

Why hadn't he just paid for intercourse, then? He had, on Christmas Eve, having convinced himself it was only a matter of "priming the pump." On Christmas Eve, an evening during which, traditionally, he could look forward to multiple partners (so many women in the city needing warmth for the holiday), he had walked up and down Elgin, along Rideau, in and around the Market. He'd spent hours walking, his voice hoarse, no nearer success than he had been for the past three months. It was then he decided to seek professional comfort.

But everything had gone wrong. It was a Monday. The foyer to the apartment building on Waller was dim, and when he pushed the buzzer for number 157, it took forever for the madam to answer, and when she did it was clear she'd been drinking. He had to repeat his name into the little silver grill and shout the password

– Abdul sent me

several times before she buzzed him through.

He found his way to the elevator, by the light of the exit sign, only to discover the elevator was not working. He walked up a flight of stairs, a little frightened by the dark and by the smell of industrial cleaner. There was no light in the hallway, either, but a woman was waiting for him at the door to 157.

– What took you so long? she asked

and then, before he could speak, she added, peevishly

– Don't you have anywhere else to go?

Confused, Walter said

– No . . . I'm sorry

and she pulled him to her, holding his face in her bosom.

– Poor boy, she said. It's such a sad time of year, isn't it? You come right in. We'll fix you up.

The living room was lit by candles. It was small but, at the far end, almost too big for the room, stood a Christmas tree that looked gloomy in the low light. On Walter's left, against the wall, there was a large sofa on which three women sat. They were dressed in negligees (red, green, white) and they were all of them blonde. More than that it was difficult to make out, because the shadows moved over their faces and throats like dark hands. On the other side of the room was a long, narrow table on which most of the candles stood, along with a two-four of 50, an ice bucket, and a row of plump, red velvet Christmas stockings.

– You want a drink?

the madam asked, not unkindly.

– No, thank you

said Walter.

– Only ten bucks

she said, a little more insistent. And then

– It's Christmas, mister. And the girls can't drink unless someone buys them one.

Walter took forty dollars from his pocket.

– Will this do? he asked.

– Aren't you going to have one? she said.

– I'm allergic, he answered.

– Well, isn't that something

she said

– Isn't that something, girls?

– Sure, said one of the women on the sofa.

And Walter chose her.

It isn't quite right to say Walter did not enjoy having sex with the woman. The bedroom was illuminated by guttering candles on top a chest of drawers. The room smelled of potpourri. The woman's breath smelled of mint and, though she didn't usually do this, she said, she washed his penis for him, with a cloth and water from the ewer and bowl on the night table.

He heard more than he saw: voices from the other room, the rustle of bedsheets, the *ploopf* of a pillow falling to the floor, and, once they'd begun, the sounds she made: a kind of deep hissing, followed by the words

– My, my, my . . . my my . . .

Even after his vision adjusted to the light, Walter could not see her clearly. He was between her and the candles, so her face, for instance, was a hundred faces: young, old, soft, hard, beautiful, ugly. Yet, in some respects, it was not dark enough. After they'd been at it for half an hour or so, and she'd begun to lose interest, and she'd given up stroking him or biting his nipples, and he'd closed his eyes, the better to feel himself inside of her, he opened his eyes and saw her as she put her hands under her arms and then took them out to smell her own sweat.

It was the kind of thing that made you think.

Not that this put him off at all. He closed his eyes, to spare her any embarrassment, and came when he wanted to, because his body wanted to and it had been through this so many times it knew what it wanted, whatever happened, but . . . for the first time in his life, he had an orgasm that was not pleasant. Naturally, he'd had all manner of orgasms in his life, from those that made you feel you were a different life form to those no more intense than tea on a sunny day. But this was different. It wasn't even on the scale. He was so distant from his own pleasure, it was as if he'd had someone else's orgasm and, to his own surprise, he began to weep.

Seeing that Walter was crying, the woman was most confused and embarrassed. With feeling, she said

– Don't worry, Tiger, you didn't go over time.

Walter waved his hand in front of his face, dried his eyes, and got dressed. The woman looked at him as she washed herself.

– I didn't know men were so sensitive, she said.

– It's nothing, he answered.

He left his money with the madam, who said

– Thanks

and he was all right until he hit the hallway when, as suddenly as before, he began to weep, but, with no one there to see him, it was worse. He sat in the stairwell, in near darkness, and cried for all he was worth.

If there was a reason to live, he could not find it.

And, being a reasonable man at the end of reason, feeling no love for the man he'd become, nor serious longing for the man he'd been, terrified by the prospect of a life in which he, his body, and his emotions were mutually estranged and . . . what else? oh, yes . . . seeing no hope for himself in the world, Walter Barnes decided to commit suicide.

The decision was accompanied by relief and, like finding the obvious answer to a subtle question, a delight in both the problem *and* its solution, in his life *and* its end. It seemed to him that he'd been on this course for years, that if he'd opened his eyes sooner he might have come to this years ago, when he was more equipped for death: younger, less confused by what he didn't know, having fewer responsibilities, undaunted by failure – failure of the means, that is. He now knew enough about poisons and firearms to worry that, instead of death, he would find only hospitals and / or a coma. When it came down to it though, he found it surprisingly easy to decide on how he wanted to go. He would throw himself into the Ottawa River. He chose the river because it was winter and, though he imagined he'd have no difficulty drowning, the cold would kill him if he found it difficult to persuade himself to go under.

The emotional preparation was straight forward: he "forgave" everyone who had in any way wronged him, anyone for whom he felt resentment or anger, from his mother to Paul Dylan. He forgave them easily, because he saw they were only stations on a road whose end had been there from the moment he'd first drawn breath. There was something suspiciously deterministic about his forgiving, as if those who'd hurt him had had no choice, just as he had no choice but to forgive. His "forgiveness" was more like the closing of a door, but it didn't matter. First, because he knew that men have their deaths, whatever their attitudes. Second, because he couldn't remember why determinism was wrong, couldn't even recall the arguments against it. Anyway, Philosophy was only a school for death and it all came to the same thing in the end: words, words, words, and then nothing. More complicated were the straightforward matters. He made detailed notes on his curriculum, for whoever it was would take over his classes. (How sad, after the dean had graciously allowed him to return to his classes after a month's leave, that he would abandon everything for good.) He cleaned his house from top to bottom, as if he were only going to Toronto, say, for a few weeks. He took special care of his houseplants, pulling back dead leaves, fertilizing those that needed fertilizing. He cancelled the telephone, the cable, the credit cards, and his subscriptions to the *Citizen*, the *New York Review of Books*, *Mind*, *Critique*, and *L'Ange*. He packed up his books. He put his clothes in carefully labelled boxes, arranged the boxes neatly in his closets, and threw away all of his shoes, save those he would wear to the river.

It might have taken even him longer than it had, if there had been any particular goodbyes to make, but, after prolonged and careful consideration, he chose to make none. Instead, he spent weeks trying to write the perfect letter of farewell, settling, finally, on a fastidiously brief note that he left on his kitchen table:

To whom it may concern,
I have drowned myself.
Yours,
Walter Barnes

and he dated it:

February 24, 1985

On the night of the 24th, he ate his favourite meal (bacon, eggs, Spam, and toast) at eight o'clock, then dressed warmly and put on his mittens, because it was cold, and walked a final time along his favourite street (Elgin) to the river. It was a cloudless night; the stars in the sky, a meaningless plethora, mimicked by the lights of Earth. The snow had been cleared from the pavement and there were soft, white ridges by the side of the street.

Sunday: little traffic, the side streets empty and quiet. Inside of him, there was a kind of muffled turbulence, like a fairground (with its Ferris wheels, roller coasters, and screaming patrons) heard from a distance. He was conscious of an excitement, some-where, but he was not part of it.

And how short Elgin was, though it was as long as Bank Street in his imagination: from Catherine to the War Memorial, walking slowly, it took only thirty-five minutes. Yet it was interminable, when you considered each of the streets and each of their vistas (Argyle, Gladstone, Frank, Somerset, Cooper), each with its own significance. As he walked along, certain sharp details returned to him, details he had struggled to recall only a month before: a woman in a white coat who lived on MacLaren, a woman with a lisp who looked down whenever she spoke, a woman so inebriated she'd said yes to his proposition while holding on to the mailbox, as if the mailbox had propositioned her. He *had* been thoughtless, to forget so much. A woman, a woman, a woman. His time on Earth was measured out in women. Time itself was a woman.

At Sparks Street, he tried to decide where he should go to jump. He didn't want to fall on the rocks at the bottom of the cliff. He walked east along Rideau, then retraced his steps. He wanted to drown. Best would be to jump from the Alexandra Bridge, but he wanted to see the river first, so, for the first time in years, he walked behind the Parliament Buildings and stood by the railing to look at the river and at Hull. The river was black and wide, but there was a shelf of ice and snow along the shore beneath him. The black water moved quickly and whirled as it approached the bridge from which he would jump. The city on the other shore, Hull, was a pattern of lights and tall buildings in outline. Above it, the stars, all of them bright, and a scimitar moon.

No, there was no pattern and the moon was not a scimitar. On the other shore and in the sky, there was only the nothing that could be turned into whatever one wanted: teeth, a scimitar, talcum powder, a bear, a sea monster. It was beguiling, but it was nothing. He supposed there were men and women who could turn phenomena into whatever they wanted, who lived in worlds of their own making, like building a bridge as you crossed it, and he wondered, briefly, what that might be like. He had never managed to turn the world into a place hospitable to him. At best, he had managed to forget, to put a veil between himself and the inevitable indifference of the universe.

No, there was no use speculating. Having seen the emptiness for what it was, there was no escape for Walter Barnes. Besides, it was cold, and there was no point wasting his final moments in useless rumination. He curled his fingers up in his mittens, put his hands in his pockets, and made for the bridge.

And for the first time in years, he stopped thinking.

18

NORWAY

As badly as things were going for Walter, they were not going much better for Paul Dylan. In the five months since he'd given Walter a thrashing, Paul had been anxious and resentful. Anxious, because he feared the consequences of his violence. Though he hadn't tried to discover how much damage he'd inflicted, he judged Barnes' pain by his own. He had broken a finger on Barnes' face. After five months, his hand still ached.

He felt anxious, also, because he'd administered the thrashing so publicly, he would not be able to hide, if there were legal consequences. There had been witnesses and, for months, he felt as if he were being watched: an excruciating self-consciousness. Naturally, he kept the details of the incident to himself, pretending, when he spoke to other Fortnightly members that he was sad for Walter, pretending, when Louise told him of Walter's state, that he was "deeply distressed" by the news. "Deeply distressed"? That sounded so like a novel, Louise looked at him to make sure he wasn't pulling her leg. He'd assured her that he had, himself, visited Walter in hospital, and how sad it had been to see the man in such a . . . state.

Paul continued attending Fortnightly evenings, relieved that

Walter seemed to have quit the club cold. (To his surprise, the others seemed to miss Walter's participation. Why should they do that? Hadn't Walter been pedantic and dull? Really, when he thought about it, he had done the Fortnightly a service.) He lived his life as if there were nothing wrong, but for five months he was as resentful as he was anxious. He was resentful, principally, because of the emotional torment he endured. He was convinced he'd done the right thing. In fact, it seemed to him he had been kind or, if not kind, at least restrained.

On the other hand, what had his actions accomplished? He had forgiven his wife . . . No, actually, what he had done was to give up mentioning anything that might lead them to talk about her infidelity. He even managed to give up doing things he had done for years: inspecting her bedsheets, surprising her with midday visits, rummaging through her clothes drawers. And yet, despite this, his home life was not what it should have been. He was anxious, resentful, and, yes, still jealous. At his worst, he felt he had accomplished nothing, and he was often at his worst. (Things were only a little better at work. One of his colleagues had, placidly, as if off the cuff, asked

– Everything okay at home, Paul?

– Everything's fine, he'd answered

politely but barely able to hide his chagrin at being asked.)

Still, all these months later, things were not as bad as they might have been. Walter, for instance, had not (would not?) tell the police about him. Walter was fading from his thoughts. Paul thought of Walter no more than once or twice a week. He was even growing accustomed to his life with Louise, growing used to his own fatigue, resentment, and jealousy. The only really unmanageable emotion was anger, and the problem was he couldn't predict when anger would overtake him.

Now, for instance: a Monday morning in February. He was at the office early, to read and sign letters, to prepare for a meeting with a prospective programmer. Through the window behind him, the city was white and grey, and the sky pale blue. What reason was there to be angry? None whatsoever. And then

– Good morning, Mr. Dylan.

Sharon, his secretary, had come in with the daily papers and a cup of coffee, for him, from the shop on the first floor. (Black, no sugar.) You could see she was in the mood for an exchange, but he was not.

– Thank you, he said

and looked down at the letter to someone in Seoul:

Dear Mr. Kim,
    This letter is to thank you for . . .

as Sharon blithely said

– Oh, Mr. Dylan? I wonder if you heard what happened to Professor Barnes.

– Who?

– Professor Barnes. You remember, we talked about him. Well, someone attacked him. The father of one of his students.

– Oh, really?

– Professor Barnes must have been doing something with the student, if you ask me. Anyway, I thought I'd tell you, in case you didn't know. First thing I thought about when I heard about Professor Barnes was how I told you I'd seen him with someone named Louise. You remember? Well, the other day I was talking to a friend from Carleton and she said . . . the woman I was thinking of? . . . it wasn't Louise. It was Adele. Funny, isn't it? I mean, Adele was one of my close friends. How could I forget? But the really funny thing is my mind must have been telling me something because Adele's name isn't really Adele. It's Løne . . . Norwegian . . . Løne Kastrupsen, but she hated it when people called her Lorna, so she changed it. Funny the way your mind works. Løne sounds a little like Louise, I guess.

– Yes, he said. That *is* funny.

– Isn't it? she said. My mind works in the strangest ways sometimes.

He was not immediately affected by Sharon's anecdote. He was startled she'd spoken of Walter when he was trying to think of anything but Walter, but this kind of thing happened all the time. It was synchronicity, nothing more. When she left his office, he tried to put the matter out of his mind and get on with his work:

> Dear Mr. Kim,
>   This letter is to thank you for . . .

(*Still, it was quite a coincidence.*)

No, that should be informal, his first name:

> Dear Roo,

or

> Dear Kim,

(*Though he was not the kind of man to make something of nothing.*)

If he had been less scrupulous where Walter was concerned, if his actions had been based solely on the word of a flighty twenty-four-year-old, why then, yes, he might have been disturbed by her confusion of Løne and Louise. Hers, however, had been but one piece of the puzzle. There had been the ruined Aquinas, the palpable emotion between his wife and Walter, the palpable shame. This Løne Kastrupsen changed nothing.

He stared at the letter to Seoul for some time before deciding it was best as it had been: formal, restrained, but not unfriendly:

Dear Mr. Kim . . .

The most surprising thing about his secretary's revelation, when he thought about it, was how little he thought about it. It was in there, certainly, but in an amusing way. Løne Kastrupsen. He smiled when he thought of the name. But it was insidious, and by the end of the day, he couldn't stop thinking of the woman's name.

The most disturbing thing was how the world seemed to conspire with him against himself. In all his years at work, he had thought about Norway how many times? Too few to mention. Yet, here, on the day he first heard the name *Kastrupsen*, it was as if Norway had overtaken him. There were letters to be sent to Gerd Manne and Hanne Hide in Trondheim. At lunch, he overheard an angry exchange in what he took to be a Scandinavian tongue – *Hvor har du vært? Hvor har du vært?* And he discovered that an assistant they'd recently hired had been born in Gol.

No doubt, none of this was significant. It was all coincidence. On any other day, the details would have evaporated. He would not have asked where Gol was. He would not have noticed the destination of his letters. He would have ignored the tall, old man crying out at the blonde, young woman. It was all raw nerves and synchronicity, but at each of these moments he thought of Løne Kastrupsen and, thinking of Løne, he heard the sound of buttons falling to pavement, and the sound of falling buttons now meant "Barnes" in the root language of his world.

As a jealous man, it was not unusual for disparate things to speak of one thing. When he was in the jaws of jealousy, he could not see a cloud, hear a jackhammer, taste salt, touch metal . . . without thinking, *Louise*. That was painful, in its way, but he had come to think of it as love, and it was tolerable because it was love. It was not tolerable that the world should mean *Walter*. That was an intimacy he could not bear, but what was he to do? Though months had passed, it was again as it had been immediately after their encounter. He could see the man's face, his broken glasses.

It did occur to him that Walter might have been innocent, but, if anything, in the days that followed the unveiling of Løne, he hated Walter even more than he had, and imagined him guilty of more (and worse) than he (Paul) thought. After all, Walter had refused to bring charges against him. What was that, if not an admission of guilt? He resented Walter more deeply because he was forced to hold more desperately to the idea of Walter's guilt.

So, how *were* things at home?

Things at home were worse than he thought. Paul was convinced his wife knew nothing of his humour. Not true. He had managed to keep quiet about his anxiety, but every word he spoke had a shadow. Behind everything from the bland
– Good morning
to the quiet
– Good night
there was a hint of things he might have said and, though she was often distracted, Louise understood something was being withheld.

She had not been happy for some time, but this new, darkly distracted husband had been poisoning her home since the fall when he'd come back with his hand broken from what he called a car accident, though there hadn't been a scratch on the car, and he wouldn't tell her where he'd gone or how he'd done the damage. Darkly distracted? Yes, she could sense that what he withheld had something to do with shame or, perhaps, guilt. She knew her husband well enough to recognize those emotions in him. (Her first thought, on seeing Paul hold one hand in the other as if he were carrying a wounded bird, was that his "accident" had had something to do with Walter, but that idea was dismissed because

Paul injured himself right around the time she'd begun a faintly ridiculous affair with a man named Enzo Cardotti ["ridiculous" because even she realized she was not over her feelings for Walter], and she wondered if Paul had found them out, though she and Enzo had not gone beyond a handful of earnest conversations and hopeful kisses. She'd called Enzo at home, to make sure he was all right, only to discover there was a *Mrs.* Cardotti, not his niece, not his aunt, but his wife, with whom he still lived. Her conversation with Mrs. Cardotti was the end of her involvement with Enzo and she blamed Paul for the loss. It was petty to blame Paul for *her* disillusionment, and she knew it, but there you are: her heart was intractable on the subject, this despite the secret relief she felt at breaking with Enzo.)

In fact, Paul had been distant for some time before his accident: staying up nights to work, sleeping in the basement, barely able to speak to her. She'd been certain that she had betrayed Walter in some intangible way – the copy of Aquinas she'd destroyed in frustration and thoughtlessly thrown in the garbage, for instance. She had always been careful about such things, because she knew how thorough Paul was. He inspected her clothes and their bed, and came home during the day, unpredictably, to catch her copulating, you'd think, though she'd have to have been . . . what? callous to entertain a lover at home.

Oh, as to lovers . . . there had been none after Walter. Though she'd vowed she would not pine for a man who did not want her, she could not help her feelings. The end of their relationship had been final proof (as if it were needed) that she had been in love with Walter, that she was *in love*, her emotions refusing to acknowledge the end, her memory tethered to their time together, her feelings a government she was waiting to outlive. In the meantime, it was almost shameful to share a life with Paul, her feelings for him, now, little more than a strained friendship.

As a consequence, though she had not been unfaithful to her husband for some time, it felt as if she were.

After Paul's accident, it was as if he were trying to make up the distance between them. That only made matters worse. He slept in their bed. He kissed her again, though there'd been weeks when he'd stopped doing that and she'd wondered if *he* were having an affair, an idea that upset her more than she thought it would. They even resumed lovemaking, though that was most disturbing of all. It wasn't that he changed what he did, but rather how he did it. He was now precise. He knew what she liked, but it was too obvious he knew, not just going through the motions but going through them in an order, as if there were a list above their bed, a list that included directions for proper lighting and time to be spent at each station on the way to completion. It all worked, but after the third or fourth session, she had the horrible, and horribly sad, feeling she was entirely predictable, and she was convinced he must be as unhappy as she was.

Why, then, were they married?

There it was, the question. It was a question she'd considered for years, taking it constantly up, as one would a smooth, black stone. The question first came to her just after their marriage. It had come the moment she realized that Paul would always do the dishes, wash the floors, cook, clean, and buy things for the house. His idea of home included the presence of a wife, and he treated his wife well, but it had little to do with her. Or, rather, it did. He always asked what she wanted. He knew her favourite colours, textures, food, and drink. Their home looked exactly as she might have wanted, except that, perversely, she didn't want, because, somewhere in the back of her mind, she suspected the home was more important to him than she was. It wasn't the kind of distress you could easily voice. What could she say?

– I wish you were less attentive (?)

– I wish the house were an unholy mess (?)

– I wish, for once, we could eat something dreadful (?)

She couldn't even ask if he loved her, because he so passionately loved the *idea* of her, it seemed petty to insist on the difference between her and his image of her. They were married. And then ten years passed; ten years of irreproachable economy. And she was not unhappy exactly, but . . . unencumbered by happiness, say. If she hadn't taken a job at the library, she would have gone mad. And, so, the question had become harder to put down.

Why were they married?

– *No reason. It just happened that way.*

Yes, it just happened. There had been a feeling it was the thing to do. They had been seeing each other for two years and there seemed nowhere else to go. It was either marriage or life without him, and though she didn't love him exactly, his enthusiasm had been enough to carry them forward. If she reproached herself for anything it was that, even then, at the very beginning, she'd had an inkling that this was how it would turn out, that his feelings would not sustain their marriage. She could clearly remember an afternoon with Fredrika, her closest friend, the two of them walking along the promenade towards Dow's Lake, Fredrika saying of her engagement

– It's so exciting, isn't it?

and she had answered

– Do you think so?

when what she meant was

– It isn't, and I don't know why

though she couldn't have said that without betraying those who believed she and Paul were a perfect couple. And she had enjoyed being part of the "perfect couple." She'd had her own vision of marriage: a shared enterprise, a gentle folly. She could remember herself at twenty-one saying things that made her wince even now:

– *Men don't want . . .*

– *Men don't like . . .*

As if she knew the secret to men. What did she know about it?
Nothing. She knew nothing, and when Fred asked

– Don't you love him?

she'd answered

– Yes, of course I do.

If she could find her twenty-one-year-old self, she would throttle her. But why should she blame the twenty-one-year-old? As
the years passed and the life she wanted was suffocated by the one
she had, she could have left at any age: at 22, 23, 24 . . . Any of her
selves might have acted. Instead, she woke one morning, in her
forties, to find that a city of selves had conspired against her. No,
that's not true. She had, in her way, tried to leave, but she had
failed. When had she first slept with another man? Years into her
marriage, just after her twenty-eighth birthday.

And was that leaving?

Well . . . she wouldn't have called it leaving, at the time. She
wouldn't have known what to call it. She had met Fredrika and Vé
for a drink and then for *The Gold Rush* and *Modern Times*, at the
Towne. She'd stayed only for *The Gold Rush*, though, finding it
unbearably sad to watch the Tramp eat his shoe. (Had anyone
else ever cried at *The Gold Rush*? she wondered.) It was the first
evening of a week when Paul was away, and she'd decided to walk
home from Vanier, the long way round: over the bridge to
Rideau, past houses and apartment buildings she'd ignored for
years. Certainly, the walk did her good. It was May, the day after
her birthday, so it was the fifth, and it was important that it *was*
the fifth, important that it was 1972, because time had never been
so important to her before. That night was the beginning of a terrible ache . . . as if she had become time, and her own passing
were a wound.

These days, she could remember more about the night (the
evening star, black water under the bridge, the smell of smoke
from a fireplace) than she could about the man she'd slept with.
Of him there remained the memory of his white teeth, his

straight brown hair, and her amusement at how his penis curved to the left when he was erect. There was also the smell of him (raw carrot) and the fact that the collar of his shirt stuck up like a broken wing over the collar of his jacket, and he had seemed to her the kind of man who would not trouble to do things for her.

It still seemed very little to remember about a man with whom she'd spent two days in bed. She wouldn't remember him if she passed him in the street, and if she did she would have no more to say to him now than she'd had then. There had been no intimate exchanges, no revelations, no longings divulged. She hadn't wanted anything of the sort. She'd wanted to be lost where someone wanted her, and he had wanted her, and it had all been, she now realized, unusually straightforward: a gift, a restoration of her physical self and her self-confidence. Hours and hours lost in sensation and selfishness and consideration for a complete stranger. If she felt guilty about anything, it was the pleasure she'd taken. It had been more intense than she imagined it would be and the part of her still faithful to her husband disapproved of it.

Having done something so contrary to her nature as she then understood it, she felt exhilaration and shame and, most important, a conviction that she could not go on as she had, that she had discovered something about herself that made it impossible to stay with Paul. If Paul had been home, if he had returned a day or two after her affair, she would certainly have told him everything and, knowing him as she thought she did, there could have been no going on. But, as the days passed, as the exhilaration dimmed, she was not quite convinced the direct approach was best. She could have told him anytime during those early days, but it seemed wrong to do such a thing long distance. And, the more she thought about it, the more practical concerns occurred to her: where would she go, what could she afford, what would she take with her? She worked at the library, yes, but that was part-time. She was a woman with a doctorate in comparative literature and no immediate prospects.

As if gloom at her prospects weren't enough, she also found herself thinking about her husband's needs in all this: what would Paul do, how would he feel, would he be all right? The more she thought about him, the more cloudy her own feelings became until, after a few days, it occurred to her that, now she was a different woman, there was the possibility of a different marriage with the same man. Though she knew it was a ridiculous and small idea, it was an idea she couldn't stifle, so that, by the end of the week, as she drove to the airport to pick up her husband, it was the only idea that remained with any clarity: she had changed, so they would change.

Thirteen years later, the pettiness of the idea was unavoidable. Not only had their marriage reverted to business as usual, but she had not even managed to convince him she *had* changed. She slept with other men, three or four, a paltry number, each time with the hope that her transgression would out or that he would notice her, her real self (quicksilver though it was) as opposed to the wife (that too solid creature) with whom he lived, or that she would have to leave, or that Paul would leave her. More empty ideas because, thirteen years on, she had become, simply, a woman who occasionally slept with men other than her husband. She had exchanged one way of being with Paul for another, equally unsatisfying.

But then, she had never told him of her infidelities, had she? Where was the courage in that? Where in the world do those who leave find the will to go? Yes, if there is *physical* abuse. Yes, if the marriage is unbearable. But hers was not quite unbearable and her husband had never touched her in anger. So, she found herself wishing for more love from Paul or for none at all. And until the balance was tipped one way or the other, she could not decide what to do.

Still, something fundamental had changed when she was with Walter: she realized not only that she *could* love another man but that she wanted to as well. There had been a night in Walter's yard, summer, the stars above, when she had offered to leave her husband and she had meant it. She would have left, if only Walter had asked. But he hadn't and, in retrospect (strange to feel this), perhaps it was better he hadn't. She would have to do the leaving on her own. She'd been devastated by Walter's rejection, but it had been a revelation to meet someone with whom she was able to forget, however briefly, her deepest concerns: the questions about her worth, her sins, her marriage. Such a simple idea, but it had taken twenty years to bloom: her concerns were deeply felt, they were an important part of who she was, but it was possible to put them aside without losing herself. In fact, it was necessary. One needed respite from oneself, rest from doubt. One needed a home, in the end, a place where one could simply "be," and this she would never have with Paul.

So, on the day her husband discovered that the woman seen with Professor Barnes was a certain Løne Kastrupsen, Louise had resolved to tell him their marriage was not working, had not been working for years. It was all her fault, yes, but the life they had shared was not the one she wanted.

{ 19 }

A CHAPTER ABOUT SUICIDE AND DEATH

The walk from his house to Parliament Hill should have been the longest part of Walter's walk towards death. It was only a mile from the cliffs facing Hull to the bridge from which he'd decided to jump, not more than twenty minutes, even in bad weather, and yet . . . Walter got as far as Rideau Street before he was accosted by a young man in a peacoat. The man didn't look threatening, but it did look as if he'd been drinking and, as he was black, Walter assumed he needed money. So, before the man could speak, Walter took his wallet from his pocket and, surprised to find he'd forgotten to put so much money in the bank, handed his last two hundred dollars over.

– What's this? the man asked.
– I'm afraid it's all I've got, said Walter.
– I didn't ask you for money.
– You look like you could use it, though.
– Why?
– Well, you know . . .
– Is it my coat?
– Yes, said Walter, it's your coat

though he suddenly noticed the coat was not as decrepit as he'd thought.

– I just bought it last week, said the man.

He seemed disconsolate.

– I'm sorry, said Walter.

– I just wanted to know the way to the Mayflower.

– Oh, well, keep going down Elgin and you'll come to it. Cooper. First street after the Elgin Cinema.

– It's a new coat.

Seeing that he'd disappointed the man, and wishing to console him, Walter said

– It wasn't really the coat, you know. I noticed you were black and I assumed you wanted money.

– It's because I'm black? But I just wanted to know where's the Mayflower.

The young man, who certainly had been drinking, wavered as he considered the case. It would have been difficult to assess, even without drink. On the one hand, Walter had adverted to his race. On the other, he'd done so in a kind voice. And if he'd spoken the truth, then the coat was not universally disliked, a thought that brought him some satisfaction, since his mother had vowed to throw it away when he wasn't looking. Also, there was the money. He didn't know how much there was, but it was enough for a few rounds at the pub. Of course, taking the money would tacitly affirm the man's bigotry, and that was reprehensible.

Walter waited for a few moments, and then he gently said

– Well, I should be going.

– I can't take your money.

– Why not? I don't need it any more.

The young man thought about this too, but before his thoughts could cohere, Walter added

– And I'd be honoured if you had a few drinks, on me.

– Why? You don't know me.

– I don't know anyone, said Walter.

– I know what you mean, said the young man.

How friendly one could be, *in extremis*. Walter thought of all the friends he might have made, if he'd decided to kill himself sooner.

– Yes, he said. The times we live in.

Again, he tried to move away. This time, the young man held him by the sleeve.

– I can't take your money, he said, unless you have a drink with me.

And because he suddenly thought it ridiculous to die with two hundred dollars on him, Walter agreed, but on condition they did not go too far out of his way. So, they walked to the Lafayette. The walk was unexpectedly convivial for both of them.

– Thomas, said the young man.

He looked young enough to be Walter's son.

– You should put that money in your pocket, said Walter.

And so the young man did, but in a touchingly awkward way. Money in one hand, he patted himself distractedly with the other until, finding what he was after, he reached into his left pants pocket with his right hand and pulled out a black wallet, into which he pushed the crumpled bills. For a minute or so, in the midst of a most mundane act, the young man was so entirely unselfconscious it was as if Walter could see something beyond this particular young man to all the young men who had preceded him on Earth, himself, Walter Barnes, included.

– Sorry, Thomas said.

They walked on in silence, each lost in his own thoughts. The Laf was not busy, but it still took time for the waiter, a scruffy old man in a green shirt, to approach them.

– What can I get you? he asked.

Thomas ordered a pitcher of draught and two glasses.

– So, he said. So . . .

to which Walter responded with a polite smile.

Their silence was not strained and, perhaps because they did not speak, it seemed to each that the other was agreeable. Still, when Thomas went off to use the pissoir, Walter got up and walked out. It made no sense to court friendship at a time like this, and he left his drink untouched, because he didn't want to die drunk, to die as if he needed chemical courage to do the most logical thing he would ever do.

(That was pride speaking. To whom could it possibly matter if he were inebriated or not? The pathologist? The undertaker? He would fall into the cold and go wherever the river went and there was no telling who, if anyone, would next see his body. Yet here it was, his eleventh hour, and he was still concerned with appearances.)

As if it were unplanned, Walter found himself at the foot of the Alexandra Bridge, looking over towards Hull, distracted by dark thoughts. He had braced himself and taken a step onto the bridge when he heard his name.

– Hello, Walter, said Mr. van Leuwen. How are you?

There was van Leuwen before him, walking back from Hull, it seemed.

– Oh, hello, Robert.

– Cold night to be out and about, isn't it?

The question was casually put, but there was clearly another behind it. Van Leuwen's head was slightly angled to one side, his hands in his pocket, as if he were expecting something.

– Yes, I guess it is, said Walter, but not as cold as last year.

– Is that right? Listen, are you all right, Wally? I was sorry to hear about your accident a while back.

– I'm fine.

– What exactly happened? I heard a few versions of the story.

– I was assaulted.

– That's terrible, said van Leuwen. Did they catch who did it?

– Oh . . . really, it was just an assault. Happens all the time.

– You're taking it remarkably well.

– I'm fine. Really. How are you?

Before van Leuwen could answer, two things occurred. First, the parliamentary carillon rang for eleven, each mournful clang clear and mournful in the clear and mournful night. And then, they were approached by an older man, staggering across from Hull, singing at the top of his voice

– Irene goodnight . . . Irene goodnight . . . Goodnight, Irene goodnight, Irene . . .

When he reached them, he said

– 'Evening lads . . .

and they could almost taste the alcohol on him.

– Lovely night, isn't it?

– It is, said van Leuwen.

– I miss home, though.

– Where's home? asked van Leuwen.

The old man put a hand to his mouth, as if he were going to spew. Walter and van Leuwen stepped back at once, instinctively, but the man took his hand away from his mouth, said

– Loughborough Junction

and, turning away from them, staggered a few yards before again breaking into song, singing the only words to "Goodnight, Irene" he could remember, the chorus, which he'd been singing from just outside Les Quatre Jeudis, and which he would sing all the way to Sandy Hill, all the way home, in fact, because he hadn't lived in London for fifty years and it was now a place where his father (long dead) would sing ("Ramona, I hear the mission bells above . . .") and look down at him as if he loved him and down at his mother (long dead) as if he loved her too. It didn't seem possible that such a place should die, though it would, because he would and he would surely take it with him, there being no one left to carry it.

Van Leuwen smiled.

– Where's Luffbro Junction? he asked.

– I don't know, said Walter.

After a pause, during which they tried to recall the thread of their conversation, van Leuwen said

– Well, I guess I better get home myself. Night, Wally. I'm glad you're okay. You know, you should come to the next evening, if you're up for it. Henry's got us reading Francis Hutcheson this Saturday. We miss you.

– Good night, said Walter.

He had already turned away from van Leuwen, turned towards the bridge, towards Hull, thinking how meaningless their conversation had been, and what a shame it would be his last. On the other hand, he was cold and ready for death and, as if it were a parting gift, his memory pushed up the words to a prayer he hadn't thought of for years:

If the noise of the flesh were silent, and silent too the phantasms of earth, sea and air, silent the heavens, and the very soul silent to itself . . .

Now, really, could there be greater consolation than Saint Augustine?

As if it were unplanned, he found himself at the centre of the bridge, looking down into the river, with Ottawa on his left and Hull to his right, the meaningless firmament above and darkness within.

It was time.

Of course, this being his first leap from a bridge, he hadn't considered the impediment of the railing. He had imagined something like a graceful jump, his eyes closed, his arms outspread. Unfortunately, he was not as agile as he had once been. He could not clear the railing without a running start. As he didn't wish to be struck by a car, he could not begin his run from the middle of the road. He would have to climb on or over the railing. But the railing was smooth and icy and he would look ridiculous doing so. Small price to pay. Walter took off his mittens, put them in his pockets, placed his hands on the railing, and was about to pull himself up when someone touched his arm and said

– Excuse me. I don't usually do this, but do you have a few minutes?

Walter turned and saw a young black woman. He answered

– Well . . . you see, it's just that I'm . . .

– Please, she said. Please.

There was something in the tone of her appeal that stopped him, something too in being accosted by a second black person on this, his final night. He thought about the woman's request. Strictly speaking, he *was* busy. On the other hand, it wasn't his intention to jump for an audience. Then again, he could see it had taken nerve for her to address him and, just then, nerve was very much on his mind.

– Please, she asked again.

Walter said

– Well . . . will it take very long?

– I don't know, she said.

She began to cry. It was no business of his, whatever it was. She would have to find her own way in this world, but he could listen, for a little while.

– What is it? he asked.

– I don't know where to start, she said.

They began walking, slowly, despite the cold, towards Hull, with Walter wondering how long it would be before he could jump in peace.

The young woman's name was, she said

– Mary

It was Mary Stanley. She hadn't planned to speak to him in particular. It might even be that, had she known Walter, she would not have been able to tell him anything at all. In any case, she was not used to speaking with strangers, and it was a measure of her distress that she spoke to this one. It was late and cold, but they walked, not quite together, in silence, towards Hull where, even on Sunday, they would find a somewhere open late. They walked without speaking, until they crossed the bridge, because Mary did not know where to start, nor what to speak nor what to hide. This is what, more or less, she said, though, naturally, being more discreet, she would have kept the intimate details to herself . . .

Six months it had been since her grandmother had tried to convince her she was a wealthy woman. Even before this "revelation," Eleanor had begun to behave in peculiar ways: forgetting where she was, speaking in a Trinidadian accent, hiding unsavoury things in odd places (dinner plates beneath the bathroom sink, dirty clothes in the kitchen cupboards, clumps of hair in the vegetable crisper), wandering away from the house with a winter coat over her nightgown. It would have been difficult to believe anything Eleanor said. Still, Eleanor had sworn Mary to secrecy and Mary had kept everything secret, in effect siding with her grandmother.

And then, Eleanor had died of a heart attack.

Two days before her death, she'd again called Mary to her side. She was now thoroughly Trinidadian. Her accent was impenetrable, but she herself was warmer and more open and, although she was lucid, it took longer for her to come to the point; the point being that everything was settled, that all was now in Mary's name, that Eleanor trusted and loved her. Her final words to her granddaughter were

– Yuh musn' fahget de blue bag, Mary. It hav' evryting in deah

before she turned away and closed her eyes and slept.

The following day, Mary did not see her at all. She worked late, ate supper in the Market, and was home at ten, by which time her grandmother was, usually, asleep. It occurred to Mary, afterwards, that she'd felt *something* when she came in the door. It was a cold night, but the house was warm and quiet. Her parents had retired early. Her brother was out. The house was still, and it seemed to Mary someone had been cooking, because the house smelled of curry. As she walked into the living room, there was a loud and startling clatter of pots in the kitchen. And, thinking there was an intruder, Mary went cautiously to the kitchen – no one and nothing and not a thing out of place. It occurred to her afterwards that there must have been some significance to the disturbance, that, perhaps, she had entered the house at the very moment of her grandmother's death. But whatever it was, if it was anything at all, Mary went up to her own room, after giving the kitchen another once over, and she was asleep by eleven.

The next morning, her mother discovered that Eleanor was dead, and the day after that they found Eleanor's will in an envelope beneath her mattress:

I, Eleanor Stanley, being of sound mind and body, leave all my property and all my earthly possessions to my beloved granddaughter, Mary Stanley.

Eleanor Stanley
15 January 1976

In the crinkled cream envelope there was, along with the will, a card on which Eleanor had written the name of her lawyer (Martin Bax) and his telephone number. It was a surprise to all of them that Eleanor had bothered to leave a will, a surprise and a source of bemusement; as if a pauper had decided to give rags and bones to her nearest and dearest.

– Aw, she was okay, the old lady, said Stanley.

No one contradicted him, but Mary was apprehensive. It was as if she'd forgotten to turn a stove off somewhere.

Eleanor was buried on Friday, December 7. A week later, almost as an afterthought, the Stanleys gathered in the office of Mr. Bax to hear a reading of the will. It was a curious enlightenment for them all. As Mr. Bax read Eleanor's will, as he formally revealed the properties, holdings, and bank accounts that had been Eleanor's, they were all forced to reconsider their impressions of the woman who'd been Eleanor, grandmother, Mrs. Stanley. Mary, of course, was stunned by the will. She felt guilt because she had not taken her grandmother at her word, guilt because she had kept Eleanor's wealth secret, guilt because she was Eleanor's only beneficiary, guilt because she was now on one side of a divide, looking back on those she loved.

Her mother looked at her with dismay. Her father looked at her with pride. Her brother refused to look at her. Mr. Bax looked at them all, somewhat quizzically.

– It's quite a will, he said. Allow me to extend my congratulations.

But the only hand he shook was Mary's.

– I have a few things to do before I leave the office. Why don't you all stay here until you've collected yourselves. You can leave by this door, whenever you like. It'll lock behind you. It's been a pleasure meeting you. And, again, congratulations.

Once Mr. Bax had gone, Beatrice turned to Mary and said

– You knew about this?

– Gran told me, Mary answered, but I didn't believe her.

– Why didn't you tell us?

– She didn't leave *us* a thing, said Gil. She left everything to Mary.

Mary's first thought was to immediately divide the inheritance, but she had no idea how to dispose of the (approximately) $8 million her grandmother's estate was now worth.

(*What was the best way to dispose of foreign properties? How should they best divide the money? Should her parents receive the greater part? Should her mother be given less than her father? Should her brother be given any money at all, at his age?*)

Her mother and father, daunted by the idea of so much money, thought this "inheritance business" a grand, inexplicable mistake. Neither believed the inheritance was real, so both believed any delay was likely to be disastrous: easy come, easy go. Because they could not believe this inheritance (if it existed) was truly theirs, they believed it belonged to someone else: lawyers, the government, the wealthy, whomever. If, by some miracle, the inheritance really, truly was theirs, then the best way to deal with it was to put it away where it couldn't be taken from them.

Stanley said

– I don't think anybody can think straight with all that money.

What he meant was: Mr. Bax, the government, whoever it was who had the money now was not to be trusted. The sooner they themselves had it, the better. There was, as always, kindness and concern in Stanley's voice. He could no more mistrust his daughter (or any of his family) than he had his mother, God keep her soul, but he wanted everything settled as quickly as possible, whatever questions and doubts there might be.

– I'm going to meet with Mr. Bax, Mary said. We need some advice.

And that was that. Or, rather, it wasn't. The four of them struggled to understand what had happened. What did it mean to be worth "millions of dollars" or to own property "overseas"? And why was it they could not touch what they owned until Mary met with *her* lawyer? For weeks they walked about, open to the kind of emotions it was difficult to express. They were stunned and excited, incomprehending and resentful. They were thrilled. At times, they were, even, reconciled to the old woman, to Eleanor.

Finally, after a sadly quiet and quietly tense Christmas, Mary had her interview with Mr. Bax. She felt relief at the sight of his black desk, his Turkish carpet, and his windows that looked out onto Elgin. She was comforted by his camel hair suit, blue shirt, and ox-blood brogues. She would have given anything to hear him say

– *I think you should divide your grandmother's inheritance in four, at once.*

but he said nothing of the sort. After shaking her hand and then settling into his chair, he said

– I think you should wait, before you decide what to do with this inheritance. You have quite a bit of capital, it's true, but you've also got some property abroad. You should decide what to do with that first.

– What about my family?

– What about them?

– This money is theirs too, isn't it?

– Yes, of course, if that's what you want. But even if you decide to sell off your properties and divide the money, it will take time and it's much easier, for all concerned, if there is only one seller. You're free to consult with them on the best course to take, but until you've decided on a course, I think it's best if you hold the reins, yeah? For a while, anyway. It's what your grandmother wanted, and I'm happy to help you any way I can.

For an hour and a half, they spoke of property, probates, and responsibility. After which, having taken notes, having agreed that caution was best, she shook his hand and walked out onto Elgin, saddened by the state of affairs. What would her parents do? What would they think?

Well . . . they listened to every word, nodding their heads at the mention of legal fees, taxes, property maintenance, and probates. Her mother shushed her brother whenever he tried to interrupt, and tried to accept that it would be some time before each was given their share of Eleanor's legacy. Unfortunately, suspicious of Mr. Bax's caution, it occurred to Beatrice that it would be best if, instead of waiting for a sum that would come *after* the properties sold, Mary arranged to give them each a deed to one of the properties. There were four buildings – one in London (U.K.), one near Dawlish (U.K.), one in Lans-en-Vercors, and one in Ottawa – and four Stanleys. Perfect. They would each, while waiting for the properties to be assessed and sold, have income from the rent their own property brought in. As well as the liquid assets, some $3 million they would share – equally.

It seemed a reasonable compromise, but Mr. Bax had already cautioned Mary against dispersing the deeds. First, Gil was too young to be given such responsibility. Second, it would take even more time for Mary to deed the buildings to her parents, and have the deeds probated, than it would for her to do it on her own and arrange the sales herself. Third . . .

Her mother frowned.

– Mr. Bax can't tell us what to do, can he? she asked.

– Fine, said Mary. I'll do whatever you want.

But it isn't always easy to know what one wants, especially with things so "unreal" as property in Dawlish, Devon. Gilbert was outraged that he, being too young, would not be given a property for his own, but the real trouble came from an unexpected quarter: her father.

Not long after she had spoken to Mr. Bax a second time, Mary and her father were remembering "the old lady" together. Stanley, despite all, missed her. Mary missed her too, but there was something else: in the surprise and confusion Eleanor's will had occasioned, Mary had forgotten the other face her grandmother had unveiled: Robert Stanley, Esq. Did she, sworn to secrecy as she'd been, have the right to mention these details now? She decided she did. Mary's impulse was generous and loving, but . . .

As a boy, Stanley had often asked his mother about his father: who was he? What did he look like? Was he dark-skinned? He hadn't pestered Eleanor, because she wasn't the kind of woman one "pestered." But when he was eight or nine, she discouraged his questions once and for all: she slapped his face and told him to mind his business. Though this was grossly unfair (whose business is the father, if it is not the son's?), Stanley took his mother's violence in the way he was used to taking it: he took it as justified. To the eight-year-old, it was suddenly obvious that his father, whoever the man had been, was monstrous, his memory a terrifying burden on his mother. When he was old enough to understand the word *rape*, he thought he finally understood the nature of his father's monstrosity and he never asked after the man again.

So, on hearing that his father was an Englishman, he understood that Robert Stanley, Esq., had taken advantage of his mother, marrying her to obscure the trace of his violence. He smiled when Mary told him about his father and he thanked her, but from that moment, Stanley wanted nothing to do with the property in England. The money the old girl had made for herself, that was one thing, but London and Dawlish now seemed to him like blood-soaked ground and he refused to have anything to do with them. It was as if, by renouncing, he were cauterizing a wound.

Now, if he'd been able to express these things, if he had been able to say to his wife

– My mother was violated by this Englishman. I won't have anything to do with his buildings

there would have been an end to the whole issue. Beatrice was not heartless. She would have understood. But, in fact, he had never been able to admit this thing to anyone, ever. Eleanor's violation was a dark, humiliating, but privately held conviction. He could not bring himself to say the first words ("My mother was . . ."). So, instead, without explanation, he shifted allegiance from his wife to his daughter. After he and Mary had spoken, he announced

– I don't want to be a landlord.

– Why not? asked his wife.

– I just don't, he answered. I'll just wait for Mary to sell those buildings off.

– Well, *I* think it's the right thing, said Beatrice.

And in the days that followed, Mr. and Mrs. Stanley grew cold to each other or, to be exact, Beatrice grew cold while Stanley made futile efforts to mollify her. He could not accept a deed to property in England, not without (to his mind) betraying the memory of his mother, while Beatrice would not accept a deed to property if she were the only one taking. She, too, felt uneasy, when she thought of the men and women who inhabited the houses they had inherited. She was wary of the responsibility, but she was determined to protect her family, to make certain they got their due before the government found ways to squeeze it out of them, as governments always do to the poor. It seemed not only perverse that Stanley wouldn't help but hostile, and that was devastating.

There was more to this. Beatrice wasn't all that avid for money or property. Rather, Eleanor had treated her daughter-in-law as little more than chattel, a servant, something her son had picked up and kept. She had cursed their marriage, refused to attend their wedding, and then, at the end, had moved in with them! If Beatrice had allowed the woman into her home it was because she understood Eleanor was her husband's albatross. Now, however, the worst of it, the thing that rankled was that she could not convince herself this inheritance, property, and money was anything more than another turn Eleanor was playing on them. Above all, she wanted them to come out of all this with *something*. And as property was at least *something*, she was wounded when Stanley, of all people, stood in the way and would not move.

And so, though it seemed they were arguing about property, or money, or what have you, Mary's parents were arguing about deeper things. Their marriage was shaken and, because it was the first time in her life she felt this tearing apart, the first time she had been compelled to imagine the destruction of her family, Mary was shattered, the moreso as she imagined the whole business was her fault.

– I'm sorry, said Walter.

These words conveyed little of what he actually felt. It was two o'clock in the morning of the day after he was to have finished with life. He and Mary had quit Les Quatre Jeudis at one. They had walked the streets of Hull. They now walked the streets of Ottawa. He'd spent hours with a stranger whose distress was not quite understandable to him. Still, there was something about the young woman, something that moved him.

They were walking south on Bank and it was the middle of the night, but Mary felt as if she'd stepped from the confessional into a quiet, late-evening church. Had she sinned? Yes. She had not spoken of her grandmother's will. She had not believed her grandmother. She had not done the things she might have. And for this she would lose that which she had taken for granted: her home, her parents, the world from which she'd come.

– I don't think you'll lose anything, said Walter. You've had a shock, that's all.

– My parents haven't spoken to each other in weeks.

– Well, maybe it's not as bad as you think, said Walter. My parents rarely spoke.

They had come to Bank and Gladstone. Mary said

– Thank you so much for listening.

They looked at each other, as if they had a history of concern, one for the other. But, of course, they hadn't. And, not knowing what else to do, Mary put her arms around him, the side of her face rubbing against his coat, and held him, for a moment, before walking west. Walter stood at the corner watching the young woman walk away. For tonight, in any case, he had missed his chance at death. He was too tired. It wasn't that he wanted to live, exactly. His mind was not to be changed by place or time. No, but for some reason he thought it awkward to die so late, or so early, and he was amazed that, on this night of all nights, he had spent hours listening to a young woman go on about lives that had nothing to do with his, about herself. It seemed to him the first time anyone had shared so much.

As he walked back to his house, along Bank, past Catherine, past Glebe, he found himself distracted from thoughts of death. Why had she told him so much about herself? What had he done to elicit such trust? Was it something she'd seen in him, or was it a matter of chance? Unanswerable. Perhaps, in the end, death *did* bring out the best in him. Perhaps it was his natural element.

Now, there was a thought with which to greet the blue-fingered dawn.

BOOK II

20

AN EVENING IN

I sometimes wonder if Franklin would have made a good politician. He believed too much in too few things (in one thing, actually) and politicians like that are almost always crushed. Ottawa was filled with them, wanderers after single ends (Senate reform, say, or flat-rate taxation, or proportional representation). They were like souls in the fourth circle of Dante's Hell, buffeted by the winds of their passion.

When Franklin himself thought about it, when he thought about the course his life had taken, he was grateful to be something other than a politician. He was, as a civil servant, working for his country, or his idea of "country," and this thought kept him in good spirits, despite the increased responsibility that was now his, and despite the anxiety he felt at the thought that Alba was such a tremendous project it was inevitable something should go wrong: he, or someone under him, would forget a crucial detail, a crucial contract, contact, meeting, greeting or . . . something.

Another source of anxiety (his occasional doubts that any prison, however magnificent, *could* improve the men who were forced to inhabit it) was dried up by two thoughts that came to him one night as he looked out on the park that was below his living-room window. The park was its mysterious, dark self, its

eight streetlamps bearded by light. Just beyond the yellow light, a
nocturnal life quietly carried on, with its mice, owls, raccoons,
and bats. He could not look on the scene without feeling just
what it was that made the park a holy place: the presence of a dili-
gent and desperate struggle for survival. It never failed to move
him and, on this night, feeling the power of this particular place,
its influence, it occurred to him that all places (even the least
memorable) had some effect or other. They led to worship or
desecration, ease or discomfort. Why shouldn't Alba, if she were
truly Art, move men to better themselves? The only questions
were: Why had it taken so long for Alba to occur to someone?
Could it really be that, from the time men had first imprisoned
other men, none had thought it would be good to hold them in
places that ennobled? Prisons were inevitably horrifying. They
inspired nothing but fear or pity. They were, as places, inimical to
the very aims of imprisonment, if what one wanted was men
who, having accomplished their punishment, returned to society
whole. Alba could do no worse than the houses of horror we
were accustomed to calling prisons. Or so Franklin thought and,
with that thought, he felt even more grateful that he had been
called (by whatever force it was that did the calling) to shepherd
the prison into being.

The feeling that he had at last discovered his destiny put
Franklin in excellent spirits and he became, for a time, convivial.
He invited people to his home and cooked for them, something
he hadn't done since university. He was a limited cook, however.
The only thing he ever made was boeuf stroganoff: braised beef,
mushrooms, and sour cream on a bed of fried potatoes. In this,
too, he had been guided by Alexandra Byeli. She had shown him
how stroganoff was done and it was the only dish he ever mastered. So, his cuisine was irreproachable but specific.

(The most remarkable thing about Franklin's meals was not
the food but, rather, the long dining-room table: rustic, at first
glance, old, and in need of sanding. But what looked like bumps

on the surface were in fact drawings in the wood, each drawing depicting a moment in Canadian history: John A. MacDonald in Parliament, the hanging of Louis Riel, the Turtle Mountain rockslide, and so on in a profusion of drawings that progressed in a spiral on the table's surface and down along its thick legs. The table, a gift from Edward, had been bought at a flea market in Plantagenet and finessed into Franklin's apartment by a handful of men. Of all the things I remember about Franklin's apartment, that table is what I remember most fondly, because, no doubt, far from home as I am, I would love to have it for myself.)

The most frequent beneficiary of Franklin's conviviality was Edward. Though he tired of boeuf stroganoff, he could not remember a time when Franklin's company had been quite so warm, or when Franklin had been so open. It was as if MacKenzie Bowell Federal Penitentiary, the very idea of it, had turned Franklin into a more generous man.

One night, for instance, when the other guests had gone, Franklin actually spoke about his family. This was so unexpected, Edward tried to change the subject, certain that Franklin had, mentally, stumbled. But, no, it seemed simply that their friendship had crossed a threshold. Franklin spoke of Anse Bleu, the grey stillness of it. He then spoke of his father and, for the first time, his mother, a petite New Brunswicker. She was, he said, a vague presence to him. She had died when he was young and he had, unfortunately, few memories of her to share: she had bought him cowboy pants, when he'd asked for them, (together) they had made a kite in the shape of a whale, and she had once broken a fingernail while opening his bedroom door.

– Well, said Edward, I bet she would have been proud to see you these days.

– What do you mean? asked Franklin.

– I mean, with Bowell penitentiary and everything.

A surge of fellow feeling ran through Edward. How rare it was, in his experience, for men, no matter how close, to speak of their mothers. And he was about to say something along those lines when Franklin interrupted him.

– Anyway, said Franklin, the important thing is to get Bowell penitentiary built.

He put his arm around Edward's shoulder.

– Thanks for coming, he said.

It occurred to Edward, then, that he had been unkind. Franklin had shared something of his past, his deepest memories, and he had given nothing in return. As soon as he tried to think of a confidence appropriate to the occasion, however, he realized there was little he had ever withheld from Franklin. He was not private in the way Franklin was. His confidences were neither as secret nor as personal as Franklin's. As he put on his coat, he remembered a small animal he had loved.

– You know, he said, when I was in Grade Seven, I had this great frog.

– The one that died? asked Franklin.

– How did you know?

– You're an open book, Eddy. That's what I like about you.

When Edward had gone, Franklin sat down to drink a tumbler of vodka with a hint of grapefruit juice, adulterating the vodka because he did not like to drink alone. He put on a record and listened to La Bolduc. (Yes, somewhere deep within, he was irresolvably Québécois.) And on hearing La Bolduc's voice, he sank into the small fissure in his being that led to his childhood.

This self-indulgence was something he rarely allowed himself, because he did not like to be reminded of the past. But on this night, pleasantly inebriated after an evening with Edward and a few guests, he allowed his memory to wander in places it did not usually go: here was his mother, her face a charming mask of pinkish makeup and white powder, there was his father looking out at the blue-green river, and there he was staring at himself in a mirror, trying desperately to pat down a cowlick at the top of his head. Touching details, all mercifully distant because Anse Bleu was a world he had deliberately left behind. And yet, it was also the place that had inspired him. In a sense, Anse Bleu, being the community he had known best, the one against which he compared every other, *was* the "ideal community" Alba was meant to protect. How strange that he should wish to protect and keep a world he chose not to inhabit. Perhaps someday, when he had made his mark, he would return to Québec, having redeemed the loneliness that had been his childhood and the blandness of the world that had made him.

And as Edward made his way home, he thought of Franklin. Though they'd been friends for years, he could not think of a time when he'd seen Franklin more optimistic, or more open. And yet, Edward had lately begun to feel a little disloyal. The truth was, he had reservations about MacKenzie Bowell penitentiary, but he hadn't the heart to tell Franklin about them. To Edward's mind, MacKenzie Bowell was, first and foremost, a prison. Its purpose was to segregate the dangerous from the innocent. If, in so doing, it produced monsters, well, that was the price a society paid. If you could convince the monsters who murdered and raped that they had souls and that their souls needed tending, then, perhaps, you could rescue them from their own filth. But how was that to be done with bricks and mortar? Were buildings really so persuasive?

That was the question, and that is where matters stood: Franklin believed places were or could be persuasive; Edward could not.

Yet Edward was not the kind of man to easily contradict a friend. His idea of loyalty had always included the duty to believe what his friends believed. This had, until now, been rather easy for him. After all, he had few friends, two to be exact: Franklin and Reinhart. And then again: once one said a thing a few times, it became a habit of mind and the road from mental habit to belief is not long. Were there not things Franklin believed that Reinhart did not? Yes, of course. Franklin believed in God, Reinhart did not. So, did Edward believe *and* not believe? Yes, exactly. When he was with Franklin, he allowed himself to be persuaded by Franklin's presence. When he was with Reinhart, he allowed himself to be skeptical. If both men had come to him and asked, point blank, if there were a god, he would, for the sake of friendship, have had to lose consciousness. And did *he* believe in god? He believed in friendship. For most other things, there was a space within him, a place for possible belief, for belief when it was called for.

Which is why Bowell penitentiary was so frustrating to Edward. He had come upon something that he could not share with Franklin, his friend. He blamed himself, of course, and his own stupidity, but there was something more: a feeling of impending disgrace. Should he, then, have told Franklin of his premonition? Another man might have, as a tribute to friendship. But Edward was not that kind of man. As he walked home that night, he resolved to put his misgivings behind him and to be supportive of Franklin's vision, to *believe* in Bowell penitentiary the way he'd come to *believe* in Art.

When he entered his parents' house, his home, he saw that a light in the living room was on. His father (insomniac, as usual) was up watching a late-night movie: *House of Dr. Rasánoff*.

– Why don't you watch it with me, Ed?

– I've already seen it, Dad.

And yet, they did watch it, until Edward fell asleep, falling just as it was getting interesting, just as the faceless girl was beginning to understand what her father had done in her name.

21

AN EVENING OUT

In the three years since his wife had died, François Ricard thought of her often and found solace in the textbooks on quantity surveying he read or reread. People spoke of the consolations of philosophy or of poetry, but he found in those things little but wasted words and obscurity. Yes, he still attended Fortnightly evenings, but he took no comfort in Plotinus or Kant, still less in Claudel or Ronsard. Even the great Allais, whose work he and Michelle had often read together, even Alphonse Allais seemed bitter:

– *Cet homme-là . . . me tromperait sur la tête d'un teigneux!*

On the other hand, the textbooks on quantity surveying, most of them in English, were, if not consolation, at least soporific. He could read Willis' *Elements of Quantity Surveying* or *Practice and Procedure for the Quantity Surveyor* with as little or as much attention as he could manage, and they led him, by way of memory . . . memory of a time when he and Michelle had only just met, both of them walking together along Laurier to Sandy Hill, where she and her friends shared an apartment on Templeton . . . by way of memory towards sleep. Not that sleep was simple. Since

Michelle's death, sleep had become a process, one decision after another: to lie down on their bed or on the sofa, to retire early or stay up late, to close his eyes or read . . .

He had other duties, of course, besides sleep, and other responsibilities. There was work, for instance. To think he'd studied so hard to end up sharing a small office at Transport Canada with his English counterpart, an office with a window that looked onto other buildings. At the beginning of his career, he had travelled to the ports along the St. Lawrence (Trois-Rivières, Port Saguenay, Sept-Îles, and points between) and had shaken hands with managers and supervisors who played the small game of making their needs seem more urgent than they were.

– *Cré moé-là, on a besoin d'bécosses en ostie toastée.*[1]

Now, as a manager, he sent inspectors out from time to time and collated their reports, made certain they were in language plain enough to be understood by the new minister, Mr. Mazankowski, and sent them along in the hope that they would, eventually, attain the minister's attention. It was not exciting work, and the less said about it, the better.

There was also his responsibility to his son. In the time since Michelle's death, they had spoken of her often, and it had been his task to comfort Daniel.

– *Papa, est-ce qu'il y a un Dieu?*
– *Oui.*
– *Papa, est-ce qu'il y a un paradis?*
– *Mais oui. Si'l y a un Dieu, il y a un paradis.*

In the beginning, they'd had that conversation so often, François had almost managed to believe in a God whose existence he doubted.

– *Papa . . . ?*
– *Oui Daniel?*
– *Est-ce qu'il y a des revenants?*

---

[1] I say, we could certainly use some water closets.

– *Non, Daniel.*

They'd both had trouble sleeping. For months, Daniel would wake in the middle of the night, or near morning, and come in to sleep with him, so that François, sleepless himself, would lie awake, waiting for his son to fall asleep. It drew father and son closer, grief making contemporaries of them. In fact, it sometimes seemed to François that his son was more mature than he was. It wasn't that Daniel recovered faster than he did, but that Daniel often tried to console *him* and, at times, for his son's sake, he allowed himself to accept the consolation.

His relations with his peers were as tentative now as formerly they had been open and confident. He shook hands with his underlings, and nodded to his superiors, but it would not have surprised him if, as he walked the narrow halls of Transport, he passed through his fellows as through pillars of cloud.

His relations with his friends were almost as vaporous. When Michelle was alive, he had enjoyed the company of a great many people, men and women with whom he could remember real conviviality. But whose company had he sought in the last year? He attended evenings with the Fortnightly, but these evenings were no longer amusing. He continued attending, in part because this was something he'd done with Michelle, in part because it was curiously satisfying to see how little comfort ideas brought. Really, Franklin Dupuis, whom he'd met after Michelle's death, was one of the few people who called regularly, once or twice a month, to invite him out for drinks and conversation or drinks, conversation and boeuf stroganoff, and François often accepted because there was something voluptuous in his lapse from the world, and he fought against it, against the voluptuousness.

It seemed odd that Franklin, who had not been a close friend, who had attended but one or two Fortnightly evenings, should choose to socialize with a man in mourning. One wondered what he drew from the long silences that were now inevitably part of

François' conversations. Though they were both francophone, their conversations took place, for the most part, in English. François could speak to Franklin in French, if he chose, and, for a few minutes at most, Franklin would use their shared language, but, somehow, they always returned to English. It unnerved François to speak English with someone who spoke French as well as he did. It made you wonder what it was Franklin was trying to avoid. Still, there was something agreeable about the man. In a word, he was diverting. Franklin was one of those men who could talk about themselves without seeming self-absorbed or blinkered, who could talk about themselves without talking about themselves. In fact, the more Franklin talked about his studies, his time with Diefenbaker, or his thoughts about prison, the more his so-called "self" seemed to recede. Listening to him was like driving along a flat road, in late summer, towards a bright but resolutely distant horizon. At the heart of the man, there was something unreachable, and it was, at once, off-putting *and* compelling.

One evening, the two of them had dinner in the Market and drinks at Wim's. It was, in most ways, a typical evening out for the two, save that Franklin spoke French as they walked to the Market. Wim's was crowded, noisy, and dimly lit. They sat near the front entrance and looked out onto Sussex Drive on a warm summer evening, the street dark from a light rain, the pedestrians mindless of the weather, animated.

– What would you like to drink? asked Franklin.
– N'importe quoi.
Franklin ordered a single cognac from the waitress.
– Tu n' bois pas? François asked.
– Pas ce soir, said Franklin. L'alcool a tendance à me distraire.
– Pourquoi m'encourager à boire alors? Ça m'distrait, moi aussi, non?
– T'es pas dans le même bateau que moi, austeure. Toi, t'as besoin de distraction.

François looked up, wondering where this new tack was heading.

– Pourquoi? he asked.

Franklin hesitated.

– Because . . . your wife is dead.

– And?

– Tu as porte ouverte sur la douleur.

– Ça c'est mes affaires, said François.

– Yes, mais t'as surement besoin de distraction de temps en temps, n'est-ce pas? À travers cette porte il n'y a que tristesse.

– Tu n'as aucune idée de quoi tu parles.

– Voilà ce que j'aime chez toi, François. T'es la franchise même. C'est vrai que je n'peux pas comprendre ta perte, même si ma mère est morte.

– Ta mère est morte? Quand ça?

– L'année passée. Et puis, tu sais, j'en parle rarement, mais j'aimais ma mère.

Both men stopped speaking. But then, as quickly as it had come, the unexpected tension dissipated. They began to laugh. For François, it was as if he had at last discovered Franklin's secret heart. The man's mother had died recently, and it was touching that he should seek out others who had been recently bereft.

– T'avais raison, he said. J'ai besoin de distraction de temps en temps. Ta mère est décédée. On va boire ensemble. Waitress! Can we have a cognac for my friend?

The waitress ran the fingers of her left hand through her hair and exhaled words that ran together and sounded like

– Cognananasaft . . .

Franklin began to speak English.

– Thank you, he said. I probably *could* use a drink.

They sat in silence until the young woman brought another cognac.

– Santé, said François

– Skol, said Franklin.

Then, as if an idea had just occurred to him and he needed a drink to quell his excitement, Franklin swallowed another mouthful of cognac and said

– Maybe I can help you.

– Comment ça, "help"?

– Well, I've been given more responsibility. You know how it is. And there's one project that's going to be big. It's not public knowledge, but it just so happens, I could use a quantity surveyor. You told me a while ago you haven't been doing work in your field. Wouldn't you like to get back to surveying?

– I already have a job, François answered.

– That's just it. You wouldn't have to leave Transport, for this.

– For what?

– For a penitentiary. It'll be a while before there's approval, but I think we're talking about several buildings. Water, roads, drains . . . the works. Rundstedt's behind the project, and I've been asking architects for designs. I know it's all a little early, but if it goes through I'd like to have figures from a quantity surveyor I can trust. Once we find the right site, of course.

– You want me to do this for *you*? asked François.

– Yes. I'd pay you out of my own pocket. I couldn't pay you as much as the job deserves, but I'd like to have the figures *before* the government's surveyors go to work.

Actually, what Franklin wanted was complicated. He wanted François' work, because he really did think it would give him an advantage to have a proper and thorough appraisal of the penitentiary's costs. François was, at very least, a conscientious man, and Franklin had no doubt his work would be professional. But he also wanted François' esteem. He needed confirmation of Alba's soundness and he sought François' admiration, because he knew how difficult it would be to attain, François being a man who thought for himself. It may have been something like superstition but, in these early days of Alba, it seemed best to bring the best along with him. Not that approval makes right more right. It was rather that Franklin still had small doubts about Alba and was insecure enough to lie about the year of his mother's passing to bring François to his side. Still, lest we forget: Christ himself wondered about the need for crucifixion, before getting on with his death.

– All right, said François, I'll think about it.

22

MR. RUNDSTEDT AND SUCCESS

W hat is a successful life, anyway?
The Right Honourable Rundstedt was not the kind
of man who could have asked such a question in
such a way. It isn't that the question, asked in precisely that way,
would not have interested him, but, rather, that he would have
thought it an abstraction. Certainly, in Rundstedt's life, there had
been elections lost, debacles, and humiliations. There had even
been dark nights of the soul, but the soul in question was never
his own. That is, Rundstedt believed his defeats and debacles were
the world's doing, so he took them easily in stride.

   – *Well, what're you gonna do?*

was his response to condolence or commiseration. In a word,
Rundstedt was not particularly self-conscious or self-aware. He
might lose this election or that vote, this money or that house,
without gaining the slightest doubt about his way of life. The
metaphysical question

   – What is a successful life?

needs a metaphysical notion of failure in order to receive a meaningful answer and Rundstedt simply did not know about "failure."

   He had a wife.

   He had children.

He was recognized in the circles that mattered to him.

And yet, a year after his election, a year after his nomination to Cabinet, he began to feel there was something missing. Not that he had in any way failed, but rather that there was a lack. It was, in emotional terms, as if he had misplaced his car keys. Take, for instance, the small matter of women.

He had a wife.

The same could be said for most of his contemporaries, it's true, but a number of them seemed remarkably unconstrained by their family ties. In public, of course, it was *de rigueur* to laud the benefits of stability, fidelity, hearth and home, but a number of his contemporaries still managed to chase skirt, from one end of the day to the other. Rundstedt was not that kind of man.

He had a wife, whom he adored.

In fact, he had loved Edwina Rotenberg from the moment he saw her: Grade Nine, Western, 1946. He had loved her for the smell of her (grapefruit), for the look of her (plump, flat-nosed, hair tucked behind her ears, green eyes), for the presence of her (she was so discreet, it was as if she were leaving a room when she entered it), and he had known, from his first look, that he would love no other girl, no other adolescent, no other woman. His fate had been decided, nuptially speaking, the moment she asked if she could sit in the desk behind his. He would have no other woman. He wanted no other, and they would, he and Edwina, have laughed at the suggestion that he did.

And yet, though the contemplation of other women had previously been enough, he began to wonder why he should not go further than contemplation, whether he wanted to or not. Whether he wanted to or not? Was it possible to be unfaithful to Edwina without wanting? Yes, because it wasn't a matter of want or desire. (Rundstedt certainly knew what it was to desire. He had only to watch Edwina undress, to wonder which she would slip from first, brassiere or panties, her back to him, dark hair falling to the nape of her neck, the sound of her voice calling his name;

he had only to think of these moments, however vaguely, to feel
the onset of desire.) It was simply that he had never felt real desire
for anyone but Edwina. (His infrequent attendance at strip clubs
and nudie bars, for instance, aroused little more than a taxonomic
curiosity about breasts, hips, hair, and haunches.) So, if he were
to be unfaithful, it would be for some reason other than desire.
And that reason would be? That a man knows who he is by what
he can do. The infidelity he contemplated was not, in the end, an
infidelity to his wife, but rather to himself. This was, perhaps,
inevitable. He was outgoing, hail-fellow-well-met, goal-oriented,
spit and polish, a walking handshake, open to the world. But he
was closed to himself. He wouldn't have recognized his "self" if it
had kicked him in the testicles and, as a consequence, he had very
little idea there were things noxious to it.

What has this to do with success? Well, Rundstedt had reached
the height of his aspirations. He was a member of Cabinet – with
no higher objective. He was respected. His ideas were given due
consideration, as a matter of course. He himself was convinced
that his commitment to building MacKenzie Bowell Federal
Penitentiary was proof he had the aspirations of a great man, an
interesting thinker, someone to read about in books. How fortunate he had been to find, in Franklin Dupuis, a man who understood the significance of his, Rundstedt's, thinking, a man who
could be trusted to carry out his wishes or, even, to fulfill wishes
he, Rundstedt, was unaware of harbouring. With Franklin as his
right hand, Rundstedt was free to concentrate on policy, free to
travel about and make speeches, free to meet constituents. So,
there was, at least for now, no position to pursue, no voters to
win over.

And yet, if this is what you called "success," it was, in its way,
the end of the road and it disarmed him.

For the first time in his adult life, Rundstedt looked to other
lives for direction and, in looking to other lives, he began to question his own, to wonder about his satisfaction, to mistrust his own

happiness. Like an earwig, self-consciousness crept into his being, bringing with it the dreadful notion of failure, the hitherto strange idea that his life might have been lived other than he had lived it. Rundstedt was still quite cheerful, you understand. You could not have told that his soul was in confusion, and he was not the kind of man to drown in darkness.

But still . . .

23

PARALLEL LIVES

P aul Dylan's wife had left him. She'd left in April. She had returned, briefly, in May. She had left for good in June. They had last seen each other in August. It was now November.

He did not like to speak of her departure, unless he were forced to by circumstance. He politely declined invitations to dinner, and he usually answered

– Fine

when he was asked how she was. To friends, he admitted the subject was excruciating. She had left him. He was not ready to talk about it.

His first reaction, in the spring, had been disbelief, a disbelief beyond words. Something had happened. He knew it. He listened to his wife explain why, though she loved him, she could not go on; but it was as if she were telling him the newspaper would not be delivered for a week, or as if she were admitting she could not stand to eat fish on Mondays. She told him in the morning, before he went off to work. Perhaps that was it. His mind was elsewhere. When she had finished, he'd said

– I understand

gathered his things, and left for the office. He even managed to drive to work without undue emotion, without any emotion, rather. A switch had been turned off, within. His thoughts were clear.

– What's she talking about?

he thought. And

– What a strange thing to say to me before work.

As if her departure had nothing to do with him. Nor, for months, was the switch turned on again. There were moments, certainly, when he was almost himself, moments when (watching her leave, for instance) he felt himself on the verge of anger. What had he done? He had forgiven her her affair with Walter, and was this her thanks? She hadn't discovered what he'd done to Walter, had she? No. She would have berated him otherwise. So, her behaviour was unmotivated and unfair, and it burned him.

Still, those moments when he was closest to his old self were welcome compared to the moments during which he woke from something like a parallel life. One day, for instance, he found himself holding an envelope that looked as if it had been attacked by stamps: neatly, in an ordered way, every inch of the envelope's surface, front and back, had been covered. He'd had to take the letter out, to see to whom it was destined

Baroness Beatrice Berg von der Hof

and have his secretary prepare another envelope in which to send it, "it" being a birthday card to a woman he'd known since university. On another day, he'd had a long, dull conversation with a janitor, concerning the best place to put the black metal dustbin he usually kept under his desk. Or, rather, he'd had no such conversation. He returned to himself, the darkness in his office almost palpable. There was no one at work but him. How long had he been talking to himself about dustbins? How long had it taken him to cover an envelope with stamps? He had no idea, and it was disturbing that his body now did things on its own, without him. No, it was not madness. His wife had left him. It was normal to go through such episodes. They were to be expected, or so he convinced himself. But then, when Louise returned for a week, it was worse. It was the end of May, spring, and she had called to ask how he was. He had answered

– I'm fine

and was surprised by his happiness at the sound of her voice. Though she'd left a number where she could be reached, he would never have called her. It simply wasn't in him to let Louise see even a hint of need. He had managed to work, to feed himself, to keep his house clean. Why should he surrender to the desire to see her, to hear her voice, to beg her to reconsider?

(– *I can change, if that's what you want. I'll change* . . .

In dreams, he'd said such things and done much worse, frightening himself awake because the image of him with his hands around her throat, or of him driving a nail through her shoulder, was so vivid it woke him and took him halfway to the telephone to call her, to make certain she was not hurt, before he realized he'd been dreaming, and there was no need to call.)

Louise had called to ask if he would mind if she stayed with him for a week, while her new apartment was being painted. His first instinct was to say

– *Yes, I would mind.*

but he said

– No, I don't mind.

– Are you sure?

– Of course.

(As if he were the most reasonable man in the world.)

– Thank you, Paul.

(As if he were a friend on whom she was lightly imposing.)

– You're welcome.

What was he thinking? How could he have imagined he'd live through her presence as if she weren't there? Perhaps he hoped she had changed her mind, that these few days would be a first step towards reconciliation. He'd imagined, perhaps, that he had overcome his grief, that he would see her for who she was and, if she were not coming back, bid farewell to his wife. He'd had no good occasion on which to bid farewell. He had been too distant from himself to intone the right words. He would find the right words. (As if farewell were ever a single moment.) He'd wished, almost certainly, for a chance to prove that he was prepared to live out, manfully, the calamity into which she'd thrown them. There would be no begging for forgiveness, on his part. (There is a difference between life and dreams, after all.)

Whatever it was that had prompted his acquiescence, though, her presence was a disaster. From the moment he saw her, three versions of Louise began their equal co-existence within him. First, there was the woman he no longer loved, the one who'd hurt him, the one towards whom he thought he could be cool.

– If you like, you can sleep in the guest room. I'll make the bed for you.

Then, there was his wife, the woman he did, in fact, as far as he could understand the word, love.

– Or you can sleep in the bedroom, if you like, and I'll sleep in the guest room.

Finally, there was the woman he wanted to murder, the one he had, not often but often enough, dreamed of hurting.

– Or, if you prefer, you can sleep in the basement.

After apologizing, again, and making certain her presence would not cause him emotional distress, Louise chose the guest room. They did not, at first, kiss or embrace, though that was strange, and then they did, and that was strange too. (Can there be a moment more awkward than one in which you attempt an intimacy you have achieved countless times, perhaps as recently as days before, an intimacy that was, perhaps only hours ago, unimpeded but is now impossible?) She was to stay for a week.

On the first night, Paul slept poorly. They had spoken little, the two of them. He had kept silent, for the most part, while his wife spoke of practical matters. She wanted nothing, really. There was nothing she wanted to bring to her new life. She would create no problems for him financially, would not disrupt his daily routine with lawyers and meetings. She blamed herself. She should have spoken sooner of her unhappiness. She hoped he could forgive her, but, no, there was really no way of going on and, though she couldn't support herself as well as he had supported her, she had money enough to see her through a year, if she were careful and, in any case, she hoped, though he certainly wasn't obliged, that he might help her out, now and then, until she found a better job. She would certainly repay him, if he did.

He had heard these things before, and he had his own feelings about them. It all sounded as if she were being magnanimous, as if he should be grateful. He looked at her, as she spoke, and he could not understand how he had given up his life for this, a thin woman who liked to dress in style, who had taken to wearing clothes that hid her neck; the bags under her eyes dark as noonday shadows, her teeth all that were visible of her when she laughed her irritating laugh . . . like a whinny.

But then, he hadn't given up his life for this woman. He had given it up for a woman who'd gone long ago. So, what could he possibly owe this horror in front of him? Nothing. Ah, but it wasn't so simple. Even if this was not the woman for whom he had done everything to create a home, still the woman he loved was buried in the rubble of this one. And the tragedy, if you could call it that, was that he could still hear the voice of his beloved somewhere in hers.

On the first night, when it was late and she had no more words to say, they said good night and went off into their separate rooms. At first he couldn't sleep, because there was an unanswered question on his mind: why had she come here? She had, she said, abandoned any claim to his house. She'd even added that she wanted nothing from this place. Now there was a sharp hook. From all their years together, was there not *one* thing she regarded as her own? No. She wanted to obliterate their marriage. She had other friends. If she wanted to obliterate him, why return? Could it be that she could not bring herself to leave, that she was still emotionally attached? Or was it, rather, that she was there to mock him, to remind him that she was there by right?

The question kept him awake until he could feel the coming of dawn: the song of birds, a small chill, a bluish light, through the curtains, that reminded him of the sea. Although, the two or three times he got up to look out at the morning, he was surprised to find the light was only from the streetlamps, and that it was still late. And then, when the question faded somewhat, he couldn't sleep because he was trying so desperately to sleep, and he would catch himself in the act of falling asleep, as his thoughts grew more peculiar, and the thought that this was sleep and that he was finally sleeping would wake him, because he couldn't shake the feeling he had forgotten something important.

And then he did, finally, sleep for a while.

And then he got up to see if his wife was sleeping.

He didn't want to disturb her so, sensibly, he went out the window of his room and walked along the window ledges, unmindful of the neighbours, until he reached the window closest to the guest room through which he re-entered the house. He was careful to make no noise. The moon outside was bright, its light like a torch; so bright, in fact, that he could see a moth on the wall: white wings, with minute green spots, shivering as it made its way. At her door he hesitated, his fingers on the doorknob, until he remembered she was a deep sleeper, that she wasn't likely to hear anything short of real commotion. (The night was so quiet, he could hear the friction of the moth's wings.)

Inside, the guest room was as brightly lit as the hall had been. There was a moth in here as well. This one was larger, with the same minute spots on its wings, and it made its way along one of the black curtains that had been parted to let in the air and the moon. His wife, looking taller and more pale by moonlight, lay on the bed. It was warm, and she had thrown off the sheets, and she lay naked on the bed, her narrow, lovely back towards him, her wide hips. By this extraordinary light, he could clearly see the down that grew along the soft groove between her vagina and her anus.

No doubt about it, he was enthralled. He forgot why he had come. But when he remembered, he also remembered how much she had hurt him, and in remembering that pain, his anger rose up so suddenly, it was as if a full orchestra had struck up inside him, not just any orchestra, but one intent on playing the overture to Tannhäuser – a music he so loathed, he put a hand over his mouth, lest the sound escape from him and wake her. Not that it helped. She stirred in her sleep, and he wondered what he would say if she turned to him. No, she hadn't stirred at all. Rather, there was a mouse that moved out from beneath her pillow. Paul was horrified she might think he'd put it there, but he was relieved there was only one, as if one were forgivable.

Ah, but there was not just one. There never is *one* mouse, is there? Several moved out from beneath her pillow, and several more climbed onto her shoulder and along her back. (They must have made their nest in the mattress. He so rarely slept in this room himself.) She was an admirably deep sleeper. And he was filled with tenderness for her. He had to do something about the mice. He took up the bedside lamp and he began to strike at them, using the lamp's metal base. He even managed to hit some of them, though not, apparently, hard enough to do serious damage. And so he began to swing very hard indeed, unmindful of where he struck, because he struck her, her head, her back, her shoulder, accidentally, but with all his force, and she woke, for an instant, or rather she sighed, before passing out again, the bed-sheets damp and white.

He was dreaming, of course. There were no window ledges along which he could have moved. The room he'd imagined her in was a room in his parents' house, not at all like the guest room.

Still, the violence woke him, and he could not go back to sleep until ten in the morning, when he heard her get up, shower, and leave for the day.

The following night was made worse by the deepening resentment he felt at her presence. Not only did he wonder why she was there, but he was now slightly fearful of sleep itself. It was one thing to dream of hurting her when she was miles away, God knows where with God knows whom. It was another to do so when she was within reach. How often one heard of sleep-walkers who . . .

And so, after another evening of attempted small talk on Louise's part, they went, at opposite ends of the hall, to their rooms. He intended to sleep. He took with him a late novel by Henry James, chosen almost at random from the bookshelf. (It was *The Ambassadors*; though, of course, almost anything by James would, under normal circumstances, have anaesthetized him in minutes flat.) He read, without really understanding its interminable sentences with their tortured and, one might say, if one were being unkind, cruel syntax, as much of the book as he could stand before he sat up waiting, listening to the small sounds of night.

He was not tired. He was not sleepy. He was increasingly anxious, because he began to feel, in earnest, the return of his jealousy. It had been adulterated by despair, guilt, shame, or it had been masked, as all his emotions had been, by what he now took to be shock, plain and simple. On this night, however, it returned to him, pure. It was not a matter of *feeling* betrayed. He knew he had been. There were no more clues to be ferreted from the little places she kept hidden from him. It was out in the open. (Even more than it had been with Walter Barnes.)

On this night, he did not believe her capable of leaving him, unless there were someone else. (Walter, perhaps. Walter, still. Walter, always.) All that remained was to have her name him.

And then?

And then, he could leave her in peace. There would be no more reason to hold on to even the most cherished version of her he possessed. This idea of liberation filled him with hope for his own release. There was no reason to feel jealous. She was no longer his, but a part of him still needed proof she was not. So, if he could get her to admit her fault, he would be freed. There was an elegance to the idea that thrilled him.

Somewhere around two in the morning, the desire (the need) to ask her the name of her new (what was the word?) man became so keen, he thought to get up and see if she were still awake.

If she were awake, he would ask her.

If she were not, he would wake her, it being close enough to morning to make little difference. He sat up, thinking this through, for an hour, an hour during which he got up from bed a dozen times, getting as far as the door each time, before deciding that, no, it was too early and, besides, wondering if he had thought things through.

Finally, he got up, opened the door to his room and walked down the hall to the guest room. He felt the carpet under his bare feet. He passed the bathroom, on his right, its door open, from which he caught the scent of a soap she used. (What was it called? Something from Neil's Yard . . . London, of all places.) The whole house smelled, faintly, of his wife, as perhaps it always had, though he was only now aware of it. (No, it didn't smell of *her*. It smelled of the commercial perfumes, powders, and nail polish she used. Those smells had become her. The thought disgusted him.)

It wasn't the moon that shone through the window in the hall. It was a light from his neighbour's backyard.

He opened the door to her room quietly.

The curtains were drawn, but a soft glow illuminated the place where the windows were. It was, at first, too dark to make out much of anything, but, as his eyes grew accustomed to the dark, he saw that a bit of light thickened and narrowed, changing as the curtains fluttered, along the wall, towards the bed where she lay sleeping. After a while, he could clearly see her profile on the bed, and then he could see her, partially covered, her white cotton nightgown bunched up so her waist was exposed.

The room smelled of her.

He felt, at once, the desire to straighten her nightgown and a fear of doing so. He stood at the door, one hand on its frame, one hand on the door itself. He stood there for what must have been half an hour, scarcely breathing, unaware of thought, though somewhere inside him someone was thinking because he felt shame and longing, and he was aware of images (lamp, cord, letter, window) whose passage through his imagination disturbed him.

He was about to leave. He had decided that, after all, it was too early to wake her, when she stirred. She turned from her back to her side, facing the wall, her back to him: an unpleasant reminder of the dream he'd had the night before, though she wasn't exposed to him, having drawn the sheets over herself as she moved.

And as she moved, she clearly said the words

– Owl . . . (something, something, something) eyes sore . . .

followed by others that were incomprehensible. And, for some reason, that is what he had come for, and he knew it, and, for a moment, he felt relieved, unburdened, not even angry. This woman was no one he knew. He turned on the lights, startling her from sleep.

– What? What is it? she said.

– I don't want you here any more, he answered.

– What? What's the matter, Paul?

– I can't sleep with you here. I don't want you here.

She turned to the clock on the table beside her.

– It's four o'clock. What are you doing?

She pulled the bedsheets up over her body.

– I can't sleep, he said. That's all. You have to go.

– I can't go anywhere now. It's four o'clock.

– You can leave in the morning.

Not before she spoke, but before he could make out her words, he closed the door and went back to his bedroom.

They had last seen each other, briefly, in August. It had been months since then, and his feelings for Louise had hardened into something he carried about with him. It was November and grey, with Christmas at spitting distance. How would he deal with that, with snow and tinsel and his parents asking if he were "all right" and why Louise could not visit them, however she felt about him.

– She's like our daughter, his mother had said.

His father added

– You should try this new . . . what do they call it? Marriage counselling? Don't know if it'll do any good, but it's worth a try, if you ask me.

– It's over, he'd said.

And so continued the slow work of obliterating his wife, her memory.

24

HALLEY'S COMET

I t had been a sombre Christmas. Despite the comet that entered Aquarius on Christmas Day, it was a dull season for Louise Lanthier. It was her first Christmas without Paul in twenty years, her first Christmas alone. She now knew the season for all it contained of bitterness and solitude. The only acquaintance she met, and that by accident, was Walter. She'd seen him walking along Clarence the week before Christmas and had stopped him to say hello, but it was as if he were afraid of her. He'd lowered his eyes and walked on, relieved to get away from her, it seemed. And how odd that had been: exhilarating and wounding, wounding though she tried to see things from his perspective, it being impossible for her to hold anything against him, despite the time that had passed.

All that Louise had known was an illusion. That was why she had left her husband. *Claro.* Yet, in looking about her, free from what she took to be the illusions of life with Paul, it seemed as if *everything* were illusory, as if life itself were an accommodation of the false. It followed, then, that there could be no marriage, no love, no home without disguise.

Yet, there were some illusions worth tending, others not. Paul, for instance. Who was he who'd been her husband? A year ago, she would have said he was a good, if neurotic, man: faithful, obsessive, but caring. He had worked hard to give her what he thought she wanted. (She hadn't known what she wanted, but something in her must have wanted the things he gave her. He hadn't provided these things in spite of her, had he?) She would not have thought him capable of the kind of instability he'd shown, recently.

Take the time, months ago now, when he had asked her to leave *his* house. She'd been fast asleep, dreaming of a field of birds, when he'd turned on the light in her room and asked her to go. Just like that, at four in the morning. So irrational. She had been more than upset. She had been frightened. Once she'd recovered from the shock of being awakened, she began to wonder how long he'd been there, watching her while she slept. She began to wonder at the violent need to be rid of her. Clearly, she had taken one side of him at face value. She had taken his kindness, his attentions, his tenderness for the expressions of love, believing that these were the signs of which he was capable. If she'd missed, throughout their marriage, an ease in him, an ability to be affectionate without demonstrating his affection, she had also accepted that this was the kind of man he was, demonstrative only in his own way.

Now, however, in this dismal season, she was beginning to see him more clearly, and the clarity was humiliating. Years ago, she'd described some aspect of her life with Paul, and her friend Véronique had said

– That sounds a little odd.

Vé had not meant to be unkind, had not said anything to wound, yet Louise *had* been hurt. Again, years ago, when she'd casually mentioned that Paul would often come home from work, unpredictably, to collect whatever he'd forgotten, Fred had asked

– Is he jealous?
and she had answered
– No, not all. He's forgetful
though she'd known very well he was jealous.

Over the years, there had been any number of moments when Fred would look to Vé, or Vé would look to Fred, and the two of them would look away from her. Neither of her closest friends would have been entirely surprised at Paul's recent behaviour. That she *was* surprised gave proof she'd spent years ignoring crucial things. Her husband had been her own creation.

So, she'd been right, morally and emotionally, to leave?

Oh, yes, of course, if you like.

But, wait a minute: why had she asked to stay with him in May?

– Because her apartment was being painted.

– Because her friends could not take her in for the week she needed.

– Because she was not seeing anyone.

– Because she missed Paul's company.

– Because, although she'd given up claim to it, she still thought of the house as *theirs*.

It had never been her intention, in leaving, to obliterate all she'd known or all she'd been. Believing that Paul loved her, and knowing that she, in her way, loved him, why would she hesitate to ask him for a hand he could easily give?

And then, he'd awakened her at four one morning and asked her to leave the house.

Worse was to come, though. When, a week or so after he'd turned her out, she tried to take money from one of their joint accounts, she discovered Paul had taken all the money from all their accounts, including the account in which she'd put her contribution to their retirement: the money her father had bequeathed her, two hundred thousand dollars. She'd been living on the pittance she made at the library, just enough to pay for her basic needs, supplemented by her savings. She needed the money much more than he did, so she was devastated to discover what he'd done. As the one who'd left, the one who'd broken the marriage, she could not bring herself to insist on right, but still . . . reasonable was reasonable.

So she'd begun to call him. At first, calling in the morning when she knew he would be out of bed, or in the evening when she knew he would be home from work. Then, because he did not answer the phone, she began to call late at night and on weekends. Then, because it was clear he *would* not answer, she wrote to him, and began to call for him at the office.

He did not answer the telephone, and he would not speak to her at work. (It was humiliating to hear the placid voice of his secretary, Sharon:

– I'm sorry. Mr. Dylan is in a meeting.

– Do you know when he'll be free?

– I'm afraid not.

– It's very important. Can I leave a message?

– If you like.

– Please tell him his wife called. My number is . . .)

So it was with some desperation that she'd returned to what had been their home. It was a Saturday in August, an afternoon because she hadn't wanted to wake him. (Hadn't wanted to wake him? After how he'd behaved?) He had answered the door, in his bathrobe.

– Yes?

he'd said, as if she were a salesman.

– Paul, we have to talk. I know you're hurt, but I don't think it's right to avoid me like this.

(More emotional than she'd meant to be, relieved that she'd found him, still convinced he would respond to reason.)

And he had shut the door in her face.

That was the last straw. Like a fool she had rummaged in her shoulder bag, looking for her key, which she found in her coin purse, though, of course, because Paul was thorough, he had already changed the lock. She'd stood outside, on their front steps, ringing the doorbell, knocking at the door, until her index finger hurt and her knuckles were pink and she finally began to understand the magnitude of her miscalculation.

If he had ever loved her, he did not now.

Four months passed, months during which she'd lived at the edge of her capacities. She did all that her feelings of guilt and shame compelled her to do. She continued to write. She continued to call. And then, having heard not so much as a peep from him, she did the only thing left to her. Exhausted by her efforts to speak to a man who would not speak to her, feeling that her efforts had only made matters worse between them, she went, in late December, to Timothy Nenas, of Nenas, Anarosh, and Komala.

– So, Mrs. Dylan, you want a divorce?

– Yes.

– You don't mind if I speak frankly, do you?

– No.

– Good, good. I'm going to have to ask you some pretty personal questions, sooner or later, so it's just as well if we just put them on the table. Know what I mean?

– Yes, of course.

– So, did your husband sleep with someone you know?

– No.

– So you're the one who had the affair?

(A brief, irrepressible memory of a pale-green summer dress, a warm night between Ottawa and Montreal, Walter's raincoat across their laps, his hand moving furtively beneath the coat, his finger sliding along the lips of her, as she held the narrow strip of her panties aside . . .)

– No. There was no affair.

– Oh, gee, that's too bad. I mean, infidelity's common grounds these days. Pretty easy too, but . . . Okey-dokey. Let's talk about the grounds then. There's no infidelity, so you and your husband are just incompatible, eh? Long marriage. What? Twenty years? Wheels just fell off the wagon?

– Yes.

– Think he'll say the same thing?

– I don't know. He won't talk to me.

– Oh? That's not good. When was the last time you talked?

– Three or four months ago, before he took all the money from our joint accounts.

Mr. Nenas, a young man of Asian descent, raised his head.

– Does he have a lawyer?

– I don't know. We used to have a lawyer . . .

Mr. Nenas wrote a few words on foolscap.

– Well, I guess that's first things first. We need to know if he's got a lawyer. You can't do much until that's settled, unless both of you were getting along, and it doesn't look like you're getting along . . . I mean, there's the divorce and all . . . but you'd be surprised how many get along until the divorce, then it all comes out.

He smiled politely.

– Why don't you leave your husband's address and phone number with my secretary? We'll get back to you in a week or so. Just out of curiosity, Mrs. Dylan, do you know what you want? You don't have to answer just now, but you should think about it, eh. I mean, you're entitled to half of everything, basically.

– I want this to be as easy as possible, but I want the money my father left me, my two hundred thousand dollars. Mostly, I want that.

– Good. So, we'll talk in a week then?

They shook hands and, as she was leaving the office, she noticed a framed print on the wall.

– It's nice, isn't it? said Mr. Nenas.

Louise looked, politely, at the reproduction of a drawing. A page from a yellowed sketchbook: it depicted a man and woman within a thin circle. Five semi-circles of flame surrounded the couple. The man wore a cap, his head bowed, his hands held up as if he had just thought of something. The woman wore a cape, fastened at her throat, one hand holding the fabric up at her waist, the other pointing off in the distance as she looks, not unkindly, on him. Near the bottom of the page, outside the circle, was the number 8.

– It's a Botticelli, Mr. Nenas said. I like to remind my clients about beautiful things. It gives them something good to think about.

– Thank you, she said.

And meant it. The Botticelli seemed to her, as she left the office, a mysterious but hopeful image to accompany her into the life she would lead from now on, *la vita nuova*, the new life.

25

FEBRUARY 24, 1986

L ittle had changed and yet everything had changed.
On this, the anniversary of his attempted suicide, Walter
Barnes sat in one of the two chairs he now owned, reading
one of his two books. Of the two, a Bible and the Arden *King Lear*,
he had chosen the Bible, not for any consciously spiritual reason
but rather because he found it beautiful and amusing, in particular the Pentateuch, of which he was reading Leviticus.

He was not aware that a year had passed since he'd first tried
to kill himself. If he had been, he would not have known whether
to rejoice or mourn; though, in any case, he might well have
chosen to mark the event in this way: reading, at home. The year
had been dull, unworthy of commemoration. He had, for the
most part, kept to himself and shunned contact with anyone
outside the university. Much of his life had been conducted
within the, what was it, three square miles that had for bound-
aries: the university, the canal, Catherine Street, and the river. And
time passed without him being aware of it.

Yes, but this home of his was a residue of the year that had
quietly passed. Time had passed, but it had taken with it so much
that had seemed important:

telephone, television, cable, credit cards, magazines, newspapers, glasses, goblets, snifters, shoes, clothes, books, books, books . . .

He had not chosen the life of an ascetic. It had not been in him to choose one style of life over another. Rather, he had decided not to have his house full of things that would eventually have to be dispersed. He expected to succeed at suicide, sooner or later, and he wished to be ready for his death at a moment's notice.

The two books he'd kept hadn't been kept so much as found. They had fallen between the headboard of his bed and the wall. He'd found them in May, after months of living in anticipatory austerity; anticipation of death, yes, but also, after his third failed suicide, of life. He read them for distraction, and for amusement, and as a way to pass the time without company.

So, little had changed?

He had changed, it's true, but in the scheme of things that was nothing at all. And he had not changed all that much. He still taught at Carleton, the books he needed kept on the shelves in his office. He still lived in his house on 3rd, however denuded it now was. He still regretted, though less poignantly, his failings, his childhood, his previous life.

So, what *had* changed?

For one thing, he now realized that death didn't want him any more than life did. Who knew that his first attempt at suicide would be his most resolute? The second attempt was a sad debacle. It was mid-March, but he had convinced himself the river would not be cold enough to do what he wanted of it, so he bought rat poison, enough to kill a townful of rats. He made his own bread, sifting a quarter cup of strychnine into the flour and kneading it into something that could, if one were kind, be called a loaf. He then made himself spaghetti bolognese, boiling the pasta in water, to which he'd added a spoonful of strychnine. He fried the tomatoes, bacon, and rosemary in a cup of olive oil, to which he'd added two tablespoons of strychnine.

He would have eaten this final meal, but two things happened.

First, after setting the table and putting the sticky pasta and thick sauce onto a plate, he went to the door to his backyard. He went to take a final, sentimental look at the night sky, but he was suddenly overcome by the most violent stomach pain. It was all he could do to crawl to the living room where he lay, in agony, for hours, thinking death was upon him.

As he was in the living room, Walter did not hear the neighbour's dachshund, Otto, come into the house. And so it was Otto, climbing up on Walter's chair, who ate most of the spaghetti. This was particularly sad, because Walter liked his neighbours, Mr. and Mrs. Molnar, and had been friendly enough with Otto to gain the dog's trust. (While he himself groaned in agony, Walter heard Otto's final, faint bark, and he'd thought it appropriate that this should be the last sound he heard on Earth, though, as it turned out, his were the last sounds Otto heard.) So when, at four in the morning, he discovered the poor dachshund's corpse on his dining-room floor, Walter was devastated. He was devastated, and he had no idea what to do. He could not bring himself to tell the Molnars that their beloved dachshund had died in his stead

– *Couldn't you have been more careful?*
– *Couldn't you have eaten the rat poison before you went out?*
– *Why do you want to die, Wally?*
had died in his house, in fact
– *Otto always loved your kitchen, Wally.*

And, yet, it seemed wrong to lie about Otto's end.

He decided not to speak of it. He wrapped Otto in newspaper, put him in a white plastic bag, and left him out with the refuse. He threw out his pots and pans (along with the dishes and silverware he'd used for his final meal), and he was as kind to his neighbours as he could be, commiserating with Mrs. Molnar in particular, genuinely sorry for her distress during the weeks when they searched for their dog. He would, he resolved, be kind to them to his dying day.

His third attempt was not, technically, an attempt at all. It was only a partial surrender to despair. It was May and all the reasons for death were again persuasive. Again, he resolved to die, going again to the river where, temperature be damned, he would jump – less likely to take anyone or anything else with him. It was the last night in May. It was warm and cloudy, though the stars were visible, from time to time, above the clouds. He thought he was as determined as he had been in February, but it was ten o'clock and, it being Friday, there were more people about. He tried to focus on death by drowning, but he also thought about swans. Why swans? They had never been of particular interest to him: great, clumsy birds, but lovely when you thought about it, and he couldn't stop thinking about it. It became a kind of frustration, a distraction to such an extent that he walked to the bridge without much noticing his surroundings, and he was surprised to find himself halfway across the Alexandra, staring absent-mindedly at Hull, at the river, mindless of the passersby, one of whom said

– Nice night, isn't it?

to him or to someone else, and it suddenly occurred to him, or he suddenly remembered there had been two swans in his life: one was a woman named Cygny Krausas, the other was a real swan that had belonged to his friend Louis Zukofsky.

Of Cygny, he could remember nothing but her name. Louis, though . . . The Zukofskys had lived on Elizabeth Street, just off Bell. Ukrainians they were, and kind.

What had that to do with him now? Nothing that he could see.

Yet there must have been something about swans, or Zukofskys or even Cygny, because, without being quite aware of what he was doing, Walter walked back along the route he'd taken, thinking about the night, which was beautiful, and about his own life, which was not, and about his death, whose moment had not yet come.

That was, to date, the last time he made anything like a con-
certed effort to take his own life. It was not the last time he would
try to commit suicide. At least, he didn't think so, which is why he
kept his belongings to a minimum and abandoned his search for
wider knowledge, for the Feminine, or for a better self. He put his
pursuits and desires on hold until the time came, if it came, when
he knew he would live, live long enough to make pursuit and
desire feasible.

It was now February 24, 1986. He had lived without any major
pursuit for a year, long enough to make death welcome, you'd
think. And yet, he thrived. Freed from his mania for books, his
quest for women, his need for acceptance, he did little more than
teach sociology and read, over and over, the Bible and *King Lear*.
Every once in a while, he went out with someone who hadn't forgotten him, but, aside from that, he had time to appreciate the
silence and solitude his new life brought. That's not to say that
Walter's misery faded, or that he resolved his conflicts, or that
his life in death's shadow was entirely restorative. There were
moments when he was assailed by the thought of his own failings,
moments when this memory or that laid him out, and he spent
dreadful hours trying to fit his old life into the new. And it was not
all that unusual, particularly in summer when there were no
classes, for him to find himself distraught: one part of him prodded
into despair, the other looking on with a kind of alarmed curiosity.

The part of him that stood beside his own emotions was not
unoccupied. At times, it was happily engaged in planning the
finer points of its own death. As others draw diagrams of their
ideal houses, sheds, or summer homes, so Walter wrote more and
more elaborate scenarios for his own end.

He began with the simple

I am drowned.

moved on to the convoluted

I am drowned in the waters of the canal, after a day of drink . . .

and, by the end of summer, arrived at the frankly inosculate

While riding the seven: I accost a stranger and start up a conversation, after which, the two of us having descended at the same stop, I invite him or her to the nearest bar where we discuss the latest news, after which, as if on a whim, I introduce the subject of quahogs and order a round of whisky, followed by another round of whisky, followed by, this being Saturday and both of us being at liberty to drink, two or three rounds of drink, perhaps whisky, after which we drink even more and I again, in a good-natured way, mention the quahogs and, if more drink is needed, order still more whisky[1] before suggesting we cement our newfound amity with a walk[2] to Chaudière Island or, better, Île Riopelle, where, I say, I happen to know the quahogs can be found, and we proceed, in a leisurely way, to Île Riopelle, to the edge of the island where I convince my companion to put his or her head under water, after I've done so myself, assuring him or her that the sight is worth the discomfort and then, when he or she claims not to see any quahogs, because after all there are no quahogs at Île Riopelle, I suggest that he or she look again and, this time, I put pressure on the back of his or her head, holding him or her under just long enough to cause real distress but not long enough to drown,[3] after which, naturally angry, he or she will, instinctively, do the same to me and, in their drunken state, hold my head under until I drown.[4]

---

[1] 10 rounds of whisky: $80.00.
[2] 8 kilometres. Perhaps more drink needed.
[3] 1 minute or less. Bring a stop watch.
[4] 2 minutes, perhaps less: pile-driving to heaven.

Now, in what way does this suggest a man who was thriving? As his scenarios grew more elaborate, so they became more playful, and as they became more playful, so the idea of suicide became more abstract, the final piece in a puzzle whose assembly was more attractive than its solution. In a word, the distraction was gradually, and at least temporarily, good for him, though it was macabre.

One might say almost as much about Walter's newfound austerity. It was distracting in a negative way. That is, having very little in his house while, at the same time, feeling compelled to stay at home, Walter was forced to rely on his own resources: reading, silence, and thoughtfulness. Although those who cared for him suggested he get out more, it was actually more instructive for him to discover how little it mattered if he did not go out, that his own limited resources were, at least temporarily, enough, that the books he had would do, that thought allowed to proceed at its own pace was not inefficient.

And what about his sensual life?

Well, during the first half of 1985, when he was thinking most seriously about killing himself, he had, perhaps not surprisingly, no sex at all. That is, it ceased to be an issue. His desire for women flickered and went out. Or so it seemed at first. What flickered, though, was the frantic longing for intercourse.

After the summer, in the first days of autumn, he permitted himself a night out. He dressed in black, something he had never done, and went to the Royal Oak, where he stood at one end of the bar, not anxious. That in itself was odd. His old self had never been able to stand at a bar without feeling there was a woman near with whom he could fornicate, if only he asked, and he had always asked, persuaded, or seduced. On this night, though, he barely noticed the women. He noticed them, but not particularly. In the past, he'd been cautious in bars, for fear he'd encounter women with whom he'd slept, and for whom he felt no longing. It wasn't so much that he'd been averse to having sex with women with whom he'd already fornicated, but rather that, in his mind, the repetition was almost invariably taken for deeper interest. So, he had tended to have sex repeatedly only with women who were manifestly drunk. That is, if, on the first night, the woman had been inebriated, he would, without compunction, sleep with her again, on the principle that she was unlikely to remember their first time, and so most unlikely to think this second liaison a sign of romantic interest.

How complicated these things had been and how pointless his rituals. It made him wonder how much he had done to protect himself, especially now that he couldn't think what it was he had that required such elaborate defence.

In any case, on this night at the Royal Oak, he needed no protection, because he wanted nothing. He looked about him as he drank his ale, interested in the shape of the bar, the feel of it, the sound of conversations, the smell of the place: perfume and powder, alcohol, smoke, beer, and roast beef. He observed the restrained movement of the bartender: quick, a little careless, mostly efficient. He watched the to and fro of three waitresses, dressed, all of them, in T-shirts and black pants. Then there was the bar itself: its large, plate-glass window looking out onto Bank Street and Barrymore's, its wainscoting . . . not an English pub, but a fair imitation, though why anyone should wish to be in England when they were not was, and always would be, a mystery.

Perhaps there was a man, a would-be publican, who so missed the land of his birth he had felt compelled to turn this little piece of Ottawa into a version of the land he'd left behind. He himself would not have been fooled by his own creation. It was not English. It was not filled with Englishmen, and no sooner did one step out the door than the absence of England was flagrant. So, if the object was to quell nostalgia, the Royal Oak would have to be counted a failure. It would be a constant reminder, to our publican, that home was elsewhere; rather an inducement of nostalgia than a charm against it. There was something touching in all this: poor John Bull . . . no home in Canada, not only exiled, but in exile in exile.

And so, the Royal Oak was born, and Ottawans flocked to it because . . . ?

Well, first, because they could drink their way to Hell and back and still do their vomiting at home. Second, because it was exotic, the words *royal* and *oak* bringing to mind places they'd heard about, or about which they'd formed vague, and vaguely noble, imaginings: knights in armour, ancient castles, damsels in distress. Third, because there were a number of Englishfolk in Ottawa, some of whom wished, on occasion, to be reminded, however imperfectly, of home, even when home itself had become intolerable.

Lost in minor but diverting thought, Walter did not hear the bartender announce last call. Nor did he hear the woman beside him ask

– Do you want another drink?

until she repeated the question while leaning towards him:

– Do you . . . want . . . another drink?

– No, thank you, he answered.

– It's last call, she said.

– Thank you. I've had enough.

She had been drinking. It looked as though she wished to sleep, and yet her words were not exactly slurred. (For the briefest moment, she reminded him of another young woman, the one on the Alexandra Bridge. Perhaps it was her voice. There was no physical resemblance, but . . . what was the other woman's name? Had he ever known it? She had saved his life, stayed his hand or, rather, stayed his feet, and he could remember the look of her coat more than he could her face or her name.)

– Well, I'm going to have a drink, the young woman said.

She smiled and ordered a daiquiri.

– You sure you don't want one? Let me buy one for you. Please?

He could not refuse without hurting her feelings, and so he found himself nursing a banana daiquiri, sweet enough to gag a maggot, on an autumn Saturday night, shortly before one o'clock. The woman did not say much, but she looked in his direction often enough to demonstrate her interest, and she smiled in a knowing way, though, really, it was unclear what it was she knew.

Still, the banana daiquiri seemed to do what she wanted, because, once she'd swallowed the last of it, she seemed less incapacitated. She got down from the bar stool and smiled.

– Do you want to walk me home? she asked.

In the moment of asking, she seemed genuinely shy, as if he were the first man she had ever asked to walk her home. Well, perhaps he was, though there was a strong undercurrent of something, an undercurrent that made it seem as if, in her question, the extremes of innocence and experience met. Quite a question, then.

– Of course, he answered. Where do you live?

– Just around the corner, she said.

Though where she actually lived was at Cooper and Elgin, a good way off, far enough to observe her struggles, for the most part successful, with balance, and to keep her from crossing into traffic, and to piece together the fragments of conversation. Her words didn't add up to anything coherent, but she herself did. He tried to imagine how her apartment would look. Would she have a stuffed animal on her bed? (Yes) Would she have a photograph of a nude woman? (Yes) Would she have a cat? (Yes) Would she have books (yes) and would they be novels (yes: Stephen King, Rita Mae Brown, Margaret Atwood) or textbooks (yes, as well: Accounting, Economics)?

And the woman herself, Brigit by name?

She was attractive, even inebriated: blonde, with brown eyes, a slightly flat nose, large hips, small breasts, long fingers that held her white jacket closed over her light-orange dress, and a graceful neck, only partially obscured by the collar of her jacket. An unexceptional woman, he might, at one time, have said, though why is that? Everything she was on this starry night (September 28, 1985) in this city (Ottawa, Ontario) was . . . what was the word? *Unwiederholbar*: gone, past, never to return . . . the very essence of an exception.

At the door to her apartment building, she invited him in for tea. He said

– That's very kind

and walked up the steps with her.

Her apartment was much as he'd imagined, but there were a thousand things he could not have predicted:

its smell: coffee grounds and lavender potpourri

a framed photograph of an elephant spouting water onto its own back

a modest collection of glass turtles on top of the television

white underwear on the kitchen counter

He watched as she threw her jacket over the back of a chair and reached behind to pull down the zipper on the back of her dress. As if it were a delicate operation, she filled a kettle with water, put it on the stove, without turning it on, and took down two black mugs, on both of which the word *Penetanguishene* was written in gold lettering. All the while, she carried on a fractured conversation with him, with herself. Something about the place, something about the night, something about tea, about her clothes, about the bar, about the tea, music, night, tea . . .

There was something about the tea.

He thanked her again for making it, though she hadn't done so, and he was caught off guard by her entrance. She returned from the kitchen with her dress around her ankles and, as he stood to meet her, she fell, or let herself fall, towards him. Their embrace was ungainly, but she said

– Oh . . .

as if there were something passionate in the way he held her up. No sooner was she able to stand on her own than she began to kiss his cheeks, his neck, his ears. Then, she pulled his head towards her, crushing his glasses against the bridge of his nose. She left her mouth open, waiting for his tongue that she then playfully bit. It had been a long time, for Walter, but the world contracted, as the world will, and his powers of observation faded.

(Not entirely . . . Perhaps because it really had been a long time between bouts, he would remember a number of things about this particular encounter. For instance, it had never really occurred to him that no two women touched, held, or stroked his penis in quite the same way. Certainly, he knew there were differences, but he had been unmindful. His pleasure, and gratitude, at being touched had been sufficient. As he walked home that night, however, he was conscious of the range: from those who were timid, who touched in an almost glancing way, to those who held on for dear life and would not let go. He would not, previously, have expressed a preference. He had sustained no permanent damage, and, besides, the sins of exuberance were, in this arena, entirely forgivable. Still, there was something about a certain delicacy . . . Brigit, though she'd been drunk, had adroitly guided her hand down the front of his trousers, showing remarkable dexterity once she'd found what she was after, not wrestling with him, but provocative. And he, how had he touched her? An extraordinary question, enough to make one self-conscious and vulnerable. How did *she* prefer to be touched?)

After some time in this embrace, after they had cooperated in the removal of his clothes, she throwing them about, he letting them fall, long after they had gone past words, she led him to her bedroom where, pushing the cats (one plush, one real) from the pillow, they lay down on the bed and continued fondling until, with some force, and sounds that sounded urgent, she directed his head to her pudendum, where, it was understood, his tongue was wanted.

And it was lovely, this, the taste of a woman: familiar, certainly, but specific as well. Some thing like . . . like . . . oh, what was it?

And in no time at all, she held his head in both hands and moved herself on his tongue and came, saying, quite clearly

– Oh Harry . . . Harry . . .

That was the first surprise. The second was that, as soon as her body recovered from its little quakes, she lay perfectly still. And shortly after that, she began to snore: fast asleep, dead to the world, inert. This had happened to him before, of course, with

other women, once or twice. It was a hazard of sex with the inebriated. He should not have been surprised.

How had he dealt with it in the past?

In the past, he had carried on, in the belief that he had their
tacit assent. Having enthusiastically reached this point together, it
seemed a reasonable thing to do, as if the woman's lack of consciousness were an annoyance to them both. Not on this night,
though. On this night, he sighed and got up, moved the covers
over her body, because the room was cool, and left, letting himself
quietly out of an apartment he would never see again.

And what, in the end, did it matter?

Certainly, he was physically frustrated, but he had gone out
with no distinct need, so his frustration was easily borne.
Besides, he was grateful to have been himself awakened. He had
been used but, more important, he had been wanted, and that,
mirabile dictu, was an intense pleasure that made the night itself
pleasurable.

He took the long way home.

Walking across Cooper to the canal, and then along the walkway, beside the black water made blacker by moonlight, facing
away from the moon then towards it, towards the university then
away from it. Nothing special, no one encountered, the sound of
water lapping against concrete, the moon at three-quarters,
Aquarius sinking slowly beneath the horizon and taking its
oddly named stars with it: Ancha, Sadalmelik, Sadalsuud, Skat,
Sadachbia, and all the little Aquarii. The slow movement of the
stars. In the half-hour it would take him to walk home, Sadalmelik
would sink beneath the skyline, but just try to catch it moving.
Like those moments, in childhood, he'd spent staring at the
kitchen clock, staring at the minute hand, trying to see it move,
knowing it did move, and yet surprised, always, that it had moved
from the one to the two to the three, as he sat at the kitchen table,

himself forbidden to talk or move until his parents had finished eating. Not a pleasant memory, but that was past, and it did no good to think about such things, because there would never be anyplace to put them where they wouldn't fall . . . and how strange to think of memories that way, that these memories were like fig-urines that fell from a shelf and, unbreakable themselves, broke everything around them . . . *pax tecum*, mother, peace on your ashes. Perhaps death wasn't any more desirable than life, perhaps it wasn't even less savage – angels and demons, the heavens and an inferno . . . a relief to be beyond all that, to say, along with Galileo, but with no fear of reprisal, *eppur se muove*, though, really, it *was* difficult to believe the Earth moved and not the stars. And what did it matter? Truth? Yes, but Truth was the flower of an instant – only the memory of it kept you going. And if the stars could be made to look down on us, what would they see? The face of Earth moving so fast, it would be impossible to catch what we call a moment, impossible to catch the clock's hands at rest. There, now: for Ancha and Sadalmelik, he, Walter Barnes, was long dead, as cold as his parents, already gone and nowhere . . . as was Brigit, whose smell was still on him, mingling with the scent of bushes and flowers along the promenade. To think the world, which had always caused pain when he let it in, could come in to console.

And then he was home; the house opened to him. A good night out, though his old self might not have said so. And what made it a good night, anyway? Think of all the things that would recede from memory: Brigit, the night, his thoughts, his feelings. All of these things would recede, though of course they would leave whatever it was you called their residue, whatever you called the influence of experience forgotten. What stayed longest, aside from the feeling of having had such a night, was the sensa-tion of stepping into his own home (at 3:35 in the morning, September 29, 1985) and recognizing it for his own. No clutter, two books, two chairs, a table, bare walls, a handful of dishes, a bed, three towels, a small desk. Less than he had owned since he was in his twenties. What made it a good night was that, without thinking he belonged, he *did* belong.

Were there many other women, then, after Brigit? Did his relationships change with this change in his world?

"No" to the first question; "not exactly" to the second. Certainly, he had sex. He was a charming, attractive man. Moreover, though he didn't entirely abandon the idea of suicide, he began to find his old, desperate self slightly ridiculous. So, in the company of others, he was modestly self-deprecating: an attractive trait in an attractive man. Still, you wouldn't have said there were "many other women." There were no more than half a dozen and, of those, none, for one reason or another, was interested in anything more than an evening's fulfillment. Yet, *he* was. Without effort, he found he remembered their faces, their faces above all, and sometimes their names. After so much time spent searching for it, a place had opened within him, a place to accommodate the details he had, in the past, despaired of knowing. He was not so much prepared for intimacy as defenceless against it, a vulnerability that was no threat at all, given how little of himself he now thought it necessary to defend.

And yet, sometime in December, months after Brigit, he'd been in the Market shopping for a Hungarian salami at Saslove's when he had almost bumped into Louise Dylan. He'd seen her before she saw him and, for a moment, he'd felt elated: recognition, joy at the sight of her. That feeling was followed by a feeling of shame and humiliation, and, naturally, shame and humiliation had stifled his first impulse, which had been to greet her and convey in his greeting regret at how their time had ended. It occurred to him, however, that words were inadequate to deal with the past and, anyway, unnecessary and, perhaps, unwanted (by her). So, instead of saying

– Louise, how lovely to see you

or

– I've missed you

he had scuttled off.

He could see himself scuttling.

This image crossed his mind, months later, as he read Leviticus, sitting at his kitchen table on a snowy night: February 24, one year after his first attempt to die. The memory of his cowardice saddened him. It was as if his old, defensive self had risen from the dead, but the memory was followed by the thought that, at their next meeting, he would say what he felt. He would not avoid her a second time, or so he resolved and, aware of the change in himself this resolution implied, he felt pleasure and relief at the thought of seeing Louise again.

26

STANLEY AGONISTES

Now that he thought of it, Stanley had *always* wondered where his mother's money had come from. While he lived with her, they had never wanted for anything essential, but he could not remember her either working or talking about work. She would never have spoken to him about anything important and he would not have asked, but the money had come from somewhere. If he'd never dwelt on the matter it was because money was only one of his mother's many hidden aspects, another of the mysteries of his childhood.

He had not had an ideal childhood. His mother, Eleanor, had a repugnance for him she would not hide. His father he did not know. So, he was raised, until he was old enough for school, by a succession of old women, all of whom were hired by his mother, most of whom were kind.

He was not a difficult child. He rarely cried. He slept through the night, from the beginning. And throughout his childhood, he was as entertained by a cigar box or a piece of newspaper as he was by rubber animals and toy soldiers, which was just as well because the cigar box and the old newspaper were what he most often got. It certainly wasn't the child care that drove the old women from Eleanor's house, it was the abuse they had to take from his mother.

As soon as he was old enough for school, Eleanor herself left him, every morning at 8:30 a.m., at the schoolyard, armed with lunch (a peanut butter and lettuce sandwich, a carton of milk). She returned for him at 3:30 p.m. After school, he was left to himself and he could, provided it did not disturb his mother, do whatever he wanted. Of course, as they had no television, and as he was not encouraged to read, "whatever he wanted" consisted mainly of playing on his own or, even better, with other children in the neighbourhood (Ottawa South, breeding ground for criminals).

Any of this might have made another child unhappy or resentful, but it did no such thing to Stanley. He learned the value of self-reliance, early on. He got such affection as he needed from his nannies, in particular from a monumentally maternal Englishwoman named Mrs. Lemon, who took care of him between the ages of three and five, treated him as lovingly as she might her own son, and who was heartbroken when Stanley reached school-going age and she was dismissed. Her leaving was the deepest wound (by far) of Stanley's childhood and, in fact, his later affection for his own mother was fortified by his love for Mrs. Lemon, the two of them somewhat mingled in his memory: his mother and the woman he wished she had been.

As to the other essentials, Stanley was taught the value of silence, caution, and a cheerful disposition by the older boys in the neighbourhood, none of whom hesitated to throttle him when he said the wrong thing, whatever the wrong thing was, or, again, to throttle him whenever he stepped out of line. If there was any lasting ill effect of this childhood, it was in Stanley's lowered expectations of himself, of life, and of those around him. Many of the boys he knew were sent off to reform school or, later, jail. He himself was careful enough to avoid either, but both were terminals the neighbourhood naturally led to.

Once he finished high school, where he did well, though not well enough to draw attention to himself, life in his mother's home ended, more or less, and so ended his childhood. He married. He found work at Canada Post. No, not work, a vocation. He sat in a low-ceilinged room with thirty men and wrote the excessively mathematical exam given to prospective letter carriers, and he passed it easily, in part because he had no idea this was to be his vocation, in part because he didn't care if it was or not. From the moment he was hired, or from the moment he began carrying letters in Sandy Hill, his life was centred. He knew where he would be five mornings a week, he knew what he would wear, more or less, and he knew who his friends would be. And he took satisfaction from all of it, from the uniforms, the friendship, and the work.

Stanley Stanley was not, save in his name, an oddity. He was not born without the capacity for pessimism or doubt. He could brood, and he had, in his life, brooded. He had even, once, harboured an idea that tormented him. This was shortly before his marriage when it occurred to him that he was not worthy of his bride. To begin with, he thought Beatrice the most beautiful woman he had ever seen.

Not to be unkind, but even those who thought her lovely would have adverted to Beatrice's personality, before, if pressed, moving on to her physical endowments. But, then, she was the third of four sisters, three of whom were striking beauties. (So beautiful were they that her father, Knolly, considered himself cursed. He adored his daughters, but he often and publicly thanked God for this one child, Beatrice, who was not endlessly pestered by the young men of the neighbourhood.) Still, Stanley found Beatrice's good looks unnerving. And then there was the way she accepted his flaws, both those he had and those he imagined himself having. And finally, there was the strange sensation of being loved, rare enough in his life to be both exhilarating *and* confusing.

For weeks, these feelings tormented him, led him to the brink of cancelling his own wedding. He was convinced Beatrice was making a mistake in marrying him and, because he loved her, his deepest inclination was to protect her. How had he escaped from that vicious groove? He hadn't. Instead, his mother inadvertently saved him from himself. Eleanor hated Beatrice. She thought the girl insipid, plain, and, though worthy of her son, unworthy of *her*. And, as she genuinely disliked the girl, she allowed herself to tell them, flatly, that she disapproved of their marriage, that she would not meet any of Beatrice's kin, that she would certainly not attend their wedding. Her only gift to the newlyweds was her assurance that they could go to Hell in the handbasket of their choice.

Beatrice was devastated, and so was her family. For months, not a day passed without Beatrice's mother or her father or her sisters trying to dissuade her from marrying Stanley. And Stanley agreed with them. He was on the verge of calling the marriage off when it occurred to him that, no matter how he explained things to Beatrice, no matter how carefully he explained his unworthiness, she might think he would not marry her without Eleanor's approval; she might think he needed his mother's go-ahead. That thought, the hint of it, was enough to bring all the resolve he needed.

And so, two people who loved each other married, despite the disapproval of their families, despite . . . well, despite everything and largely because, although he loved her, Stanley did not wish to stand, or be seen to stand, on his mother's side.

And now, there was the matter of Eleanor's will. It had led to the only serious disagreement between Stanley and Beatrice since their wedding.

A few months after their daughter's meeting with Mr. Bax, months after Stanley had declined to take on property in England (or elsewhere, for that matter), they had overcome the deep bitterness between them, but the matter lingered there, painful, in part because neither understood what it was the other wanted or feared. Eleanor's will, in other words, was a broken toe their marriage had to endure.

Nor did it help when Mary, on her own initiative, tried to appease them. She asked Mr. Bax to sell one of Eleanor's (Mary's, actually) holdings, in the hope both her parents would be happy with money, with something tangible. They had looked into the markets and found it was a good time to sell in England. So, Mary put the London property up for sale. Weeks later, it sold.

Did her decision please anyone?

Not really. Beatrice was further frustrated by this new turn. She took no comfort in the prospect of money. Her frustration was with Stanley's refusal to own property, with its implication that *they* could not do as well as Eleanor had done. This implication, of course, touched on the deepest source of Beatrice's pain: her resentment at the way Eleanor had treated her and her family, as if they were menials. Beatrice could not bear the suggestion now that they were in any way inferior to the woman. How convenient for Stanley, she thought, that Mary had decided to divest. Now, it seemed, he would not have to deal with Eleanor's heritage, would not have to assume his responsibilities.

Stanley was not disappointed by Mary's decision, but he could see the sale upset his wife, could even see that it looked as if his daughter had liquidated in order to please him. So, on hearing the news, he'd said

– That's great, Mare, but you should have asked us first.

A sentence meant to gratify his daughter while mollifying his wife, a sentence that failed miserably on both counts. Mary began to cry and Beatrice, who thought his words hypocritical, looked at him as if he were low.

Gil, who, by parental fiat, was cut off from his grandmother's money until he reached twenty-one, was also unhappy. However, he was a teenaged boy. It was difficult to tell this new unhappiness from the unhappiness that was his usual state.

After Mary's failed gambit, things grew slightly more tense. Stanley and Beatrice still spoke, but it was easy to see she would have avoided him if she could. He even began to feel uncomfortable with her in bed, and this was devastating. The two had first slept together after their second night out and they had both known, despite their youth, that this was a thing they wished to do endlessly. (Three things, actually: copulating, softly speaking, and sleeping.) And in all their years together, there'd been no end to the mystery that was their pleasure in each other.

Where was Stanley to sleep, if not with his wife? A good question. And then, after a long, vacationless summer, Stanley himself proposed he sleep in the living room ("just for a night or two, because I've got the insomnia"), and Beatrice reluctantly agreed. She took his abandonment of the marriage bed as an admission of defeat, however, and on her first night alone, she began to mourn the loss of her husband. On her second night, she began to wonder if this was divorce: irredeemable solitude.

The separation worked on Stanley in a way that was more devious. On his first night in the living room, he slept soundly. The following night, he slept just as soundly. It was as if he had rediscovered sleep. On his third night, though, he didn't fall asleep. He passed into the place between sleep and wakefulness, kept there by a handful of words that settled on him, like aphids:

"*mother . . . selfish . . . moon . . . lake . . .*"

Some of those words came from Beatrice.

– You're as selfish as your mother, she'd said.

But the rest were from a mysterious sentence that had come to him when she compared him to his mother: "The moon is not a . . ." What was the word? Lake. "The moon is not a lake." The sentence returned to him, on his third night in the living room, bringing a particle of the past with it . . . something about his mother, selfishness, the moon and . . . not lake, not lake at all . . .

He could not sleep until he recovered this connection, which had something to do with lake, but neither could he, quite, remain conscious: the very act of thinking, or meditating, on words was enough to tire him out, but it was not quite enough to pull him clear of consciousness. He tried to jog his memory. If not *lake*, then what? Pond, straight, lagoon, cove? (He dreamed, briefly, that he was a fjord into whose waters his own bare feet plunged, catching himself in the throat.)

Then, after hours of near sleeplessness, it returned to him, gently. It was not *lake*, it was *estuary*. It was not water. It was a word.

He was eleven. He had taken one of his mother's books: something by Shakespeare. It was evening. The sky was darkening, the moon pale, outside his bedroom window. His coverlet was white wool. And he was reading by waning daylight. His mother never came into his room. She never troubled him, after they'd said good night. Nevertheless, she had come in. She stood beside his bed. She wasn't angry, or at least he didn't remember anger. She'd asked what he was reading and, when she saw the book, she said

—. . .

something he couldn't remember. What he did remember was that she had taken the book and, smiling, asked him the meaning of three words: *estuarie*, *Cybele*, and *bedizen*. He knew none of them. She smiled and took the book from his room.

Such a peculiar moment. Why had it taken so long to recall? Because it was inconsequential? No. Although he could not recall the moments that preceded it, nor those that came immediately after, it was painful. Painful because it was sharp: he could remember what his mother wore, the pattern on his pyjamas, the disposition of the moon. Painful because, although he could remember none of her words, it was one of the few moments in his childhood in which he hated his mother, hated her with a purity so astounding that the fifty-year-old who recalled the scene apologized, reflexively, to his mother, wherever she was. God grant her peace.

Had he really felt such hatred?

Yes, he had. To this day, he hated those three words. He hated Shakespeare. He hated the bedroom that had been his. He hated the bed. He hated the window through which the moon had come. Everything, everything. The moment had poisoned the crucible in which it had been fired. The question wasn't "Why had it taken so long to recall?" but, rather "How had he ever forgotten it?"

And yet, he'd been right to forget.

To begin with, the old lady was dead. It would do no good to hate her now, if it ever did good to hate. Also, what a thing to carry around. It would have made him miserable to relive such moments. In any case, she hadn't hit him, she hadn't even raised her voice. Where was the lasting harm? He had left home early and he had, since then, avoided Shakespeare; no great loss on either front. She hadn't always been a good woman. Granted. But she had been turned into the nettlesome woman she'd become. Someone, one of the many about whom he knew nothing at all, had made her so.

Besides, the world was rank with complaint: my mother was this, my father did that. In the end, it all led to talk about talk about talk. Words, words, words. *He* wasn't going to carry on about the sins of the dead.

But what if, in trying to avoid being his mother, he were to become like her all the same? Weren't there things she, too, had sought to avoid? With her high culture and precious books, her haughty behaviour and squirrelled money, hadn't she, in her turn, tried to run from someone or somewhere or something? Yes, almost certainly yes.

And behaving as his mother had, selfishly, was exactly what Bea had accused him of doing. On his third night sleeping on the living-room couch, a moth-eaten green blanket pulled over his legs, he finally saw his wife's point. And, as had happened before he was married, even the hint he could side with Eleanor against his wife, however unconsciously, was enough to change his mind.

Which is all to say: a moment from Stanley Stanley's past resurfaced and woke him to his present. He recovered his sense of direction: his wife was North on the only compass that mattered. And, the following day, on seeing her, he felt gratitude for her presence, and he resolved, in light of the gratitude he felt, to do whatever Beatrice asked of him, without regard for his fears and humiliation.

{ 27 }

HOUSES AND MEN

When, after a long time in Limbo, her family returned to a semblance of itself, Mary began to long for her own house and, perhaps, a family of her own. This desire, naturally, changed how she thought of herself and the world. Ottawa, for instance, became the city to which she could say she belonged. It was here she *wanted* to live, somewhere downtown: off Elgin, say, or near the Market; though, of course, she could afford to live wherever she wanted and this made the whole process more difficult, there being so much choice.

Her longing was also accompanied by a feeling of imminent "homeness," the sense that she would shortly discover the place she was meant to live, and this affected her feelings about work as well. Did she belong there? Was it fair for her to go on working when she had so much money? Difficult questions for a young woman who had never dreamed she might live a "life of leisure." The "life of leisure," when she tried to imagine it, consisted of mixed drinks sipped in dark bars, an interminable version of something by Donna Summers playing on and on while hirsute men, shirts unbuttoned to their navels, leaned back on long zinc bars, allowing themselves to be admired: *Cloud Cuckoo Land.* And was she obliged to live there, simply because her grandmother had left her property and wealth?

Making the question of work still more difficult to resolve was the fact that she began to see Rundstedt's department for what it was: a place with a clear purpose. It was, according to Franklin, dedicated to the preservation of culture, her culture, her country's culture. And she believed him. That is, she began to see it as an interested citizen might. Rundstedt and Franklin were there to keep criminals from remaining the scourge they were. She wanted to help them in this. So, how could she leave?

With the desire for home and family and work, there came the question of men. One of her friends had lightly asked what she looked for in a man and Mary was surprised to find she had not, until that moment, thought of the matter in quite that way. What, in fact, *did* she look for in a man? Too difficult to answer. Were there men in her life for whom she felt more than admiration or respect or friendship? No, there were not. What there were were negative exemplars, men for whom she felt the opposite of longing: Edward Muir, for instance.

What was it about Edward?

He'd left a bad first impression, certainly. On first meeting, it seemed to her that Edward had leered, looking her over in a way that suggested handcuffs; whether for her or for him was unclear. She'd had much time in his company since, and he had not made the slightest untoward suggestion or undignified comment, yet it seemed to her that the leer still lurked in him, and she was never able to shake the feeling that Edward wanted something sexual from her.

Was she alone in these feelings? No. Most of the secretaries who knew him, including Mr. Rundstedt's personal secretary, Ruth, found him off-putting, though, to be fair, a few of them, taken perhaps by his boyish looks, were enamoured. Mary had heard one of them say she wouldn't mind if he "nuzzled her tits for a few hours." A thought, amusingly put, that left an unpleasant impression, but it proved Edward was not without admirers.

There were other points in his favour. He did his work well. Even she, uninclined to look kindly on him, could see he was efficient. He navigated through Parliament and parliamentary sludge like an expert. (His years as a page had served a purpose, no doubt.) From time to time, he could be very funny. He did expert imitations of a handful of MPs, and his Joe Clark was strikingly good. His humour was bitter, as if those he imitated had done him some personal wrong. But talent is talent and Edward was talented.

So, again, what was it about him that was off-putting?

At heart, it had something to do with his imitations. Though he had never imitated Franklin, where Franklin was concerned Edward was not his own man. He was openly faithful to Franklin, in a way that suggested not following but toadying. He repeated, in his own way, things Franklin said. There was, or seemed to be, nothing in him that was not connected to Franklin. So much so that one could have said Edward's problem was Franklin, and it made you wonder if he wouldn't have been a better man elsewhere, working for someone who did not take Edward's devotion so much for granted. At least, it seemed to Mary, Franklin took Edward's devotion lightly and, at times, it was as if Edward believed the same thing or felt himself in thrall or felt himself in the wrong place. One afternoon, he'd said, apropos of nothing

– I've got a good memory for figures, you know. I think I'd have made a good banker or something.

Another afternoon, he'd asked, again without prompting

– You ever wonder what it would be like if we spoke Latin? *Ave Maria, gratia plena* . . .

On both occasions, he'd seemed bewildered, and confused by his tone, she had laughed at him and had then been embarrassed by her own laughter. Whoever Edward was, he was more vulnerable than she had imagined, and yet she disliked him still.

What about Franklin, then, if we're speaking of men?

No, that was now a closed book. Though he was as friendly as ever, Franklin had become a man with a mission. It was a worthy mission and he had not lost his soul. Every morning, he asked how she was doing, and he asked after her parents, but it had been some time since she'd wanted to share the details of her life with him, because she felt it was important to keep out of his way. Now that her parents were reconciled and she no longer felt guilty about their discord, she did not think her life and concerns worth the distraction from politics and penitentiaries. But perhaps she was being too cautious. Hadn't he invited her to his apartment for boeuf stroganoff? Yes, he had, and the evening had left her feeling flattered, impressed but out of place: flattered by the invitation, impressed by the stroganoff, but uncomfortable in the company of Edward and Franklin and two clerks from Parks and Recreation. No, that's not quite right. The company was fine. What was odd was convivial Franklin, his spare apartment, his Russian books, his love for classical painting. On seeing his apartment, Mary realized Franklin was not the person she thought he was.

Whatever it was she wanted in a man, he was not for her any more than Edward was.

Of course, as to men . . . they were not the necessity (to her, home was), at least not for now. Though she admired her parents and held their marriage as something of an ideal, she was Eleanor's granddaughter in her independence. She was not cantankerous or niggardly, as her grandmother had been, but she imagined she, too, could live without a husband, as Eleanor had done, if she had to.

And it was with this thought, the thought of Eleanor living proudly on her own, that the idea of keeping Eleanor's house first came to her granddaughter.

28

DEMOCRACY

*I*t is a beautiful room: high-ceilinged, though not as high as one imagines, wide, though not as wide as one imagines, with a tall chair at one end (stately is the chair) and, at the opposite, the doors by which Members enter (stately, too, the doors). Wood, wood every-where, and stone: the magnificent wood of benches rubbed smooth by the arses and elbows of a thousand men (mostly) and women (occasionally): stately the arses, stately the elbows. Oh, I sing the body electric, for every atom belonging to me as good belongs to you . . . It is the House of Commons: Question Period, all the accents come at once.

Speaker:	Will the Honourable Member . . .
Oshawa (NDP):	What?
York Centre (L):	Mr. Speaker, will the . . .
Speaker:	Order. The Honourable Member from Oshawa has the floor.
Oshawa (NDP):	Mr. Speaker, will the Prime Minister please tell us why public funds have been wasted looking . . .

Wasted? He can't say that, can he? There is loud, grumbled resentment from the Conservatives, but Oshawa presses on.

Oshawa (NDP):   Why funds have been *wasted* on commissions looking into prisons? Why funds have been wasted . . .

Now, really, that was just provocation. More grumbling drowned him out.

Speaker: Order! The Member from Oshawa has the floor.

Oshawa (NDP):   Thank you, Mr. Speaker. Will the Prime Minister tell the House why the public needs new prisons?

Essex-Kent (L):   (aside, to Essex-Windsor) Young Cassius has a green and hungry look.

Essex-Windsor (L):   What?

Essex-Kent (L):   (points to Oshawa) Young Cassius . . . he has a *green* and *hungry* look.

Essex-Windsor (L):   What the hell are you talking about?

Essex-Kent (L):   Oh, for heaven's sake. Jim was right. The NDP are going to try to make something out of this prison thing.

Essex-Windsor (L):   Oh . . . well, yeah, of course. Why didn't you say that?

Gander-Twillingate (L):   What are you boys talking about?

Essex-Kent (L):   Julius Caesar. Young Cassius with the green look.

Gander-Twillingate (L):   Who?

Essex-Windsor (L):   Exactly.

The Prime Minister rises to answer the Member from Oshawa.

Prime Minister: Uhh, Mr. Speaker . . .

Gander-Twillingate (L):	(aside) The chin that walked like a man . . .
Prime Minister:	Unlike the Liberals and the NDP, the . . . uhh . . . Conservative Party has never wasted public funds . . .

Now that was uncalled for . . . provocation, grandstanding . . . The hue and cry of the Opposition, the appreciative noise of the Conservatives drowns out the messiah from Manicouagan.

Gander-Twillingate (L):	Wipe the shit from your chin, lad!
Qu'Appelle-Moose Mountain (PC):	That's telling 'em, Brian!
Cariboo-Chilcotin (PC):	'ear! 'ear!
Speaker:	Order! The Honourable Member from Manicouagan has the floor!
Prime Minister:	As I was saying, Mr. Speaker, the . . . uhh . . . Conservative Party does not play with public funds. Nor do we play with the public's trust. We have always been the defenders of law and order . . .
Cariboo-Chilcotin (PC):	'ear! 'ear!
Brandon-Souris (PC):	Hear! Hear!
Davenport (L):	Aw, go on!
Prime Minister:	We have always . . . uhh . . . defended law and order, because we are not only interested in the economic health of this great land of ours, but also . . .
Oshawa (NDP):	Answer the question!
Burnaby (NDP):	Answer the question!
Beaches (NDP):	Hear! Hear!

Essex-Windsor (L): They're on their own on this one, eh?

Gander-Twillingate (L): Who?

Essex-Windsor (L): The NDP.

Gander-Twillingate (L): That they are. It's a motherhood issue, boys.

Essex-Kent (L): What?

Gander-Twillingate (L): It's a motherhood issue. No one wants to shoot down a few good penitentiaries. We could use a few prisons out our way, I'll tell you.

Essex-Kent (L): Really?

Gander-Twillingate (L): Yes, sir. I'll tell you, we haven't got a big population, but it's mostly crooked. I'm with the Tories on this one.

The Prime Minister, the boy from Baie-Comeau, the Magus of Manicouagan, has given the floor to the Right Honourable Cabinet Councillor to the Secretary of State, Albert Rundstedt by name: Westerner, well dressed, crookedly smiling.

Rundstedt (PC): Mr. Speaker, if the Communists . . .

Oshawa (NDP): What Communists?

Rundstedt (PC): I mean the Socialists, Mr. Speaker. If the Socialists had bothered to ask before making these accusations –

Burnaby (NDP): What accusations?

Oshawa (NDP): We asked a question.

Speaker: Order! The Minister for Prisons and Correction has the floor.

Rundstedt (PC): Thank you, Mr. Speaker. As I was saying, if the Communists had

bothered to ask, before accusing us
of wasting public funds, they would
have found that . . .

There follows a steady, lengthy thrashing of the Opposition, a peroration
on need, a moving description of citizens, fawnlike in their innocence,
prey to the wolves of Have-not, to the lawless who will stop at nothing to
take what is earned, earned with dignity, by the sweat of a brow, by a
bone-wearying day's work, work gone for naught, there being wolves
here and jackals there, wolves and jackals whose rights are protected by
Liberals and Communists, I mean Socialists, who show deeper, more rev-
erent concern for criminals than they do for victims, because we live in
woeful times when the straight road has been lost and we are in a dark
wood where it is evening and the sky is bruised and we are far from
shelter . . . a stirring speech but familiar, ignored by all present, includ-
ing Rundstedt's fellows, who know a victory when they smell it and who
are loath to pay attention when attention is not crucial.

Gander-Twillingate (L):	I wonder who's Rundstedt's tailor?
Essex-Windsor (L):	He does have a fine jib.
Essex-Kent (L):	But he sounds like a sewing machine.
Essex-Windsor (L):	That's true.
Davenport (L):	You boys hear the latest?
Gander-Twillingate (L):	Oh God. No, my son, leave humour for them that knows how.
Davenport (L):	No, no, this is a good one.
Gander-Twillingate (L):	So tell it.
Davenport (L):	Why don't blind people skydive?
Essex-Kent (L):	I don't know. Why?
Davenport (L):	It scares the hell out of the dog.
Essex-Windsor (L):	Oh, for God's sake.
Essex-Kent (L):	I don't get it.

Across the aisle, Members of the ruling party weigh more weighty matters:

Joliette (PC):	Je suis allé diner avec un ami hier soir, puis il m'en a sorti une bonne.
Chambly (PC):	Enweille donc.
Joliette (PC):	Bon. Paraît que mon ami a une cousine qui n'est pas trop smart. Franchement, là, est complètement tarla. Puis, y'a deux ans, elle s'est mariée avec un gars aussi cave qu'elle. Alors, tu comprends pourquoi la famille avait peur qu'ils aient des enfants. Et c'est c'qui est arrivé. Elle était enceinte et là là tout le monde avait peur qu'elle donne un nom ridicule à l'enfant. Mais non, l'enfant est née puis on l'nomme Barbara. "Barbara," c'est pas si pire. La famille se rassure, et puis . . . un an plus tard, voilà qu'elle est enceinte encore une fois. Mon ami appelle sa cousine pour la félicitér. Puis "Qu'est-ce que tu vas nommer le nouveau?", qu'il demande. Sa cousine répond, "On va l'appeler 'Poil de souris.'" "Mais comment ça 'Poil de souris'? T'es pas sérieuse. C'est pas un nom d'enfant, ça." "Pourquoi pas? dit sa cousine. On a nommé la première 'Barbe à rat.'"
Chambly (PC):	(laughing) Ah oui, j'ai toujours aimé celle-là. Mais elle est vieille.

Joliette (PC): C'est-tu vrai? Moi j'l'ai entendu
      pour la première fois hier.

Chambly (PC): Bon, moi j'vais te passer une plus
      récente . . .

And back again:

Davenport (L): I wonder how long Rundstedt's
      going on for this time.

Essex-Kent (L): Could be days.

Davenport (L): Why're the NDP carrying on with
      this prison protest business, then?

Essex-Windsor (L): They're desperate for something to
      call their own.

Davenport (L): This isn't a clean government.
      There's lots of other things they
      could go on about.

Among Rundstedt's confreres, there was the usual wonder that Rundstedt could, when speaking of his portfolio, talk for so long without coming to a point. They applauded at the occurrence of words like justice, duty, and responsibility. They suppressed their mirth as, first, the NDP and, then, the Liberals tried to interrupt his going on, tried to move to other business. As far as the Conservatives knew, Rundstedt's department was efficient, not at all profligate. His doings were of interest to them, though, not because anyone cared about Rundstedt's philosophy but because the man might, he just might, win approval for the building of a new federal penitentiary. The money, the employment this would bring to the province that built the prison was, naturally, of deep, even reverent, interest to everyone. So, his confreres applauded and shouted, "Hear! Hear!" from time to time, to show their respect for Rundstedt? Yes. For Rundstedt's efficiency? Yes that too, but, above all, for the wealth Rundstedt might bring to them and to their constituents.

(Strange though it seems, I can't think of the House of
Commons without a longing for home. It's as if the cacophony
itself were my city, the waves of voices held by *Robert's Rules of
Order* the way the ocean is held by a narrow reef or the wind by a
picket fence. All those who were raised in capitals could say as
much, I'm sure, but my city's squabbles have so decisively influenced my view of the country, I have affection for the arguments
themselves.

Quebec, for instance . . .

I remember driving with friends along the Trans-Canada
from North Sydney, I think it was, going home to Ottawa. This
was just after high school and we had, because most of us had
nothing better to do, taken a dresser and a mirror from Ottawa
to Port-aux-Basques.

We might have chosen a more scenic route. The Trans-Canada
serves few provinces well and, frankly, it betrays others. It flatters
Nova Scotia, but it murders New Brunswick, which, along the
highway, looks as drab as an old man's drawers. Still, we took the
Trans-Can because it's well maintained and we wanted to get
home as quickly as possible. We'd been travelling all day and left
New Brunswick near sundown. And, as if a curtain parted, we
entered Quebec. It was particularly beautiful. The water was high
in places, in places almost touching the highway. The hills were
coddled in evening. The land was green and soft.

From Matapedia to Ste-Florence, it felt as if no one has been
here before us and no one would come after. It was the first time
I understood how beautiful my country was, the first time I felt
love for the land itself. We were in the province that sometimes
wishes it were not, and as we made our way through Quebec (Lac
au Saumon, Rimouski, La Pocatière, Montreal), I couldn't help
taking leave of it. As if we were all in the same elegiac mood, the
conversation suddenly turned to "indépendance." Someone said

– The problem is plebiscites. They don't always mean what you
think they mean. Say you and your friends have been drinking,

and now everybody's hungry. You ask people if they want fish for dinner. Six out of ten say yeah to fish. Well, it's no mystery: most of you want fish. And even if you want lamb or chicken vindaloo, you bow to the majority, okay? You can argue about the kind of fish, but in the end you all know, more or less, what you're going to get. Now, you take these same friends, and you ask if they want freedom. Ten out of ten will say they want freedom, but, at the end of the day, you're no closer to knowing what it is they want. Even after you've asked each of them what they mean by freedom, you're bound to come up with incompatibles, contradictions, and diametrically opposed notions: freedom from, freedom to, freedom within the bounds of social democracy, freedom within the bounds of the anarcho-communist collective, anarchic freedom. There are more "freedoms" than you have houseguests. And *nation* is closer to *freedom* than it is to *fish*, okay? There's no way to tell what Quebecers want when they say they want a nation, and they haven't even managed to say that much.

And someone answered

– Well, Jesus, wherefore Democracy if you can't trust the word of the people?

– Calm down. You'll miss the turn off at Ste-Anne de Bellevue. Look, a plebiscite is useful for deciding if your neighbour should be allowed to turn his Victorian mansion into a rooming house, but otherwise . . . metaphysical questions can't be resolved numerically, okay? As far as I'm concerned, democracy is an endless argument about democracy, but it's infinitely preferable to the silence of tyranny.

– No, no, no. Democracy is rule by the people, or by the people's chosen representatives. It isn't an argument, it's a form of government. And the problem is our chosen representatives behave one way when they're seeking election and another way once they're elected. Once they're elected, they serve power and money. It bugs me that Canada is Canada, for them, only as long as it's economically viable. Canada isn't only a name. It's a place with a history. Now, there's your long conversation: Canadian history. And it needs Quebec to go on. It needs Saskatchewan, Manitoba, Alberta . . .

– Look, there's the turn to l'Île aux Tourtes. You know, I remember when I first read Whitman. How does it go? Somewhere he says that every atom of himself is shared by all and vice versa. I remember thinking you have to be either a poet or insane to think that way. You know, we're all one and so on? Still, the poetic is noble and selfless, and wouldn't it be great if we were all poets? If we were all poets, we wouldn't need countries, don't you think? We'd all be part of a true democracy.

– You're insane. Poets need countries *more* than everybody else. They're all about the particular. Besides, if we were all poets, who's to say we'd be Whitman? What if we were all Philip Larkin? You'd see a lot of small, sour little states.

– You're missing my point. I'm talking about an ecstatic way of being in the world. Poetry's the only thing that comes close to taking the world in ecstatically. The world is too much for the mind, because world and mind aren't equal. Our minds prey on the world, but a mind can be poetic or prosaic. So why shouldn't it be ecstatic? And if it's ecstatic, what do you need Canada for, eh?

– Okay, now you're just getting overheated. The problem with ecstasy is that it doesn't care about anything but itself. No Canada, no Quebec, no democracy, nothing. Ecstasy is paradise, and paradise means the end of the world. Anyways, close the window a little, will you?

– You cold?

– Yeah. It's cold out.

It was night and the sky was cloudy and when we left Montreal, we left the light. Ontario was dark and quiet. The land smelled of wet earth and rotting wood. The windows in the farmhouses, small illuminations, nicked the vast darkness. It's true the future ripens in the past and the past rots in the future, but how difficult it is, at times, to remember the long parade of the dead, their struggle for every yard of highway, every tree cut, every brick laid. From Rigaud to Castleman, however, I thought about the dead and wondered, as I often wonder still, if their arguments were so different from ours or if it's the land itself that sets the agenda.)

When Rundstedt finished speaking, the House voted on whether to begin construction of a new federal prison, location and so forth to be determined later. They voted their overwhelming assent and MacKenzie Bowell Federal Penitentiary took a step closer to being. It was a complete success for Rundstedt, perhaps his greatest day in office. And after the vote, pleased with himself, he had dinner with Franklin, where, in great detail, pausing only to savour the memory of his parliamentary grandiloquence, he related the particulars of his, of their, triumph.

And, in a bout of optimism, they toasted the new penitentiary with Pernod and ice water.

29

CHANCE

einhart had not actually accepted Franklin's invitation to
design a prison, but Franklin had said
– There is no night
or words to that effect and something in Reinhart had shifted and
caught his attention.

Months had passed. Months, perhaps a year . . . and the sedi-
ment of this moment had thickened. He was no closer to understanding why Franklin's words had affected him, but from the
moment he'd heard them he'd begun to meditate on the idea of
night, to create with night in mind. In effect, then, Franklin's
words had been a presage, the onset of a task whose sense would
not come until the task was done. When Franklin said
– There is no night
it created, in Reinhart, sense without meaning, or meaning
without sense, so that it was up to him to recover either sense or
meaning. Or, if you prefer: one of the muses descended and filled
the artist with longing for something (or somewhere) that did not
yet exist.

So, Reinhart was inclined to accept Franklin's invitation, but
he never said so, because there was an element missing: the *where*.

Over the months, Reinhart had often asked *where* the prison was to be built. Buildings were part of a landscape, after all, and Reinhart could not create one without the other, could not figure the scene without some idea of the ground.

Naturally, Franklin was as frustrated as Reinhart, maybe even moreso, but the prison's destination depended on things far outside his control: government approval of the project, a committee's recommendation for ideal location . . .

And then, after a sequence of events, the penitentiary came into clearer focus:

– A Royal Commission found Canada's penal system wanting.

– There was (Conservative) assent to the commission's findings.

– There was (Conservative) assent to Rundstedt's plan to investigate possible solutions to the system's flaws.

– There was (Conservative) assent to the idea that, for technical reasons, more prisons were not an unpalatable idea.

– There was, from Minister Rundstedt, (qualified and not entirely heartfelt) acceptance that, for "economic" reasons, the best ground for MacKenzie Bowell Federal Penitentiary was somewhere in Quebec. The Cabinet had collectively chosen Quebec. Where exactly in the province seemed of little interest to anyone in the federal government. (It did not interest Rundstedt at all, as he couldn't have told you where the Gaspé began or Montreal ended.)

All of this created a real climate of "perhaps" for Rundstedt's prison, and it happened in good time, politically speaking. The Conservatives were elected in 1984. The commission released its findings in June 1985 and, a few months later, the government of Quebec generously suggested three acceptable locations for the federal government's prison: the area around the Gatineaus, the area around Ste-Thècle or, finally, the area around St-Félix-D'Otis (which everyone called "Ostie St-Félix" or "St-Félix, ostie," depending).

Now, Franklin would have chosen a part of the province not on offer for MacKenzie Bowell, but the Gatineau Hills would do. The hills and the land around them were not unlovely and the site was close to Ottawa, so Franklin decided to begin his assessment of the three locations there. He had nothing deeper in mind than a cursory look. He invited Edward along to take photos of the terrain and, of course, he invited Reinhart, just in case the land proved interesting.

None of them knew the Gatineaus well, but Edward drove because neither of the others wanted to.

As Reinhart and Franklin were distracted by a conversation about Apelles, the Greek painter whose paintings no one has seen, Edward lost the right road. He inadvertently turned onto a narrow lane that declined along sharper and sharper curves until, finally, it stopped dead before a tangle of fallen trees, rotten branches, and jutting rocks. (Chance.)

Reinhart, feeling cramped, got out of the car to stretch his legs and wandered off, over the tangled branches, out of view. (Chance, again.)

For fifteen minutes or so, Franklin and Edward sat together in the car, more or less silent, waiting for Reinhart's return. They would have waited longer, but, suddenly and from a distance, they heard what sounded like a cry of alarm. Both men went cautiously from the car, unsure the sound they'd heard had been human, but as they stood up to look around they saw Reinhart. He was some fifty yards before them, on the other side of the fallen trees.

– Come and see this, he called.

And as they approached he pointed down towards an impossibly beautiful valley. Immediately to the left, invisible from the car, a stone hill ascended. Not a hill, really, it was more like a large, scalene triangle that went on for a hundred yards. At its highest it was, perhaps, thirty feet and, near its summit, there was a tree:

leafless, almost as grey as the rock on which it had managed to thrive. Ten strange birds, with pinkish wings, alighted from the tree in strange formation. The hill, or triangle, was some five feet wide, and its width was smooth, as if the hill had been a road. Beyond the hill, the land dipped sharply, and the three men looked down onto a valley's valley, through which a wide river ran, making a bluish Sygma among the trees. Though it was November, and the sky was more ash-grey than blue, the place was inspiring.

– Where are we exactly? asked Reinhart.

– I don't know, said Edward. We're a little lost. I think.

– Why didn't you say something before? asked Franklin.

Reinhart was intently taking pictures.

– Take some photographs for us, Eddy, said Franklin suddenly enthusiastic himself.

– I think, said Reinhart, if this *is* the place, I wouldn't mind drawing something for it, you know? A few buildings, maybe.

But he was not thinking of architecture. Rather, he was overcome by the place itself, as if he had dreamed this very corner of Gatineau, not as a lieu for a prison but as a kind of crèche for his imagination. This landscape (which was, as chance would have it, part of the land proposed by the government of Quebec) was part of him, and he knew this immediately.

Franklin was not thinking of architecture, either. He looked out on the land, the river, the trees and thought, almost casually, So this is the place. How did he know? He, too, recognized it, but in Franklin's case the recognition was unmysterious. The place reminded him of Anse Bleu: water, rock, sky. To think he had come so far only to discover that his "destiny" was in this piece of land that looked torn from what had been home. And yet, on reflection, Alba had been born with him in Anse Bleu. It was only reasonable that it should find itself here, that *they* should find themselves here. So, it wasn't that the land belonged to him, it was, rather, that he and Alba belonged to this part of Gatineau.

And so, the ground on which MacKenzie Bowell Federal Penitentiary would sit (if either man had anything to do with it) insinuated itself into the minds of Reinhart Maur and Franklin Dupuis.

One wonders, given the difference between them, if one should say that here were "two minds one place," "two minds two places," or, even, "two minds no place at all," as both saw the land as somewhat other than it was. There was a third man with them, of course, and he saw only what was there: a dark river, pebbled shores, ground thick with pine trees and undergrowth, and a steep hill. Edward did not find the land inspiring, but he suspected his outlook was influenced by certain thoughts he'd been having.

First, there was a foreboding, a persistent feeling that something was going to go wrong. And, in light of the foreboding, he'd begun to think up arguments against the prison, searching for one that would, like a key, open Franklin's mind to caution where this penitentiary was concerned.

One might have thought this moment (standing with his closest friends before a rough landscape) a good time to reveal his misgivings. But he kept his opinion to himself and suffered, principally, not from his doubts but from the feeling he had been set apart from his friends, both of whom were captivated by a plot of land that did nothing for him. To be kept from the joy Franklin and Reinhart were evidently feeling was, for Edward, like being unable to enter a promised land.

And what did he do? He simulated joy, or tried to, nodding his head and smiling, before saying, once the others had stopped speaking:

– Make a great place for a penitentiary. So isolated and all.

At which, Franklin and Reinhart both turned to him and stared. It was as if he'd said something ultramundane and they were struggling with its sense.

– Yes, said Franklin, I guess it *is* a little out of the way.

Reinhart added

– Make sure you take pictures, Eddy, in case something happens to mine.

Which Edward did. And the resulting photos were sharp and well lit, though, as Edward had unwittingly cracked the camera's lens cover while climbing over a tree trunk, there were spidery lines that made the photos look like small jigsaw puzzles.

30

LIBERTÉ, ÉGALITÉ, FRATERNITÉ

Some time after his modest parliamentary triumph, Minister Rundstedt was in Paris. He had been in Oslo, representing the government at a conference on the social sciences. He had given a short address, in a hall filled with sociologists and minor politicians, and then, duty done, he had gone to Paris. He was in Paris to attend a conference on penal reform. There he gave the same speech he had given in Oslo. He attended a dinner in his honour at the embassy, and he was his usual gregarious self. Then he took a few days to see the city.

Paris?

As far as he could see, there was nothing much to the place. The river was fine, as rivers go, but you could only take the "fly boats" so often, and the Seine was not clean. He had been disappointed by the Eiffel Tower, and bored by most everything save the traffic. (The traffic was not interesting, you understand, but it needed careful attention.)

He had long heard of Paris' reputed charms, its historical significance, its legendary prospects. He was to spend three days in the city of lights, but all he had to show for it, after two days, was the vague feeling he should be elsewhere. He had bought a few trinkets for Edwina: a glass globe in which a copper miniature of the Eiffel Tower was enclosed, a menu from one of the famous brasseries (Lipp: an expensive, disappointing haunt), an illustrated history of the Bastille on whose bright cover a faded republican held up the faded head of Louis XVI, and a book he had bought at the Louvre.

The book from the Louvre was emblematic of his stay in Paris. He'd bought it for Edwina, because its cover was striking: a woman in a long dress seated on a brown bench, in her arms and on her lap a naked child in one of whose hands there is a ball; the child leans away from the woman to cull roses from the flower bed beside them. All done in painted terracotta: white, white, blue and green. Rundstedt assumed it was the Virgin and child, which it was. He assumed it was French, but this it was not. It was Italian, which he discovered only when he'd returned to his room on Rue Chevert. So, the most beautiful work he saw in Paris was not French.

Perhaps part of the problem with Paris was the unspoken assumption that superior men would find it superior. The embassy staffers had pleasure at the thought of introducing him to their wonderful city. Theirs was the delight in Rundstedt's first views of the Pont Alexandre III, the Musée Rodin, the Tuileries. Every man has two cities, he heard said, his own and Paris. It did not occur to luteciaphiles that there were some cities inimical to Paris. You couldn't truly love Calgary, as Rundstedt loved it, and love Paris, unless of course you were damned indecisive, and Rundstedt was not indecisive. His heart beat faster by the foothills. The Bow River ran through his happiest memories. What was this collection of old stones, Paris, to him?

Still, once he decided he and Paris were quits, once he resigned himself to his hours in the city, he began to unwind. Travel to foreign cities was one of the rewards of his position and if, like most things in life, it was less than it was made out to be, so be it.

The sky on this late November day was cloudy. Rundstedt crossed the avenue to Les Invalides, for Napoléon's sake, but despite the encouragement of his guide, an embassy secretary named Morgan, he did not go in. When they had walked to St-Germain, Rundstedt dismissed the woman.

– I hope you don't mind, he said politely, but I'm tired.

– Not at all, said Morgan.

She hailed a taxi, gave the driver the address.

– Have a safe trip home, she said.

Before the taxi pulled away, Rundstedt put his head out the window and asked if she knew where he might eat supper.

– Somewhere good, he said.

– Of course, she answered.

She took a square of paper from her purse, wrote the words

Au Pied de chameau
rue Quincampoix

and handed it to him.

As it happened, the taxi driver knew English passably well.

– What she say? he asked.

– What? said Rundstedt.

– There. On paper. What she say?

Rundstedt peered at the paper for the first time.

– Pee eh duh sham oh, he said.

– Pied de chameau?

The driver held his index finger up and moved it from side to side.

– Is marocain, he said. You like marocain?

– Sure, said Rundstedt. Why not?

– No American can like marocain, the driver said bitterly.

– Je suis Canadien, Rundstedt answered.

– Ah . . . , said the driver.

And he was silent for the short ride to Rundstedt's hotel.

– You go to Pied de chameau? he asked.

– Later, said Rundstedt, later. Thank you.

He paid the man, then got out of the taxi. He went up to his room, slept for an hour, woke up to write letters to his constituents, to plan the coming week, and to read Franklin's report on his favoured site for a federal penitentiary: the Gatineaus. (Rundstedt himself would have preferred MacKenzie Bowell in Alberta. He accepted, however, that it would do the party most good if it were built in Central Canada. The Gatineaus? Sure, why not? As well there as elsewhere, if the party approved.) Then, though there were almost twenty-four hours before his plane left Orly, he cleaned his room before sitting on the bed to read a few pages of an old Tony Hillerman: *Dance Hall of the Dead*.

Rundstedt had decided to try a small restaurant on Boulevard de la Tour-Maubourg when, as he stepped out of the hotel, he was met by the taxi driver.

– You go to Pied de chameau? he asked smiling.

How long had the man been waiting? Rundstedt was not quite pleasantly surprised, as if he'd met an acquaintance about whom he was ambivalent. He was going to tell the man he'd decided against Pied de chameau when the man said

– I take you. No money.

– No money? asked Rundstedt.

– Je ne peux pas prendre votre argent, he said. No money.

As it turned out, the man was Moroccan, and he was sincerely sorry for having suggested Rundstedt was American.

– American? said Rundstedt. That's no insult.

The man held up his index finger and moved it from side to side.

– Is insult, he said. I pay back.

He would take Rundstedt to the Pied de chameau, free of charge. He insisted, and it would have been impolite to refuse. Besides, the man was honourable. He had been called Algerian or Tunisian or Lebanese so often in Paris, he could not bear to have called a Canadian an American. He was honourable and kind, and his kindness brought out the politician in Rundstedt. During the twenty minutes it took to reach Quincampoix and Molière, they spoke warmly of their respective homes. Ah but Safi was a wonderful town, and how important it is for a man to have children. And they agreed: there is nothing in life but children and land, yes, and God willing they would both shortly return to their own.

– Amen.

– Inch' Allah.

By the time Rundstedt stepped from the taxi, the men were confreres. Now it would have been wrong to eat anywhere but Au Pied de chameau. Whatever Moroccan food was, he would try it. He stepped from the Parisian street into the restaurant. It was dimly lit, not dark, and, without knowing the Middle East, Rundstedt thought it Middle Eastern. What figured it as such? The colours (brass, pomegranate, amber), the fabric that hung down as if they were inside a tent, the waiters?

– Est-ce que monsieur a prénoté? asked the maître d'hôtel. You have a reservation?

– No, said Rundstedt.

The restaurant was not full, but you could sense it would be. There was bustle. It was early but, just as Rundstedt had made himself comfortable, he was asked if he would share his place. There were, after all, many reservations.

A young woman was shown to his table.

– Thank you, she said.

– No problem, answered Rundstedt. Your first time here?

The woman was not as young as he first thought, but she was attractive and she had an accent that mingled German with a highly correct Anglo-English.

– Yes, she said, but I have heard the food is exquisite.

– Oh yeah? said Rundstedt. Maybe you could help me order. I can't make much of this menu.

She looked at him. Their eyes met.

– Neither can I, she said. But I've been told the tajines are very good.

– What's a tajine?

– I am not certain, she said, but I shall try one.

– And I'll have the lamb and couscous, said Rundstedt. At least I've heard of those.

Both dishes were good. So thought Rundstedt, who, having been invited to do so, tasted his companion's tajine with chicken, onions, lemon, and olives. It smelled of lemon. It was not the kind of thing he would care to eat often, but isn't it odd how the presence of a beautiful woman distracts the palate? She was certainly dressed to distract: décolleté without being vulgar, her bosom accentuated by a red dress that had a deep-V wrap bodice, long sleeves, and padded shoulders.

– My wife would love this stuff, he said.

– And what sort of woman is she, your wife? she asked.

– Edwina? Ahh, Edwina's great. We've known each other since high school. Listen, what's your name again?

– Gudrun.

– Well, Gudrun, I've been married most of my life, and I'm a happy man.

They had eaten, largely, in silence. The Pied de chameau had accumulated patrons. The mood, the accents of the place, the unbuttoned humanity had done its part for conviviality. Rundstedt, naturally talkative, had made only tentative efforts to bring Gudrun out, but he had certainly taken her in: her blue eyes, her long fingers, a gentle precision. Well, she was European. There were no crumbs in *her* butter: young, elegant, perhaps even, if he'd been younger, arousing. Arousing? Now there was a word on whose neck you had to step.

– Will you have a drink? asked Gudrun.

The restaurant was full and lively, yet it was only eight.

– I would like to buy you a drink, she added. You have been kind enough to share your table.

– No, no, said Rundstedt. I'll stay, but only if you let me buy. What'll you have?

She had the thé à la menthe.

He had a liqueur distilled of figs.

– And what is it you do, Herr Rundstedt, if you do not mind my asking?

– I'm a politician, he answered.

How that word needed an entourage. Politician? For a moment, it seemed to him the word was meaningless without its formal trappings: its leather-backed chairs, its solicitous secretaries. Rundstedt felt not bashful but naked. He was in a city where his language and position mattered only to a few who were themselves strangers. For the first time since meeting Edwina, Rundstedt was awkward in the company of a woman.

– And what do you do? he asked Gudrun.

– I am a hair stylist, she answered.

– It's a good profession, he said. Edwina sees her hairdresser, what, once or twice a week? Must be interesting work.

– It is not very interesting, said Gudrun. I have always wished to do other professions. Habit has confined me to my work. Only now that I am dying, I have begun to do the things I would like.

– Oh, said Rundstedt. Well that's just, that's just very sad.

– Forgive me for saying it, said Gudrun. I should not like to hide it any more, you see? That is why I am in Paris. I have always wanted to visit Paris.

– Yeah, it's quite the place.

– Would you like another drink?

Rundstedt had finished his alcohol without realizing.

– No, he said. It's getting late and I have to pack.

– I see, said Gudrun. You have been kind. I hope I have not spoiled your evening.

She put her hand on his, momentarily.

– No, no, he said. It's nothing. Happens all the time.

– I do not understand, said Gudrun. Do you know many people with cancer?

At a table nearby, a man said
– My wife thinks I'm in Oslo – Oslo, France, that is.
Rundstedt said
– I don't know a lot of people with cancer, no.
Gudrun smiled.
– You are fortunate, she said. Thank you. I, too, should go.
Again, she touched Rundstedt's hand with her impossibly long fingers.
– I hope you will have a nice flight home, she said.
She stood up, and how beautiful she was standing beside him: a hint of rose water, a discreet smile, a manner both serious and distracted. Her dress was swiftly swallowed by her beige coat, and then she was gone.
It is true Rundstedt was, at times, a shallow man, callous even. He was never unfeeling, however, and he felt he had been petty. He had, at the mention of her death, wished himself as far from Gudrun as possible. Year after year, he had listened to dire stories followed by requests for assistance. It had hardened him to the most heartbreaking tales, and hers had not been the most heartbreaking.
Still, Gudrun had asked for nothing. He had needlessly flinched.
He felt even smaller when, having given her enough time to leave the vicinity, he approached the bar and discovered she had paid for his meal and his drink and had left a note:

I Thank You . . .
Gudrun Lindemann

He *should* have had another drink with her, although a man in his position had to be careful. Rundstedt decided to walk. He skirted Les Halles. The night was starless, wet, and cold, the streets uncrowded. So much for the city of light. He passed something Egyptian as he crossed Place de l'Hôtel de Ville and then, miraculously it seemed to him, he found the Seine. By then, however, it had begun to rain and he'd had enough. Rundstedt hailed a taxi and, once inside, struggled to remember the address.

– Onze . . . rue . . . Chevert.

– Yes sir, said the driver.

As he stepped from the taxi, he was thinking how much he missed Edwina, Edwina who spoke French so much better than he did, Edwina who might have found this city charming, Edwina who would have had them taking tours and attending embassy functions. He was not thinking of Miss Lindemann, but it was she who preceded him into the small lobby of the hotel. He was beside her, at her elbow, as she turned away, without seeing him, and took the stairs up to her room.

Rundstedt was startled. He did not think to call her name, to follow her, to thank her, to wish her good night, and by the time he recovered from his surprise, the night clerk had repeated

– What is the number of your room, sir?

Well, well. Will wonders never cease. What were the chances of them sharing a hotel?

Rundstedt approached his room thoughtfully, heavy key dangling. He had just put the key in the lock when he turned to see, two doors away, Miss Lindemann struggling with the lock on her door. This time, she turned towards him and

– Herr Rundstedt?

She seemed upset.

– Please? Why do you follow me?

Rundstedt laughed.

– I know it looks bad, he said, but this is my room.

– So. You are staying here also?

– Yes, I am. Listen, thanks for the dinner.

– It is nothing. Good night.

She turned away and continued struggling with the door.

– Can I give you a hand? asked Rundstedt.

Some of the spirit seemed to go out of her, at his question. Her (padded) shoulders sagged; she sighed; she stepped away from the door.

– Perhaps you will be able to open it, she said.

– Sure. Let me, said Rundstedt.

With no effort at all, he turned the key and her door opened.

– You just have to push it when you turn the key.

– Thank you so much, said Gudrun.

Her room smelled of rose water. Its windows looked out onto Rue Chevert. Her bed was neatly made.

– I am disappointed I cannot invite you to spend the night, said Gudrun. You are married. However, I am very lonely. Will you come in to talk?

They were standing before her doorway, a hand span between them. Miss Lindemann's coat was open and Rundstedt, not much taller than she, could see the freckles that began between her breasts. He was both relieved and disappointed he would not spend the night.

– Sure, he said. Why not?

Though many might not believe it, talk is what they did: with him in a chair, coat across his lap, and her beneath the covers of the bed, unselfconsciously naked save for a brassiere and a St. Christopher's medal.

And what did they talk about? Home, his wife, her parents. It was wholly innocent and completely satisfying. For the first time in his life, Rundstedt had the pleasant feeling that he was . . . no, not desirable. He knew he was that, to Edwina, but . . . strong, *strong* is the word: confident and self-assured enough to, after a few hours, relax in the company of a woman he found attractive. That is, a woman who was not his wife.

31

WHAT IS IT, PAUL?

I n the year and more since he'd turned his wife out, Paul
Dylan's life had been unsettled, all aspects of his life constantly disturbed. Had he not founded Dylan Programming,
for instance, were he not "the boss," he might well have been
shown the door. He would certainly have dismissed himself, circumstances permitting. There was no justifying his absence. He
was at his desk every morning at nine and he left in the evening,
well after everyone else, it's true. But it had been some time since
he had done more than sign the documents that needed signing
and approve decisions made by his more dedicated employees. In
fact, his head of operations had, for at least a year now, been the
company's most important employee.

In his own defence, he might have pointed out that he had not
interfered with operations and the company had thrived. He
might also have asked if he were not entitled to coast, from time
to time, seeing as it was his business.

Yet, no one had questioned his entitlement or his right to coast.
For months there had been peculiar looks and polite queries
about "things at home." Then, after a while, there was a kind of
abatement. Those who worked closely with him accepted that his
was the kind of burnout that accompanied success. It wasn't that

he did not keep up with the latest developments – the move from
C to C++, for instance. He did, and for some time now, that and
his support for new ideas were all they expected of him.

He had tried to be more involved in work but, despite his
efforts, he could not shake the woman who had been his wife or,
more exactly, he could not shake her lawyer. What had he done
to deserve the hounds? He had behaved honourably, he felt, and,
considering the circumstances, with restraint. *He* hadn't ended his
marriage. Its end had been decreed; this though he had (more or
less) looked the other way at his wife's infidelity. But over time, it
became clear his wife had been wounded by his silence, his with-
drawal, and his discretion. She wanted his house, his money, and
even his assent: his assent that she was within her rights, his assent
that she had behaved fairly, his assent that she was entitled to
whatever she thought herself entitled.

Evidently, Mr. Nenas, her lawyer, thought she was entitled to
whatever she wanted. Nenas had summoned him, as if he were a
two-bit lackey, but Paul refused to have anything to do with him
until his own lawyer had advised him to meet the Polynesian
bastard. It was imperative. Paul stood to lose half of everything he
owned if he did not agree to meet with his wife and her lawyer.
So, he had gone, though he would have preferred to burn every
little thing he owned and let her sift through the ashes.

He and his lawyer, Perry Newman, had waited in a meeting
room. The floor was carpeted. They'd sat at an exceptionally long
table. There were no windows, and the place was flooded with
fluorescent light. If he had not already been on edge, the room
would have put him there. Though it was very like the conference
rooms in his own building, Paul had never felt so confined by
walls and light.

Then, after making them wait, Mr. Nenas had walked in with
Louise.

Paul's anger had turned to loathing. Anger had something of
love to it. He'd felt anger when it seemed possible to retrieve what

was lost. Now, however, he wanted none of it. He saw Louise for what she was: a perfumed harpy. Every inch of Louise was pathetic: hair, lipstick, the tilt of her head, the way she looked down at the tabletop.

Whereas, previously, the thought of Louise's suffering would have been gratifying to him, at that moment he'd felt only that he wanted her excised, taken away and put somewhere he would never see, find, or even think of her. (There was a thought: so well hidden, he would not even discover the memory of her.)

The first words from the Polynesian's mouth had been:

– I think we have a bit of a problem here.

– Why don't you tell us what the problem is? Perry had asked.

– Your client has been extremely uncooperative.

– How so?

There followed a litany, a nebula of complaints, until Paul said

– I didn't abandon anyone. I worked twenty years to make a home for my wife, then she abandoned me.

Gently, Perry had put a hand on his arm and said

– Let's let him finish.

On the other side of the table, Mr. Nenas was sitting up stiff-backed. The former Mrs. Dylan had also straightened up.

– We're not, said Mr. Nenas, contesting that it was Mrs. Dylan who initiated this separation, but she didn't surrender her rights by leaving. And you've been pretty cruel, haven't you? You took her money from your joint account. You've refused to see or speak to her, and you've left us no alternative but to take you to court. If I were you, I'd listen to your lawyer, eh.

Paul couldn't help himself. He said

– You Polynesian prick.

– Who's Polynesian? asked Mr. Nenas. I'm from Moose Jaw.

Again, Perry had put a hand on Paul's arm.

– Let me do the talking for a bit, he'd said gently. Listen, Tim, if you've come here to insult my client, we can adjourn right now. First of all, this joint account business won't fly. Any account the

Dylans held in common was for use by my client as well as yours. There was no formal agreement as to its management, so don't be provocative. Second, it was, as you've said, your client who walked away from the marriage. She did not give her husband occasion to express his opinion on the matter. Despite that, here we are, Tim, in your office, talking to you and to your client. Mr. Dylan was not obliged to speak to your client. He waited until he heard from her representative before making himself available, so there again he's done nothing wrong. If you'd like to be serious instead of provocative, let's stick to terms. What would Mrs. Dylan like?

That had pinned Nenas' ears back for him.

– Fair enough, said Mr. Nenas. My client would like exactly what she's entitled to: her own money back and half of everything Mr. Dylan owns. House, business, assets. The works.

– You must be kidding, said Perry.

– Not at all, Mr. Nenas answered.

– Mrs. Dylan instigated the separation. She does nothing to save the marriage and, as I understand it, she's the one who had an affair.

Mr. Nenas' eyebrows had circumflexed.

– What affair? he'd asked. There was no affair.

Until that instant, it had been as if the former Mrs. Dylan did not exist. She'd sat quietly by her lawyer, humiliated that it had come to this: begging for what belonged to her. The issue was Paul's behaviour, his theft of her money, his refusal to speak to her or, until Mr. Nenas threatened to proceed against him, her lawyer. Now, for the three men in this sterile room, the issue was her morals. With whom had she slept and when? They'd turned to her, waiting for her to deny her infidelity But why should she deny? Why should she swallow the lie beneath all this: that she was entitled to her belongings only if she could prove she had lived blamelessly for twenty years, that she had earned what was hers through fidelity?

– Yes, she said, I did have an affair.

Mr. Nenas was caught off guard, but he recovered.

– It changes nothing and you know it, Perry. Mrs. Dylan is entitled to half of all property and assets accrued during the marriage. So, what we're doing here, today, is asking for Mr. Dylan's cooperation. We'll need his business statements, bank records, the works. We'd rather not go through court to get them, but we will if we have to.

How strange it had been. The sounds of the lawyers' voices had faded softly or gone out of focus, as if they were speaking through felt. How strange, too, that such an obvious truth

. – Yes. I did have an affair

delivered with contempt should have so influenced him.

As if the thought had just occurred to him, Paul had said

– And are you finally going to admit who you slept with, Mrs. Dylan?

Her lawyer had come immediately to her defence, putting his hand up as if to ward him off.

– That's not our business, he said.

Exactly what she herself might have said but, again, the indignity, the being made to feel these men held the strings to her fate, was too bitter. She had moved Mr. Nenas' hand from before her and said

– Walter . . . Walter Barnes.

She'd spoken Walter's name clearly, looking straight at Paul for the first time, allowing herself to feel the full measure of her anger.

Paul had blanched, and kept quiet from then until he walked from the conference room.

That first meeting (so far, the only one) had been in March. Louise's mention of Walter Barnes had had as profound an effect on Paul as she had hoped, but for reasons she could not have guessed. If Paul had been devastated, it had not been, as she'd thought, because he'd felt the humiliation of her infidelity but, rather, because it had become clear to him that she had *not* slept with Walter Barnes. His conscience, which he had managed to stifle since the day his secretary had mentioned, "Norway, Løne, Lucy, Louise," returned to torment him. He had hurt an innocent man. From the moment Louise had spoken Walter's name, he'd recovered his sense.

He understood, the instant she had said Walter's name, that she was lying. The hesitation, the look on her face, the way she'd spoken. She had lied to protect someone else. When Louise named Walter, Paul understood not only that he had misinterpreted the signs that pointed to Walter's guilt but that his previous version of Walter, that he was too much the academic to copulate, had been true. He now saw just how circumstantial his evidence had been, and it shamed him to think he had cobbled bits of hearsay, meaningless signs, and the testimony of a college girl into a case against so gentle a man. No, Walter was innocent and Louise was utterly despicable.

What was he to do? It wasn't only a question of guilt and expiation. The guilt was sharp enough, but it had been a long time since his contretemps with Walter and, besides, if asked, he would have said it had not been his fault. Really, if it came to fault, Louise was the one who'd flattened Walter. She was the one who had driven him to do it. He had been her instrument. He had been used. He and Walter had both been deceived by a woman without morals.

But who was there to warn a man about marriage and women? There was song, it's true

– *Mujer, si puedes tú con Dios hablar . . .*

but one could not live a life by the bard. And there was the Bible

– *. . . he that heareth, and doeth not, is like a man that without foundation built a house upon the earth . . .*

but how much more dangerous was holy writ as a guide to life.

He was alone, and it seemed to him he'd been alone for decades. The friends he'd had at school had fallen into other lives like pebbles into a deep well. The friends he'd made since had, most of them, for one reason or another, passed from his life. He now avoided the other members of the Fortnightly Club, for instance. His community had dwindled to one, to himself, and its purpose was lost, or its purpose still had something to do with Louise, though it was not clear what that something might be.

Almost without meaning to, having no end in mind, he'd begun to follow Louise. No, that's too easily said. He did not follow her. Rather, he put himself in her vicinity. It was a matter of curiosity. Weeks after the meeting with Nenas, Perry had told him, gently, that it might have been better had he, from the beginning of the separation, kept the lines open.

– But what's done is done, Perry had continued.

Barring some fantastic revelation, say that Louise was not who she claimed to be, she was, by law, entitled to half of whatever he had made during their marriage. They could stall. They could prolong the process and, if that was what Paul wanted, Perry would do his best. But was there not, Perry wondered, a chance Louise would still accept less in order to avoid a long wait?

– I could speak to her, said Perry.

– Whatever you like, Paul had answered.

But he'd been thinking on Perry's fantastic notion: that Louise was not whom she claimed to be. What if Louise were not Louise? And how could one tell if anyone were who they claimed to be? Though Perry had not meant the notion seriously, it was an idea that sang to Paul's psyche. Or, rather, it provided a pretext for his budding obsession to see his wife again. Whatever the case, shortly after this meeting with Perry, Paul had begun to track Louise down, as if she were a science project, waiting to observe her at the places he thought she might be.

The first wait had been tedious. He'd sat in a rented car and watched, from seven o'clock until nine, on a night in autumn, parked across the street from 371 Powell, the house she shared with her friend Fredrika. And what a strange sensation it was to see

Louise approach, walking west, pass his car without seeing him, cross the street, fumble with her keys, and step into Powell. He'd felt shame, resentment, and pleasure. His pleasure was an echo of the pleasure he'd once felt at the sight of her. His resentment was more natural; she was, after all, a woman he now loathed. All of these emotions had passed through him simultaneously.

She entered the house at eight. It took Paul an hour to recover, to keep himself from knocking at her door, to reassure himself that he had done nothing wrong (he had done nothing at all), and to resolve never to repeat his "experiment."

He managed to hold to his resolution for weeks. All was well. As if the incident had led him back to the straight road, he found himself able to work, to concentrate, to put the small matters behind him, to take care of business. He became, again, meticulous. So it was all for the best. It had all been for the best. He had recovered clarity. The strange current that had run through him at the sight of her had been liberating. He knew where he stood. He could dispense with her. He felt such freedom, he imagined he could easily give up his money, his home, his business. He could give it all without flinching. To her, even.

No, actually, no he could not.

His second vigil, two weeks later, had not been like the first. For one thing, he he'd been on foot this time. For another, on this occasion he'd hoped to meet her casually, as if it were unplanned. He would encounter her on his way to, let's say, a movie at the Somerset, though the Somerset was not *that* close.

He'd walked along Powell, from Bronson to Bank Street.

At eight o'clock, already dark on a dark day, he'd had to be attentive, though not suspiciously attentive, to the few pedestrians who approached and then passed him by. Not a woman among them, though one young man wore a long white raincoat that could have belonged to Louise, and Paul found himself resenting the times in which they lived.

This second vigil had done nothing for him. Having failed to catch sight of Louise, he reproached himself for the effort. He should not have bothered. He would not bother.

His third vigil, days after the second, was, again, in a rented car, parked almost exactly where he had been the first time. It was, again, fruitless. Perry had spoken to her, and she had said that it was now too late to negotiate. She wanted no more talk. The court would speak for her, for them. She was prepared to wait for the word from a judge. Abetted by Perry, Paul had resolved to speak to her himself, but he found himself incapable of leaving the car. What was he to do? Beg? No, his spirit could not be taken from him. He would have nothing more to do with her.

And yet, there was a fourth vigil.

And a fifth.

And a sixth.

And a seventh.

And so on.

It was now autumn. He hadn't seen Louise since the first night in ... April, wasn't it? He could no longer say why he was on Powell. It seemed he came, these evenings, because he had come in the past. It was frustrating, but the frustration was a strong emotion, almost a drug. The street itself had its charge of bitterness. He could not approach Powell without feeling shame and humiliation along with the need to eradicate shame and humiliation.

Powell Avenue made him feel this way, the house at number 371 even moreso. He knew its façade well: wooden porch (white), short banister (white), front window through which (curtains open) he could see a living room, through which (curtains closed) he occasionally saw a blurred silhouette belonging to God knows whom, and a second floor, with two windows, more opaque, and a third floor, with a gabled window, more mysterious still. He did not know the house's layout, had no idea what sort of warren it held, but he disliked it anyway.

The street itself was a poison: beginning with this house shared by Fredrika and Louise (371), it infected the street (Powell), which poisoned Bank, which poisoned Bronson, which poisoned the Queensway. He could no longer pass Bank, Bronson, or the Queensway without being reminded of Louise, without being reminded of the emotions he felt at the sight of her, at the thought of her. Eventually, the whole of Ottawa would sicken and wither, and he would have to leave because there would be nowhere left for him to find peace, no sanctuary, nowhere he would not feel her presence, and that was exactly what he wanted now: sanctuary, a place where his murderous feelings would not find him.

Murderous? Yes, because it had suddenly, clearly, become a struggle to the death between himself and his wife.

Murderous, even when he was not dreaming? Yes, because he could not sleep, had not been able to sleep for months.

Travel did no good. He had gone, on business, to San Francisco and Fort Worth, and had returned to the same hatred and misery. Nor did the society of others. There was no going out in Ottawa, no distraction, and though he could be polite in a room of strangers, there was no place in him for friendship.

And then, on this autumn night, when he'd been sitting for an hour, in darkness, thinking only that he had come to the end of a road, that this was the last evening he would spend waiting for the sight of a woman he did not want to see, Fredrika and Louise stepped out the door of 371, stood for a few minutes on the porch, laughing.

Everything about their sudden appearance filled him, suddenly, with loathing.

The women were dressed in dark raincoats.

Fredrika dropped her keys, and stooped to pick them up.

Louise's hair was in a ponytail.

Both women looked down at the ground as they descended the steps.

They were arm in arm as they walked towards Percy.

It was all just too too, and it seemed as if it were done to him, with him in mind, as if to say

– Your suffering is part of our amusement.

Without forethought, but as if it were what he'd had in mind from the beginning, Paul started the car and drove towards the two, intending to run them over.

No. There was no intending. Paul Dylan ceased to exist. Thought, emotion, and personality were reduced to will and trajectory. The idea of killing the women was so clean, it seemed to have existed before time itself. He would, later, remember that, at the moment he drove towards them, his mind harboured a single question: when should I floor it?

The women had crossed Percy. They were on their way to Lyon when he stepped on the accelerator, pointed the Mustang at them, and drove up onto the curb.

How could he have missed them?

They had been walking quickly, when Fredrika's keys again fell from her hand. They both stopped, turned back, leaned down, lightly knocked heads, and the Mustang, like a sudden wind, fluttered the back of Fredrika's raincoat.

And that was it.

November 2, 1986: no harm done, but it was hours before his hands stopped shaking. He had narrowly avoided murder, but his first feeling was disappointment. It seemed to him that, for better or worse, his life would have been simplified by Louise's death. Now, he had to live on with her *and* with his failure to do what he should have done on their wedding night: kill her, that is.

And was he the kind of man who could kill?

In the hours following his attempt on Louise's life, Paul sat in his car by Brown's Inlet recreating the fateful moment over and over, sometimes hitting her, sometimes hitting both women. Fredrika. Now, there was a woman for whom he felt little. He had never liked her much, yet he could not dismiss the vision of her in a raincoat, fumbling with a set of keys, bending to pick them up. He'd known Fred since high school. He knew her parents, could remember the liver spots on her father's hands.

Had he really come so close to killing her? Yes.

What manner of man was he, then?

There had been other dark nights, other harrowing moments during which he'd struggled to maintain a clear sense of himself, his life, his worth. This night was different, though. He could scarcely imagine a darker descent or, rather, he could: himself, bereft of even the smallest things that pointed to who he had been, himself lost to himself, which would leave only death to put an end to annihilation.

What manner of man was he? No answer from Brown's Inlet. No answer from the stars. No answer within. So, long after any reasonable man would have told him to seek help, Paul Dylan decided that, yes, perhaps, he did, if only for this night, need company. He thought of Henry Wing. He had always respected Henry, and Henry's discretion.

It was midnight when he left the car on Metcalfe and walked to the house on Cooper, Hercules and Lyra above him. He had no idea if the right words would find their way out, but it was already a relief to see the façade of 77 Cooper, to feel, before he entered, its peculiar stillness of books and banisters, blue rugs and elaborate moulding.

He felt hope as he knocked at the door.

– Oh . . . hello, Paul.

Paul had so expected to see Henry, it was, for a moment, as if he were hallucinating, as if Henry Wing had become Walter Barnes. But he was not dreaming. It was Walter who opened Henry's door, Walter who greeted him and asked

– Are you coming in?

{ 32 }

TO DAMASCUS

I t was unusual, but not odd, that Walter should be at Henry's.
They were friendly and, as he slowly recovered something of
his former conviviality, it was natural Walter should gravitate
to Henry Wing, who was, after all, a sympathetic man. It's true
that, for some time after his most recent attempt at death, intellectual matters were of little interest to Walter. He had abandoned
the Fortnightly Club at least in part because he would have found
it difficult to feign interest in, say, the difference between the Latin
word *Natura* and the Greek word *Phusis*.

Intellectually, he was content, when he was not rereading the
Bible, to reread *King Lear*, amused at how suddenly and deeply his
allegiances changed, how he could, one week, feel sympathy for
Edmund and, the next, revulsion, wishing him dead earlier
though it was ridiculous to wish Edmund anything at all, ridiculous but inevitable because his familiarity with *Lear* had become
something like intimacy with a living acquaintance. The book
had come to *seem* a living acquaintance. He had been reading it,
once or twice weekly, for a year or so: distractedly, attentively,
with disdain, disbelief, admiration, barely able to keep his eyes
open, unable to put it down.

Not that he had mastered the work.

– *Why should a dog, a horse, a rat have life, and thou no breath at all?*

Here, for instance, he wondered why it should be "dog, horse, rat" as opposed to "horse, dog, rat," which would have been more orderly, or even "horse, rat, dog," which would have put the pest in the middle. But it did not trouble him. It was in these unanswerable questions that one felt the presence of another mind, of Shakespeare, if you like, and that was company enough.

As he recovered from his descent, however, pleasures came back to him and became pleasures again. He allowed himself to collect a few things for his home: African violets, Aspidistra, napkins (cloth), ewers (2), Armagnac (1 bottle), pots (cast iron, 2), pans (stainless steel, 2), a delicate wooden egg (Lithuanian), in which there were two grains of corn on which the whole of the Torah had been inscribed.

He permitted himself to walk in the city. He went wherever he liked. There was the walk along the canal: always along the east side, along Colonel By, on the city's crooked spine, by the houses looking down from Echo Drive, to the Pretoria Bridge, with the university in the distance and Hull beyond. Or through the experimental farm: along Prince of Wales, past the arboretum, to the pavilion at Dow's Lake. Really, it hardly mattered where he went. The city had its own tone, rhythm, and reason that conflicted or accorded with his own. It was beautiful or wretched from step to step, moment to moment, and he was part of its conversions.

One day, for instance, he had walked along Echo, gone up the stone steps, and wandered in a nest of streets he did not know (McGillivray, Herridge, Drummond, Hazel . . .). It was evening. The snow was deep and the winter sun turned the rooftops crimson. As he approached Hazel, he heard a melody he knew.

– Mild und leise wie er lächelt . . .

How odd to hear the *Liebestod*, here. He stood at the corner of Drummond and Hazel and listened until the final chord faded. No doubt, somewhere someone was pounding on a wall to have the music turned down, but it was momentarily marvellous for Walter to imagine that Isolde also dies here, steps from a pharmacy and a busy street. A vivid moment, but not all that unusual, a moment that needed him, the music and the waning light to come into being and pass away again. It was lovely to feel that one belonged, that one was necessary to the errant and erratic creations of his city, Ottawa, Ontario, 1986; to feel, however briefly, that one would not live anywhere else.

It was on one of these walks that he met Henry Wing. He was walking along Elgin, had passed Mags and Fags, when he bumped elbows with Henry.

– I'm sorry, he said.

– Paul? said Henry.

– Walter, said Walter.

– Yes, yes. I'm sorry, Walter. I'm distracted these days. It's a pleasure to see you.

It was a pleasure to see him, as well. It had been years. They shook hands, as people passed.

– How are you, Henry?

– I'm a little sad, but I'm well.

He looked older, though, and more frail.

– I was just thinking about you the other day, Walter. I was reading Paracelsus.

– Are you sure you're okay, Henry?

– What? Oh, yes, I'm fine, Walter. I'm as fine as fifty-nine can be, but how are you? Shall we walk? I need the exercise.

They walked, Henry slightly bowed and stiff-legged, Walter tired but happy for the society of a man with whom he felt at ease. They spoke, moving along the evening streets, the sun sinking through the last of the clouds.

They had met at seven o'clock. It was eight o'clock, and they were approaching Vanier before they realized how far they had gone, how hungry they were.

– I don't know that I have much to eat at home, said Henry, but you must come and have something with me.

It was odd to enter a house he hadn't visited in years. It was much as Walter remembered it, but he felt as if he were stepping into a past. The house was neat, clean, and warm. In the kitchen, where they went to eat their chicken and lentils and drink grappa, there was, on the wall beside the table, a vivid print of a mysterious scene: a woman on a balcony was pulling at her hair; a plank from the balcony had fallen and a child had fallen with it; the child was in mid-air; in the street below, spectators were aghast, but from somewhere, from the clouds perhaps, a monk was also in mid-air, falling towards the child. The print was a memento of something or other, but there had always been something mysterious about Henry's home.

For hours, as their food grew cold, the two men spoke and drank. Neither would have said he had much to say about anything at all, but then communion is always a little surprising. Every so often, Henry would say

– You should eat, Walter. It's good

and they would both pause for a mouthful of chicken, but it was the company that mattered.

Henry did not often speak of personal matters but, when they had finished eating, he said

– Have you been in love, Walter?

– I'm not sure what the word means, said Walter.

(True, but he knew *who* it meant. Louise came to him, as if she were part of his instincts.)

– Neither am I, said Henry, but –

– It means so many things, I wonder if we should name it at all. Henry put his hand on Walter's arm and smiled.

– Of course, he said, of course. It's in the nature of these things to be vague. At the end of time, when everyone who has spoken the word is gone, some interested party may finally be able to say what the word *love* meant to humans, but until then, we give it the meanings we must.

Henry took his hand away and had a sip of grappa.

– I am in love, he said.

– I'm happy for you, said Walter. Is it someone I've met?

– No, I don't think so. In any case, she is leaving Ottawa.

– Does she love you?

– I've always thought so, but, you know, Walter, that isn't so important any more. It gives me pleasure to think Kata loves me, but I find I want what's best for her. Maybe I'm not selfish enough. When she said she wanted to leave, I could have begged her to stay. I could have offered to go with her, but I don't think she wants me to, so I'll stay. Most of the time, I manage to think about other things, but it isn't always easy.

It occurred to them both, at the same moment, that this was the most Henry Wing had ever spoken of his private life to Walter Barnes. The thought momentarily broke their intimacy. Henry said

– I'm sorry to burden you, Walter.

He looked his fifty-nine years: slightly frail, thin, his face a sharper version of the face he must have had before Walter knew him. Walter felt a deep sympathy for the man.

– More grappa? asked Henry.

After the grappa, their third or fourth, Henry went in search of a book he wanted Walter to see, and it was then that someone knocked at the front door. After waiting to see if Henry would answer, Walter went to the door himself.

He was surprised, and a little displeased, to see Paul Dylan.

– Oh . . . hello, Paul, he said.

The man looked pale, distraught, and frightened.

– Are you coming in? asked Walter.

– Yes, said Paul.

He stepped into the foyer, avoiding Walter's hand, stepping around him.

– Where's Henry? he asked.

– Aren't you going to shake my hand? asked Walter.

Paul did, apologizing:

– I'm sorry, Walter. I'm a little distracted.

It is difficult to say for whom the moment was more peculiar. Paul Dylan had distressing things on his mind. There was no room, in his thoughts, for past transgressions. He spoke to Walter as if nothing of significance had transpired between them. Walter was, at first, troubled. His first thought was to throttle Paul Dylan, and as he shook Paul's hand, it occurred to him that he could easily strangle the man. So, after all, he had not risen above their encounter? No. He resented the humiliation, the time in hospital, the despair? Yes.

– Where's Henry? Paul asked again.

– He's gone to find the *Hypnerotomachia*.

– The . . . ?

Henry came down the stairs, carrying an oversized leather book.

– Paul, he said. How wonderful. An impromptu meeting of the old Fortnightly.

He put a hand on Paul's shoulder.

– Is everything all right? You don't look well. Why don't you have a grappa with us?

It suddenly seemed to Paul he had made a ridiculous mistake. Even if he'd found Henry alone, what would he have said?

– *I've tried to murder Louise, and I'm afraid I'll try again?*

What was the answer to that? Yet, part of him wanted to say just that, wanted to hear the answer in a voice that was not his. He did not want to stay, but neither could he leave.

– Yes, I'll have a grappa, he said.

He drank the first one quickly, looking as though he might swallow the delicate shot glass. Henry refilled the glass. Paul drank this one almost as quickly. Henry refilled his glass and, this time, both he and Walter watched as he drank.

– I'm afraid that's it for the grappa, Paul. Can I get you something else?

– No, said Paul. I have to drive.

– Some water?

– What would you say if I said I wanted to kill you? Henry smiled.

– I'd say I was sorry there was no more grappa, he answered.

The three of them sat at the small kitchen table: Henry at one end, Paul at the other, Walter between them. It was quiet. Lights were on all over the house, as if guests were expected or had just left. At the mention of killing, Walter, who'd been looking at the painting on the wall, moved his chair closer to Henry, turned it to face Paul as Paul said

– What if I wanted you to kill me?

– That I couldn't do, said Henry.

– Why not?

– It isn't in me.

– It's in everyone, said Paul.

– I don't believe it is.

– Haven't you ever wanted to kill someone?

– No, said Henry. What's this about, Paul?

Paul rubbed the tip of his tongue with his finger, then said

– We should talk about something else.

Which, being accommodating, Walter and Henry tried to do. The ease they had felt in each other's company was gone, however. With Paul brooding at one end of the table, it was difficult to think of anything to say. It did not seem appropriate to open the *Hypnerotomachia*. It did not seem appropriate to speak of books at all, nor to speak of the things that had entertained them for the past, what was it, five hours, six hours?

Paul sat staring at the oven as if it had offended him.

After a bit more of Paul's silence, Walter rose from the table, annoyed.

– It's getting late, he said.

He smiled as he shook Henry's hand.

– We should do this again.

– I'd like that very much, said Henry.

. Walter politely said good night to Paul, and then Henry accompanied him to the front door.

– I'm sorry to leave like this but . . . Do you want me to stay?

– No, no. I understand. We'll see you again, Walter. Good night.

Henry returned to the kitchen where, at his entrance, Paul said

– I tried to kill my wife.

It was one in the morning. Henry was tired and mildly inebriated. He would have preferred to say a few words to Paul, usher him from the house, and retire for the night, but there was nothing to be done. Paul Dylan, whom he had known for years, whom he did not know at all, looked as if *he* had suffered but it was of Louise that Henry thought first.

– You failed, I hope.

– Yes.

– And you want to talk about it?

It wasn't a matter of want, but, yes, he also wanted. From his nightmares and jealousy to his effort to kill Louise and Fredrika, Paul told Henry everything, in detail.

Henry sat quietly and listened. The night deepened. The lights in the house grew more yellow until, as morning approached, they grew wan again and faded into the blue morning light that came in through the kitchen windows. He had no idea why Paul Dylan had chosen him for a confessor. He did not think that Paul respected him particularly, and his most enduring image of Paul, before this night, was of a man with a smirk: agile, but not deep. Yet, as he had listened to a long, alarming, and confused story, the depth of the man's obsession came through in the telling: repetitious, circling back to Louise's betrayals, to his knowledge of her betrayals, his regret that he had not killed her, his self-pity . . .

And it was difficult to know what was expected of him. He was meant to listen, obviously, and he listened, interrupting only once

to have Paul repeat the account of his near-collision with Louise.
(After which, Henry said, beneath his breath:

– You've lost your soul.)

At dawn, the house was cold. Paul stopped speaking. Henry
rose from the table.

– Do you really think I've lost my soul? Paul asked.

– I don't know, said Henry.

And he turned away to make breakfast: four eggs, salt, pepper,
half a Scotch bonnet. He spoke as he scrambled the eggs and
cooked them, his sadness coming as much from a feeling that he
had nothing meaningful to say as from the situation.

– If you had lost your soul, you wouldn't have come here last
night. You must have imagined there was some escape from the
life you're leading, don't you think? Anyway, I don't believe in
damnation. I know how hard it is to be practical, but if you don't
want to feel the way you're feeling now, Paul, you have to change
your life.

(Oh, that was easily said. Could he, Henry, change the way he
lived, even if change meant he could keep Katarina? Far from
certain.)

He had spoken in a calm voice, careful to avoid scolding. The
world was not his to remake. Paul Dylan was not his charge. Yet,
when he turned to give Paul breakfast, he discovered the man was
overwhelmed by emotion. Paul Dylan sat with his back to the
wall, facing Henry, an apologetic smile on his face, a short man
dressed in a blue, pinstriped suit, a cream shirt, a lilac tie. His
clothes were slightly rumpled. His face was shaded by a day's
growth of beard. His arms were folded, held close to his chest, as
if to make himself more compact. His tears fell, but he did not
wipe them away.

Though Henry was a kind man, sympathetic to the full range
of human distress, he felt revulsion at the sight. He stood still in
the centre of his own kitchen holding two plates, on which there

were eggs, rye bread, sliced tomato. The while, Paul sat watching him, or so it seemed, though there was no way to know what it was Paul actually saw.

Finally, Henry said

– You should eat.

and put breakfast on the table beside him.

A CHANGE OF HEART

F or three days, Paul Dylan had trouble eating.
Though Henry Wing assumed he'd said nothing of depth,
a handful of his words had sunk to the deepest place in
Paul's being. The words
— *You have lost your soul*
had sunk and detonated so that Paul heard little thereafter save
— *You have to change your life.*

In another place, at another time, the words might have been
as meaningless to him as they had been before. But in that place
(Henry Wing's kitchen) at that time (six in the morning), they held
the charge of perfectly chosen words. And as the days passed,
away from work, wandering about a house that was now strange
to him, it even seemed as if his life had been tending towards the
moment when Henry's words would make sense.

How he had struggled against the very idea of soul, or at least
against the idea that lay behind it: God, the great intruder. You
could not have one without the other, no soul without God, and
he had always felt disdain for the idea of God, for the idea of
divine presence, for the idea of a merciful watchman.

And yet, he had lost his soul.

It wasn't that Henry had led him to the realization. He had not been persuaded. Rather, he heard the words and knew they were true. The minute he heard them, he felt not only the desolation in their meaning but also the exaltation. The words held him like a mirror. They called out for that which he had never been able to accomplish: surrender.

But what did it mean to change and to whom or what would he surrender?

Of course, this is all said as if he could choose. Could he have chosen, he would have avoided the very idea of soul, the idea of surrender. Could he have chosen, he would have avoided God entirely. God, however, was no longer an idea, for Paul. God, understood as an idea, understood as he had formerly understood it, was no more than an intriguing equation, wonderful, no doubt, but only an aspect of thinking, leaving its imprint on thought and, so, subject to the visions and revisions of thought itself.

He did not surrender to an idea. Rather, *soul* and *change*, words almost casually spoken by Henry Wing, were signposts at the border of a world he had avoided. And Paul Dylan was like an amnesiac who, reaching into a coat pocket one day, discovers a passport to that very world (his photograph on the second page), just the document to jog his memory. Memory recovered, it was baffling to think he had spent so long in exile, that he had, even, denied a provenance that was now so obvious.

That is, as he had recognized himself in Henry's words
— *You have lost your soul*
so he came to recognize himself as belonging in God. The recognition was sudden, exhilarating, and irrefutable. The world as he knew it fled before enlightenment. It fled the moment Paul came to himself in God. The life he had lived lost its purpose. It had led him to this point, so it was not to be despised, but had he really spent so many years nurturing an enterprise, gathering money, flying about the world in order to nurture an enterprise, gather money, and fly about the world? It seemed so. But he was not obliged to go on nurturing, gathering, flying.

Paul was ecstatic, but he was also frightened that the joy he felt was the result of a delusion, frightened that it was evanescent, that he would return to himself and the world wherein he had no soul and there was no God. That is, he was frightened of the man he had been. At the root of his fear there was new selfishness. Though he was willing to turn away from all he had coveted, willing to give up the material possessions he had worked so hard to possess, he could not bear the thought he might lose this: God the Father, the keeper of souls. The thought filled him with anguish because, in his desperation, it did not occur to him that God was not his possession, not a thing to lose.

There was also, at the root of his fear, a feeling of unworthiness. He was unworthy because he had wandered so long in the wilderness, because he had betrayed the holy within him and without, because he had sinned and had not known it. He could not see how he merited this sudden dispensation and, there being so little connection between the life he had led and this moment in it, he felt anxious.

And then there was the stain on his conscience: Walter Barnes.

You would think, after all he had done, that Louise would loom in his conscience, but in those moments of revelation, Paul did not think of her. He had wronged her, perhaps, but she had put herself in the line of fire, whereas Walter had been innocent. In attacking Walter, he had put his faith in the very thing that had also kept him from God's grace: Reason. He had trusted observation, induction, and deduction. It was what he had done to Walter that kept him from deserving, that stood in the path before him. It was this sin he had to expiate before he could live fully in God.

How was he to expiate a sin he had committed so long ago?

There was nothing he could do for the man: no service, no kindness, no deed that would undo what he had done. Nor was there anything to say: no blandishments, no kind words, no words of comfort. Nevertheless, he needed Walter's forgiveness.

He needed this from a man who had no reason to give it, because it seemed to him that, without Walter's forgiveness, he would be what he suspected himself to be: unforgivable.

He had last seen Walter a few days previously. They had shaken hands in greeting, and then three days had passed, days during which Paul Dylan had come to being in God. Perhaps, now, he had the right to hope that this final thing would be granted him.

And for the first time since his childhood, Paul Dylan prayed.

He went down on his knees, because this is how he had been taught. He prepared a place in himself for God to enter, closing his eyes, listening to the sound of his own breath. And when it seemed the world was only darkness and the sound of his breathing, he prayed for forgiveness.

The following day, Paul set out for Walter's home. He did not know what he would say, did not know how he would ask forgiveness.

It was Sunday morning. There were few people on the street, not many cars on the road. There was no one about as Paul pushed on Walter's doorbell.

As it happened, Walter was at home. He had woken early, with the dawn. He had lain in bed for an hour, thinking about a book he would write: a sociological study of table manners. It was an unusual idea, for him. Properly speaking, the work was outside his province. He was no anthropologist. And yet, he found the idea compelling.

He had eaten breakfast, abstained from showering, and he was happily immersed in plans for the book, sheets of paper spread about the kitchen table, when the doorbell sounded.

– Just a minute, he said to himself.

He completed a sentence before going to the door.

– Yes?

Both men were startled at the sight of the other, but Walter was also alarmed. He immediately, instinctively, stepped back. With more dislike than he intended, he said

– What do you want?

– Walter, I just want to talk.

– What do you want to talk about?

– I want to talk about what I did.

– What you did? When?

– When I attacked you. A few years ago.

– Oh. Well, I'd love to reminisce, Paul, but I'm busy.

– Please, Walter.

The man before him looked so wretched, Walter almost regretted his initial hostility. And yet, here was a man who had dragged him from his house, kicked him unconscious, and left him for dead. Now he wanted to talk about it. The idea was bizarre, but Walter entertained it (briefly) before saying

– Some other time

and stepping back to close the door.

– Walter, please.

Dylan was so abject, he reminded Walter of himself. It would have given him no pleasure to shut the door.

– All right, Paul. What is it?

For a moment, Paul struggled with the words, and then he said

– Forgive me.

Not quite hitting it.

– Fine. I forgive you, said Walter.

– No, no. You don't understand. I mean, I finally realize I was wrong. I was misled. I thought you'd had an affair with Louise. But I was wrong. So I'm asking you: if it's possible, please forgive me.

Walter's first thought, on hearing these words, was that he could not imagine a more obscure charade. What did the man expect him to say? Paul knew very well he'd had an affair with his wife. That was why he'd attacked him in the first place. Was this all a prelude to further violence? He put a hand on Paul's shoulder, to hold him off, and he said

– Paul, I *did* have an affair with Louise.

And Paul Dylan, who had been unable to look up at Walter, looked up.

How few moments of deep feeling there are in life, yet here he experienced another, a moment almost as devastating as the one following his attempt on Louise's life. In an effort to spare him pain by making it seem as if he'd deserved a beating, Walter Barnes was lying. Paul now felt the full measure of his own unworthiness.

Falling to his knees on the doorstep, he managed to say
– Forgive me, Walter. Please forgive me
and a lifetime's anguish came out with every word.

Walter was moved. No, this was not a charade. Yes, Paul was asking for forgiveness. He helped the man up and said
– I forgive you
surprised at how sincere his words sounded.

Yet, as he said them, he began to resent having had to say them at all. This was a new invasion, a forced intimacy, more insidious than a physical encounter. What business of his was it that Dylan wanted forgiveness? How was it his duty to comfort the man? Were there no bounds to Dylan's selfishness? Walter felt as if his humanity, his fellow feeling had been drawn from him to serve another, and the more he thought about it the more disgusted he was by his own submission.

He took his hand from Paul's shoulder.
– I've got work to do, he said
and closed the door, leaving Paul to his own conscience.

Walter's morning was slightly ruined. He blamed himself for having opened the door in the first place, for having listened, for having succumbed to a weakness in himself. He was perturbed until, at noon, having spent hours doodling on his pieces of paper, he finally persuaded himself of his good fortune. He had given Paul Dylan what he wanted and now they were quits. There was no further business between them. In other words, Walter was aggrieved but liberated.

When you thought of it in this light, you could say things had gone in his favour.

Paul, on the other hand . . .

From the moment Walter said

– I forgive you

Paul felt and accepted forgiveness. He barely noticed Walter had closed his door to him. He had heard the words, and felt humbled. There was no victory, no exultation, only the conviction that he had been right to surrender to the spirit within him.

To Walter's door, he said

– Thank you

and turned away from Walter's house, grateful. He'd had a wife. He had behaved badly, but all that was in another country and, besides, the man he had been was dead.

{ 34 }

INSPIRATION

Reinhart hadn't had peace since his visit to the Gatineaus.
At his first view of the land in the Gatineaus, something
had ignited in him and he had scarcely been able to think
of anything else, save during the relatively brief moments of
respite brought on by exhaustion.

This was different from other bouts of inspiration he'd suffered. The paintings he'd done of Christ, for instance. Something
in the image of Christ had made itself familiar to him, long before
he'd begun to paint Edward on the cross. Something in the image
had made itself at home, within him. There was no other way to
put it. He had been daydreaming, one day, when it dawned on
him that he had a relationship to Christ. No, not the kind of relationship that precedes belief, something a little more banal. It
was as if, all his life, he had heard news of someone, had seen his
image: a thousand voices, a thousand perspectives. And then,
perhaps not surprisingly, voices and images had become solid in
him, had taken form and shape. So, Christ, the unknown, was
within. His paintings were a way to bring *Him* out. There was, as
far as he could see, no theological significance to his work. He
was resolutely atheist and, besides, he had, at times, felt something of the same thing for Elizabeth Taylor, say, or Audrey

Hepburn: women about whom one heard others speak, whose images built up to something solid within. But neither of them was, for Reinhart, makeable. Christ was makeable. Christ was not exhaustible. He could imagine painting Christ as an ant, a dunghill, a dog, a cantaloupe, a river, a forest (green), a forest (razed). In fact, he could spend a life painting Christ without coming to the end of Christ. You could, if you wanted, call Christ (as he was within Reinhart) a symbol or a touchstone, but only for convenience. Christ was neither symbol nor touchstone: not symbol, because possessed of no fixed meaning in Reinhart's psyche; not touchstone, because inconstant. Christ was a kind of mysterious fountain within him. Nor was Christ the only idea, in Reinhart, that could not be exhausted. There were a handful of things or ideas to which he found himself returning, sometimes to his own surprise. For instance, he had finished a still life with two dead rats and a porcelain bowl when he noticed he'd spent most of his time painting the water in the bowl, the blue of the porcelain, the folds of the tablecloth. He hadn't managed to do the rats any kind of justice, but you couldn't call the painting a failure, for all that, because there were some things that were roads to other things, and some things that were the things themselves. Meaning: what he wanted from his own work was an avenue to further work. A successful canvas, for Reinhart, either solved a problem or provoked one. It wasn't a matter of doing something perfectly (or even, at times, well), because he did not begin with an ideal version of the work.

With his own work, he threw himself in deep water, every time, with the faith he would emerge. But, then, he knew how to begin a painting. At some point, a mark had to be made on canvas and that was all there was to it. As far as sketches for a prison were concerned, though, he had no idea how to go about it and, having no idea how to proceed, he spent months doing little else but looking. For the first time in his life, he read assiduously. He read whatever suggested itself to his imagination: the *Odyssey*, Xenophon's *Anabasis*, Ovid's *Metamorphoses*, Pliny's *Natural History* (Books 2, 7, and 8), Nezami's *Seven Princesses*, *Tirant lo Blanc*, *Orlando Furioso*. He looked at everything. He spent days in the gallery, hours at flea markets. Nothing was too small or insignificant to contain some grain of the thing he was chasing. When such and such a cup or fish knife proved disappointing or unsuggestive, it meant that he had, at least, eliminated some portion of the universe from consideration.

A tiresome process, then, but also inexpressibly absorbing and exhilarating. He was looking for an external manifestation of something that existed inside him. It was tiresome to sort through the things that were useless, but it was exhilarating to discover a clue in, for instance, a large bowl of brilliant aquamarine glass with a decorative design of swirled ribbing and lily pads (found at a flea market), or in passages from ancient, dusty books.

The idea, which was not an idea so much as it was a wager or a hope, was that the various objects, words, and impressions would point to something, would give a coherent picture of that which united them, of the somewhere that lay behind them. He also hoped that he would recognize the "picture" of MacKenzie Bowell when it came, and that it would be singular, original, deep.

And then, while in bed with a man named Giovanni, more precisely, at the sound of the word
  – *Anche*
something in Reinhart opened. He carried on as if he were still present, but Reinhart couldn't decide which distraction he resented more: Giovanni or the curtain that slowly parted, in his imagination, to reveal . . .

To reveal (later, long after Giovanni had gone and Reinhart had been alone for hours) a vision that had nothing to do with buildings:

Through a window, in a room he did not know, he saw olive trees.
The trees were beneath the window. In the distance, on a hillside,
there were the lights of a small town. The sky was cloudless and
dark. The moon, off to his left, was full, as bright as the sun, with
Mars just beneath it and off to the left. He knew none of the con-
stellations by name, but the stars were so clear, he could have
drawn lines between them to make the gallery he wanted: the open
book, the falling chair, the stethoscope . . .

It was not a vision in the usual sense. It was an hallucination.
He could feel the room through whose window he looked. There
was something Turkish about it. As he had never given much
thought to the sky or the moon, it was as if the hallucination
belonged to someone else. And, belonging to someone else, *he*
could find no personal significance in it. He could not have said
what it was, in the sky he imagined, that was meant for him. The
sky he envisioned seemed to have no bearing on his own work,
yet at its presence Reinhart let himself go. He began to draw.

It was noon the following day before he looked up from his
desk. He looked up because, outside his window, a car horn
sounded and would not stop. It was then that he discovered what
he had drawn. It was, though not unpleasantly, puzzling. He
imagined he'd been creating buildings of startling modernity:
light towers, stone walls, a barren courtyard . . .

But MacKenzie Bowell Federal Penitentiary was not as he
might have imagined. It was as if he'd had a fifteenth-century
vision, something Masaccio or Piero, even, might have had while
in a fever. It was all marble and coloured stone, with a piazza (no
other word for it) and octagonal plinths. Not at all what one
would have called a prison compound, not what one would have
expected to find in the Gatineaus, but still, it was what had been
called out of him and, without stopping to eat (urinating, when
nature called, in a jar by the desk, a jar that had once held honeyed
kumquats), he went on drawing buildings, perspectives on the

compound, and views from unusual angles, until seven o'clock in the morning when it finally occurred to him he hadn't eaten in a while, he was tired, and it was time to go to work. He looked down at the drawings he'd made, pages and pages filled with details that seemed to have come through a narrow gate in Time, slipped to him by one of the artists he'd admired as a boy.

None of it was what he'd expected (it never is) or what he wanted (it is never quite that, either), but he was so exhilarated by what he had gone through that he forgot to eat or bathe before going out. No matter. It was almost summer and the world (or Ottawa), with its blue washed sky and lime green buds breaking out from the tips of grey branches, seemed to be going through an inspiration similar to his own.

35

MISÈRE ET CORDES

D aniel was now thirteen. He had lived six years without his mother, six years already, and François Ricard was afraid she had become, for his son, a fading memory. Though he was still thoughtful and inquisitive, Daniel now rarely asked the questions he had asked before:

– *C'est quand que tu as rencontré maman?*
– *Comment est-ce qu'elle était, toute jeune?*
– *Est-ce qu'elle nous aimait?*
– *Est-ce que tu l'aimais?*
– *Est-ce qu'elle m'aimait?*

At school, he was unfocused and easily distracted. He could no longer remember, for instance, the simplest poems

Par les soirs bleus d'été, j'irai dans les sentiers . . .

and he now failed *dictées* he would have found simple only a year before. In the past, his mother had made a game of memory. They'd competed to see who could recall the most of a poem heard for the first time and Daniel had often won. He had a wonderful memory, but, these days, it seemed to have gone underground.

Something had to be done, but what? François and Daniel had

begun to lose the closeness that had come with Michelle's death. François made efforts to recover it. They went walking through Sandy Hill and Lowertown. He bought Daniel the skates and hockey equipment he wanted. They stayed up late to play chess. They read, before bedtime, whatever Daniel wanted as well as books he thought the boy would love: *Le Grand Meaulnes*, *Le Père Goriot*, *L'Odyssée*. But they could both sense – behind the outings, readings, and chess – a falseness, an intimation that they did these things together because they were the things a father and son who were close would do. The ease had gone from their relationship.

As for Daniel, his mother had died and the vacuum she left was part of everything he did and felt. Her presence was, as Père Laurent said of guardian angels, not a shadow exactly, but a shadow made of light. You might be doing the most innocent things, throwing stones into the river, say, and you would sense their presence, said Père Laurent, the way plants sense the sun. So, one day, he had asked Père Laurent if his mother were a guardian angel, and Père Laurent had answered

– Mais non Daniel. Elle est avec le bon Dieu qui la tient dans sa miséricorde

Père Laurent's answer, delivered in the mildest tone, had upset him, because he had no idea what *miséricorde* meant. The word, or was it words, had tormented him.

Misère et cordes?

Miséri corde?

Had God bound his mother? In his darkest thoughts, he imagined his mother suspended above the world, just out of reach. How long would He bind her? Was it just a matter of time before she fell, as souls are said to fall, into the pit? Yet Père Laurent had said the word as if it were a glorious thing. Perhaps, God being God, the cord never broke.

– Papa? Les cordes de Dieu sont plus puissantes que nos cordes à nous, pas vrai?

– Mais quelles cordes Daniel? Dieu n'a pas de cordes.

– Mais, Papa, tu sais, l'aut' jour . . . Père Laurent m'a dit que Dieu tenait les âmes dans sa misère et ses cordes. Il n'a pas dit vrai?

– Misère et cordes? Daniel, la miséricorde n'est pas une chose mais une idée. Miséricorde veut dire une sensibilité à la douleur d'autrui. Et puisque Dieu est supposé être plus grand, plus noble, plus je ne sais quoi d'autre que nous, Il est aussi plus sensible à la douleur.

Now, this was an answer that comforted Daniel, and the boy went off to his room, but it did not comfort his father. François understood the boy was asking about his mother and wanted reassurance, but he thought it wrong to make clear a word that was not at all clear. He put Le Devoir up between himself and the world and thought about "mercy." As he did, other, truer responses to his son's question occurred to him. He called Daniel back and was about to say

– Daniel, no one knows if God is merciful. It makes no sense to say God is loving, merciful, or good, because none of the living have even so much as seen Him. The only inheritance you have, as a man, is ignorance, and you're old enough now to take what's yours: nothing

when he realized what he was doing. He was going to tell a thirteen-year-old that everything men saw, touched, and imagined was built on illusion and nothingness. But when his son stood before him, he could not. Instead, he asked

– Veux-tu jouer aux échecs?

– Je n'peux pas, answered Daniel. J'ai des devoirs.

– Ah oui? Alors allons voir où t'es rendu.

And off they went to check Daniel's homework.

That moment with his son stayed with him for days.

Would it really have hurt Daniel to hear the truth from his father? It was inevitable that a conscientious human being would, eventually, arrive at the same thought: man is a synonym for ignorance. Partial ignorance, not even absolute ignorance.

But it was easier to look on the abyss with your hand in another's, wasn't it? He should have looked down on the void with Daniel and said

— *There, you see? And yet I'm with you.*

When his mother died, Daniel must certainly have looked down on darkness himself. It broke your heart to think of it and, feeling guilty, François wondered if he had not, for six years now, in some measure, abandoned his son. Though he had seen to Daniel's material needs, sheltered him, allowed himself to be (momentarily) distracted from thoughts of Michelle, it was not until his son asked the meaning of *miséricorde* that he began to see that he had, since his wife's death, withdrawn from his son. The thought was unbearably sad. For six years, he had behaved as if mourning were his only life: to mourn the death of his wife, to give life to her memory through mourning. He had neglected his son's needs and, so, he had neglected life itself.

Was mourning over, then? No. As with people who, in love, feel not as if they've begun to love but as if they have, rather, discovered a fount of love within themselves, a fount the beloved brings to notice, so it was for François' grief. Michelle's death was not the beginning of grief, but a discovery of a grief within; grief, like love or language, being a source that reveals itself.

Yes, all right, grief has no end, because it has no beginning.

Still, in thinking of his son's needs, the pain of missing Michelle was not over, but it was adulterated.

On Sundays, François and Daniel visited Michelle's grave, changed the flowers they had left the week before: irises for lilies, lilies for irises. They had visited the grave together so often it had become part of Daniel's childhood. Through the repetition of certain details, they had even created for themselves a small ritual:

— park on St. Laurent
— walk to the cemetery, whatever the weather

– stay for fifteen minutes of silence
– then, home for the Parisiennes they made the night before

But what endless variation these few steps produced. No two vigils were alike. There was, first, the weather: clouds, precipitation, blue sky, dark sky, evening light. Then, there was Time itself. Though they rarely stayed for longer than fifteen minutes, it sometimes felt like five and, at others, like five hundred. Then, again, there was the mood in which one set out or the strength of Michelle's presence. The only thing father and son did not do was speak. In the beginning, when the sight of Michelle's headstone overwhelmed him, François forbade his son from speaking. And ever after, even when he no longer felt the depths of grief, he maintained silence. So, both were surprised when, one Sunday in autumn, after changing the flowers and standing silently together for a while, François said

– C'est comme si on était içi depuis des heures.

Daniel looked up at his father. They were standing side by side. There was, as there often was, a cluster of mourners not far from them: older, heads bowed before a pink granite headstone.

– N'est-ce pas? said François.

– Oui Papa, said Daniel.

– T'as pas froid?

– Non . . . un peu.

François smiled and put his arm around his son's shoulder. Then they stood in silence until their time was up.

After that, François was not joyful, exactly. The memory of his wife was not, suddenly, indifferent to him. Rather, a capacity for happiness, something he'd had since childhood, gradually returned.

It was around this time that Franklin Dupuis called to ask whether they could, for a few minutes, meet officially, though it was a weekend. François agreed and, early on a Sunday afternoon, Franklin knocked at his door. He was dressed in a long black raincoat, its collar turned up.

– I really can't stay, he said, but . . .

From beneath his overcoat, he took a cardboard cylinder.

– You remember I asked if you'd do quantity surveying for a new penitentiary?

– Vaguely.

– Well, said Franklin. I've got something to show you.

He walked past François, into the living room, looking around before stepping into the dining room. There, he took the plastic cap from the cylinder, eased three scrolls from within, and unfurled them on the table. Both men looked down at the drawings. Franklin admired them, his pleasure obvious, but François had trouble deciphering what he saw.

– Beautiful, isn't it? asked Franklin.

– Sure, said François. But what is it?

– It's MacKenzie Bowell Federal Penitentiary.

To François, it looked to be architectural drawings of a town centre somewhere in Europe, or the reconstruction of a lost city: a neighbourhood in Pompeii, for instance.

– It would be a real favour if you did this, said Franklin. Give me a sense of the costs before the construction bids come in. I'd be paying you myself, so there wouldn't be much money.

– Where are you going to build it?

– In the Gatineaus.

– Hmm. You know, Frank, this calls for a lot of marble. It's going to be prohibitively expensive, and I haven't done any surveying since I joined Transport.

And yet, as it happened, François was in just the mood to accept Franklin's proposition. He had recently been told to actually *take* a vacation. He would lose the time owed him, otherwise. He found the idea of working as a quantity surveyor appealing.

He was ready to take any assignment that might bring diversion. So, after a brief look at the oddly antique plans, and without thinking about it all too deeply, François smiled and said

– Okay, Frank, je l'ferai pour toi.

– Wonderful, answered Franklin. I can't tell you how much it means to have people you trust working with you on something like this. I'll call you next week with the details.

– Would you like a drink of something?

– No, I don't think so, said Franklin.

He rolled the drawings tightly up, inserting each one in turn back into the cylinder.

– These are the only ones I have, he said. I'll have copies made for you.

He slipped the cylinder inside his raincoat, then moved forward to embrace François with one arm.

– This is a real project, he said. I'm glad to have you with me.

And as suddenly as he had come, Franklin was gone.

François would come to think of this as an almost hallucinatory visit, as vivid as if he'd dreamed it, though the image that stayed with him was not of Franklin but, rather, of Daniel's shoes. Moments after Franklin had gone, and as if on cue, his son had come in from the yard.

– Papa, he'd asked, qu'est-ce qu'on a à boire?

– Daniel, enlève tes souliers, s'il te plaît. Bon, allons voir s'il nous reste du jus d'ananas.

As they were walking into the kitchen, François noticed that his son's shoes, one lying on its side by the front door, were as dark and crumpled as those in a van Gogh he'd seen, with Michelle, in New York. He no longer remembered why they had gone to New York, or when, but he recalled the painting as distinctly as if he'd seen it moments before. How strange that these unrelated things (Franklin, van Gogh, New York, his son's shoes) should be so intertwined in his memory.

36

A COMMITTEE MEETING AND A SMALL SETBACK

I n April, after Rundstedt had met with the men from Corrections Canada to describe the kind of penitentiary the government wanted ("a new kind, one that embodied a bold new way of thinking"), Franklin took over. He met with this person and that, to see that Corrections Canada understood precisely what MacKenzie Bowell entailed. After that, the dates were set for the competition for architectural designs. And then, when the due date was past and the ministry had received and organized dozens of submissions (some of them quite striking), he sat on the selection committee assembled by the Department of Public Works and made certain that Reinhart's work was on the short list delivered to Minister Rundstedt, who, in turn, presented the designs to Cabinet, downplaying the cost of MacKenzie Bowell.

How quickly that last paragraph reads, but if you consider that each of its words represents hours or days, noon-hour lunches, evening cocktails, friendly cajoling, near bribes, bribes, finger-numbing paperwork, hastily met deadlines, finagling, haggling, posting, sleepless weeks, the arduous creation of an illusion of fair competition . . . if you consider how much patience, resolve, dedication, single-mindedness, humour, and humourlessness . . .

if you consider that Franklin worked harder than anyone else to see that everything went according to design . . . then you will have an inkling of how powerful Alba's hold was on Franklin's imagination. And thanks to his hard work, the months and months that passed as he did his bureaucratic duty, things were going his way: the men at Corrections Canada were on his side when he explained the thinking behind MacKenzie Bowell, the men at Public Works were swayed by his ideas, which, in a way, was very like having them on his side, and the member from Hull-Aylmer, near whose riding MacKenzie Bowell would sit, was, especially after an expensive meal and good drink, favourably disposed to the whole enterprise.

Franklin's initial progress was not entirely unimpeded. One of the men from Public Works let it be known that, whatever the thinking behind the new penitentiary, he thought Reinhart's plans horribly expensive and, though Franklin had spoken about culture civilizing criminals, he was not convinced. Had Franklin not heard of National Socialism? Ahh, he had. And had he heard of its love for Mozart, Goethe, the Icelandic sagas, all the highest culture? And yet, these same Mozartians had murdered millions. How did Franklin account for that? In 1939, the only thing civilization did was help vile men systematize their worst urges. Is that what the minister wanted?

– Good point, said Franklin, but you don't think Canadians are the same as Germans, do you? I just don't think we're like that. We're *different* and our criminals are different too. They just want a chance to belong. Besides, if culture and art aren't civilizing, what are they?

– They're window dressing, said Mr. Public Works, exasperated. It's all window dressing and you don't pay millions for window dressing.

– That's a little shallow, said Franklin. I don't think you believe that. I know *I* feel changed when I read a great novel or look at a great painting. Don't you?

– I do too, said someone from Corrections. I think Mr. Dupuis is spot on. You get a troubled soul to read Wordsworth and you'll save a life, I always say, and these designs by Mr. Mauer are just what I mean.

In the end, Mr. Public Work's feelings were immaterial. After Franklin admitted his own "qualms" about the cost of Reinhart's plans and asserted that the minister would take these costs into consideration, the other members of the committee nodded in agreement and voted, with Franklin, to include Reinhart's designs at the *head* of the short list.

After that tricky and significant victory, it seemed almost certain that Mackenzie Bowell would see the light of day sometime in the not-too-distant future. There were, of course, other problems, but one in particular held Franklin's attention, though he might have called it more of a distraction than a problem, as it was less about MacKenzie Bowell itself than it was about fidelity. Franklin wanted everything done just right, however, and as all true aesthetic visions demand purity, it would have to be dealt with.

If Franklin, Reinhart, and Edward had approached the site in the Gatineaus in the usual way, that is, from the main road, they would have seen immediately that there were summer residences quite close to the proposed ground. As it was, they did not discover until much later that four men and two women, all of whom lived in Ottawa, owned land that abutted the site. Two of the men had done nothing with their property. They sold to the government immediately and for very little. But the four remaining owners had built small cottages on their land, places that looked like gingerbread havens, sanctuary from the city.

Now, Franklin had sympathy for all who sought refuge. (At the time, the Vietnamese were still fleeing Vietnam, there were refugees from Iraq, and, of course, the memory of Biafra still haunted.) But buying a cottage was not, to Franklin's mind, the act of a refugee. That is, he did not believe that men and women bought cottages in desperation, that they chose cottages over death. In fact, he felt that cottages almost inevitably despoil a land. (In this case, they were an eyesore, a blight that would mitigate the influence of Alba.) So, unable to grasp the significance of second homes or summer houses, he assumed the remaining owners could easily be persuaded to give up their properties, and he sent Edward to sound them (unofficially) out.

Edward had no trouble finding their names:

> John Fields
> Colleen Thompson
> Robert Burr
> Marilyn McAllister

All of them lived around or near the centre of town. All of them, thought Franklin, were estival do-nothings who headed to the Gatineaus in late spring, their gas ranges and Scottish terriers in tow. Moneyed enough to afford the near wilderness, they would no doubt insist on market value for their properties. On the other hand, it was likely the Fields, Thompsons, Burrs, and McAllisters were Conservative and, being Conservative, sympathetic to the ideals and aspirations of the party. Now, *that* was wishful thinking on Franklin's part. The Fields, Thompsons, Burrs, and McAllisters were moneyed, yes, but not wealthy, and they were all Liberal. They did take their poodles and terriers with them to the cottage, but with the conviction that wilderness was ennobling, ecologically priceless, and in need of preservation. The last thing any of them would have done was to sell their properties to a government bent on using the land for a prison.

Unaware of their attitudes and, so, unjustifiably confident, Franklin had Edward arrange to visit the McAllisters at their home in the Glebe, on the pretext that he wanted to buy the lot beside theirs, property that was unoccupied. The arrangement was easily made but, darkly, Mrs. McAllister let him know there were certain considerations of which he might not be aware.

Considerations?

Edward wore a charcoal-grey, silk and wool suit, a white shirt, a pale indigo silk tie, and new black oxfords. His coat was full length, light wool, navy blue. He had, perhaps, overdone the cologne: a citrus-based scent. However, before knocking at the McAllisters' door, Edward stood at the corner of Clegg and McGillivray allowing the wind to dissipate his fragrance.

Mrs. McAllister, a thin, birdlike woman, met him at the door, frowned, and thereafter treated him with excessive courtesy. She did not look him in the eye. She moved concernedly about within the bulky cage of her grey Shetland sweater.

– Do come in, Mr. . . .

– Muir, said Edward.

– Muir, she repeated. If you just wouldn't mind leaving your shoes by the door. Our floors are pinewood, you see.

The floors looked newly waxed and strangely untrod, as if the McAllisters hovered more often than they walked. There were two dogs with Mrs. McAllister.

– Oh, we don't have to be formal. Call me Marilyn, please.

There was a standard poodle, cream coloured, uninterested in Edward.

– This is Lucy, said Marilyn.

The poodle looked him over before padding away.

– And this is our baby, Heraclitus.

She leaned down to stroke a russet Havanese that wriggled happily and yelped as it began its inspection of Edward's grey socks.

The McAllister home was a curious meeting of land and sea. There seemed to be an aquarium in every room. There were two in the living room: one for the gouramis, another for the loaches and the green terrors. On the other hand, the armchairs in the room were covered in studded leather and, over the back of the chesterfield, there was a sheepskin. On the walls, there were paintings of fields, streams, dogs.

– Would you like some tea? Marilyn asked. We have oolong, Prince of Wales, chai, Earl Grey, and, let me see, Russian black, chamomile, mint, peppermint, and morning glory. My husband's just on the telephone. He should be with us in a second.

As if on cue, Mr. McAllister entered as his wife spoke of him. Mr. McAllister . . .

– Doug. Just call me Doug

was, like his wife, barefoot. He wore a bleached blue shirt and black jeans. He had one hand in his pocket and his eyes seemed impossibly wide apart on his narrow face. It gave the impression of a man looking in two directions at once.

– You get some tea? he asked.

– I was just asking him, said Marilyn.

– Well, does he want some?

– No, thank you, said Edward.

– So, said Doug. Mar told me you were looking to buy land in the Gatineaus.

– Yes, said Edward. I'm interested in –

– Look, I've got to tell you straight off we're against it.

– It isn't anything personal, said Marilyn

– 'Course it's not personal, said Doug. We don't even know you, do we? I'm sure you're a great guy and all, but we talked to the other owners and, to tell the truth, we all pretty much decided it would be a bad idea for there to be another cottage out there.

– I don't understand, said Edward. If I wanted to buy the property, how could you stop me?

Doug McAllister sat in the armchair facing him.

– I don't like the way this is going, he said. I don't want you to take this personally. It's not about you personally, and I don't want you to take it personal the way I'm telling you all this. I'm telling you straight up, 'cause I think that's the best way for both of us. But, listen –

– Just hear us out, said Marilyn kindly.

– That's it. Just hear us out. I don't think you'd want a place out there if it was the same as the city, would you?

The question was not rhetorical. They waited for his answer. Edward said

– Well, no, I guess not.

– There, you see? said Doug. The more people that build out there, the worse it is for everybody.

– It would be terrible for the environment, said Marilyn.

– And that's another reason, said Doug. It'd be hard on the ecosystem.

– The ecosystem? said Edward.

– You don't look like the kind of person who cares about the ecology, said Doug. Maybe I'm wrong, but if you do care about it, you'll want to build somewhere else anyway, won't you?

Bewildered, Edward said

– I'm not sure I understand what you're . . .

Doug stood up, put his arm around his wife's shoulders.

– Look, Mr. Muir, he said, we've been really straight with you, and maybe this isn't what you wanted to hear, but let me answer your question. You wanted to know how we could stop you, and the answer is we can't stop you, except that the lots left up there you have to go through our property to get to. And the only road in there doesn't belong to the municipality. It belongs to us. It's private property and you can't use it. You can pay to have your own road put in, but it'd be pretty expensive, *if* you get permission, and you'll have to pay to maintain it. Well, maybe you're rich and you can afford it, but we'll fight you all the way.

Edward stood up.

– I see, he said.

– That's the spirit, said Doug. You know, there's lots of places in the Gatineaus just as beautiful. You'll find something.

It had been a miserable skirmish. Edward had not even managed to make his real intentions known. The McAllisters had dismissed him so completely, he felt abashed as he walked from their home. He had let Franklin down. He had not been able to accomplish even this small, easy task. It would serve him right, if Franklin were to chastise him.

But Franklin did no such thing. He listened sympathetically to the details of Edward's failed mission and asked questions about the McAllisters: the kind of people they seemed to be, the way they lived, the strength of their convictions, etc.

Here, too, Edward felt he had let Franklin down. He had been so overwhelmed by the McAllisters he'd given little thought to the kind of people they were. Although, when he actually thought about their behaviour . . . They were arrogant, certainly. Malicious? No, not particularly. Cunning? Not at all, unless their directness was meant to mislead.

– So, normal? asked Franklin.

– Yes, I guess they were, answered Edward.

– Good, that's good, said Franklin. Maybe we can use reason.

37

PHANTOM MORALS

The Stanleys made no secret of the wealth they stood to inherit. So, the friends and acquaintances who did not hear of it directly learned of the Stanleys' good fortune from those whom they had told. Naturally, the thought of so much money brought serious questions.

Should Stanley keep his job?

Should Mary keep hers?

Should Gilbert pursue his education?

Should they buy a new home, or two, or even three?

The advice the Stanleys received was both varied *and* consistent. It was varied in that it was often contradictory: Some advised them to stay where they were and invest their money, while others, believing money was meaningless until spent, urged them to buy whatever they wanted. Some believed wealth would bring joy, others that the Stanleys were now as likely to enter Heaven as a camel was to pass through the eye of a needle. Some revealed their own pressing needs, others pleaded on behalf of those who could use a hand. The advice was consistent in that it was all based on an idea of wealth the Stanleys themselves shared. Being lower middle class, and having assumed it was the duty of "the wealthy" to be responsible, humane, and generous, they found themselves constrained by a morality they had created for others, for "the wealthy." That is, they believed it was their duty to help the "less fortunate," but had no idea where or how to begin.

This phantom morality, a moral code they had built for those "above" them, certainly influenced their decisions. For instance, almost everyone felt the Stanleys needed a new house. Now that they had money, it made no sense, it seemed, for them to remain on Spadina. Spadina Avenue was not where the wealthy lived. None who knew them well wished to see them leave, but none could stand the thought of their staying, either. In urging the Stanleys to leave, their acquaintances drew the darkest picture of the neighbourhood in which they themselves were confined. Spadina was crime-ridden, drug-ridden, dilapidated, and fading. They would stay, because they had to, but the Stanleys could not stay without, whether they meant to or not, rubbing their neighbours' noses in the dirt that was Spadina Avenue.

The Stanleys, being faithful members of their community and class, felt similarly. If sudden wealth had afflicted someone of their acquaintance, they would have suggested Rockcliffe or the Glebe as more appropriate neighbourhoods while secretly shuddering at the thought of lavish homes and snooty neighbours. So, though they found it painful, they understood why, in a remarkably short time, men and women they had known for years began to take leave of them. The Stanleys were now the kind of people who could live "elsewhere." Wasn't it only a matter of time before they got gone?

For Stanley and Beatrice, the most peculiar thing, more peculiar even than having to adjust to a morality they had themselves created for the people they now were, was the awareness that they had become exiles in their own city. Without changing language, habits, or outlook, they were on the other side of a border, looking back on friends and the familiar, and it was as if they now had to consciously create "home." But how was that done? Their first home had evolved from who they were and where they'd felt comfortable. This was different. The new life started from different principles, first of which was the assumption they could consciously create a better home for themselves.

They tried to be optimistic, but it was difficult to tell from what side this "new life" should to be approached.

It was not as traumatic for their children.

Spadina Avenue represented their childhood and, as so much of childhood is in the turning away from childhood, it was inevitable that both would, sooner or later, turn away from Spadina. Their friends were envious, but they were not resentful. They had not yet lived lives that led to unelected termini. So, it was amusing for them to think of Mary or Gilbert with money, amusing to imagine it could happen to them as well.

Mary's parliamentary friends were pleased for her and sensible about the problems she would face. But talk of her wealth took up less time than did speculation about the scandals and doings of the government. Then there was the election. It was a year or so hence, but it was still of greater moment than Mary's money.

Mary herself wasn't sure what to think about her fortune. It had been overwhelming to sit in Mr. Bax's office when, after selling off the last property in England, his secretary had brought in a wicker tray on which there'd been two crystal flutes for champagne. Mr. Bax himself had opened the bottle of Krug Clos du Mesnil, and they had celebrated her family's continuing good fortune: an intensely hopeful moment.

So much to look forward to, and yet something was not quite right.

To Mary's mind, Prisons and Correction had set out on the right foot. There had been a Royal Commission on the status of prisons, and that had gone very well. She had been busy for months, helping to coordinate bodies, reports, and press releases. She had felt part of something grand and significant. She herself was Liberal and thought prisons a sign of collective failure. If there were prisons, it was because society was imperfect and could not (or did not) care for all of its citizens alike. But she was intrigued by Franklin's idea of prison reform, and pleasantly puzzled by the idea of Art as the means to change.

After the commission's report, after the lobbying for MacKenzie Bowell, after parliamentary approval of the project, there had been the plans for the new prison, further reports, feasibility studies, statistics, preparations for the selection committee. Paper, paper, paper. Paper is the lifeblood of a government department, proof of its vitality. So, she was a member of a department that was doing well.

But paper has its laws, cycles, and stages. It has to be copied, signed by the minister, sent to various places, returned, signed again, initialled, and filed (in various cabinets) before it comes to rest in the archives. Each stage must be properly completed and signed before the next begins. And it was just this that was troubling Mary. She had seen Rundstedt's signature thousands of times. She knew it particularly well. So, she was more than a little surprised to see what appeared to be forgeries. From her first sighting of a suspicious Rundstedt signature, she'd been keeping an eye on all the documents that required his name, trying to figure out if there were, perhaps, a pattern, if the suspicious signatures came only when Rundstedt was away. So far, she'd been unable to detect a pattern. So, she kept quiet about the whole business.

As if all that weren't enough, there was also the question of St. Pierre and Mickleson.

One Wednesday, she had taken a call:

– Mr. St. Pierre speaking. Can I talk to Franklin . . . Dupuis?

– He's not in at the moment. May I take a message?

– You're his secretary?

– Yes.

– Ahh. Listen, miss, what'd you say your name was?

– It's Ms. Stanley.

– Okay, then, Miss Stanley, would you please tell Mr. Dupuis that Mr. St. Pierre called to confirm our appointment for Friday afternoon. My partner and I will be there Friday at three. Okay?

Before she could answer, he had put down the phone. Franklin seemed happy to hear the message and mentioned that they were land consultants and that Friday at three o'clock exactly the two men walked into the office without knocking. The first was tall, broad-shouldered, and well dressed: a full-length impermeable over a navy blue suit, a pale yellow shirt, and, incongruously, a black silk tie. Even his fingernails were immaculate though, oddly, his cheeks looked as though they had been imperfectly rouged.

This was Mr. St. Pierre.

– We've come to see Mr. Dupuis, he said.

The second was almost as tall, but he stooped, and he was more shabbily dressed. Where Mr. St. Pierre was dark-haired and recently coiffed, Mr. Mickleson was almost blond and his hair stood up as if windblown. Mr. Mickleson said nothing. He stood behind Mr. St. Pierre, his hands in his coat pockets, looking down at the carpet. When he walked into Franklin's office, Mary saw that Mickleson had a slight limp.

She heard Mr. St. Pierre say

– Hey, how're you?

before the door closed.

If it can be said that some men are accompanied by darkness, it should be said of St. Pierre and Mickleson. Without knowing why, Mary felt uneasy in their presence, uneasy when they were in Franklin's office, uneasy knowing of their existence, even. They were not right, though one couldn't have said how they were wrong.

Franklin did not speak to her directly about their visit, but a week later Edward filed a request for a short-term contract for something called "land consultants." A week after that, their names (Robert St. Pierre, Robin Mickleson) were on a document awaiting Franklin's initials and Rundstedt's signature. It would have been irresponsible of her *not* to make her misgivings about the men known to Franklin, so she took the contract to him herself.

– Franklin?

– Yes, Mary?

– Here's the contract for the land consultants.

– Oh! Thank you. I'll initial it right away.

– Uhm, Franklin, I just wanted to mention, I saw those men, Mr. St. Pierre and Mr. Mickleson, and I think there's something funny about them.

– What's that?

– They don't *look* like consultants, do they?

– They don't? What does a consultant look like?

– You're right, but there's something about them . . .

Franklin smiled.

– I know what you mean, he said. They're like Mutt and Jeff.

He signed the document and returned it to her so that she could leave it for Ms. Rees, who would leave it for Mr. Rundstedt.

Though it was Franklin the men had come to see, Mary so mistrusted Edward, she was inclined (perhaps even determined) to see Edward's hand behind St. Pierre and Mickleson. She suspected, with no proof, Edward was trying to finagle funds for his friends. It seemed the only reasonable explanation. Those men, Mickleson and St. Pierre, were no more "land consultants" than she was a horse. They had to be Edward's friends. So, from the moment she decided Edward was, somehow, behind St. Pierre and Mickleson, Mary tried to keep closer track of Edward's doings in the department.

That is, while doing a job she was now less certain she wanted, Mary made more work for herself. She did not have time to think of the anxiety that comes with a change in fortune. When she thought of them at all, her grandmother's money and property seemed mere facts of life, though it had been only two years since she (and her family) had inherited Eleanor's wealth.

38

REINHART ABANDONS MACKENZIE BOWELL

R einhart had completed the plans for the penitentiary in ecstasy, but it wasn't an unfamiliar ecstasy. He had been overwhelmed, exhilarated, and sleeplessly impassioned by any number of his own works. There had been perhaps a dozen paintings that had taken his life over as completely as this design had, and the experience had been just as important for him, the artist.

The difference here was in the project's origins. To begin with, he would not have guessed that a mere building would so capture his imagination. And then, the penitentiary was strange: not Canadian, not Québécois, though, to his mind, it belonged in the Gatineaus because the Gatineaus itself had prompted it, had called it out of him. He could not have imagined the penitentiary without seeing the land on which it would stand, yet it was a mystery to him that that tract of land had inspired these particular buildings. But, then, who knew the imperatives of a land, the deep reasons behind the things a land brought forth – its languages, painting, buildings, and song? No one. They were discovered in building, in imagining, in creating. Once the penitentiary was built, if it were built, the public would discover, as Reinhart had, its rootedness in the place; though, no doubt, some would think it strange or even foreign, until they were used to it.

In the days after he had given the plans to Franklin, Reinhart would have hurt anyone who suggested they be modified to serve monetary or political ends, so convinced was he that he had managed to put architecture to dignified use, perhaps for the first time since Leon Alberti. It did not trouble him (it never had) that his design was not very like a prison, that *his* penitentiary was, in some ways, impractical. Its purpose did not concern him. So long as it was built as he'd imagined, it might have held cows or swine: no matter. The vision was all.

The first thing to make him reconsider the merit of his designs was, strangely enough, Franklin's response. Franklin did not simply *like* the designs for MacKenzie Bowell, he was enraptured by them, and Reinhart felt oddly put off by Franklin's enthusiasm. It was as if he had painted an extremely flattering portrait of Franklin himself, something he had not set out to do. Besides, approval is always a disturbing thing, isn't it? Reinhart's work had met with indifference for so long, he expected some form of rebuke. So, Franklin's rapture prompted him to look at his designs from another angle. It was painful to discover this other angle, but as soon as he began to question the value of what he'd done, he found a number of things that displeased. The penitentiary was classically beautiful, it's true, but its beauty robbed it of originality. It made use of classical material, but wasn't there something *vieux jeu* about so much marble?

And wasn't it, just a little, facile? Yes, it was. Franklin Dupuis would not have adored it otherwise. How could that have happened? He had spent months absorbed by the very idea of "prison." He had despaired of finding inspiration, but when inspiration came, it was pure and he had surrendered to it because he'd had no choice. That is, he had surrendered to his deepest instincts and, in a fit of feeling, he had produced . . . designs that thrilled a civil servant. Now there was a thought that made you want to break your own fingers. No, he was being hard on himself. One is always vulnerable at the end of a work. MacKenzie Bowell had much to recommend it. It was boldly backward-looking, eccentric, practical, and . . .

The problem was, having become acquainted with the vision's flaws, he could no longer look away from them and, as time passed, Reinhart found himself less and less interested in the penitentiary's fate. This was, in fact, consistent with his attitude to his own work, with the way in which he pulled himself out of one work in order to throw himself into another. He was not interested in his paintings once they were finished, and he sometimes thought his finished work an impediment to the work he had yet to do. Looking at one of his old paintings was like meeting a slightly tiresome former lover. It was fascinating, up to a point, if a great deal of time had passed. It was sometimes interesting, if the piece had solved a puzzle or led him in a new direction. But, for the most part, looking at his own work was embarrassing. He didn't do it often.

The one most affected by Reinhart's alienation from his own work was Edward. Reinhart's enthusiasm, his commitment had helped to eclipse Edward's doubts about MacKenzie Bowell. Yes, he should have known Reinhart would abandon the prison. He abandoned everything he created, but Edward had hoped this work was different. Why? Because he needed the reassurance that came with Reinhart's belief in the project. This belief had helped Edward deal with the uncertainty he felt about Franklin's confidence. When Reinhart abandoned ship, Edward found it more difficult to ignore his misgivings and, worse, his original doubts came back, bringing new ones with them. Now, for instance, there was the matter of St. Pierre and Mickleson.

St. Pierre and Mickleson were, initially, his doing. Edward had heard of them a year before, had heard of them from a secretary to the minister of agriculture. The woman had been flirting with him for months and, after going out for drink with her, Edward had allowed himself to be seduced. She was slightly older than him, but the sex had been surprisingly good and, afterwards, he had not minded lying beside her to talk, a thing he almost never did after sex, usually preferring to leave as soon as was convenient. And she had been talkative. For hours, they'd spoken of everything: nail polish, nuclear weapons, single-malt Scotch, the perfect margarita, and life on the Hill. While talking about this minister and that, she (rather indiscreetly) mentioned having once had to use fixers. Fixers? Yes, you know, rat poison, men who solved problems in unusual ways. Not murderous, but responsible, well organized, quiet as nuns. Like, a certain minister, "you can guess who," had been having trouble getting his neighbours to let him expand his swimming pool. He didn't know what to do, but she got her brother, who "lives at the bad end of the block," to recommend a couple of men and they were really good. When the minister expanded his swimming pool, his neighbours didn't raise a squeak, not a *squeak.*

Edward had not seen the woman in some time, had avoided her even, but when Franklin mentioned, off the cuff, having explored any number of reasonable means to sway the McAllisters, Edward had thought of the "fixers" straight away. And, to help Franklin, he had gone out with the woman again and, *après les ébats amoureux,* which really were surprisingly wonderful, had asked how he could get in touch with her so-called fixers. And she had told him, because she found Edward appealing, though she had added, in a serious voice:

– They're very thorough, if you know what I mean, okay, Eddy?

He'd had no idea what she meant. He was naive and would, too late, regret his naiveté. But after assuring her he would tell no one where he'd got their coordinates, he'd passed the information on to Franklin, who had met with the men himself. Edward had been in the office the afternoon St. Pierre and Mickleson had come to meet with Franklin, but he had not been invited to speak with them, so his first impression was fleeting but memorable: St. Pierre seemed amiable, though a little odd-looking; Mickleson was quiet. Their presence was intimidating but professional. And yet, as they were leaving the office, Mickleson let out a laugh that sounded like dogs choking, a laugh that abated as abruptly as it had begun.

Franklin had not said much about the men afterwards. So, on the surface, it had all seemed unremarkable, "business as usual," and Edward might not have thought twice about the men were it not for the sound of Mickleson's laughter and, later, the fact that Franklin hired the men as "land consultants." Edward had no way of telling if they *were* land consultants, but they didn't look like the kind of men who were up on land or geography or anything of the sort. So, it seemed to him an obvious and public untruth, given that the department would be paying for St. Pierre and Mickleson's services. The subterfuge and the memory of Mickleson's laughter unsettled him and provided yet another doubt he didn't need.

After Reinhart's change of heart about the penitentiary, when Reinhart abandoned MacKenzie Bowell, Edward was left to think for himself, to sort out his feelings about it, and this was not something he enjoyed doing at all.

BOOK III

39

MOVING DAY

S tanley Stanley and his daughter walked together in Notre
Dame. Much time had passed since Eleanor's death, but
they were still the only ones to regularly visit her grave.
Stanley could have forced Gilbert to accompany them, as he had,
once or twice, in the months following Eleanor's death, but it was
not worth the trouble or the distraction. Gilbert was like a
monkey let loose in the cemetery, wandering around the monuments, scratching himself, impatient, scarcely able to stand still at
his grandmother's headstone. Nor could his father hit him a good
one, considering the place, and the respect due the dead. So, it
was better to leave Gil at home.

As for Beatrice: she had come, in the beginning, but had felt
hypocritical.

It was sad to think how resentment endured, but Stanley did
not want remembrance to cause pain, so he and Mary went on
their own.

They were not awkward together. If there was tension, it was
only in Stanley's awareness that Mary had, as she grew, become a
woman of whom he was proud but with whom he did not, he
felt, share intellectual ground. She had gone beyond him. She
thought about the world in ways more subtle, it seemed to him,

than he could. She would, for instance, happily speak of politics and ideology and, despite his best efforts to understand, he was inevitably left behind after a while. Still, he would smile as if he understood, to encourage her, because he was proud and because he loved the seriousness with which she spoke.

For Mary, there *had* been tension. Younger, she'd been embarrassed by his difficulties with her words. At his instigation, she would recount the things she'd learned, going on about this or that until she saw he was not paying attention. She'd been insulted by his lack of attention and had stopped speaking to him about bookish things until, one evening, as they sat together on the sofa watching Tommy Hunter, he said to her, in a kind voice

– It's too bad we don't talk any more, isn't it?

– What do you mean, Dad?

– I miss you talking.

– We talk all the time.

– Not about anything that matters.

– Like what, Dad?

– I don't know, but we used to talk about all sorts of things. I don't always know what you're talking about, Mare, but that doesn't mean I don't want to hear it.

After that, she spoke to him about whatever was on her mind, finding a language they could share: a third language, somewhere between the one in which she'd been schooled and the one her father spoke. It was like building together, each from his or her own side, a bridge on which they could meet. In fact, one of the unexpected gifts of Eleanor's death was that the two who missed her most, or the only two who missed her at all, grew closer as they visited her grave, their common ground. It was not that Stanley loved his daughter *more* after his mother's death but, rather, that he met the adult his daughter had become and he liked her very much, would have liked her even were she not his daughter.

So, Stanley and Mary walked together in the cemetery that held Eleanor's remains. There was no anniversary to mark, but it was a significant occasion nonetheless. It was the day they were to take possession of their new house in the Glebe. Beatrice, Stanley, and Gilbert were to take possession. Mary had, to her family's surprise, moved into her grandmother's house.

The move had been quite a process. She'd had to give the tenants notice, and then have men turn the building back into the Victorian home it had once been. And, even so, she was still up to her neck in the many and mysterious shorings up her home required. As if that weren't enough, there were the small but unignorable concerns she had about work: particularly the four or five irregularities around Rundstedt's signature she'd seen since she'd decided to keep track. They were a real puzzle, as it was unclear who was forging the signatures or why. She was inclined to blame Edward, but what if behind Edward there were Franklin, or behind them both Rundstedt who, because he was often away, might have approved the false signatures. It was hard to think straight with such a conundrum in mind. And though she might have wished to let her father in on her concerns, she felt honour-bound to keep them to herself.

As they walked through the cemetery, the sky was bright blue with slow-moving clouds moving slowly above. It was windless and warm and, as much to ease her own mind as to distract her father from his thoughts of moving, Mary asked

– Dad, what do you think it means to be loyal?

– You mean, answered Stanley, if your friend's wrong, what are you going to do? I'm not sure I'm the one to ask, Mare. I've only ever been loyal to your mother.

– No, you mean *faithful*, Dad. You've been *faithful* to Mom.

– Well, it's pretty easy being faithful to my wife, Mary. But I mean *loyal*. Whenever there's something to do or when I'm think-ing about buying something, let's say, I think about your mother first. How's it going to affect her. That's what I mean. I'm not one of these guys who're loyal to a hockey club or something. I just don't care about anything as much as I care about your mother and you and your brother. So, if someone I knew was fouling up I'd say something about it. Right is right and I don't care what anybody says. I'm not saying I'm perfect and maybe I haven't always been as loyal as I should be, but that's how I try to live.

– Hmm . . . , said Mary.

She was going to point out that, unfortunately, she did not have someone on whom to ground her life, when she saw her favourite headstone: a stone that had obviously been in the cemetery for centuries. It was of sandstone, worn down, wind-shaped, the name of the dead obliterated. All that was left was a wing, which had, perhaps, belonged to a graven angel and a hand, its finger pointing downward. Mary could never pass it without mentioning her amazement that a hand and a wing should be so mysteriously clear, while time, wind, and rain had wiped everything else from the face of the stone. It was as if the elements had contrived an obscure but intriguing message.

– There's your stone, her father said.

And both of them stopped to admire it before moving on. Perhaps feeling he hadn't properly answered her question and wishing to draw her out again, Stanley asked

– What's Mr. Rundstedt doing these days?

– He's in his riding, out promoting free trade.

Mary paused. She reaffirmed her admiration for Rundstedt. He worked hard. He was a tireless campaigner and, in only a few years, he had managed to completely quell her doubts about his character and merit. Still, there had recently been a minor incident. Ruth Rees had been away, so Mary had been opening mail addressed to the minister when she came upon a package from overseas: a flat, brown envelope that smelled of soap. In the package was a stone carving of the Eiffel Tower: grey, unremarkable. That, in itself, was not at all strange. People sent the most peculiar things: bars of soap carved to look like penises (or was it grain silos?), nail files, cookie tins filled with cookies or dead mice (and, in one case, an elegant blue tin filled with shortbread cookies, beneath which there had been a dead robin), and so on. Security was supposed to catch these things, but they almost never did. The stone came with no explanation, just a piece of paper with two small letters stamped on it: "GL, from Paris." A receipt?

She had handed him the package when he was next in the office.

– *What's this?* Rundstedt asked.

– *I think it's a souvenir.*

He had smiled, pushed the package away, and said

– *Keep it for the office*

when he noticed the square of paper with the initial on it. That was the interesting moment. He held the paper up between his thumb and forefinger, considered it for a second, and then turned briefly beet red.

– *I remember now,* he'd said. *It's for my wife. I forgot.*

– That was nice of him, said Stanley, buying something for his wife.

Mary was going to say Rundstedt should have had no cause for embarrassment, but they had come to Eleanor's grave.

– Dad? she asked. Don't you think Gran should have a bigger headstone?

Eleanor's headstone was a rectangle of granite, rust coloured, three feet high, and her name was so deeply engraved it was legible from quite a distance.

Stanley thought about it.

– No, he said finally. She wasn't fancy.

He walked slowly around the stone.

– I don't think it matters anyway, he said. Do you think it matters?

No, it didn't matter. It was for their benefit, not hers, and it was good the way it was.

– Did you love her, when you were a boy, Dad?

This was the first time anyone had asked him that in quite that way. Stanley looked down at the name on the stone:

ELEANOR STANLEY

Yes, he had loved her when he was a boy, although . . . is it love at all, the feeling one has for one's parents, or is it something else, an instinct say, a feeling like a pilot light that won't go out? He loved his daughter. This he knew because the instant he had seen her small, perfect self, he had felt that love. There was a before and an after. Before there had been nothing and, then, at the sight of his daughter, love came to, within him. Where Eleanor was concerned, there had been no before. He had, as far as he could say, been born with this feeling for his mother and, over the years, he'd had to protect it . . . from her most of all, from the one person who seemed intent on snuffing it out. And what did he feel now she was dead? Well, relief, disappointment, sadness, and, despite all, the feeling (whether "love" or "instinct") he'd always had: helpless pleasure at the thought of her and an equally help-less dread at the thought of what she might say or do. Did he love her, then, when he was a boy? Yes, he'd certainly thought so. So,

– Yes, he answered.

Mary sighed.

– Isn't it sad, she said, that you never knew your father?

Taken aback, Stanley asked

– Why would I want to know *him*?

– Well, he was your father, wasn't he? My grandfather?

– By mistake, said Stanley. He wasn't much of a man.

– But Gran loved him. She kept his picture all those years.

– I don't think so, Mary.

– What are you talking about, Dad? Didn't you ever see it?

– No, I never saw his picture.

Now it was Mary taken aback. She had always supposed her father discouraged mention of Robert Stanley because the subject was painful, because he did not want to discuss the longing he felt. It had never occurred to her that he might be incurious or even troubled by his father's memory. She hesitated to show him the photograph. A distant echo of the promise she'd made to her grandmother momentarily stopped her, but it seemed wrong to keep this from him.

– Look, she said, here's his picture.

Ever since her grandmother's death, she kept the photo of Lord Robert Stanley with her at all times, in the pages of whatever book she was reading. She kept it there along with a photograph of Eleanor as a young woman, but it was Lord Stanley she found most interesting. He stood before a chapel with a tall bell tower. He was squinting at the camera, the sun in his face, smiling nonetheless. He was dressed in a white linen suit, had on a dark tie, and his right hand was in the pocket of his jacket. To Mary, his face was like a familiar and cherished thing seen from an unusual angle.

The photograph did not, at first, have any effect on Stanley. He politely took it, glanced at the sepia face, felt a shudder of dislike at the sight of the man's demeanour, then turned it over. There on the back of the photo was his father's name written in what was unmistakably his mother's hand, along with the words *Mt. St. Benedict*. That in itself was surprising. His mother had never, as far as he knew, been sentimental. She had been unsentimental on the subject of his father. To see her handwriting on the back of Robert Stanley's photo was a strange revelation, an intimation that his mother had been more mysterious than he'd imagined, and he had imagined her mysterious indeed. Why had she kept this from him? The man, slight and dignified, did not seem capable of violence. So, what could she have been hiding? Her love for him? Why would she hide that? Was she the one who'd taken the picture, and was his smile for her? No, no, no. It was too late. His contempt for the man he assumed his father had been was too deep for this moment to be anything but unmanageable dissonance. He would never see Robert Stanley as his father, never accept him, and yet . . . when he gave the photograph back to his daughter he did feel a certain release, a certain lightness. Had his "father" been there before him, instead of this sepia image, Stanley might have felt, well, a little less hostile, perhaps even curious.

After he had returned the photograph to his daughter, and when sufficient time had passed so Mary would not confuse his affection for gratitude at her mention of his "father," Stanley put his arm in his daughter's arm and they walked a little way, arm in arm, until it became uncomfortable because each had his or her own rhythm and because, as they returned to the world outside the cemetery, their worries and anxieties returned to them and, so, returned them to themselves.

The house Beatrice had chosen was relatively modest. Its ceilings were tall enough (ten feet) but not impressive. Its backyard was of a decent size, but it was plain. Its basement was spacious, dry, and high-ceilinged, but the floor was concrete. The whole had recently been painted a flat white and the effect was of near Quakerish severity, but Beatrice had taken to it on first sight.

The house's owners, Mr. and Mrs. Molnar, an older Hungarian couple, had had the For Sale placard put up only a day before the Stanleys offered to buy it. They had put the house on the market for more than it was worth, not because they were greedy but because they had been indecisive. They'd spent twenty years in the house, had cared for it as if it were their last home. And it might have been their final home, but age, the long staircase, and the sadness of having lost Otto, their beloved dachshund, had convinced them otherwise. Since Otto's death, the house had begun to feel like a mausoleum. It was far too big for them. They needed something smaller, or so they thought and, in a brief fit of decisiveness, they had put the house on the market.

Now, if you had to live in the Glebe, this was the very place to do it. The house was understated but dignified. For Stanley, however, this purchase was accompanied by the persistent feeling they had done wrong. It wasn't displacing the Molnars that troubled him. Mrs. Molnar had said

– We're so happy the house is going to good people.

No, it was rather that Stanley was troubled by the idea they had not earned the home, had not worked to make it theirs, did not deserve the good fortune that came with his mother's legacy. He hid his feelings from Beatrice, because he did not want to dampen her pleasure, but on the day they took possession of the house he was ambivalent and quiet.

From the cemetery, Stanley and Mary had driven to 3rd, where they met Beatrice and Gilbert.

– How was Granny? asked Gilbert.

It was all Stanley could do to keep from striking the boy. He glared at him, but then smiled bravely at Beatrice as she turned the key in the front door. The house opened up to them, and it was like seeing it for the first time: wooden floors, polished and gleaming, walls white and uncurved, tall windows in every room. And how quiet it was, until Beatrice opened a window in the living room and the sounds of the city made their way in.

Gilbert, overjoyed but feigning boredom, went up to the third floor where he had three large rooms for himself, an apartment with which he could do as he liked. Beatrice and Mary went together to the kitchen to make tea in the kettle and cups Beatrice had brought from the house on Spadina. Stanley stood in the drawing room, which led to the dining room, which led to the kitchen. In an hour or so, men from the Bay would deliver furniture: sofas, a loveseat, armchairs, an enormous oak table, high-backed wooden chairs (that reminded him of medieval artifacts), floor lamps, side tables, brass beds (three), china, silverware, an aquamarine rug from Pakistan and another from Iran (chosen by Beatrice for their colours; she had never seemed so keen on colour before), a new stove, a new refrigerator . . .

Well, it wasn't so bad, was it?

As he stood in the drawing room, he thought about work. He had retired from the post office. It would not have been right to take work from someone who needed it, but this was the first time Stanley would be without a job. What would he do exactly? What was home without work? Wasn't it work that had made home home?

– Here's your tea, Dad.

Mary handed him one of the cups from the old house, his favourite: a mug on which the words IF YOU'RE CLOSE ENOUGH TO READ THIS, BUGGER OFF! had faded to near invisibility. Beatrice stood beside him, her arm around his waist.

– By tomorrow, it'll look just like home, she said.

– Looks like home already, Stanley answered.

Which, perhaps, it did, if your version of home happened to include estrangement, loss, and the nagging sense you were in a museum.

The house was home to neither of them, and would not be for a long time, if at all.

Home was now, as it had been at the start of their life together, each other. The house would have to get used to them, which it would do as they did the small things: putting up drapes, dressing the beds, sweeping the floors, sitting out in the garden, making the place theirs, inhabiting its interiors, learning its drafts and warm currents.

– Well, it isn't rocket science, thought Stanley.

Which was true, astrophysics being easier than homemaking.

40

ST. PIERRE AND MICKLESON

St. Pierre and Mickleson were not land consultants. Their line of work had no name, though it had a long and obscure tradition. And although they had markedly differ-ent personalities, St. Pierre and Mickleson shared two qualities that suited them for each other and for their work: a sense of humour and an abiding respect for professionalism, for things done not just rightly but precisely. Also, they were both intellec-tually placid, untroubled by ideas or ideology. They felt no scorn for others nor any sense of their own superiority. They needed no justifications for their actions and could not be put off by pangs of conscience.

They had been asked to persuade Mr. and Mrs. McAllister to sell their property in the Gatineaus. The McAllisters were the last of the cottagers to hold out. All the others (Fields, Thompsons, and Burrs) had sold their holdings and moved on, shortly after discovering their places would be near a penitentiary. The McAllisters, however, were hard-headed. They seemed genuine in their concern for the environment and, as they owned one of the only roads into the land on which the prison was to be built, it was, perhaps, their hope the government would reconsider the location of the penitentiary.

St. Pierre and Mickleson had done all sorts of research on the McAllisters, charting their comings and goings, listening in on their telephone conversations, listening in on their most private exchanges, all in order to discover the kind of people they were: successful (yes), sophisticated (not really), cultured (not particularly), honest (not especially), faithful (not inevitably), brave (no, not at all). They were a couple with a deeply held belief in their own moral superiority; they seemed to enjoy (or Mr. McAllister seemed to enjoy) exercising authority; they had worked hard for what they had and, as with a good many adults who have no children, they adored their pets: a poodle and a Havanese.

In other words, they were almost statistically normal.

On a Saturday night in spring, when Mr. and Mrs. McAllister were at home in Ottawa preparing for bed, St. Pierre and Mickleson knocked at their front door. It was Mrs. McAllister who answered.
– Yes?
she asked, holding the door open only enough to let her face out.

Mickleson entered first, kicking the door open and knocking Mrs. McAllister backwards. The Havanese, Heraclitus, jumped up and down excitedly, barking at the intruders. So as he shut the door behind him, St. Pierre took a pistol from his coat pocket and shot the dog. The report was soft, there was the sudden sharp stink of gunfire, and the dog looked to have been pulverized: bits of fur clung to the walls and the floor, and there was blood everywhere.

Mr. McAllister, in pyjamas and housecoat, was there on the staircase. This made Mickleson's task much easier. He moved quickly to Mr. McAllister and hit him first in the solar plexus and then in the mouth, straightening him out, and knocking him backwards onto the steps. He then went up to the second floor and checked its rooms for guests.

From the moment Mickleson forced his way in to the moment he struck Mr. McAllister, not one minute passed, but for Mrs.

McAllister it was as if an eternity unfurled. She did not know where to look, what she was supposed to feel, what she was supposed to do. When she saw her husband lying on the stairs, she began a scream that was immediately cut short by St. Pierre.

He put a hand over her mouth and said (resolutely, reassuringly, just loudly enough to be heard above the commotion)

– If you make a sound, I'll shoot the other dog. You understand?

She understood exactly. The poodle, Lucy, had wandered in to observe the disturbance. Though usually an excitable dog, she sat up quietly, puzzled, looking from Mrs. McAllister to Mr. McAllister and back, before thoughtfully licking some of the blood from the floor. Mrs. McAllister, though she was on the verge of hysterics, bit her own tongue to keep herself quiet.

As he descended the stairs, Mickleson helped Mr. McAllister to his feet, guided him to the living room, and allowed him to fall on the sofa. St. Pierre did the same with Mrs. McAllister, one hand on her elbow, guiding her around the poodle. When the McAllisters were sitting, St. Pierre asked

– Are you comfortable?

but as neither answered, Mickleson fired into one of the aquaria in the room. Gallons of water and a handful of gasping fish wet the carpet and the floor.

– Are you comfortable? St. Pierre repeated.

This time, Mr. McAllister managed a groan that was like

– Yes.

– Good, said St. Pierre. I want your complete attention, okay? We're not going to kill you.

– Really? asked Mickleson.

St. Pierre smiled, looked at his watch, and addressed the McAllisters.

– We have friends, he said, interested in your property in the Gatineaus. Apparently, you have a lovely cottage there. Is that right?

It would be difficult to exaggerate the confusion St. Pierre's question aroused in the McAllisters. Mr. McAllister, still bleeding from the nose, was not rightly conscious. Nothing seemed real, save the possibility of his own death, and it was absurd that his death should have anything to do with the Gatineaus. He couldn't stop himself from saying, to himself as much as to the intruders

– The cottage is closed. We haven't opened it yet.

As if there had been some mistake.

Mrs. McAllister was convinced her silence was the price of her dog's safety but, hearing her husband speak, understanding his tone, she ventured a few words, in the sudden, bright hope they would clear matters up.

– You must have the wrong house, she said. Our cottage is still closed.

– No, we have the right house, said St. Pierre. Our friends would like to buy your property.

– It isn't for sale, said Mr. McAllister.

As if he had discovered a key.

– No, it isn't, said St. Pierre, but it will be.

– When? asked Mr. McAllister.

– As soon as possible, said St. Pierre. Tomorrow or the day after. Soon. You have a week to put your property on the market. If not, we'll have to remind you how interested we are.

Again, St. Pierre looked at his watch.

– Our friends will put in an offer for $25,000, and you'll accept it immediately, okay? And one last thing. I know I don't have to mention it, but it's good to get these things out in the open. It would be a bad idea for you to go to the police. You understand? The only thing we've done so far is kill Toto. How long would they put us away for that?

– Not long at all, answered Mickleson.

– That's right, said St. Pierre. The system always favours the criminal.

His voice was the voice of a well-wisher.

– Another thing, he said. You work for the *Citizen*. It would be unfortunate for the people you love if anything about this saw the light of day. You know what I mean?

Mr. McAllister was confused, and looked it. St. Pierre repeated
– We wouldn't want to hear about our business in the newspaper, you understand?
– Yes, said Mr. McAllister. Yes, I understand.
though, in fact, he did not.

St. Pierre and Mickleson then walked out of the living room, and out of the shambles they had made of the McAllisters' home. It had taken them less than fifteen minutes.

The McAllisters were thoroughly and permanently traumatized. Though the physical damage they suffered was not severe or permanent, they never recovered. Nor did they need any further persuasion. Frightened as they were, it was not in them to fight for land that was, in the end, recreational. Their cottage in the Gatineaus was on offer a week after the invasion. And it was bought by a numbered company that paid them exactly $25,000 for their loss. And so, a few months after St. Pierre and Mickleson visited the McAllisters, the last of the private property that abutted the prison's site belonged to a legitimate, numbered corporation that sold its holdings to the government at a profit.

41

FRANÇOIS' SCRUPLES

F or very little money, in order to help a friend and to distract himself from concerns that had been weighing on
him, François had agreed to do quantity surveying for the
new federal penitentiary. He hoped his work would be useful,
that it would give Franklin a "heads-up" where costs were concerned, but really he had taken the project because numbers,
research, tidy organizing all brought him peace and reacquainted
him with work he loved.

Still, after some time with the architect's designs, it seemed to
François as if he'd been asked to cost out a hallucination. It wasn't
that he'd had difficulty figuring the costs of the penitentiary. The
difficulty was in accepting that a civil servant (Franklin), an
architect (R. Mauer), and a Cabinet minister (A. Rundstedt)
would think of building such a compound, never mind building
it as a prison.

Here was MacKenzie Bowell Federal Penitentiary:

An immense marble piazza, in the centre of which was a circular building, also marble, with four entrances: north, south, east,
west. The entrances were classical: marble columns with plinths
supporting marble vaults, the doors oversized (24 feet high, 12 feet
wide) and bronze. The circular building was itself immense, built

of green and white marble. The first floor was some 48' high, surrounded by 24 Doric columns that supported the second floor (16' high) which itself used 24 (smaller) columns to support a vaulted roof (green and white marble) at the very top of which was a small-scale version of the entire building: narrow columns supporting a vaulted roof. At the south end of the piazza, there were two fountains, one on either side of the central building: marble, octagonal basins. Then there were the buildings that surrounded the piazza on three sides (north, east, and west).

Something classical must have inspired the architect's delirium. Not all of the buildings were of marble, but most of them had arches or columns, or arches *and* columns. A building on the east side was typical. It was three storeys high, a rectangle. Doric columns supported the second floor, which was notable for its profusion of tall windows, *trompe l'oeil* pillars, and elaborately moulded windowframes. The third floor had pillars that supported the roof, but it was unusual for its balcony, a generous balcony that went round the entire floor, affording a view onto the piazza.

In a word, there was nothing practical about Mauer's design. There were no fences, walls, or obvious guard posts. The compound was as porous as a small city, and it was difficult to see how the prisoners would be effectively watched. There was, perhaps, something humane in all this. It was as if a society had decided to keep its scruff in a Renaissance setting, sending rapists and murderers to Bassano del Grappo, say, or Arezzo. Thought of in this way, there was something almost touching in Mauer's design, but it took little experience with materials to understand that the buildings would cost the public millions and, even if baser materials were used, would do poorly what it was designed to do.

You could see it from here or, at least, François could see it, now, after months of consideration: MacKenzie Bowell was a white elephant. Months after he had submitted the figures for the cost of the penitentiary, months after it had been approved by the selection committee, and to his own surprise, François Ricard was offended. He was not *personally* offended. The intellectual he was could find reasons to approve of MacKenzie Bowell: it was fantastic, innovative in its retrospection, perhaps even a moment in the rethinking of incarceration. Rather, he was *civically* offended. His communal self was offended by the thought of spending so much money on what was, in effect, a wager. There were so many needs. A certain class of citizen was doing well, in Canada, but there seemed to be more, and more evident, poverty. He had visited Toronto for a conference and been overwhelmed by two things: the pace of the city (mindlessly brisk) and the number of unfortunates living on the street. The shame he'd felt at the sight of bodies wrapped in dirty overcoats, curled up on the pavement like dogs, returned to him at the thought of the penitentiary. There were vagrants in Ottawa, of course, but there were more of them in Toronto. In Toronto, when François remarked on the number of homeless, his companion had sighed and said

– It's pretty sad, eh?

But it hadn't seemed sad to François. It had seemed hypocritical and cruel. Cruel, for obvious reasons: who could live while men and women froze to the grates they clung to for warmth? Hypocritical, because he lived in a country where poverty was thought to be a foreign gentleman. Poverty lived in Africa, visited Asia, was in South America on vacation. Thinking about the plans for the penitentiary, François thought of domestic poverty and it seemed to him that this prison was a poisoned chalice.

Why? Money.

Though Franklin might justify the expense, he could not prove that spending on marble and polished brass was better for society than care of the homeless. Or, if he could, François wanted to hear the proof for himself. Perhaps it wasn't too late to have the ministry reconsider the choice of materials if nothing else. In light of the estimates he'd given them (and the price for the marble alone was, one would have thought, prohibitive), MacKenzie Bowell seemed the product of a ministry (or an administration)

intent on social experiment, which made Franklin the *porte-parole*
of good, if misguided, intentions. However, late or not, someone
needed to be told that there was more to government than interesting ideas or good intentions.

François called Franklin's office and arranged to meet him the
following day at two in the afternoon. So, when he arrived, he
was surprised to find Franklin was away.

There was only one person in the office, a young woman who
looked oddly familiar.

– May I help you? she said. Puis-je vous aider?

There was something about the way she spoke, an ease.
François considered her for a moment before speaking, in French,
though she was almost certainly anglophone. He said

– Je m'appelle François Ricard. Je suis venu voir M. Dupuis.
Nous avions rendez-vous à quatorze heures, je crois.

– Ah, she said. Malheureusement, M. Dupuis n'est pas encore
de retour. Mais je m'attends à c'qu'il revienne bientôt.

Her French sounded Belgian, Liègeois, say, though she was
dark-skinned, perhaps Caribbean.

– Et vous vous appelez . . .? he asked.

– Mary Stanley, she answered.

Touching the back of a chair a few feet from her desk, he asked

– Ça vous dérangerait si j'attends içi, Madelle Stanley?

– Pas du tout, she answered, je vous en prie.

François now had the curious feeling they'd met in high school,
though this was improbable, as she was obviously younger. But
the feeling was pleasant and, when he was not reading his novel by
Modiano, the two of them carried on sparse but light conversation (about the Byward Market, mostly, and how one used to be
able to buy live pigs, goats and chickens . . . and about Parliament)
until almost three thirty.

Having relaxed in François' company, Mary inadvertently
spoke English. She immediately apologized.

– No need to apologize, said François. I speak English.

– I'm glad, she said.

And blushed, not certain which language to use, until François said

– This new penitentiary of yours is quite the project, isn't it?

– I'm afraid I don't know much about it, she said politely.

And looked down at the papers in front of her. After a while, he said

– Look, I'd love to stay a little longer, but I'm afraid I must go. Please tell Franklin I was here. And I hope we'll talk again, the two of us.

– Yes, that would be nice, said Mary. Thank you.

As he got up, François handed her his business card:

François Ricard
Transport Canada / Transports Canada
1-800-535-1177

– I enjoyed talking to you, he said. Maybe we can do it again sometime.

It was difficult to figure why a man from Transport was interested in the penitentiary, but she let that pass. The important thing was the impression he left. She'd felt, instinctively, she could trust him. The one she was unsure of was herself. She found she had actually *wanted* to talk about the prison as if that might have led to talk about the goings-on around her. Something was not right in the ministry and she felt, knowing things were not right, part of something shady. This feeling of "shadiness" was actually more disturbing to her than if her suspicions (about forgeries) or her fears (about St. Pierre and Mickleson) had been confirmed. That is, being a person of strong moral backbone, Mary found doubt unbearable.

Though she had tried to share her initial suspicions of St. Pierre and Mickleson with Franklin, she'd told no one of her subsequent investigation of the duo. Of course, her "investigation" hadn't got very far. She had tried to track the men down, to check their references, only to discover that none of their references added up. They had both listed their most recent employer as

Far Western Land, Inc.

but when she'd called Far Western, she had got

Carol's Hair Salon

In fact, all the telephone numbers they'd left, including their business numbers, were for salons. She had dialed all of them, a few of them more than once, and by the end she had felt oddly disturbed, as if she'd had a waking dream about telephone numbers. She had expected to discover that the men were not what they claimed to be. She had intended to report her findings to Franklin, to warn him. Instead, she kept the episode to herself because, for all intents and purposes, St. Pierre and Mickleson were ghosts or, worse, the kind of men who *could* not exist even when they clearly did. She was not frightened exactly, but she was disturbed. It was clear to her that the non-existence of St. Pierre and Mickleson could not be revealed without some understanding of why the men had hidden themselves (or were hidden by others) or who knew about their non-existence. Did Franklin know? He had hired them, after all.

She'd had no right to verify the references given by St. Pierre and Mickleson. The official business of the department was not, strictly speaking, her concern. And yet, she had verified and she was concerned. Could she follow her father's advice, she would have told someone something, but her circumstances were such that she neither knew *what* to tell nor to *whom* she should tell it.

She turned François' card over, as if there might be some clue to the man on its reverse side, and wondered if she should call him, nothing more in mind than tea and talk. She also wondered, as she always did, how soon she should call, if she were to call at all, and if it were polite to suggest a simple tea after work or, perhaps, a meal somewhere, the Khyber Pass, say.

On entering the Khyber Pass, Mary looked for a table away from the other diners.

When François arrived, not long after her, she had to stand and wave at him, feeling graceless.

She might have enjoyed the physical attraction that flared up at the sight of him: well dressed, nicely shaved, his hair dark but not oily, his nose straight. But the attraction made her feel frivolous, as if it were wrong to take him in *that* way, what with them being mere acquaintances, two civil servants talking, that's all, though it pleased her to be with a man she found attractive. And why shouldn't it, she thought, why shouldn't it?

After words about the weather (cool), the Liberal campaign (ineffectual), John Turner (untrustworthy), and Brian Mulroney (a self-important martinet with a heartfelt vision of the country), they were surprised to find the waiter beside them waiting for their order. Neither had even glanced at the menu.

– A moment, please, said François.

– Of course, said the waiter.

Mourgh, aush, qabili pilau, kofta nakhod, lamb and spinach . . .

– Have you been here before? Mary asked.

– Yes, I have, answered François. I've liked everything. This was a good choice.

It was Mary's second visit and, as she couldn't remember what she'd had the first time, she let him order: qabili pilau (rice with lamb, carrots, raisins, cumin, and saffron . . . an intoxicating fragrance) for her, lamb and spinach for himself, a Riesling for the table and Bride's Fingers for dessert. The most enjoyable meal she had had in years or, at least, it would be in retrospect. She was distracted from the taste of pilau and wine by her interest in him.

How open he was, without being effusive, and how attentive. He had told her about his son, his late wife, the work he did at Transport. Moved by his quiet generosity, Mary spoke of her own concerns, but sideways. She asked if he believed in astrology. (He didn't, though he knew he was Sagittarius.) And then she asked if he didn't agree handwriting is a better indicator of personality. He agreed in principle, though he was skeptical here too. And finally, they began to talk about what "evil" handwriting might look like. Would it be sloppy, ill formed, ragged, or, perhaps, on the contrary, smooth as silk?

At this point, their conversation was interrupted by a woman who said

– François? I thought it was you. What are you doing hidden back here?

François smiled and stood up to embrace Louise Dylan. The man who was with her came forward as well.

– Walter! How nice to see you, said François.

He introduced both of them to Mary, then asked

– Where's Paul?

– I don't know, said Louise. We're divorced.

– I'm sorry. I didn't know. I haven't seen anyone for a while. Is everything all right?

As the three spoke, Mary was, briefly, left out of the conversation. These, then, were François' friends. The woman had an appealing smile. Attractive. There was something in the way she held herself, the way she dressed, that reminded Mary of her mother. The man, Walter, was a different matter. Even in the dim light, he looked familiar. He was tall, slender, and quiet; quiet, even when he spoke. Perhaps he was English: confident and a little cool, as she thought the English, though she didn't know any Englishmen.

Walter looked at her and smiled, his head to one side.

– Do we know each other? he asked.

– I think so, Mary answered. But I can't remember how.

Walter was about to politely echo her thought when, as if a light had been turned on in a dark room, he had a vivid and precise image of her: her hand on his arm, as she asked him to listen to the story of her . . . what was it? Someone in her family?

– We met on the Alexandra Bridge, said Walter.

– Oh, yes, said Mary. What a good memory you have. When was that?

– I'm not sure, said Walter. Two years ago?

When had he tried to jump from the Alexandra? A long time ago, it seemed. And yet, yes, though she clearly did not remember, this was the young woman who'd stopped him from jumping. She had saved him, perhaps it was natural he remember *her* more than she remembered him.

Louise reached back to put her hand in Walter's and asked

– You two know each other?

– No, said Walter. But we've met before.

– That's wonderful, said Louise.

Their collective causerie lasted no more than five minutes, after which François suggested they should all meet on some other occasion. Then Walter and Louise walked out of the Khyber Pass, bodies close, a sight that unexpectedly saddened the two who stayed. Mary and François finished dessert in distracted silence, trying to recover the thread of their own conversation. François was sad at the thought of how perishable love was while Mary was saddened by how elusive love seemed to be.

When they returned to their conversation, both were slightly more formal.

– Would you like to walk for a while? asked François. It's still early.

– Yes, that would be good. I can work some of these calories off.

– You certainly don't need to, François said.

In the moments that followed his payment of the bill, as they rose from the table, François heard (as if it had suddenly flared up) the music that was playing on the restaurant's stereo. It was something ineffable, like a Middle Eastern blues, the perfect accompaniment to the wistful pleasure this evening had become.

– Please, what is the music? he asked the waiter.

– "Gol-e Yakh," the waiter answered.

It was said quickly, as if merely to jog François' memory, though this was, in fact, the first time he'd heard it.

– Oh yes, said François. Thank you.

As if his memory had indeed coughed up what was needed.

They walked at the edges of the Market: from King Edward to St. Patrick, St. Patrick to Dalhousie, Dalhousie to Clarence and Clarence to Majors Hill. They did not speak much, but they recovered an ease in the surrounding quiet of the evening. At one point, Mary thought to mention her grandmother but did not. François recounted how he'd broken his thumb playing street hockey on Guigues, an admission that made her feel suddenly protective of him or, rather, protective of the boy he had been when he had broken his thumb.

When they came to Majors Hill Park, they gazed at the Parliament Buildings and over at Hull and then, as if the walk had loosened their tongues or triggered a need, they began to talk. About nothing in particular, at first, and then about themselves: parents, homes, and childhoods. And when, after an hour or so, it was time to go their separate ways, they shook hands and kissed each other's cheeks, awkwardly, and agreed they would see each other again, there being so much left to say about home and childhood.

42

A TROUBLED LUNCH

On the afternoon Franklin was to have met François Ricard, he and Edward had a long lunch at the Mayflower. They often ate lunch together, often at the Mayflower. The food was passable and it could be eaten away from parliamentarians, most of whom ate in the Market or on Bank Street or in the (God grant their senses reprieve) cafeteria.

For the first while, they spoke of MacKenzie Bowell. Rather, Franklin spoke. Cabinet seemed certain to reduce Reinhart's design to such a shadow of itself, it seemed to him the penitentiary would be more valuable for the bricks and copper used to build it than for the effect it would have on anyone, let alone its inmates. But it hadn't come to that yet. And a great idea, as this penitentiary was, would surely find its way into the world.

During what was, in effect, Franklin's effort to boost his own spirits, Edward contributed what encouragement he could. He asked the occasional question

– Is the prime minister behind the penitentiary?
and made the occasional point
– Maybe Cabinet doesn't get it
but, in fact, his mind was on something else. He did not quite take in Franklin's words or mood, because he was himself upset.

Why? Because, a week gone, he had met with Mickleson in the Gatineaus.

Actually, Edward was to have met St. Pierre. Franklin had asked him to take new pictures of MacKenzie Bowell's site when St. Pierre called to arrange an exchange: he had an envelope for which he wished to exchange money. What was in the envelope, Franklin never said, but as the prison's site was halfway between Ottawa and the place where St. Pierre and Mickleson were "at work," he suggested Edward take the photos *and* make the exchange.

All might have gone well too, save that St. Pierre's mother had died suddenly and he'd left the vicinity to attend her funeral. So, it was Mickleson who met Edward in the Gatineaus, at the site of the penitentiary, alone, in midafternoon.

To Edward, the landscape was unnerving. He found it unlikeable and antagonistic, as if the ground, a living being, after all, reciprocated his dislike. The day itself was filled with short, sharp sounds, the rain was persistent and cold, and then there was Mickleson himself. You could feel he was a peculiar man. It wasn't his looks, though he was not handsome, but his being.

Edward arrived at the appointed time, but at first Mickleson was nowhere to be seen, and Edward cursed him, *sotto voce*. Then, as he was about to return to his car, Mickleson suddenly appeared and said

– Nice day for it.

Edward jumped backwards, into the branches of a spruce, bringing a shower's shower on them.

– Jeez, you scared the heck out of me, he said.

Mickleson looked him over and smiled. He patted Edward on the back, as if to say "that a boy," and pointed in the direction of a car that, Edward now saw, was parked near his own. Without another word, Mickleson preceded him, opened the car door for him, and, after he himself had climbed in, handed over an envelope.

It all seemed so very odd. Edward was in a Volkswagen with a man who intimidated him, yet he was relieved once he'd taken the envelope and handed his over. Although the day had been too dark and wet to take any clear photos, he had accomplished this one useful thing, at least. He felt a little petty for having cursed Mickleson's lateness. He now tried to be considerate.

He said

– Thanks

and then, after a pause

– So . . . must have been quite the job getting the owners to sell, eh?

It was none of his business what Mickleson and St. Pierre did and, moreover, Edward did not want to know any details. He had simply asked the kind of question one asks to be polite. He expected no more than a perfunctory answer, after which he would have left Mickleson's car in a good mood. His question unexpectedly upset Mickleson, however. Who knows why? Perhaps Mickleson was upset by his partner's loss, or Mickleson hated the sight of Edward Muir, or Mickleson disliked the weather. Whatever it was, when Edward said

– *Must have been difficult . . .*

Mickleson thought

– Fuck you, you ugly little time-server.

For Mickleson, Edward was part of a world that pretended he and St. Pierre did not exist, until they were needed, that is. These were the people who treated them like dogs. Mickleson had a mind to hurt Edward Muir, to break a few of his fingers. Instead, he did something thoughtful. He described, in lurid detail, the damage he and St. Pierre had done to the McAllisters, their dog, and their home. It gave Mickleson pleasure to feel Edward's horror and to make an accomplice of him, to warn him that if word got out about the McAllisters, if he (Mickleson) heard any of his own stories back, he would have to damage Edward and Franklin and everyone who worked in the office with them.

Edward fully felt Mickleson's malevolence, but he had no idea what he'd done to deserve it. He understood Mickleson was an unpleasant man, but he could not quite understand the story he'd been told. It didn't seem possible for St. Pierre to shoot a dog. He looked to be too proper a man. So it seemed unlikely Mickleson had told the truth. On the other hand, unless Mickleson were insane, it made no sense to invent such an elaborate story and then threaten retribution if Edward should breathe a word of it. The threat was as ridiculous as the story. Mickleson and St. Pierre were shadowy. The last thing they wanted was the light of a public inquiry, an inquiry that would certainly follow an attack on Franklin or Rundstedt. Mickleson was not making sense. He was being absurd. So, Edward did the only thing that seemed right. He laughed.

Mickleson, surprised, also laughed.

At which, Edward stopped laughing just long enough to say

– I'm sorry I asked.

After which, Mickleson, not all that amused, grunted.

And Edward got out of the car.

For Edward, the encounter had been disturbing, but as it had ended in laughter, he was inclined to dismiss it. Then, two days after meeting Mickleson, he got a call from St. Pierre.

– Edward Muir? It's St. Pierre. I want to apologize for my partner. Mickleson loved my mother more than I did. Her death was very hard on him. Anyway, I want to apologize for him. He told you things he shouldn't have. I think it'd be better all around if you both forgot your conversation, okay?

– Sure, okay, I . . .

– That's great. It's been a pleasure.

In some ways, this brief conversation with St. Pierre was more troubling than the episode with Mickleson had been. Edward had convinced himself that Mickleson's story was not to be taken seriously. And he had, in so doing, almost overcome the horror he'd felt at the thought of Mickleson and St. Pierre violently unhousing the McAllisters. Discounting Mickleson's account of little dogs and pistol whippings, he was able to imagine more lawful transactions: persuasion, an agreement in price, or a slightly fraught accord. However, St. Pierre's apology and his sinister insistence on forgetting made it clear that Mickleson must have told some version of the truth, that Mickleson and St. Pierre had killed a dog and tormented its owners, in order to secure a drab piece of land in Quebec.

He had not seen the assault on the McAllisters, but it was possible for him to imagine the most vivid torment, possible to imagine the dog's death in brutal detail. Actually, it was difficult to imagine it in anything *but* brutal detail. In his mind's eye, the dog was always petite, a Yorkie, say, or a Bichon Frise. It was possible for him to imagine the McAllisters getting "what they deserved." It was not possible to imagine the same for their dog.

He had kept the apprehension he'd felt since the call from St. Pierre to himself. He'd kept it to himself for some time, before he felt he *had* to say something. He'd been rattled by Mickleson's threat to keep him quiet if he spoke a word of what he knew, but his apprehension also had, in part, to do with Franklin. He was certain Franklin knew nothing of St. Pierre and Mickleson's methods, was certain Franklin would be horrified when he heard about them. But what if Franklin, on discovering the truth of St. Pierre and Mickleson, assumed Edward must have known about them all along and, worse, approved? It was mortifying to think Franklin might take him for someone who would recommend thugs capable of such violence, as if he (Edward) were indifferent to the suffering of others, indifferent to the suffering of the McAllisters, for whose fate he felt responsible.

When they had eaten and Franklin had finished talking about MacKenzie Bowell or, at least, paused long enough to make it seem he had, Edward delicately ventured that there was something he wished to talk about, if there was time.

– What is it, Eddy?

They had taken the booth farthest from the front of the restaurant, a booth beside the waiters' station, one that looked onto Cooper, not Elgin, across from a slightly morose apartment building: volutes, plinths, stone work from the Thirties. In a low voice, Edward described his meeting with Mickleson: the dark and the rain, the look on Mickleson's face, Mickleson's presence in the small car that smelled of cigarettes and pine cones, and then the curious threat to keep Edward quiet. You could almost feel the pride Mickleson felt in recounting what he and St. Pierre had done, the pleasure in threatening Edward's life, as if Edward's life were of no more consequence than the rain, the cigarettes in the ashtray, or the scented and yellowing paper pine tree than hung from the rear-view mirror. It had been frightening to be in a car with the man, as frightening as contemplating the details of St. Pierre and Mickleson's methods, which had come with special emphasis on the fate of the dog.

All of this had been unnerving but slightly incredible, until the final thing, the thing that had disturbed Edward most: a brief phone call from St. Pierre, proof, it seemed to him, that Mickleson had been telling the truth. Otherwise, why should St. Pierre have bothered to ask him to forget Mickleson's words? More than anything else, Edward wanted Franklin to understand the enormity of that phone call. These men: he was now sorry he had recommended them. They were ruthless and dangerous and their attention was on him.

Edward spoke in whispers, stopped speaking when the waitress was near, fidgeted, nibbled at the remains of his salsa burger, and repeated himself until Franklin said

– My God, Eddy. That's terrible. I had no idea.

– What if, said Edward, they're killers?

Franklin rubbed his nose.

– No, no, Eddy. From what you say, they put down a dog. They're not really killers.

– Will that be all? asked the waitress.

– Why don't we have a drink? Franklin asked. I have an appointment at two. That gives us a few minutes.

To the waitress, Franklin said

– Two Zombies. And make mine without pineapple, please.

Once the waitress had brought their Zombies, Franklin said

– I understand you feel bad about this, but you feel bad about something you couldn't have known. I'm glad you told me all this, Eddy. I certainly didn't know anything about St. Pierre and Mickleson, so it's as much my fault as yours. But we all make mistakes, and I think we should just move on from this one, eh. Just move on.

When they had finished their drinks and Edward sat staring at the life on Cooper Street, Franklin said

– We should be getting back to the office, but I want you to take the rest of the day off.

– Why?

– I think you deserve a few hours off. You've had a difficult few weeks. Anyway, I want to think this through on my own for a while.

Edward nodded and said

– Okay, Frank, thanks

then added

– I worry about St. Piere and Mickleson, you know? I wish there was something we could do.

Franklin looked down at his watch, his face in shadow.

– I'm late, he said.

Franklin did not return to the office. He was too preoccupied for that and his walk home was sobering. There were three matters to make him thoughtful. First, there was Edward. Then, there was the question of St. Pierre and Mickleson. And finally, there was Rundstedt.

He took things in order, Edward first.

How upset Edward had been. He had cause, of course. Mickleson had threatened him. Mickleson's presence was off-putting, at the best of times, no doubt about it. Franklin himself found the man disturbing, the kind of man of whom one suspects the worst even before talking to him. A military man, a Catholic, had once told Franklin that men who have killed, no matter the reason (duty, self-defence, whatever), lose something of them-selves, become slightly dead inside, freezer burnt. So it was with Mickleson. It was not surprising Edward should be intimidated. But frightened people are unreliable. He had calmed Edward down and Edward was, whatever else he might be, loyal. That was something, at least.

This is not to say Franklin was remorseless where St. Pierre and Mickleson were concerned. He had assumed the men would have to use a certain force to clear the cottagers off, but he had called on them because he'd believed in the perfection of Alba and that the site on which it was to stand should be inviolable.

The irony was that once he'd read François' estimates, he real-ized there would have to be compromise of some sort. There would be no perfection. François had put the price of MacKenzie Bowell Federal Penitentiary at $225 million. A quarter of a billion. Reinhart's pure, unsullied vision might have stood a chance with the Liberals in power, but no self-respecting Conservative govern-ment would put up that kind of money for convicts. Among other things, this meant that the violence done the McAllisters had been done in the name of a purity that *could* not be achieved. St. Pierre and Mickleson had been used for what now looked like groundless optimism. In retrospect, Franklin regretted his haste, realized he should have known better, and felt slightly stricken for what he had provoked.

The third thing that preyed on Franklin's mind as he walked home had been on his mind for a week: a conversation he'd had with Rundstedt. The minister had returned to Ottawa for a few days and they had spoken after the government's own quantity surveyors had sent official estimates of MacKenzie Bowell's costs, estimates that were slightly higher than François': almost $226 million.

– Well, he'd said, your Dostoevsky idea about treating convicts like human beings was pretty good. Everyone in Cabinet understood, but a quarter billion is just too much, "Djustawhiskey" or not. It looks like most of the buildings will have to go, if we want to keep a least some of these plans. I don't have to tell you how people get when big money is involved.

Though Franklin had expected a scaling back, he'd been struck by Rundstedt's almost casual tone. Had Rundstedt given up on the penitentiary? Was Cabinet on the verge of shutting it down? Or was it that Rundstedt had begun the long process of campaigning and had simply distanced himself from MacKenzie Bowell?

– I'll have to talk to the architect, said Franklin.

– Yes, answered Rundstedt. You talk to him, but make sure you tell him there's no way it's going to go forward like this.

As if the idea had just occurred to him, Franklin said

– Maybe we could use other material.

– It's a thought, said Rundstedt, but I don't think that'll make the kind of difference we need. Talk it through with your architect and let me know what he thinks. I don't have a lot of time to go over details, just now, but since Brian put me in charge of this himself, I feel personally responsible to bring it in under $100 million. Say, around $80 million . . .

– But, said Franklin, if it's just another pen . . .

Rundstedt had put his hand on Franklin's shoulder and said

– I know, I know

and turned away, already on to something else, preoccupied as usual.

But there it was: nothing approaching Reinhart's designs could be built for $80 million. MacKenzie Bowell Federal Penitentiary would not be anything like Alba. And yet, though the moment had come as a shock, Franklin had not panicked. The first thing he'd done was arrange a meeting with Reinhart and he'd begun furiously thinking what it was the penitentiary could lose while retaining its essence. If it were not to be the *Mona Lisa*, might it be a *Venus de Milo*, armless but serene?

As it happened, Reinhart seemed not to care. When they spoke, it was almost as if he were a different man. Reinhart referred to the "architect" (that is, himself) in the third person. He understood that a proper architect might be horrified by this dissection of his art by philistines. He understood that a vision realized is part of the usual process, for architects, but he himself had been satisfied by his drawings, by the lines he'd made on paper. And he had moved on. As in:

– The man who drew these plans isn't here any more, Frank. And I don't feel like his agent. I don't feel a connection. I'm not surprised the government's too chintzy to go ahead, but you do what you think's right, okay? I've got complete confidence in you.

His words should have been bracing but, somehow, they weren't. It was as if, in abandoning ship, the captain had hastily given Franklin his cap and formal jacket, transferring authority just before the ship went down. Still, it meant Franklin would have, briefly, a certain leverage vis-à-vis changes to the design, not much, enough to put forward his suggestions as to which buildings in the complex ought to be dropped, which kept, suggestions, also, as to materials. It was important, for Franklin, that marble be used, enough to allow its influence to be felt, its cool and beauty.

So, Reinhart's abdication was, to a minute extent, promising. On the other hand, Franklin would now have to get Rundstedt's attention. Formerly, that would not have been a daunting task. It had become daunting.

Lately, Franklin was anxious and often sleepless. It took all his concentration to maintain equanimity, to perform his duties conscientiously. To say the least, the image of St. Pierre and Mickleson invading a home and brutalizing those within was not conducive to poise, and neither was the thought of Edward's fear and the chaos it might lead to.

{ 43 }

A SUDDEN AND UNEXPECTED DOWNFALL

At the moment Edward and Franklin sat down to discuss St. Pierre and Mickleson (noon), Rundstedt was working hard in Vancouver, preparing for an election and trying to decide how best to report to Cabinet on the costs of MacKenzie Bowell. He had, in spite of his conversation with Franklin, decided to deal with the matter himself, and he'd already chosen, without Franklin's counsel, the buildings that would stand. More than that, he'd just received a report from Bush, Boshari, and Hawes, the quantity surveyors, on the price of what was, now, a rather lovely medium-security prison in the Gatineaus: $60 million. In view of how much the Liberals had spent on museums of Art and Civilization, no one could object to that.

Rundstedt's four years in Cabinet had changed him. He was more exacting (of himself), more forgiving (of others) and, lately, more absorbed by work. His closest friends thought him deeper and more conscientious, and though he was also a little more pre-occupied, they approved of the change and, at times, compli-mented themselves on their premonitions of his greatness.

His wife, Edwina, also heard the talk about him and felt not pride exactly, but satisfaction that the world now knew the worth of a man she had loved and admired from the moment they met.

There was something "off" about him, though. His public self had never entered their home before. She could, without exaggeration, have said she did not know well the politician who shared her husband's name. Albert Rundstedt MP was a federal politician who represented her riding (rather well), shook hands with anyone who extended their own, believed in the values they shared: home, family, education, protection from lawlessness, protection from money-grubbing Liberals who, you could be certain, were rooting around the stinkpit for another Pierre Trudeau.

Lately, however, it was Albert Rundstedt MP who walked under the lintel, Rundstedt MP who, in his crowd-oiling voice, praised her cooking, her housekeeping, and, once, her body as she undressed. She'd been naked save for a brassiere and she had slapped his face, not playfully: the first time she'd done anything like that, so surprised had she been that Albert could, even inadvertently, humiliate her that way. Her slap had brought him 'round. He behaved as if his words had all been larks, but he'd returned to her. The incident was, perhaps, more resonant for her than it was for him. It made her wonder if there were something deeper at work, and wonder if she was right to let him go off on his own: months in Ottawa while she took care of home and children in Calgary. Still, he had returned to her, and it was as if they had passed through a mirage together, although, from then on, she could not fully share in the joy Rundstedt's success brought his friends, his constituents, his children even.

Rundstedt had felt slightly embarrassed at Edwina's slap. He had laughed at their mutual discomfort and downplayed the misunderstanding between them. He himself would not have said he "returned" to Edwina thereafter. He was more attentive to her, yes, but that was in part because, despite himself, he often thought (and not happily) about the woman who was now constantly on his mind: Gudrun Lindemann.

The peculiar relationship of Albert Rundstedt and Gudrun Lindemann had begun innocently, in Paris, had continued innocently, with an exchange of presents, and, until Osaka, was still innocent, though it might, in a certain light, have been taken for a more carnal relationship.

But wait . . .

After Paris, Ms. Lindemann haunted Rundstedt's imagination. (And how suitable the cliché: she seemed to move about the world with him, sitting in this chair or that before he did, parting the curtains of a room, turning down the bedclothes in an anonymous suite.) They had been chaste and intimate, a situation both wonderful and agonizing, for Rundstedt. Wonderful, because it involved no physical contact. It's true he had seen Gudrun in a state of undress, but they had had nothing but the most perfunctory touching: greeting, farewell. Nor did he take her lack of clothing for provocation. It seemed to him, simply, that Europeans had different standards of modesty. Had his family, the von Rundstedts, not moved from Deutschland generations ago, he would not have noticed Gudrun's lack of clothes. In other words, Rundstedt could *be* with Gudrun without the twin oppressions: copulation and frottage. (They were oppressive, because he could not keep himself from desiring them. So it was: the more chaste and innocent their intimacy, the more he thought of her in carnal terms. And that, of course, was the source of his agony.)

Their second meeting, in Osaka, was like the first, though there were severe and unfortunate variations.

He and Gudrun had not spoken or corresponded at any length, so she could not have known he was to attend a conference in Osaka. He himself had not known until rather late. The justice minister had declined to attend, but it was a formal invitation. Someone with some symbolic weight had to attend, and so Rundstedt attended.

It was a conference on international law.

He arrived the day before he was to give a commencement address.

He delivered a short address, dry as toast.

He departed two days later.

It was a bland and formal duty undertaken by Rundstedt, though it meant time away from his campaign, because Rundstedt's seat was certain. He did not need to campaign as vigorously as others. His flight left on a Wednesday and arrived on Friday, with Thursday disappearing somewhere west of Hawaii. The flight left him so tired, he booked into his room at five in the afternoon and slept until eight when, too tired for anything else, he ate at the bar of the Kitahachi, his hotel.

The Kitahachi was anonymously "Western." Its chief virtues seemed to be a relative absence of occupants and a relative proximity to the university where he would speak. There was, then, no compelling reason for Gudrun Lindemann to have chosen the Kitahachi. And yet, she had.

Rundstedt walked into the bar, which was brightly lit in spots, dim in others: lurid light and dark shadow. It was meant to be both convivial and intimate, no doubt. There was music playing that sounded like hymns shot through with electric somethings. The place was not busy. He sat at the bar, ordered a rather expensive cocktail with lychee, and did not look up until he had finished eating what tasted like a North American version of Japanese food. When he did look up, he discovered he had been sitting beside Gudrun Lindemann for some time.

Difficult to describe the emotion. He felt her presence before he saw her. He turned to look for the hostess, noticed how familiar the woman beside him seemed, turned away, turned back (she looking straight ahead) convinced it *was* Gudrun, turned away (aware of how ridiculous the very idea, though . . .), turned back (she now looking at him, smiling quizzically, not in recognition . . .), and said

– Miss, uh . . . Lindemann?

And, now, she was startled.

– Excuse me, ya?

Bewildered to find herself next to . . .

– Herr Rundstedt? Liebe Gott. Was tunen sie hier?

And again

– What do you here?

as if forgetting her English in the turbulence of their encounter.

– I came to lecture at the university, said Rundstedt.

They embraced, turning towards each other while sitting on bar stools that did not swivel. There was, for Rundstedt, a pleasure in recognition, a tincture of home in this place so far from it. Gudrun was not from home, except in the limited sense that Europe, being closer to Canada, was "home" when he was in the Far East. Yet, he associated her, instinctively, with the familiar, with that which belonged to him. What Gudrun felt, beside surprise, was difficult to make out. She did not seem unhappy to see him, but he got the impression she blamed him for this intrusion into her private life. Perhaps she felt unlovely. Her hair was so short, it was as if she had been brush cut. She was thinner than when he had seen her last, and he supposed that her illness had made its way to some deeper place.

Well, all things come to an end, he thought. We must all die.

– Are you travelling through Japan? he asked.

– Yes, she answered. I will go to China after.

– China, eh? That sounds interesting.

(Now, why would anyone want to go to China? he wondered.)

– You're going to Hong Kong? he asked.

– Yes. Hong Kong and then Kowloon.

There was, then, an awkwardness between them. The bond that surprise had created loosened. Who was this woman, after all?

He was tired. He wanted to sleep.

– Well, said Rundstedt, it is late.

– Yes, said Gudrun. Good night, Herr Rundstedt.

(It gave him an indefinable but intense pleasure to hear his name spoken as she did, spoken as if he were his great-great grandfather.)

– Good night, he said.

Rundstedt was in bed, having perused his itinerary for the following day, and he was on the verge of sleep when it occurred to him how improbable it was to have met Gudrun in this place (Osaka). It was so improbable it seemed like a sinister design, and he felt a momentary panic. He was in the midst of something; he was sure of it.

Yet, life was made of these serendipitous encounters. His grandfather had, at a country fair, vomited on a duck that belonged to the farmer who would, weeks later, introduce him to his future bride. His father had, in the Second World War, been taken prisoner by the man who, after the war, bought the house next to theirs in Calgary: Mr. Reineke. He himself had, as a boy, saved from drowning the boy who would, years later, as a man, save his (Rundstedt's) son's life.

What if this? What if that?

It was all God's doing, part of a design it was not ours to fully see. Better to allow these moments to run their course. It might take years before their significance were known. Still, it was sad that they had not had occasion to speak, he and Gudrun. There was something about her, especially here (in his hotel room) and now (on the verge of sleep). And, convinced he would not see Gudrun again, he allowed himself to feel disappointment.

The following day, Rundstedt was shepherded through his duties. He was met in the morning by a well-dressed young man who, deferentially, guided him to the stations he was to visit, most of them at Osaka University. Though he was politely greeted, politely guided, and carefully supervised, Rundstedt had the impression it was resentfully done. The trip itself was something of a mild rebuke: second-class hotel, polite but cool guidance, and, after he had delivered the address, complete indifference. Perhaps, as he was not the man they wanted, his hosts had been offended. Perhaps, there was some dereliction of duty or confusion, on the part of his hosts. In any case, once his address had been given, his duties fulfilled, he was left to his own resources until his flight home.

Now, Rundstedt's resources were fine, but his imagination was a little stunted where Osaka was concerned. There was nothing he wanted to see, nowhere he wanted to go. He did not speak Japanese, so the theatre did not interest him. He was not a drinking man, and he was not wantonly sociable. That left little for him to do save what he actually did: read (W.P. Kinsella), call campaign headquarters (Calgary), call home, eat, sleep, wander around the blocks closest to the hotel (cautiously, so as not to get lost).

There was the first day gone.

That night, he went to a restaurant called Painappuru, sat alone at a table for six, and was, as he considered ordering a dish that resembled fried chicken, accosted by Gudrun, who, as if they had made this engagement long before, sat in the chair beside his and said

– I think you are pursuing me, Mr. Rundstedt.

Because he was grateful for company, and because this second encounter was not as extraordinary, Rundstedt smiled and answered

– Miss Lindemann.

And invited her to dine with him.

She was a cultured woman. She had, she said, mastered only a basic Japanese, but she seemed to know the country, its theatre, its food. She pointed out that Rundstedt had chosen a wonderful restaurant. She congratulated him and, with his permission, she ordered for them both, taking pleasure in the sounds of the language, pleasing their waitress with the peculiar cadence of her Japanese.

They ate

yaki-nasu (broiled eggplant?)

kinpira-gobo (what exactly is burdock?)

oden (fried bean curd? sardine dumplings? who knew?)

and mochi (you could glue your hand to a plate with mochi).

They talked of food, of theatre, and, after a while, of Gudrun's failing health. It pained her to admit that, yes, she might not live beyond a year or so. There would be fewer and fewer occasions for her to explore the world as she wanted: on her own. (It was a shame such a lovely and personable woman should be on such intimate terms with her own frontier.) Having encouraged her to speak of her health, Rundstedt felt as if he'd darkened the mood. How thoughtless of him. Here was a woman travelling the world in order to unburden, to lose the darkness, to, what was it, "break the surly bonds of earth"?, and the best he could do was remind her of her ties to this world.

– This was really good, he said, pointing to their meal. Let me pay for it.

– Thank you, no, she answered. It would not be . . . correct.

How circumspect she was. There was no one around who knew either of them: no one to see him pay for her, no one to see her acquiesce.

– Let me buy you a drink, then.

– Very well, she answered. I will have a . . . Pink Lady.

– A Pink Lady? You a socialist?

He'd smiled as he said the words, but it was clear she was offended.

– Not at all, she said. I am Green.

She was a member of the Green Party? As he understood it, that was a socialist word for socialist. Well, what of it? As far as he knew, half the Germans were fascist; the other half socialist, and as Edwina was Jewish, he knew which side he preferred.

– Let's go somewhere else, he said. Is there a bar nearby?

– Yes, certainly, she answered. I know of one.

Ms. Lindemann's choice was unusual. It was a French brasserie called My Cosey Corner Girl, and it seemed to be a strip club. No, it didn't *seem* to be a strip club. It was exactly that. As they entered the smoke-filled room, there were four women on stage, dressed as English schoolgirls, dancing what seemed to be a combination of jig, cake-walk, and maxixe.

As Rundstedt and Gudrun sat at their table by the stage, the women shook their plaid skirts, then lifted them to reveal white, crotchless bloomers: their vaginal lips lightly rouged or naturally scarlet.

– I have heard, said Gudrun, this is the best bar. Is it all right?

– Yeah, said Rundstedt. Okay.

He had certainly been to a strip club before, though not with a woman. This, he thought, would be much like the others: raucous, entertaining, a pleasant lieu for a drink, though the music was not to his taste. And so it seemed, until the dancers crouched, spread their legs, and invited spectators to the side of the stage so they might enjoy more proximate views of pudenda. This was unexpected, as were the magnifying glasses used by some of the patrons for an even closer look.

Gudrun, one of a dozen female customers at the Cosey Corner, got up from the table, once she had ordered her Pink Lady. She approached the stage matter of factly, taking up a magnifying glass that lay there and inspecting a dancer's vagina. She did it in a way Rundstedt thought typically German: with disinterest, as if to (exhaling) say

– Yes, yes. It is a vagina.

Smiling, one eyebrow arched, she turned to give the magnifying glass to Rundstedt, only to discover he had not followed her to the side of the stage. She held it out to him, as if it were simply his turn and, in that instant, Rundstedt felt it was most natural to step up to the stage and examine the lips of a woman's vagina. He did so as a Canadian might, however: slightly embarrassed, putting on a brave but mocking face, as if to say

– Well, yes. I guess it is a vagina.

Not quite comfortable, under the circumstances, but aware that this evening, these circumstances, would make for good conversation. (The evening was one he longed to share with Edwina, but he would, when the time came, tell it his own way.) When he had finished not-quite looking at the woman's pudendum, Rundstedt returned to the table to drink his beer and keep company with Gudrun.

Rundstedt had not inspected the dancers with the polite enthusiasm the white-shirted Osakans did, but he felt he had been respectful of Japan, its customs, its inhabitants and, feeling this way, he relaxed. He gave his full attention to Gudrun, who, once she'd seen what the Cosey Corner had to offer, turned her attention to Rundstedt. In this way, they managed to recover something of the closeness they had discovered in Paris.

(How odd that two strange cities, Paris and Osaka, should afford him such intense intimacy; a gift, one felt. It's true he would have preferred to be somewhere he knew, but the presence of a woman with whom he was at ease made even Osaka seem familiar.)

They spoke of nothing too troubling: fate, its unpredictable underpinnings, Japanese beer, its inferiority to German brew, the collegiate atmosphere in which they found themselves. Until, finally, when it was time to go, and Gudrun had, in jest, bought for Rundstedt the panties of a dark-haired stripper, they wandered back to the hotel and, as she had in Paris, Gudrun invited him to her room.

He demurred and then relented.

They spent another night together, talking, on the verge of sleep, though here in Osaka she teased him for his prudishness. Had he not just spent the evening at a burlesque club? Would he not make himself comfortable? Would he be troubled by *her* nakedness?

– Well, no, I guess not . . . , he answered.

So Gudrun took off her clothes and sat on her narrow bed as they spoke. Curiously, Rundstedt was, on this night, not at all attracted to Gudrun. He was not tempted to rise from the narrow chair facing her, to sit beside her on the bed. This was curious, to Rundstedt, because, despite her cropped hair, she was the most beautiful woman he had seen that night. Her body was, no doubt about it, strikingly desirable and, every once in a while, she would touch his arm (to emphasize a point) or absentmindedly touch one of her breasts (while speaking of her life). Yet, Rundstedt was convinced of the innocence of her gestures and deeply impressed by the ease of her nudity. Gudrun could not have seemed more chaste and friendly if she had been draped in flannel.

There was only one moment when he felt discomfort, but it was a moment he would remember for the rest of his life: Gudrun had begun to talk of her childhood when, after an unexpected shift in her mood, she confessed she had been molested by an uncle, Georg, her mother's brother, who'd made her sit on his knees in a certain way, and face him so she could fasten the buttons of his shirt that, when they were alone, always seemed to be undone. A sad story. And then Gudrun seemed to lose herself and, before he could say or do anything, she rose from the bed, sat astride his knees, unfastened his shirt buttons and fastened them again, all the while imitating the sounds her uncle had made so many years ago. Rundstedt was genuinely distressed. If he'd felt any desire for her, it would have been crushed by her demonstration. Not that Gudrun seemed to notice. When she had finished buttoning his shirt, she laughed in a melancholy way and returned to her bed. She had forgiven her uncle long ago, or so she said. It was some time before she spoke to Rundstedt again, and when she did she hid her legs with a coverlet.

(And isn't it odd, the familiarity one allows without consent-
ing. Had he been asked, before entering Gudrun's room, if he
would care to participate in a re-enactment of abuse and incest,
he would almost certainly have said

  – *No*

but he had entered and, in entering, he had accepted the terms of
a contract with which he was somewhat familiar. In the past,
Gudrun Lindemann had been friendly, naked, and nostalgic. So,
he could not now (or later) claim he hadn't expected her familiarity, nudity, or nostalgia. Whatever he did or did not expect, however, the moments when Gudrun undressed, sat on his lap, and
relived her past were moments of pure betrayal. And all her art
consisted in having duplicity pass for closeness.)

Rundstedt left Gudrun's room just before dawn: pleased by his
restraint, convinced he now knew Gudrun as well as he had
known anyone, and that she knew him in his stuttering, inartic-
ulate, and vulnerable depths, because he had finally managed to
speak of himself, of his own life, with someone who, unlike
Edwina, did not know it as well as he did. And he felt this communion with her as a communion with all he was and might be:
an exhilarating night, despite Uncle Georg, a night of true
feeling, in which he encountered himself through the interces-
sion of Gudrun.

  He returned to her room eight hours later, because he had forgotten the souvenir she'd bought him, and because she had not
told him her plans for the day and he hoped to spend time with a
woman with whom he was, whatever else one might have said,
well acquainted.

  She was not in her room.

  He returned to her door periodically for four hours before,
finally, asking for her at the desk.

  She had checked out at seven.

  No, she had not left word for Mr. Rundstedt.

Rather, yes, she had, perhaps, as there was an envelope for Mr. Rundstedt: oversized, manila, closed with red string wound about a red-paper button, his name neatly written in Gudrun's hand. How strange the premonitions of disaster. When he took the envelope, it was five in the afternoon and Rundstedt was, finally, hungry. He had slept until noon. He had been distracted by thoughts of Gudrun, but now, with her envelope in his hand, he thought of food, a return to the place they'd been the night before, if he could remember its name. He thought, in other words, of ways to avoid opening an envelope that, in some part of his soul, he knew to be trouble. There was something about the handwriting. He could not have said why, but Gudrun's handwriting disturbed him. She had written his name plainly, precisely, but as if she were writing it for someone else. A ridiculous thought, yet he did not open the envelope at the front desk or in the elevator. He opened it in his own room, but only after he had showered and shaved and put on clothes for the evening.

In the envelope there were two photographs of himself and Gudrun. In the first, he was in the chair while she sat astride him, naked, his hand on her waist where she held it. In the second, he and Gudrun were in the Cosey Corner: he was smiling stiffly, as he examined the pudendum of a plaid-skirted dancer.

On the back of the photographs, the date and locations where the pictures had been taken were written in Gudrun's neat, impersonal hand. It was as if she herself were not implicated in the pictures though there she was (Gudrun Lindemann, if that was her name), her expression jubilant in both photographs. It looked as if she were having a wonderful time.

And they say the camera doesn't lie.

Rundstedt did not remember Gudrun looking as she looked in these photographs. In fact, the difference between his perspective and the perspective revealed by the photographs was, at first, a source of puzzlement. He tried to imagine the vantage from which the photographs had been taken.

Where had the photographer hidden?

In the first picture, it was as if the photographer had been on the ceiling above him. Rundstedt's face was clearly visible. Gudrun's back was to the camera, but she was in profile: her left nipple visible, her eyes closed, her tongue slightly protruding. In its way, it was a perfect picture. You could see Rundstedt had kept his shirt on, but you could not see if he still wore pants. Even to Rundstedt, it looked as though he and Gudrun were sexually engaged. This picture alone would have been trouble, but no doubt there were others, taken from the same camera, or from another in the same room.

The second picture had been taken by someone just behind them, but as the bar had been crowded, it could have been anyone at all, from the waitress to the patrons. Here, too, it would be surprising if there were not more photos very like this one with him bent forward, peering at a young woman's genitals, and smiling like a . . . What would Edwina say? An ignorant chicken farmer, a plucking idiot.

Along with the photographs, there was a short letter, neatly written of course:

> Dear Mr. Rundstedt,
>   I hope you will enjoy the pictures.
>   We will meet again in Vancouver, Canada, on
> October 15, 1988, at 5 p.m.:
> > *Hotel Georgia*
> > *801 West Georgia Street*
>   I am sorry we will not talk before then, but it is very
> important for you to be at this hotel, at the correct time.
> >   Yours truly,
> >   Gudrun Lindemann

The months passed, months during which he threw himself into his work. And here it was, October already, and Rundstedt was in the midst of an arduous campaign. Arduous, because it might go either way. ("Either way" for the Conservative Party, not Rundstedt. Rundstedt was so far ahead in the polls, it would be difficult for him to lose, were it not for Gudrun, were it not for this business in Vancouver.) Arduous, because he was afraid his world could collapse at any time. (He tried to think of other things but, every so often, he imagined the worst: a newspaper on whose front page was a picture of his face poised over the neatly trimmed pelt of a young woman.) Arduous because, for the first time in his life, he was not convinced of his suitedness to serve. (He had been genuinely attracted to Gudrun Lindemann. He had allowed himself to play at a fire set for him. So, you know: whither judgement? But, wait, was he really idealist enough to wonder if a corrupt man could serve the good without corrupting it? Yes, he was, though he knew any number of corrupt men who had, despite themselves, served "the good." It was late in the day to discover such raw idealism in himself and positively disturbing to experience the insecurity it brought here, on the campaign trail, where he had never been anything but confident.)

The most gnawing and distracting aspect of his predicament, however, was the lassitude he felt where Vancouver was concerned, lassitude despite the memento he'd been couriered: panties from the dancer at Cosey Corner. It was as if, whenever he thought of Vancouver, a great, grey weight were on him, dampening his emotions, tiring him out. Vancouver should have been an easy decision. He had worked for years to achieve what he had. He had the confidence of everyone. Martin Brian himself had shaken his hand, clapped him on the shoulder, and treated him like a friend. He was a great man, was Brian, and the party was now, only now, a servant of the people: east, west, and all points between. He, Rundstedt, belonged. He wanted to belong to the Progressive Conservative Party. So, Vancouver should have been an occasion to discover the nature of Gudrun's menace, to find what could be salvaged and at what cost.

And yet . . .

He was not interested in Vancouver, not interested in Gudrun. Though it would mean the end of public life, the end of belonging to the PC, Rundstedt seriously considered avoiding Vancouver, avoiding October 15, and dealing with the consequences later. He believed his life was worth certain sacrifices. He would, if he could, spare his wife and family the humiliation of a public disgrace. Then again, he would *not* do so irrespective of price. (Again, what an unfortunate time to discover such principles in himself.) He would give money, a little, if that was what Ms. Lindemann wanted but, really, that was all he would give and as he suspected Ms. Lindemann was after more than money, he thought it useless to go to Vancouver, head bowed, like a mourner at the funeral of his public life.

He went, though. He contrived reasons to be in Vancouver and went alone, waking up early, on the morning of October 15, to write letters, go over speeches, and talk to his campaign manager, the good Mr. Yanovsky, who believed Rundstedt was in Vancouver visiting a bedridden acquaintance. Rundstedt was at the Empire Landmark, but at 4:45 p.m. he stood outside the Georgia, entering the lobby at 5:00 exactly, precisely on time for the first time in his life.

He was disappointed. Ms. Lindemann was nowhere to be seen. He gave her five minutes, and then called up to her room from the front desk.

– Yes, hello?

It was a man's voice: foreign accent, but unrecognizable.

– Gudrun Lindemann, please.

– Ah. You are Mr. Rundstedt.

("Rundstedt" spoken in the German way.)

– Yes.

– Wonderful to hear your voice. Would you care to come up to the room?

– No, I wouldn't, said Rundstedt.

Pause.

– I'll come down then, shall I?

– Sure, if you want to. Where's Gudrun?

– Ah, you see, Ms. Lindemann is not here.

– Then there's nothing to say.

– No, no. I think there is, Mr. Rundstedt. There is much to say, if you'll allow me a few minutes of your time, yes? I want to talk about certain photographs, and to put your mind at ease, you see?

It surprised him to say so, but Rundstedt said

– We don't have anything to talk about.

The voice on the other end of the line grew more ironic. You could hear the smirk in it.

– Come, come, Mr. Rundstedt. This is not what you think. Besides, you owe your family and your party to listen. I will not be long. Stay in the lobby. I know what you look like. I have seen your picture.

With that, the man hung up. And Rundstedt, though he knew there was extortion in this somewhere, politely waited in the lobby: for ten minutes. (If there was one thing he couldn't shake, one thing worse than scabies, it was manners. Though the man kept him waiting, he couldn't bring himself to walk out.)

Two men came towards Rundstedt at the same time. The first was almost archetypically German. Neatly dressed: three-quarter-length black leather jacket, grey slacks, blue V-neck sweater. He was lantern-jawed, had a day's growth of beard and closely cropped blond hair. He had nothing to do with anything. He walked by Rundstedt without stopping.

The second man resembled Rundstedt or, at least, Rundstedt's version of himself: somewhat portly, if that was the word, well dressed but perhaps more relaxed within his overcoat, tie, and shoes than Rundstedt, hair nicely parted, but fingernails a little dirty.

– Mr. Rundstedt, he said

extending his hand.

– And you are? asked Rundstedt
shaking hands with the stranger.

The man smiled politely.

– Why don't you call me Larry? he said.

– Fine. What's this about, Larry?

– It is not what you think, Mr. Rundstedt. Shall we walk?

Larry moved his hand in the direction of the street.

– It will be easier to talk outside.

They stepped out, and went southwest on Howe.

As if they were tourists, Larry said

– A beautiful city, isn't it?

It had never seemed so to Rundstedt. You couldn't have a conversation in which Vancouver figured without someone mentioning its supposed beauty, but without the mountains Vancouver
was Fredericton done over and over. He preferred Calgary.

– No, he said. It's too big.

– Yes, said Larry. I suppose you're right. Listen, you are probably thinking this is about money.

– Isn't it?

– No, not at all. No one wants your money, Mr. Rundstedt. How
can you put a price on a man's life?

Larry took an envelope from a pocket of his overcoat.

– These are for you, he said.

Rundstedt knew what they were, but he stopped to look at
them anyway, stepping from the sidewalk into a doorway. There
were photographs of Rundstedt in Gudrun's room at the
Kitahachi. Gudrun was naked, of course, her hands on his shirt
buttons, but most of these photos were from different angles than
the one he'd first seen. How many cameras had there been?

– I don't want them, he said.

– Keep them, said Larry. You can show them to your wife.

Rundstedt thought of taking offence, but he didn't. This man,
this "Larry," had nothing he wanted and held no sway over him,
though he thought he did. He was distraught at the idea of losing

the life he had built for himself and his family, but Rundstedt had resolved to finish this business here. In the months between Osaka and Vancouver, he had imagined a million scenarios. At the end of all of them, however, there had been only one thing: uncertainty. Even in those moments when he'd considered giving whatever was asked of him, he knew his old life was dead. In fact, it had died in Osaka. (For one giddy instant, it occurred to Rundstedt to throw all the photographs up in the air, let them fall into the hands of those going home.) He might have given Larry a modest amount of money to go away, but nothing else, and, as Larry did not want money, they had no business to conduct. It was simply that Larry did not know it.

– If you don't want money, what do you want?

– There, now that's more like it. I was beginning to think you weren't a serious man. This is about so much more than you and your family. This is going to be a close election. You wouldn't want to jeopardize your party's chances, would you?

Rundstedt sighed.

– No, he said.

Larry laughed, politely, as if at a particularly dry witticism.

– That's good, he said. I was beginning to think you were right we didn't have anything to talk about. You see, the truth is we have quite a few things in common.

– Yeah? Who's we?

– Now there's a very intelligent question, and I wish I could answer it, but we need to know a little more about each other first. And first you've got an election to win, yeah?

They had come to Smithe Street, stopped at the light, and it suddenly seemed to Rundstedt that he had lost his hold on reality. He was in Vancouver, at the corner of Smithe and Howe, talking to a man who wished to be called "Larry," a man who had pictures of Rundstedt being used by a woman named Gudrun, if that was her name, a man who did not want money but, rather, electoral success for the Progressive Conservatives.

Really? Where was the sense in all this?

It took no genius to see that if this was not petty blackmail, it was political blackmail. If it was political, it was about Rundstedt's influence. If it was about influence, then Larry here was looking to get a hand on the rudder, for himself or others. So he, Rundstedt, was being set up. Now, who in the world would seek influence through a minister whose portfolio was so particular: prisons and prison reform?

– You're East German, aren't you?

– No, no, I apologize for my accent. I am Estonian.

So, he was at Howe and Smithe talking to an Estonian.

– Where is Estonia? he asked.

– It is in the Soviet Union, Larry answered dryly.

– And what do the Estonians want from me? asked Rundstedt.

Larry turned to him, astounded.

– Nothing, he said. Nothing at all, as far as I know. Ah . . . you misunderstand me. I am not Estonian any longer.

No, this had gone far enough. Rundstedt stopped mid-stream, so pedestrians had to move around them.

– Who are you, and what do you want? he asked.

Larry smiled sheepishly, self-deprecating.

– I am working for an eastern government, he answered. I would like your cooperation.

– Why should I cooperate with you?

– First, because I have these photographs. They could cause pain to you and your family, and they could cause pain to your Progressive Conservatives. In the second place, I will not ask you to do anything dangerous. Nothing dangerous to you or your family or your party or your country. Let us keep walking. We are in the way. Look, no one is asking you to do something dangerous. You are not that kind of man, okay? But you are a Cabinet minister. You hear all sorts of things. Most of what you hear wouldn't interest us, but some of what you hear about America would interest us a great deal, perhaps.

– You want me to spy?

The Estonian Larry seemed genuinely hurt.

– No, no. We want you to listen and if what you hear is good for us we will be happy to pay you for it. Why should you spy? All you would do is listen, and we would pay you if you heard. The more you hear, the more we pay. It is very simple.

– It is spying.

– It is listening, and I know how much you have enjoyed working with Gudrun, so maybe you work with her again. This is my proposition: you help us a little and we help you very much. We kill the pictures and we give you money.

– And if I don't win the election?

As both men suspected: a long shot.

– That, said the Estonian Larry, would be unfortunate. Very bad for the party, but . . . What do the English say? Man disposes, God supposes? If you lose this one, there is always a next one, yeah?

So there it was: he was invited to spy for a foreign country.

– What do you say? Larry asked as they reached the corner of Nelson.

He could have a political life, the life he had wanted from as far as he could remember, but it would not be his own. He would have to share it with Larry and his masters. Every victory, from now to the end of his days, would be a victory for himself and the GDR, *if* "Larry" was working for the GDR.

As he walked along Howe, beside the Estonian fellow, Rundstedt looked up at the sky, could not see the mountains, could not see the ocean but felt, for an instant, the weight of Vancouver within him. It was now clear to him he would lose everything. (Vancouver would forever be the anguish within.) He would miss the friendship of his peers. He would miss the expression of shared (or partially shared) ideals that made friendship possible. He would miss power; not the things he had taken for it (the late luncheons in dimly lit steak houses, the journalists waiting on his wit, the pleasure of walking with the powerful . . .)

but, simply, the conviction that what was important to him was as important to his compatriots or could be made so. He would be left with wife, family, home.

Was that so bad?

No, but what *were* those things without the world that had given them meaning?

He looked over at the Estonian, who was talking on about something or other. The man had recently shaved. The skin of his cheek was pink with, beneath his ear, a red blotch. Fine black hairs stuck up where the razor had missed. A human being, a man with parents and children, perhaps. When Larry turned to look at him, a crooked half-smile on his face, Rundstedt nodded and turned away. It was all he could do to hide his distress.

{ 44 }

ROMANCE

On the afternoon Minister Rundstedt met the Estonian Larry, it was evening in Ottawa and Louise Dylan sat down to supper with Walter Barnes. Things had been going fairly well for months and her good fortune seemed to have somewhat to do with Paul. Given the feelings her departure had aroused, the unpredictable behaviour it had provoked, you would have thought Paul the least likely avenue for good fortune, and yet . . .

After fighting her for every scrap, concession, and word, Paul had suddenly come around. One day, his lawyer had let it be known that they had removed all obstacles to an equitable distribution of Paul's holdings, and by "equitable" Paul meant, it seemed, whatever Louise took to be equitable. The change in his attitude was so sudden, unexpected, and detrimental to himself, Louise considered asking for less than she had. She then wondered what kind of trap it was he was trying to spring and, remembering the misery he had put her through, she asked for four-fifths of everything he owned, every asset, thinking this the best way to find out what Paul was after.

And, the following day, Paul's lawyer, Perry Newman, informed Louise and Mr. Nenas that Paul agreed to *whatever* Louise thought fair. This was the man who'd refused to speak with her, who had stolen her money, who had flayed her for whatever it was she'd done, yet she was concerned for his state of mind.

– What's wrong with him? she asked.

Scarcely able to contain his consternation, Perry said

– He's found God.

– But he's an atheist, said Louise. How did he find God?

Both men looked at her as if to say, Why would you ask a lawyer *that*?

– Never mind, she said.

But she lowered her demands. She wanted only what was equitable: the house and the two hundred thousand dollars he'd taken from her. This she was given, months later, without a word of protest. It was odd, after so much conflict, to take the keys from Perry and to walk into what was now her own home.

She did not, at first, like it. She had asked for the house because she thought it a fair exchange for the humiliation he had put her through, because she loved her neighbourhood (Ottawa South) and knew it well, because it was not so far from the main library where she worked. It was a good home for her, but though Paul had taken the furniture (and donated it to charity), the house still felt as if it were steeped in him.

The man himself seemed to have disappeared. He did not come to collect the scraps he'd left (books, boxes, a radio). He did not call on her to apologize for past behaviour. It seemed he wanted nothing to do with her. But then, out of the blue, Paul visited her on a Sunday. He was dressed simply, but without elegance: black suit, black shoes.

– I hope I'm not disturbing you, he said. Do you mind if we have a few words?

Given the cooperative side he'd lately shown (and her curiosity about his conversion), she felt almost obliged to say

– No.

There was something unlike him in all of it: appearance,

demeanour, humour. The Paul she knew would not have dressed so severely, would not have smiled on being invited into his own home, would not have approved of the changes she'd made to the house.

– It looks lovely, said Paul.

As he sat at her kitchen table, he chose his old place, at the head, and rubbed the tabletop with the middle finger of his right hand as he waited for the coffee she made. There was little else to suggest the Paul she had known, but Louise had always found the rubbing, its implied impatience, offensive. She found it offensive on this Sunday too, but she wondered if it had anything to do with impatience. This Paul did not seem at all impatient. Perhaps, he could not help the motion of his finger. Perhaps, he never could. Odd to discover a new context for an old grievance.

– What is it you want, Paul?

He looked away from her.

– I need to tell you something important.

– What is it?

He drank from his coffee. Then

– I have tried to kill you, he said.

Now, what could you say to that?

– I'm glad you didn't.

– So am I, he said. I have a soul.

– I'm happy for you, she said.

– You don't understand a word. I tried to kill you, but I couldn't. I want you to know I don't hold your behaviour against you. I've forgiven you.

– Let's just get on with our lives, she said. Let's put all this behind us, okay? I'm sorry for whatever I did to hurt you.

He brought his hand down on the table, making his cup jump, startling her.

– You're not listening to me. Please listen to me. I could have killed you. I could do it now, but if I did that I would be killing myself, and my life no longer belongs to me.

He drank from his coffee. She did not know this man. The false humility, the sneaking arrogance. To come here with his murderous feelings, expecting what from her exactly? Gratitude?

– Get out, she said.

– I will, he said.

He reached for his coffee, but she took it from his reach. He was momentarily surprised, but he rose from the table and said

– Thank you.

And walked out of what had been their home.

A dramatic exit, but its significance was unclear, as was the purpose of the encounter. Was he threatening her? Letting her know he wished her dead? Forcing her to be confessor to his sins? A mystery. A mystery still, because, from the moment he stepped out of her house, Paul vacated her life.

It was the last time she *saw* Paul, but it wasn't the last time she would deal with him. It wasn't only because she'd found his visit disturbing that Paul lingered. It was also because she had begun her new life in earnest and this new life was played out against the backdrop of the old. In a word, Louise began going out. One might have thought that seeing other men would have occluded Paul further, further buried him beneath an avalanche of new impressions: darker skin, lighter skin, more beautiful hands, longer eyelashes, pale scars in different places. And so it did, but not enough.

Naturally, she did not look for men like Paul. In fact, it displeased her to discover some aspect of a man that was too close to some aspect of Paul: a way of speaking, for instance. But Paul's ghost was summoned whenever she found herself in the presence of a man with whom she relaxed because, feeling relaxed, she thought of Paul and of all that marriage had taken from her. And so, feeling relaxed, she would tense up again, as if to say to the man with whom she found herself:

– I'm sorry, but I'm not ready to let myself go.

Certainly, from time to time, she desired the solace of sexual intercourse, or thought she did, and so she would, if she felt safe, as opposed to "at ease," cooperate in her own pleasure. But freedom from Paul had not brought more occasions for loving. It had brought fewer. To be fair, it wasn't simply a matter of Paul Dylan. His ghost was one of two that haunted her. (Walter's was the other, but Walter's presence was inconstant. It wavered in her memory, like a candle by an open window.) And then there was the problem of "going out." "Going out" was often an excruciating, perverse wager. Principally because, though Fredrika was a precious friend and knew her well, she was a poor matchmaker.

For instance:

. One day, Fred announced she thought Louise had found her equilibrium and that it was time she took some "sexual healing." Louise tepidly allowed herself to be convinced and, not surprisingly, Fred had a man in mind: Ronald Atkins, an accountant with enough energy to, in his own, rather mysterious words, "sustain a colony of anteaters."

Their first impressions were dreadful. Louise could not understand how a grown man could care so passionately for basketball, while Mr. Atkins could not fathom a mature woman who filled her mind with sludge like Thomas Aquinas or Proust.

– You don't really read that stuff, right?
he'd asked when, at his prompting, she'd named a few of the writers she admired.

– You'd have to pay me to read Proust again, he said.

– Again? she asked. You've read Proust?

– Every friggin' word.

He shook his head from side to side, as if disappointed.

– Why?

– Cooze, he answered. Any man tells you he reads Proust 'cause he likes it? He's lying. All that stuff . . . literature, philosophy . . . the only reason you read that is you want what her panties are holding. You know?

Yes, she knew.

– Hope you don't mind hearing the truth, he said. Some people don't like my being so direct.

– No, not at all, she said.

She regretted having come, regretted having stayed, regretted Fred's judgment, but there was something amusing about Mr. Atkins. She wasn't sure if she wanted to prolong the conversation or end it immediately, but curiosity got the better of her.

– What have you read to impress women? she asked.

– Christ, I can barely remember it all. Let's see . . . Proust, Kant's *Critique of Pure Reason*, *The Man without Qualities*, *The Brothers Karamazov* . . . jeez, I don't know what all.

– And did you get the girl?

– Yes, I did. I wouldn't have kept reading if I hadn't. When I was at Carleton, if I liked someone I'd find out what she was taking and I'd read one of the books on her course list and then, next time we'd talk, I'd slip in a little bit about Flaubert or whatever, and we'd go from there.

– Tell me about *The Brothers Karamazov*, she said.

Atkins smiled. He looked at her over the rim of his glasses. This approach of his had been working for years. Or he thought it had. You could see that. But what was it that attracted exactly? His knowledge, his sense of humour, his boyish pretense at "honesty"? Perhaps he'd even come to this very point in a conversation so often he could tell what kind of woman she was by the title she'd asked him to discuss. Why *had* she chosen *The Brothers*?

– I don't remember it all that much, he said. Have you read it recently?

– A few years ago, she answered.

– Oh, well . . . , he said. The way I see it . . .

There followed a most unnervingly passionate performance. Mr. Atkins lovingly recounted the story. He then discussed the differences among the brothers, expressing his admiration for

Ivan, above all, and his loathing for Smerdyakov. Then, as if he could not quite remember the details, he told the story of the Grand Inquisitor. At times, during the monologue, he paused to spit peanut shells to the floor; at times, he stopped to ask if he'd got the details right, or to solicit her opinion. His eyes did not leave hers or, at least, whenever she looked up he was looking at her.

– So? he asked. Did I get it right?

She did not know what to think. It was . . . interesting that a man should choose this route to her attention. (She thought of peacocks.) It was even, in a way, flattering and, yes, because he seemed so passionate about the book, stimulating. She was certain he could, if she wished, go on talking about Dostoevsky. But it was, finally, disturbing that something for which she had deep respect should be used for such petty ends. It was as if he had read Proust, Flaubert, and Dostoevsky without being touched by the work. No, no one who knew *The Brothers Karamazov* as Atkins did could have remained untouched by the work, but he was almost monstrously disrespectful of it. He wanted to sleep with her, that's all. Why bring in Dostoevsky? Atkins was the kind of man who made her wish for plain speaking. Let him ask a clean question

– *Would you care to sleep with me?*

politely, allow her the time to decide what she wanted, and they could go from there.

She looked at his smiling face. There was something about it that made you want to scratch him. Perhaps it was his smile that turned her off.

– Very impressive, she said.

Then:

– I'm feeling a little unsteady.

– You shouldn't have drunk before we ate, he said.

– I think you're right. I wonder if we could have dinner some other time.

He surprised her. He rose from the table and said
– Let me get this.

He was, suddenly, all business: solicitous and efficient. He did not try to persuade her to stay. He became, at the end of the evening, the kind of man who might have held her interest. It was too late, though. She had left him long before they stepped out of the bar.

Of the dozen men with whom Fredrika tried to set her up after her divorce, Ronald Atkins was the most interesting. The others she saw were, by comparison, a faceless and uninspiring lot, none of whom had made the slightest effort to woo, let alone seduce. She slept with two of these others, but then the timing had been right and, more importantly, she had felt so desperate for contact that she had forgotten how true it was that "no sex" was, in fact, preferable to "bad sex."

How could it have been anything but bad, bitterness and desperation being emotions that did not lessen her fear of engagement or vulnerability. The single time she managed to clear her thoughts, the only time she came close to letting go, her lover, a *chartered* accountant, had put on the music of The Miracles. Louise wept quietly at the first notes of "Ooh Baby Baby," a song that intensely recalled her mother and father, their home. She might have recovered from her emotion but, sensing the degree to which she was moved, her lover stopped mid-caress, asked if she were okay, and, seeing her tears, began to weep himself: a moment of such vertiginous intimacy, it frightened him and he asked her to leave.

This was the last of Fred's associates with whom she went out. From that time on, she discouraged talk of "appropriate" men or "distraction." She thought it better she should find the way on her own. And so, without rancour or arrogance, Louise resolved to give up men for a year, a year being, she thought, the time she needed to reorient herself in the world.

However, six months into her moratorium on men, just as she was beginning to feel the quiet within her, she was reintroduced to Walter Barnes.

It was June. Fredrika had begun to insist that Louise needed company or she would lose the capacity for others; she would become a prematurely withered woman. It was not easy to say no to the near daily proposals that they go to such-and-such a bar with so-and-so who would bring the brother of this or that friend, a brother who was, inevitably

– *A really interesting man.*

But Louise did say no until, finally, because she could not stand to go on denying Fred the chance to do this little service, she decided to say yes to the next invitation to meet the next eligible prospect, whoever he might be.

However, it was not Fredrika who next proposed she go out on the town. It was Véronique; Véronique who had stayed out of her way, who had encouraged her to get as far away from Paul as she could, who had waited until Louise was clearly over her husband before offering a hand, not guidance.

– Lou, there's this man. I'm interested, but I don't want to go on a "date," you know? I wonder if you'd mind coming out with us? I know you're tired of blind dates, but if you could just keep me company. John'll bring a friend. It'll be four of us. I wouldn't ask you, Lou. I know how you feel, the whole swearing-off-men thing. But you wouldn't have to say much. I just don't want to put any pressure on John. I think he's serious, but I don't want to scare him away. It's easier if it's not just two of us, you know?

Yes, she knew, and she would do this because it was for Vé and this was the first time in years, it seemed, she could do something for someone else.

They were all to meet at the Brigadier's Pump. If she'd even vaguely suspected Vé of setting her up on some blind date, the place would have immediately dispelled the thought. The Pump would have suggested romance to no one save, maybe, a lonely student, and unless you were dying for fish and chips, you wouldn't have chosen to eat here. Also, you could see that Vé was anxious on her own behalf, nervous about going out with a man for whom she had secret feelings. She had dressed on the verge of casual, on the verge of romance: a knee-length mauve dress that came in at the waist and then fell; over this, a jean jacket that was too big for her. And on her feet: low-cut, crimson leather boots, with mockingbirds embroidered at the ankles.

The women arrived early and Vé ordered a Strongbow, which she sipped from a pint glass. Louise did not want to drink. She ordered a soda, to be sociable, and listened as Vé's conversation alighted on whatever subject occurred to her. Politics, fashion, books, the price of bread. There was something inexpressibly moving, seeing Vé like this: nervous and sincere. Louise felt she had been right to come along.

Then, John Patterson, Vé's friend, entered, followed by Walter Barnes, whom Louise did not immediately recognize, Walter being the last person she expected to see on this evening, of all evenings, when she was out, principally, to accompany her closest friend.

For Walter, the encounter was as unexpected but not as surprising. John Patterson was a man he did not know well, a professor of comp lit with whom he had had two conversations at Rooster's Pub; during the first, they had discussed Atwood and Hegel; during the second, Hegel and Tolstoy. Not the deepest of exchanges, but they had kept each other entertained long enough for a spark to pass from one to the other, and it was in memory of the spark that Patterson asked Walter if he would mind "tagging along" for a little conversation with a friend of his, Véronique, and a friend of hers.

– You need a chaperone? asked Walter. Is it love?

He was kidding, but Patterson answered

– Yes. I think so, yes.

To which there was no other response but to ask for the coordinates and to accompany Patterson wherever, love having preemptory precedence, even between men who did not know each other well. So, on the appointed night, Walter followed John Patterson into the Brigadier's Pump, and smiled as he recognized Louise Dylan. Véronique introduced them.

– Walter, this is my friend Louise.

– So pleased to meet you, said Walter.

– Enchanté, answered Louise.

And she stood up, uncertain if they should embrace after, what, three years, was it? Or was it four? So much time gone, and yet . . .

It was an odd kiss. It wasn't quite recognition or recollection. It was that, for a moment, their bodies failed to acknowledge the time that had passed. From their bodies' perspectives, their kiss took place in 1983. He leaned down; she looked up. His right hand went, without thought, to the place on her waist where it always rested. There was nothing indelicate about their embrace, and nothing drawn out. Time returned as soon as they parted.

Patterson and Véronique congratulated them on their fortuitous reacquaintance and then, for an hour, ignored them, more or less, so pleased were *they* to be in each other's company. One might have said, looking at the quartet, that John and Vé were the more intimate duo. They did most of the talking. They played host to the other two, made half-hearted efforts to include them in conversation and, after a time, shepherded them from the Pump into the Ritz, for pizza. Patterson and Véronique used talk as a means to test the bond between them. They were both wary of losing the friendship they enjoyed, so they made constant efforts to demonstrate friendliness, and what better way, under the circumstances, than with talk, through talk, and across talk? Their apprehension was successfully hidden by conviviality.

The case was, naturally, different for Walter and Louise. First, their proximity having abolished and then reinstated Time, it was as if they had unwittingly crossed a threshold, and they were both a little bewildered. Neither could be certain the other had felt as he had, as she had. There was no anxiety in their ignorance, though. Neither wished anything of the other, or not exactly. They sat facing each other, aware of the absurdity of their situation, and there was, in both of them, a desire to talk, there being so many things to say, along with the desire to say nothing at all but, rather, to touch, their first moment having been so . . .

What's the word for it?

After the initial, erotic charge between them, after the fig and goat cheese pizza, after wishing farewell to Patterson and Vé (who walked off together, happily), Walter Barnes and Louise Dylan (née Lanthier) walked home together, along Rideau, along Wellington, along Bank: west, then south.

A lovely night in June, eleven o'clock. It had rained while they were indoors. It rained lightly as they walked home. Clouds covered the city, and so hid from them, first, Gemini, well above the horizon, and then Virgo, beneath whose feet the moon.

– It's good to see you, Louise. I knew I'd see you again, but I wondered when.

– I thought you were trying to avoid me. Last time, you took off as soon as you saw me.

– I didn't mean to. I wasn't very happy back then.

– I'm sorry. What was wrong?

– Well, that would make a long story but, you know, after Paul put me in the hospital, I wasn't a happy man.

– Paul? Paul who?

– Your husband.

They were at the corner of Bank and Slater, Prospero Books on one side, nothing much on the other. He touched her arm as they crossed against the light.

– I'm sorry, said Walter. Of course you didn't know. He didn't tell you. Why would he?

He recounted what he remembered, and it was as if she remembered some aspect of it as well. Principally, Paul's finger: broken because . . . a car accident, wasn't it? And so, on this night in June, years later, she felt guilty, as if she should have known Paul had done this to Walter. Her fault, because Paul had done this to her as much as to Walter, as she should have known he might.

– I'm so sorry, she said.

And they waited at another light, standing beside each other, until Walter, having said

– It wasn't your fault, Lou

said

– Why don't we walk a bit more.

It being clear that all this, from which he himself had long recovered, and which he did not wish to revisit, was newly traumatic to her.

They continued to walk along Bank, because Walter lived a few blocks farther on. Louise thought she might walk him home, and then go home on her own. Walter assumed they would walk a bit, and he would accompany her home. Instead, they walked on and, at 3rd, both of them turned, without speaking, towards Walter's house, as if it were home to both of them.

Walter said

– Let me make you something

and they went in together.

It was as if two dreamers passed unexpectedly into the same dream, occupying not only the same forest of symbols but also, briefly, the same consciousness. Walter put on the kettle and prepared a cup of tea: Prince of Wales, her favourite, a sachet of which he must have (unconsciously) saved, anticipating her return, perhaps, since he never drank Prince of Wales himself. Louise sat where she could: in one of the two chairs at the dining-room table. They said nothing, until she had taken a few sips of her tea, and then she asked

– Where's your furniture, Wally?

A simple question, but one that took hours in the answering, hours during which much that Walter did not want to recall was recalled and much that Louise had kept to herself was shared with Walter:

> suicide (its failure)
> divorce (its success)
> displacement (hers)
> the discovery of home (made by both)
> regret and longing and . . .
> confusion (of the emotions)
> confusion (of the intellect) and
> bewilderment (of the soul, always supposing . . .)

They talked until five fifteen in the morning when the sun began its ascent.

For Walter, who managed at last to be open and truthful with her, this night was both exhilarating and painful. He admitted, at last, that he had lied, that he had, in fact, loved her (if *love* is the word . . . a question difficult to decide, since he was a stranger to the emotion in question). And it was like confessing he was "slow." How shameful not to have known these feelings until so late in life, and how shameful to have fled from them when they came. He had denied, all those years ago, that he loved her and, from that moment, he'd suffered as if he were wounded. He sincerely wished he could take his words back.

It was early, and it was late. Morning light came through the windows. Though she did her best to stay awake, Louise was exhausted. It was gratifying to hear, years later, what she might have wanted to hear at the time, but it was difficult to know what to think about the past, about Walter, about her own feelings. Though she was happy to see him, she had resolved her feelings for Walter long ago. She no longer felt for him as she had.

– We should maybe sleep now, said Walter.

– Yes.

Which they did, sharing Walter's bed for a few hours until Walter, who did not dare sleep too deeply, for fear he would not wake in time, rose to make himself coffee: eight thirty. Three hours rest, and it would have to do because, as it was, he barely made his nine thirty class: summer courses, a handful of students, a review of his lectures on Thorsten Veblen.

Louise woke at noon, in a bed she did not immediately recognize, awakened by an unfamiliar silence. Even when they'd had their affair, she had rarely risen with Walter, in Walter's house, and she found it disconcerting. She made the bed. She opened the bedroom window, though it was cool outside and a rude breeze mingled with the air inside. Yes, it was noon. A grey day, but noon nonetheless.

On the table, Walter had left a note, a nearly indecipherable scrawl on the back of a card:

> Lou,
> I have . . . house, but . . .
> We should . . . anytime . . .
>   Love,
>   Walter

His hand had never been neat, but this scrawl was worse than usual. It took her ten minutes to make out as much as she did. She took the time, however, because it was thoughtful of him to have left this proof he'd been thinking of her as he rushed out. Anyway, whoever chose a man for his handwriting? If it came to that, whoever *chose* a man? She herself had never collected a set of characteristics that added up to the man she wanted, and it was odd to hear women speak as if they had, as if the ideal man were Frankenstein's monster. No, now she thought of it, she had always imagined a *place* she wanted, not a man: a place with wooden floors, and tall windows that looked out onto a garden with hawthorns, wisteria, and willow trees, a west-facing garden on which the sun would shed its last light of the day. And in that imagined place she was happy, and part of her happiness was the presence of a man whose face she could not make out but of whom she could imagine, if she let herself go, strong hands, a muscular back and shoulders.

Did it not matter, then, who was with her in that place?

Yes, actually, it did. Paul had influenced her version of home, but his real presence had cut away from her imaginings all that was haphazard and mysterious enough to hold her interest. That is: she had surrendered her imaginings, for Paul. The home inside her changed to accommodate the man she had married. From the moment she married Paul Dylan it had seemed possible their life together would be an overcoming of difficulties she suspected they would have. She had lived with Paul Dylan as if he were her husband, husband in the particular sense of one whom one has encountered at the heart of oneself.

She might have said the same thing about Walter, that he had influenced her version of *place*, that she had wanted him because her imagination was more expansive when they were together. Strange: this was something she had not known until now. ("Now" being early afternoon on June 16, 1987, as she made tea for herself and ate the closest thing to a meal she could find in the man's fridge: a crust of bread, which she had toasted, and a solid piece of buckwheat honey that had rattled in its plastic container.) What she had always felt, with Walter, was this expansion of the possible.

Yes, but . . .

As she washed the dishes (her plate and knife), she thought of all she knew or imagined she knew and how little any of it had ever helped her. Better to let life take its course. If she and Walter were fated to be friends, they were fated to be friends. More than that she did not need. She'd wait until she knew what she would have to give up to keep this "friendship," then they'd see.

As it was a day off from the library, she stayed until Walter returned from Carleton. She sat at his dining-room table reading *King Lear* (one of a handful of books she found, this because of Walter's troubles, his self-indulgent sadness, though it wasn't generous to think of unhappiness as self-indulgent. She wondered if it were possible to love someone one knew well, and then wondered if it were possible to know anyone well).

Walter returned to her life.

That's easily said, as if the two took up where they'd left off four years previously, but of course their feelings for each other were not, initially, as vivid as they had been. They did not inevitably see each other, night after night, they did not mingle their finances or friendships, they did not know each other (biblically speaking) until a month had passed, and they did not begin to know each other (metaphysically speaking) for some time after that.

In effect, the two of them drifted towards each other, Louise cautious, Walter puzzled, Louise fearing more hurt, Walter unsure just how one lived with a woman to whom one has confessed one's feelings. He had, of course, read of such situations and, by all accounts, it was his duty to woo (an obscure and peculiar word). And because he found the whole thing slightly perplexing, he went about it in a perplexing way. For instance, he'd heard that women appreciated chocolates or flowers. So, he bought neither for her, on the assumption she would have had enough of cocoa and pollen by now. Instead, he surprised her with the kind of thing *he* adored: a Japanese grasshopper in amber, a chestnut in which there was a small carving of Abraham Lincoln in profile, a pair of wooden earrings painted to look like Kronos eating one of his children.

Now, few women would have found earrings in the shape of Goya's Kronos attractive, and Louise did not. She thought them "interesting" and unusual, but she adored them because, as it happened, she had had enough chocolate (Charles Baelde's truffles with dark chocolate ganache) and flowers (columbine, above all), the things her husband had given her.

Was this why they resumed their physical relationship?

No. The resumption of their sexual relationship was an accident, say, something that happened despite her better judgment, because, after a night out (latkes and applesauce at Nate's, *The Apartment* at the Towne, a languorous walk home during which she put her arm through his as they crossed King Edward and they walked together like that until Sussex when he pointed to the constellation above them, Gemini, the twins brightly skeletal on this moonless night . . .), after an intimate and unhurried night out, desire got the better of her, or got the better of them.

– It's late, he said, do you want to stay the night? There's just the bed, but it's big enough for both of us.

Walter had blushed, not because he was consciously thinking of anything sexual but because he felt foolish telling her about his bed. She knew its dimensions as well as he did, because she'd slept with him there. And *that* thought, the memory of a particular moment between them – facing each other, her leg beneath him, she reaching down to put him in – that simple image made him blush again. But how strange to feel shame at such an intense memory. He remembered everything about that remembered instant: the colour of her eyes, the cut of her hair, the warmth of her body, the feel of her leg beneath him.

– I don't know if I'm ready for that, Wally. Can I think about it for a while?

– Would you like some tea? he asked.

– Yes, she answered.

It had surprised her to see him blush. She assumed he was thinking of lovemaking. She was thinking of the same thing and the thought was arousing, but what did she want? Uncertain. What did she feel? Lucid confusion. But why should it matter, in the end? They were not young. They knew the differences between minds and souls, bodies and hearts, didn't they?

They went into the kitchen, she following behind, inadvertently admiring the nape of his neck, his lovely hands, inadvertently remembering a trip they had taken together (the only trip they had ever taken) on the spur of the moment, by train to Montreal (just for somewhere to go, because Paul was away) and back the same day, or rather, the same night, she sitting by the window feeling both embarrassed and excited as he touched her, his hands slowly moving under the dark raincoat he had put over them as if it were a blanket.

Now *she* blushed, and was grateful he did not see her as he put the kettle on the stove and took the tea down from the cupboard above the sink. She waited for as long as she could, but as he turned towards her she took the step between them and, slipping her arms around his waist, held him while looking up to kiss his lips. Unfortunately, he was not ready for the weight of her and he staggered slightly, backwards.

It was surprising how sweetly it went. True, it seemed to take forever to come, to climax, and she was conscious of every moment and that consciousness held her back, but that was all to be expected, wasn't it? Part of her still could not forgive him for having left her, did not quite believe he would not do it again. That part of her was like a needle in an apple. It would be difficult to extract.

Still, having something to forgive him for was the very essence of domesticity, wasn't it?

Some months later, leaving the Khyber Pass after an unexpected encounter with François Ricard and a young woman, it suddenly occurred to Louise that her life had changed. It had changed completely, but it was at that moment, walking home with Walter, that she realized it had changed. And, her life having changed, it felt as if it might easily change again.

Intoxicated by the idea, by the freedom uncertainty offered, she pressed Walter's arm in hers, was aware of holding his arm, aware she was walking along Elgin with a tall man who was dressed in a long, dark brown wool coat (one side of its collar turned up), light brown pants, ox-blood brogues.

He was not an easy man to be with. He was moody, absorbed by his work, by a book he'd begun to research. She could leave him, if she chose, when she chose. She could go. She felt no deep obligation to him and the exhilaration this lack of obligation brought was profound.

Still, is it in the nature of love to seek freedom or bondage?

She held Walter's arm and leaned towards him. How strange her feelings were these days, but how wonderful to know them strange.

45

PAUL DYLAN ECLIPSED

T he sun was shining and the city was heedless of the
coming winter. Paul Dylan walked at his own pace along
the promenade, west past Bank, west towards Carleton.
It was warm in the sunlight, and the curves the canal took on its
way to Dow's Lake seemed, to Paul, meandering and sacred.
Then again, on a day like this, every clump and curve of earth
seemed sacred.

He had given up his possessions and his business. (The
moment to divest had come suddenly, as these moments will, and
he had divested, giving what he could to Louise Lanthier, keeping
only enough money to save him from charity or, rather, to save
charity from him.) He had paid a final, unnerving visit to the
woman who had been his wife. (And how devastating it had been
to discover a pool of hatred, unstanchably within. He had left
his former home as if fleeing a demon.) And, on the day of his
eclipse, the day he was subsumed by God, Paul Dylan was contentedly walking by the canal, on his way to Carleton to look for
a book (*The Fire of Love*) and to talk with the man who'd recommended it.

He was approaching Bronson when he saw, walking along the
promenade before him, a familiar figure, a familiar amble. Not

knowing who it was, but certain that he should, Paul quickened his pace and was surprised to discover he had caught up to Walter Barnes.

On seeing him, Walter looked wary, but said

– Hello, Paul.

– Walter! I recognized your back, but I didn't know it was you.

The two of them walked in awkward silence towards Carleton. The trees had changed colour. There were patches of yellow and red everywhere and, from time to time, a school of dead leaves, their bellies scratching along the promenade, would tumble into the canal.

Without so much as a cough, Walter said

– You know Louise and I are together, don't you?

And it was odd that, after all that had altered within him, Paul still had trouble saying (and meaning)

– I hope you're very happy.

What else was there to say?

Walter did not look happy, however. He looked burdened.

– Listen, Paul. There's something else you should know –

– No, no. Not at all. There's nothing. You don't have to say anything, Walter. I understand. These things happen and, anyway, it's not my business any more.

The university was in sight. They might have gone their separate ways, he and Walter, after a few more yards, after a few words of farewell, but, no, Walter wished to speak.

– I'm not sure what you think you know, he said, but Louise and I were close long before now. We had an affair while you two were still married.

Walter was beside him, his back to the water. He was not lying. Paul could feel both the truth of what he said and his wariness. And in a flash, he (fleetingly) re-experienced all he had been through and it was, for a bladelike instant, as painful and humiliating as it had been at the time: the suspicion, the word of his secretary, the "proof" (Walter's embarrassment, his philandering),

Walter's innocence (Louise's deception; Løne Kastrupsen, not Louise), his apology to Walter, at Henry Wing's home . . . What was all that supposed to mean?

– *Had he been right to question his wife's fidelity?* (Yes, clearly)

– *Had he been right to assault Walter Barnes?* (Yes, but his assault had been based on false reasoning, so: no)

It was bewildering. If he had trusted Louise, he would not have hurt Walter. But if he had not assaulted Walter, would Louise have left him? No, because the man she left was the one who mistrusted her and who had hurt Walter Barnes. If he had not come to question his wife's motive for telling him she and Walter had had an affair, would he have found the anger in himself to try to kill her? No. Each hurt, every resentment was needed to drive him on to his true life, the one he was living now. If he had not tried to kill his wife, he would not have come to God.

No matter how you looked at it, it all led to God.

As the truth of this hit him, Paul suddenly clutched at Walter's sleeve.

– Thank you, Walter, he said. Thank you so much.

Walter, wary, looked guardedly at the man before him, then deliberately pushed him away.

– I've got a class to teach, he said.

How lovely it would be to have a word other than *forgiveness*, a word that does not suggest mutual understanding, forbearance, and the acceptance of pain given and pain overcome. Walter Barnes and Paul Dylan did forgive each other, but neither would have said forgiveness was preceded by understanding, forbearance, or acceptance. There had been no accord, no meeting in fraternity, and their final moment together (September 30, 1988) had different significance in the life of each man.

For Walter, it was an embarrassment, something of a failure. He had tried to erase the last misunderstanding between them. Instead, he had provoked an inexplicable reaction: not understanding but some peculiar form of gratitude. Still, and this was no small thing, he felt he had done his duty to the past and to Paul. From the moment he walked away, it was as if all business between them were settled.

For Paul, their final moment was a revelation. He had been, initially, stunned by the truth, bewildered by the emotions it called up. He did not know what to think, did not know what to feel, but it was at that moment, in the midst of bewilderment, that revelation came to him:

– This has all been done for me.

That is, in his bewilderment he saw his behaviour in light of the ground he had covered and the place he had come. He saw the trajectory, from lovelessness and anger to peace, as clearly as if it had been drawn on a map. He could not have come to this on his own. So much had had to happen for his life to reach this particular harbour, one could not deny the hand behind it, the navigator. How unlikely it seemed that his experience had been unguided. Even this, this moment with Walter depended on the "accident" of his having failed to recognize Walter's walk.

With the recognition of trajectory, there came a momentary vertigo: the will behind his fate was almost terrifying, terrifying because beyond comprehension, terrifying in its surpassing elegance. But in its purpose, how loving: to lead him to this, this revelation that freed him from doubt.

He had held Walter's sleeve, as much to keep to his feet as to communicate the depths of feeling for this man who had, unwittingly, given him the final piece of the puzzle: if all this had been done for him, it was because he was loved. He *knew* himself loved, and it was the force of God's love that overwhelmed him.

And "forgiveness"?

At the moment of recognition, there ceased to be, for Paul, anything to forgive. What was there to forgive about Truth? In fact, the two men had moved beyond "forgiveness" understood as that which can be given or taken. Rather, they had reached a *state* of forgiveness, a state in which each became *almost* anonymous to the other. Neither was an object of scorn or dislike for the other, neither an object of attention. Each was, for the other, *almost* one of the crowd. Neither of them granted nor accepted forgiveness and yet the matter between them was overcome.

In a way, these were the final moments in the life of Paul Dylan. As he walked away from Walter Barnes, he became the kind of man who could live in God, eclipsed by the light of God: Fra Paulo, in other words. And it was only a matter of time before he would make the pilgrimage to Santa Maddalena.

46

KIND WORDS FROM REINHART

Reinhart was in an expansive mood. He would not have predicted it, but from the time he abandoned MacKenzie Bowell, leaving the details to Franklin, he'd begun to paint with the kind of passion he associated with the pursuit of, let's say, a young man with long red hair who had to be seduced. This new fertility was so striking, he came to think MacKenzie Bowell a kind of Calvary: that which had to be endured in order to find something greater.

Actually, he thought of MacKenzie Bowell in many ways, trying to reason it through: perhaps, in his immersion in the thousands of images, words, ideas that preceded his design of the prison, he had discovered the key to something in himself, something he had not recognized at the time. If so, he could not think what this "key" was. Then again, perhaps it was his reimmersion in the world, post-penitentiary, that was the source of inspiration.

Whatever the prison had done, whatever it had brought about, it was amusing to Reinhart that his least successful work (most derivative, though he couldn't quite tell from what it derived) was the one that, for a year now, had given the most back to him.

It was this Reinhart, a Reinhart at peace with the world, that Edward visited one afternoon. He was not posing for a portrait or any such thing. But as, over the last months, Edward had not seen his friend, he went seeking an ear and company. Franklin's injunction to "move on," to forget St. Pierre and Mickleson and what they had done, had been neither tonic nor practical. Edward still thought about them and was easily spooked. It seemed there was no easy way, once one knew of their savagery, to put the two men out of one's mind. They hung about his imagination like the smell of smoke from a woodstove in a winter cabin. And, of course, as often as he thought about Mickleson and St. Pierre, he thought about the McAllisters, about fish tanks, sweaters, and tea, and he was troubled by visions of bloodied lap dogs. He had avoided Reinhart for this very reason, not wishing to disturb him.

They spent the first of his visit as they always did: drinking and looking at paintings. That is, Reinhart looked at paintings and Edward, when he had had enough, looked out the window. Inevitably, this is the time Reinhart liked best. He appreciated Edward's company at the beginning of the looking, but appreciated even more that Edward left him to himself after one or two canvases. In fact, Edward was one of the few with whom Reinhart ever shared his work.

When they'd finished looking and had sat down to eat olives and a stale Boko baguette, Edward began to tell Reinhart what had been on his mind for so long.

Far from disturbing Reinhart, this recounting brought a closeness they hadn't shared in years. When Edward had finished, Reinhart asked

– Did you tell Franklin about all this?

– Yes and he told me to just let it go.

Reinhart said

– That's good advice. You're not cut out for this, Eddy because it was clear Edward was not ruthless enough to swim with Micklesons and St. Pierres. It also seemed, to Reinhart, that Franklin had not been thinking straight when he'd hired the two men.

– Franklin's not a bad guy, said Reinhart, but it's a real can of worms using men like that. Once you use them, where do you stop? Anyway, he's a civil servant. Maybe sometimes he doesn't think about consequences.

– I'm a civil servant, Rein.

– But you're not ambitious.

– What does that mean?

– It means you wouldn't do just anything to climb that ladder and get your name in some ledger in the National Archives.

– I *am* ambitious, Edward said.

Reinhart smiled.

– Eddy, you've spent years working for Franklin. Why? To please Franklin. But what about you? You've got to find something for yourself.

Edward knew, or in any case felt, that Reinhart had said the truth, but it was a truth that illuminated his friendship with Reinhart as well. His ambition had always been for his friends, never himself. It seemed he himself did not have the kind of mind that wanted. He had no talent for wanting. He knew his immediate needs, and satisfied them, but what was it to want something it would cost years to achieve? In the end, he felt, he lacked imagination.

– In the end, I lack imagination, he said.

– You've got great imagination. Otherwise, you wouldn't care about others.

Reinhart brought Edward's coat, put it around his shoulders.

– Let's walk, he said. My hands are tired.

They walked west along Gladstone, north on Bronson. This was, now that Reinhart thought of it, the first time, since childhood, he felt obliged to offer serious advice to a man who was, after all, a friend of almost forty years. Wasn't it interesting that

Edward had managed to impose so little on him? It was at moments like these that the person beside you is illuminated, some essential trait revealed, a thread one could pull to unveil the nature of the nothing within.

(The last time Edward had asked anything of him was in Grade Eight when he asked Reinhart to "help him" with Albert Cohen. Reinhart blushed at the memory of the beating he'd inflicted on Albert and of Albert following him around thereafter, like a puppy. How unpredictable sexual memories are in their intensity.)

They walked in silence, the night surprisingly warm – not sultry, you couldn't call Ottawa sultry, in November, but it was as if the city had moved south, to Maryland, say, or North Carolina. The weather was unusual and it may be it provoked in Reinhart a strong sensation of time, a vision, almost, of himself and Edward as they had been as children.

– Listen, Eddy, you know I care about you.

– Well, yeah, of course. You know I care about you too said Edward, embarrassed that Reinhart had spoken words their friendship made superfluous.

– No, no, just listen. What I mean is, you've got to move on. I think you should leave this job with Franklin. How are you going to get anywhere chasing after his vision? I just don't see what's in it for you.

– But you designed it.

– Yes, I did, and I'm glad I did, but my work is done. That's the last time I'll do anything like it. I wasn't an architect at the start of all this, and I'm no architect now, but the point is I'm not wasting away in someone else's universe. Let the things that don't belong to you go. It'll be better for you. Anyway, Eddy, you're being taken places you don't like.

What if he *did* have imagination? Should he dissociate himself from Franklin's means and Franklin's ends?

At Somerset, he asked Reinhart

– What would you do?

And Reinhart answered

 – I'd quit.

Edward had the same sense of foreboding he'd had for some time, but he simply could not quit and leave Franklin to fend for himself. It wasn't in him. He was loyal and loyalty meant something. He would stay put and stay quiet until all this was over, until MacKenzie Bowell was built. Only then, if even then, would he be able to resign with a clear conscience.

– I can't quit, said Edward

– Well, look, said Reinhart. You really didn't have much to do with these guys. I don't see how it could hurt you, if you just keep quiet and do your work. Anyway, I know you. You'll find your way.

– Yes, said Edward. Sooner or later we all find our way, because there's only one destination.

Words so uncharacteristic of Edward Muir, Reinhart stopped mid-stride.

– Where'd you hear that? he asked.

– What? Oh. Dad used to say it.

– Really? Your Dad's a pretty happy guy.

– Not after his sister died.

– Oh, said Reinhart. That's true.

Reinhart had a sudden memory not of Mr. Muir but of Edward's mother, the sound of her, the first adult he had seen weep: he and Edward walking into the kitchen where she sat, head down until she heard them and got up to find them something to eat, rubbing her eyes as she did.

Even by streetlight, Edward looked very like his mother. No wonder Reinhart couldn't stop drawing or painting Edward's portrait. However he disguised him, against whatever background he was set, Edward was inevitably hearth, for Reinhart.

They were almost at the river. It was time to turn back.

Reinhart asked

– How's your mother?

But as Edward answered, Reinhart had an unexpected vision of Edward dressed as Federico da Montefeltro in della Francesca's portrait. (How the Old World had colonized his imagination! Or was it his imagination that had colonized the Old World?)

– I'm sorry, Eddy. What were you saying?

{ 47 }

EDWARD SPEAKS UP

It would have been sensible for Edward to keep quiet about
Mickleson and St. Pierre. There was no upside to speaking.
Why, then, did he speak of the men to Mary Stanley? Well, to
begin with, Mary was the one who broached the subject one
afternoon when, after a day in which there'd been little to do,
she had casually asked if he was acquainted with St. Pierre and
Mickleson.

– No, he'd answered. I couldn't be friends with animals like
that.

– How're they animals? Mary had asked.

– I'll tell you some other time, he'd said.

He'd had no intention of saying anything "some other time."
He was speaking to a woman and he could not keep from trying
to make himself seem interesting or, at least, possessed of interesting information. *Amour propre* demanded it.

– Hmph, Mary had said
not fooled by his deferral.

– No, I'm serious, said Edward. We should go out for coffee
sometime. We've worked together all these years and –

– Edward, would you come in here, please?

Franklin had heard this exchange between Mary and Edward. After calling him into the office and closing the door behind them, he turned on Edward and said

– What do you think you're doing? Why? Why would you be talking about St. Pierre and Mickleson?

Caught off guard, Edward answered

– No, no, Frank, you're overreacting. I was just talking. That's all.

– Well, stop it. It's irresponsible.

Edward, feeling almost parentally castigated, was sheepishly defensive.

– You're right. I'm sorry. But, you know, those guys deserve to be punished for what happened to the McAllisters. I know I shouldn't say anything about them, but I wish there was something we could do.

– What are you *talking* about? asked Franklin.

– Nothing, I'm just saying, if you look at this objectively, there must be some way to punish them for what they did. That's what I'm saying. If you could tell the *right* people about them, it wouldn't necessarily be bad, don't you think?

Franklin stared at Edward for a moment, before recovering his sangfroid.

– Look, Eddy, this is all ancient history. Just let it go.

Later that day, as he walked out of the office and down the quiet halls, Franklin wondered just how well he knew Edward Muir.

They'd been acquainted for more than twenty years. In that time, Edward had seen him through the worst: his despair while running for office, his despair after losing. Edward had encouraged him when he decided to translate Avvakum and Edward had welcomed him back to the Hill when his self-imposed exile ended. Edward's admiration for him was plain and, ultimately, the admiration gave pleasure. That is to say: for more than twenty years, Franklin had enjoyed Edward's company.

And yet, what *did* he know about the man? Only the trivial: the physical details, the brown eyes, dark hair, and so on, the personal data, that he lived with his parents, was left-handed, had studied history, that his best friend was gay (and, be it said in passing, Franklin had his suspicions about Edward, on that score). Edward was geniality itself when he was with friends, sometimes thoughtless when dealing with others. And, most pertinently, he was expansive when drunk.

That was, more or less, the extent of Franklin's knowledge and, before this, it had been sufficient. But, on hearing Edward off-handedly express his opinion of St. Pierre and Mickleson it suddenly seemed to him that his ignorance of the man had become a liability. How sharp was Edward's judgment? He did not know. He wondered to whom else Edward might have spoken. Reinhart? His parents? Nameless drinkers in neighbourhood bars? He wondered just how discreet Edward had been over the years, how careful with the details of ministry business. There was no way of telling.

So, as well as hard feelings about the dismemberment of Alba, hard feelings about Rundstedt's having decided, without telling him, which buildings would, in the end, be built, uncertainty about the fate of the ministry, and pessimism about life itself these days, there was mistrust of Edward Muir. It was too much. Think of all the years he'd spent in a city he disliked, a city in which he'd made only one friend, a friend who, it turned out, was as mysterious to him as an enemy might have been. The full extent and depth of his solitude sprang up in his imagination like a field of spiny, black bramble. He found himself resentful of Edward, and he began to consider how to free himself of what was, now, an acid presence, a reminder of his isolation.

It being a warm evening and, having no other duties to fulfill, Franklin left the office and walked. He walked along Rideau all the way to Record Runner, where, after a browse, he bought Glenn Gould playing Gibbons and Sweelinck. He bought it on the advice of a clerk who swore it was better than Gould's final recording, an "abominable" *Goldberg Variations*, but Franklin would have bought anything the man suggested. After that, he ate at Marcel's, a bistro in the Market, and passed a not unpleasant evening out. He then returned to his apartment and fell asleep to the music of Orlando Gibbons.

And yet . . .

Though Franklin would not have said he'd been overly upset by this day, it proved curiously persistent. For years afterwards, Franklin remembered the wainscotting at Marcel's (painted reddish brown), the ruddy stains on a white polyester tablecloth. Besides the waiter's clothes, he remembered the stubble on the man's chin, a furtive tuft of hair on the second knuckle of his left hand, and the smell of his breath. He remembered the name of a businessman sitting at the table beside him ("Hi, I'm Roger") and the voice of a woman sitting across the room from them. Nor was his memory confined to the inside of Marcel's. He also remembered the weather, some of the cars he saw along Bank Street, and the sound of the trees shaken by the wind. In fact, it sometimes happened that a number of these details came back all at once, so that he began to think the memories of this day were like a cloud of midges.

Worse, the details of this day often brought with them the worst despair, a despair very like the anguish he'd felt as a child in Anse Bleu. Had it not been that MacKenzie Bowell might still prove effective, might still redeem all of his choices, he would almost certainly have succumbed to his own depression.

Days after the unpleasantness with Edward, Franklin and François met for lunch.

There was no agenda to their meeting. They had spoken since their missed appointment. François had passionately presented his objections to the architect's designs, decrying the expense the prison represented, reminding Franklin that there was poverty in the land and the homeless to be seen to. Franklin had listened distractedly, before letting François know that, although he could have refuted these concerns, there was no longer call for objections or refutations. The architect's designs were too expensive to stand, as François' own estimates had made plain, and Franklin was now awaiting the stripping down Cabinet would impose on the designs, awaiting the results of a surgery that would permanently damage his "child." That being, more or less, the end of that, the two men had gone pensively on to the other things: governmental gossip, philosophical issues, and so on.

If they had spoken more frequently than they usually did since then, it was because François now (perhaps unconsciously) sought occasions on which to see or speak about Mary. On this day, for instance, François would have preferred to lunch with Mary, but as they had recently seen a movie together (a rather strange movie, *The Last of England*, in which, among other seemingly random occurrences, a man eats and then vomits up a cauliflower, a scene that still poisoned François' meals when he thought about it) and he did not want it to seem he was pursuing her, he instead invited Franklin, who had time on his hands, for lunch. But François went to Franklin's office early so he had a chance to speak to Mary for a while before he and Franklin left.

The restaurant they chose (Don Alfonso's) was, in its interior, plain but not drab. They ordered gazpacho and tilapia for Franklin, gazpacho and paella for François, and a white Rioja they shared. Franklin asked after Daniel, mentioned a covert wish for children of his own, denigrated his knowledge of women, and adverted (glancingly) to the one woman he had loved. He was, in other words, expansive and reflective.

When they had finished eating, as they were drinking the manzanilla Franklin ordered, François said

– You know, I miss the Fortnightly Club. I haven't been going as often as I used to.

– It seemed like a waste of time to me, said Franklin.

– Not at all, answered François. I went the other evening and they were talking about Plato's *Republic*. The question was if a republic can be moral when it's based on immorality. Getting rid of artists, forcing people to do the jobs you think they're suited to ... how can you have a morally good state founded on injustice?

– That's a naive question, answered Franklin. *All* states are founded on injustice. Someone rules, someone serves, and power keeps things in order and running. You should judge a state by what it *does*, not how it's founded.

– It isn't so simple, said François. A good monarchy starts with an enlightened monarch. A corrupt democracy starts with a corrupt populace. Origin influences character, don't you think? Plato's republic begins with the idea of control, not justice. So, how can it ever be just, except by accident? Look at it another way. What if MacKenzie Bowell Penitentiary ...

Here, François argued that Franklin's prison, if it had been made by corrupt men, would have carried with it a stink of hypocrisy that would have turned its inmates cynical and inoculated them against whatever nobility the place held. This Franklin easily answered, comparing Bowell Penitentiary to a work of Art that, despite its origin, ennobles. Think, for instance, of François Villon: murderer and thief, hanged (or was it banished?) for being a villain. And yet, is there a deeper poem than *Ballade des dames du temps jadis* or, better still, *Le Grand Testament*, which he wrote on his release from jail:

> En l'an de mon trentiesme age
> Que toutes mes hontes j'euz beues,
> Ne du tout fol, ne du tout saige
> Non obstant maintes peines eues ...

In fact, François' argument was so feeble, Franklin (more bitter than joking) asked

– You really want to drive the last nail into MacKenzie Bowell's coffin, don't you?

François laughed.

– Not at all, Frank. I'm not disappointed it won't be built the way it was designed, but part of me is sad for you. I know you believed in it.

The park outside Franklin's window was striped by waning sunlight. A portion of it was in pinkish light, a portion in shadow. A strong wind moved the tree branches from time to time and rattled the panes on the doors to the balcony. The world, if it was any one thing, was a correlative to his emotions: of two minds and agitated. The meal with François had not been unpleasant, but it had filliped his impatience with philosophical debates. The morality of Plato's republic? Just the kind of thing to turn you against thinking itself. And yet, he could not let it go, because he had felt, rightly or not, implicated, felt that *he* had been François' quarry and that the real question was not "what is a good state?" but "what is a good man?"

So, what *did* it mean to be a good man?

Was it not to pursue, selflessly, ideals that spoke to a greater good, a good beyond the self? Had he been pursuing a *personal* vision with Alba? No, he had not. He did not need any of the renown that would have come had the prison been built as it had been imagined. He needed only to feel that his time on Earth added up to something solid, something of value to those around him. He had found the thing he could believe in and, believing, he had felt less estranged from the world. Now that he had failed to shepherd Alba into being, what was left?

What was left for the good man who has failed?

Hope, of course. That and the knowledge he *is* a good man, whatever missteps he may have taken.

{ 48 }

IN WHICH: RUNDSTEDT LEAVES THE SCENE

What was it that undid Albert Rundstedt? Was it "Larry" with his photographs of the minister and a woman named "Gudrun Lindemann"? No, of course not. You can't blame the guillotine for the walk towards it. Besides, neither Larry nor Gudrun was about when the end came.

Was it, then, a question of longing or desire?

Yes, to an extent, but both of these were heightened by the change of fortune that promoted him from ambitious but honest drudge to a position of power and influence.

Was it, finally, a lack of self-awareness?

Yes, this it certainly was, because Rundstedt was a man who had no idea how principled, well intentioned, and honourable he was. He'd had, in other words, no idea what mattered most to him.

Immediately after his meeting with the Estonian Larry, Rundstedt had considered, momentarily, cooperating with whomever it was Larry represented. The photographs of himself and Gudrun would lacerate his family, his friends, and his party, a party that had suffered through more than its share of scandals. If only to protect those who trusted him, it was tempting to carry on as if there were no Gudrun, no Larry, no espionage. To do that, however, would have been an even greater betrayal. So, the question was how to lessen, as much as possible, *if* possible, the pain others would feel. To do that he would have to suffer as much or more than anyone else. That is, he would have to abandon the goals he cherished and the standing he had attained.

Before leaving office, however, there were three communities to inform: his family, his constituents, his party. Each would have to be handled in its own way. To his family, he would have to be brutally frank – honest with Edwina and then, though the idea crippled him, with the children.

So, for the first time in his life, after more than five decades on Earth, Albert Rundstedt was obliged to look coldly at what he was and at what he would be. It might have been worse: he might have had to confront himself in Vancouver or, God help him, in Ottawa. Instead, he was allowed the consolation of his own city, Calgary. On the day he decided to tell Edwina what had happened, Rundstedt walked along or above Memorial Drive from Centre to Crowchild. The river was a thoughtful companion, as rivers sometimes are, and this was the first time he had walked this far in, what?, thirty years? If he were to be banished, better to be banished here where he could accompany the Bow. If he had to lose everything, better to start again here.

By 14th Street, the understanding he might lose the only woman he had loved filled him with such anguish he wondered how he would survive. He had been thoughtless for an instant, had looked away from the road, and suddenly, there was an oncoming car. How true it was that men did not know what awaited them, all of life an illusion until one came to a moment that was almost tangible, a moment that would not leave.

What a dark train of thought. But how ridiculous that a man his age had not seen it before. He had sat by at the deaths of his parents and at the passing of Edwina's brother. He had visited hospitals and hospices up and down the province, had shaken hands with paraplegics, had commiserated with those who hadn't seen the car coming, hadn't checked the safety on the pistol, hadn't noticed the rust on the railing. He could barely remember the words of solace he'd spoken, but he knew that, had they been offered to him now, by the side of the Bow, he would have drawn little comfort from them.

And yet . . .

He was not the kind of man to take refuge in darkness. What good would it do to go over and over the tangle of the last four years? What good to decide which moment he might have avoided: the election itself, his appointment to Cabinet, his trip to Paris? He did not have the capacity to discover the speck of poison in a bushel of grain. Nor would he turn to heaven and decry his fate. His belief in God, fervent and unswerving, did not extend to blame, certainly not for mistakes he himself had made.

He looked down at the river, back at the island, and stopped thinking about himself. He thought, instead, of Edwina, of the red hat she'd bought to wear at her brother's wedding. How amusing it had been . . . like a red shoe . . .

It was not as difficult as he'd imagined it would be but, in a way, that made it more painful.

They were alone, he and Edwina. She knew there was something wrong the minute he walked in the door. There had been something wrong since he returned from Vancouver, but he'd hidden whatever it was so well she'd almost managed to push her concern to another part of her consciousness. Still, no use pretending. Things had changed so much that she had been able to conceive the inconceivable: he was having an affair. She had been wrong to stay at home while he was stranded in Ottawa. Though she and the children had lived in Ottawa for most of his political life, she had pleaded to stay in Calgary for this one term. It was all her fault. She was willing to admit it, had admitted it to him already, in her mind. Bound to happen. Albert was a desirable man and lonely, and it had been nonsense to let him go off on his own.

She almost said as much when he admitted he had something terrible to confess. She almost said

– *It doesn't matter, Alby*

but the look of him stopped her. He looked not "different" but, rather, "the same," the way he'd looked when his mother died.

– What is it? she asked

suddenly afraid for the children.

– Oh, Ed, I didn't have an affair, but it looks like I'm having one.

He spoke mournfully, and he assumed his words made sense, but, really, he had spoken the most obscure sentence she'd heard from him in their long life together. They were in the dining room. They stood beside the table her father had given for their wedding: a long rectangle, darkly stained, worn smooth and flat in some places, smooth and dented in others. She had set the table hours before, choosing, first, the good china, then the yellow Fiestas, then the good china again, distracted beyond words.

They would not be eating for hours.

– It only looks like I'm having an affair, he said again.

Edwina nodded sympathetically, as if she'd understood this time, but then she came to herself and said

– What do you mean, Alby?

Rundstedt, who had kept his coat on, took the incriminating pictures from an inner pocket and, an excruciating thing to do, he gave them to his wife. This had, at first, minimal effect. Edwina sat down. She laid the photographs out before her in a fan. She peered down at them, interested but seemingly oblivious to their content. She squinted as she looked so that Rundstedt, concerned, was about to ask if she wanted him to turn on the chandelier.

– Who's the woman? Edwina asked.

– She said her name was Gudrun.

– Oh, so she was German?

It seemed to Rundstedt that his wife did not understand the depth of their misfortune, and he was confused. Edwina always understood or foresaw the consequences of moments and incidents before he did.

– She said she was German, anyways.

– Oh. Who took the picture?

– I don't know.

– They must have been very close.

– There was no one in the room but us.

She held up the photograph of Rundstedt, magnifying glass in hand, nose to the pudendum of a dancer.

– Why'd you need a magnifying glass, Alby? Was it . . . different?

– Was what different?

– Down there.

– You can see for yourself, he said.

– That's true, she answered. She looks normal. So I don't understand the magnifying glass then.

Truth be told, Rundstedt, who had made use of the glass, didn't understand its purpose any more than Edwina did. He told her the nature of the bar, described how he had come to be there, and explained how Gudrun had persuaded him to get as close as he could to the dancer, but, in the end, this was a matter one either understood or one did not. There was not, and there never would be, reason for him to peer so closely at what was, all things considered, not so unusual.

After her questions about the bar in Osaka, Rundstedt was convinced Edwina *would* not understand the significance of his photographs. She did not seem to mind that her husband was in a hotel room, a young woman on him like he was made by Schwinn. As if she'd found the photographs entertaining, she asked

– Are there any more, Alby?

– No, he said, that's all he gave me. Aren't there enough?

– Who gave them to you?

Edwina understood the significance of her husband's photographs. She understood entirely, and suspected they might bring about his fall from grace, but the photographs themselves were appeasing. They left no doubt that Albert was wrong. He'd said, "It looks like I'm having an affair," but it looked like nothing of the sort. He was so obviously unhappy to be touched by the woman on his lap, one wondered how she had managed to get on him in the first place.

He had been thoughtless to be taken like this. It was thoughtless to endanger everything he'd worked for, but that was, perhaps, her fault as well as his. Hadn't her own mother warned her, so long ago, about letting her husband out of the yard? She'd said

– Eddy, a husband's like a bad dog. You shouldn't let him out the yard on his own.

Her mother's attempt to share wisdom, and the only advice she remembered receiving from Hannah, who, Edwina was certain, was not thinking of Albert so much as she was of Oskar, Edwina's father, whose reputation had been well known. In fact, her mother had almost certainly loved Albert more than she did her own husband, and had died thinking him a good son, but Albert was a man and, for the women of her mother's generation, it was a great shame men were issued their parts without proper training. To her mother's mind, finding a responsible man was akin to finding a civilized savage. God works in mysterious ways, but not often.

Edwina had always thought Albert an exception. It had taken some forty years to discover that the man she thought incomparable was, in the end, comparable. In that time, however, she had also come to know herself, and in coming to know herself, she thought she had come to understand her mother's words more fully. It wasn't that men were lesser than women, nor that they were contemptible. It was, rather, that their flaws were different. They did not have fewer of them, nor more. Their flaws were the price women paid for loving men, and vice versa, and it had always been, to Edwina, bearable.

That, in any case, is what she hoped her mother meant because, whatever the meaning, her mother and father now lay in the same cemetery, side by side, their flaws forgiven (if there is a God) or forgotten (otherwise).

When he finished telling her all about "Larry," Edwina said

– You're not going to give him anything, are you, Alby?
and Albert, as if it were unbearably sad, or as if he were betraying her further, said

– No. I'm sorry, Ed.

They went into the kitchen and began, distractedly, to cook.

– You'll have to resign, she said.

It was not possible for him to resign immediately, though.

He and Edwina planned his departure, wrote a modest speech for his resignation, and he left word with Al Jackson that, if they would have him, he wished to return to lawyering where he had left it: for the firm of Jackson, Washington, and Dunn LLB. He did not want to return to law, but as he was about to make a life in politics difficult for himself, he had little choice. He might have asked those who knew and admired him to direct him to more prestigious firms, but, really, the only life he wanted would soon be beyond him, so what did it matter where he worked?

There was no question, he had to go, and yet . . . The word before the election was that it would be close. If he resigned before election day, he might hurt his party's chances. To be, himself, out of the ring was one thing; to help defeat the Conservatives was another. He believed in its ideals. He believed in free trade. He believed in Mulroney's vision. Even though it meant a moral compromise, he did not see how he could endanger its progress. And what if it were close and power depended on his seat in Parliament? What if his resignation crippled the government? He would cross that bridge if he had to.

It was said, before the election, that his opponent (Jock MacCallum, a school principal running for the Liberals) was popular, that it was a good thing Rundstedt was at his post for this election, but, as if the people themselves knew resignation was on his mind, there was, for this election, an outpouring of support for his campaign. He had never felt quite so appreciated.

You might almost say circumstances conspired to have him run. So . . .

He ran.
He was elected.
Then, after a suitable time, he resigned.

Having done his all for the Progressive Conservatives, satisfied after his trouncing of the Opposition, relieved that the PC did not absolutely need his vote in Parliament, Rundstedt returned to Ottawa to clean house and prepare for the end. (Edwina went with him.) There were two pressing duties to perform. First, before anything else, he had to speak to Martin Brian. After all the man had done for him and for the country, it would have been unforgivable to tell anyone of his resignation before he told the prime minister. Second, he would have to inform Franklin. Until Cabinet appointed someone to take Rundstedt's portfolio, Franklin would have to see to the ministry's remaining business.

When did Brian Mulroney become Brian Mulroney?

That is the question that occurred to Rundstedt as he walked into the prime minister's office. He was filled with admiration for Brian, but he was aware that he had not always admired the man. Was it that he had not always been able to see what was admirable in him? Was it, rather, that in leadership the man's best qualities had a sharper profile? Or was it, perhaps, that the man with whom he now spoke was not the same man he had met four years ago? Whatever it was, they were ill at ease. They were not best of friends, never would be. They were politicians, one of whom did not know what the other wanted of him. At the best of times, they were only as friendly as actors competing for the same part, and now that Rundstedt had requested a one on one, the prime minister was on his guard.

And yet, yes, the man was a strong symbol of himself, self-confident, crafty, blunt, and warm. He was six inches taller than you thought, however often you'd met him. His mouth was a dainty slash above the expanse of his chin, his eyes lovely. One felt that Brian would never find himself in the situation Rundstedt had. He was not that kind of man or, if he was, that aspect of him was profoundly hidden.

Martin Brian was a politician's politician. He shook Rundstedt's hand, as if they were close friends. He said

– How you doing, Alby?

as if he were genuinely concerned. Then, solicitous, he put a hand on Rundstedt's shoulder and directed him to the chair beside his desk.

– What can I do for you?

– I've got some bad news, Brian.

– What's the matter, Alby?

Rundstedt took the photographs from his pocket and laid them out before the prime minister.

– I want you to see these before they become public, said Rundstedt. I think I'm going to have to resign.

Martin Brian said

– Ahh . . .

as he examined the pictures of his Cabinet member in the embrace of an unclothed young woman, and then he said

– I didn't know you had it in you, Alby.

– No, said Rundstedt.

– Well, this is a real kick in the nuts.

The prime minister sat down. His first impulse was to make certain Rundstedt was all right. At times like this, his anger was momentarily quelled by an instinct to protect those close to him, and Rundstedt though not close was close enough. But, really, this was too much. How was it possible to choose a Cabinet, *two*

Cabinets in which there were so many careless people? How had he come to be saddled with Suzanne Blais-Grenier or Robert Coates or, now, Albert Rundstedt? It seemed to him, at times like this, that the Blais-Greniers of the world, to whom he naively extended a hand, fooled him by appearing normal. This one, for instance. He had taken Rundstedt for a solid man, responsible and popular and, above all, lacking in the imagination that led to this: lurid and embarrassing photographs that would shake the public's faith in the prime minister, in his Cabinet, and in the party. He looked at the man before him. Rundstedt was dressed in a dark blue suit, a kerchief like a crimson coxcomb in his breast pocket, a brilliant white shirt, button-down collar, a solid yet faintly irides-cent crimson necktie, and cufflinks in the shape of Lilliputian six-shooters. You had to give the man credit. He still *looked* trustworthy.

After an hour or so, they agreed Rundstedt would face the public manfully and resign. He would step down before the photos were made public. They would minimize the damage to the party. There would be:

1) A simple press conference, no questions: reasons of state.
2) No dissemination of the evidence: it would be unedifying for the public to see Rundstedt with a naked and nearly bald woman. (If the photos were made public, Rundstedt would be seen to have done the right thing in resigning to protect his family.)
3) Rundstedt would use all his resources, if any remained after his resignation, to help elect his Conservative successor.
4) Foreign Affairs would deal with the East Germans, though this blackmail was most unlike the East Germans, who were generally interested only in West Germany. It was much more like the Soviets, even down to the incom-petence of the agent who had tried to turn Rundstedt. In any case, the whole sad business would be shared with the Americans and they would take it from there.

At the end of their time together, the prime minister asked
– Where did you get your cufflinks, Alby?
Rundstedt looked down at his cufflinks.
– Les Cheveux Rouge du Forgeron, he answered.
– Here in town? They look Western.

Rundstedt tugged at his shirtsleeves until they descended far enough to reveal his cufflinks to best advantage. Then, he leaned forward; and then, he got up, put his left wrist by a window so the cufflink might be seen in daylight, daylight as it washed over the washed-out city. Hull, the city on the other shore, looked anemic beneath the anemic blue sky, and the river, not quite frozen, was now like a long tail separating one shore from the other. As the prime minister politely examined the cufflink, the winter landscape momentarily hypnotized poor Rundstedt. Once he resigned, he would not be back here. He would not see any of this again. The city he had known for thirteen years would recede in his memory.

All for the good.

Good riddance.

Rundstedt's resignation from Cabinet was unnerving (and slightly humiliating for its trivial finale: a man at the end of his career displaying clever cufflinks to another too polite to admit indifference), but his final meeting with Franklin was closer to what he expected. You could see Franklin was not prepared for the news. He was incredulous, full of concern, and outraged that communists could do this to a faithful servant.

– There must be something we can do, said Franklin.

– There's nothing, answered Rundstedt. The only thing would be for me to play along with my blackmailers and that'd be worse, in the end. Anyways, you don't need me. MacKenzie Bowell is in good shape. I'm proud of what we've done. Maybe I'll even come back when construction's finished.

Franklin nodded at Rundstedt's remarks, but you could see he had his doubts. He seemed genuinely upset to see him go, and

Rundstedt felt that this was what he would miss most: like-minded men. True, there was a hint of desperation to Franklin's commiseration, but Rundstedt took it as proof of Franklin's commitment to the penitentiary, despite all the changes made to it, and as tribute to their work together. Good to know there were a few faithful associates about.

He spoke to the others in his office in vague terms. He spoke of neither cause nor calendar when he told Mary and Edward of his imminent departure, but he thanked them for their loyalty and wished them the best in their careers.

With that, there was only the public to inform.

There had been rumours of something, a scandal or change of the guard. So, Rundstedt's former campaign office was filled with journalists and photographers. There was barely room for everyone. Rundstedt, his wife, and both of their children all sat in foldout chairs behind a black-metal desk. When the journalists had settled and there had been a call for silence, Rundstedt stood up to speak. He said

– I'm sorry, boys, but I won't be taking any questions.

– Now or afterwards? someone asked.

– Neither, said Rundstedt. I've called this conference to announce my retirement from politics. My press secretary will take questions.

There was disbelief, disappointment, and some surprise, but mostly there was a surge of professional current whose accompaniment was the whirr and click of cameras.

– I've been a politician most of my adult life, said Rundstedt. And it's been a pleasure serving the voters of Calgary South. But I'm faced with a family crisis, a serious personal matter that has to be dealt with. It's been an honour serving the people of Calgary South, them and all Albertans, but I'm a husband and a father first. I'll be speaking to my constituents personally, in the next few days, to make sure they understand, but my decision is final. Mr.

Yanovsky will answer your questions about the timetable for an election. And I want to thank you all for your support.

As soon as Rundstedt tried to move away from the desk, the questions began: Minister Rundstedt this and Minister Rundstedt that, but Rundstedt was true to his word and left the questions for his press secretary, Mr. Yanovsky, who felt he had been thrown to the dogs.

All in all, this press conference was a painful duty done and a relief to have finished. For a while, it even seemed his blackmailers had decided to do nothing. Whoever the Estonian worked for, however, "Larry" was not a charitable man. Having been thwarted, he (or his masters) sent all the photographs of Rundstedt (Rundstedt in Gudrun's arms, Rundstedt "window shopping" at Cosey Corner) to the Calgary papers anonymously and free of charge, a week after Rundstedt's resignation. And although Rundstedt was a well-liked man and a respected politician, it would have been asking too much for the *Sun* to refrain from publishing at least one of the photographs (with Gudrun's nipple blacked out) under the headline:

"FUNSTEDT" IN FLOOZY FAUX PAS

It was an unpleasant surprise to find this moment in Osaka everywhere in Calgary. Worse, this image of him was one that stayed in the collective mind, despite his years of faithful and untroubled service. And later, when his department's role in funding "gorgeous prisons" came to light, the public was inclined to believe the worst of Rundstedt. Again, the *Sun*:

"FUNSTEDT" IN FOUL FUNDING FIASCO

Still, neither the pictures nor the eventual outrage at MacKenzie Bowell were the end of Rundstedt. Far from it. Though he lost his influence and his hold in the political world, he was left with the things he had first set out to protect and preserve: his home, his wife, his children, his profession (law, after all). The fire he'd passed through left him in full possession of all that mattered. He had his sanctuary in the midst of the city, Calgary, for which he was made. He had managed to keep his principles, to serve his party, to help with the promotion of free trade, of national unity. And yet, how does a man learn satisfaction with what he has? How does a man whose profession (politics) was restlessness itself learn contentment?

To begin, he had to unlearn the self-consciousness public life had, in his final days of service, imposed on him. Then, he had to learn satisfaction with the life he was living. Neither was easy to accomplish, but he was helped by two things. First, he was by nature outgoing and his ease in his own skin came back to him gradually after his resignation. And then, when he'd had time to think things over, he actually felt proud of himself. He had chosen to abandon the life he wanted rather than allow "Larry" to blackmail him. As a result, he felt free to condemn the lack of principles many of his contemporaries showed, the Liberals, in particular.

– At least I knew when to step down, he'd say.

And after a while (not a long while, either) a fair number of his former constituents agreed with him. They remembered him as a flawless MP, the kind of man who'd always stood up for them, the kind of man who, compared to any Liberal of your choosing, was pretty darned honest. In fact, it was common to have someone say to him:

– You know, Alby, you should run for office again.

To which he would answer

– You know, I just might.

49

TWO HOUSES, ONE HOME

It is so difficult to say why certain places are hospitable. It's a matter of feeling and sensation, something that can be conveyed only after one has surrendered to a place, been filled with it. (On the other hand, I remember a room in Arezzo to which I could not surrender. It was during my early days in Europe, before I entered Santa Maddalena. I'd gone to see Cimabue's "Crucifix" and planned to spend the night at a bed and breakfast by the Ospedale Vecchio. When I went into my small room and closed the door, it was as if I were nowhere: no smell, no dust, no sense of history, no sense that anyone had ever occupied the room before me. It was a perfect blank, a whiteness, and perfectly unnatural. I could not sleep in it. I took my bedding and slept in an armchair in the living room, preferring the company of the mice to the nothingness of my room.)

Mary's new house, the one that had belonged to her grandmother, was immediately hospitable. She no sooner entered it than she felt the house had been waiting for her. It had nothing to do with Eleanor's presence, its residue, but was rather like finding her geographic centre. One could as easily have said that Eleanor, who'd felt at home in few places, had been the house's caretaker, keeping it for its rightful owner, Mary.

Before moving into her home, Mary did all she could to restore it to its best self: painting every inch of its interior, having its exterior painted, pulling up the yellowed linoleum, exposing the wooden floor beneath, wooden floors she had had sanded and revarnished. She replaced all the windowpanes and converted the house from one that had been forced to accommodate three families to one that was hers alone, the rooms painted white or celadon or cream. She kept two of the bathrooms, one of the kitchens, and left the basement as it was: stone floor, brick walls, dark, cool and dusty.

And how did this relationship with eleven or twelve rooms change her?

Outwardly, relatively little, but the change was still remarkable. Aside from becoming less earnest, a change that had begun at the death of her grandmother, Mary became more sturdy, if that's the word, or more grounded. She had been changing over the four years since her grandmother died, so it's impossible to say which had greater influence, death or homeowning, but on moving into the house on MacLaren, she fully assumed the independence she'd been working towards. It was, in fact, after moving in that she'd decided to leave her position at the ministry, giving a generous six weeks' notice. Her decision had less to do with the house, of course, than with the worsening atmosphere in the office. Coolness reigned: Franklin seemed unhappy with Edward, Edward unhappy with the unhappiness. A note of annoyance was detectable beneath every word Franklin spoke to Edward and, worse, beneath the words he spoke to her, as if he thought her in Edward's camp. Her other concerns – Mickleson and St. Pierre, the false signatures – had moved into the background or, rather, she had divorced herself from them, accepting her helplessness in these matters, but they had influenced her decision nonetheless. Not unexpectedly, the trouble of years lifted off her conscience when she told Franklin she was leaving.

– I'm very sorry to see you go, Mary. I hope it wasn't anything I did.

– No. I just think it's time for me to move on.

– Is there anything I can say to change your mind?

– No. Thank you for asking.

And that had been that, save for waiting the six weeks out, of course.

Finally, it was also on MacLaren that she understood and accepted that, well, yes, she wanted François; though, of course, it was unsettling to admit desire so openly to herself. She thought of it, rather, as making a place for him, and it was she who'd invited him to see the film by Derek Jarman, something about England . . .

Though we'd known each other since childhood, since the years my father was in medical school and we lived in the Stanleys' neighbourhood, I had not seen Mary in a while when I dropped by her home in May. I interrupted her gardening. She was wearing a white T-shirt that read *Mighty Sparrow*. Her jeans were a little baggy, so that one could see the elastic of her light blue underwear. And on her earth-darkened feet, lime green flip-flops. I had come to see the place, encouraged by my parents who'd heard from Mary's parents that she had moved.

We sat together in her kitchen, drinking mint tea – mint from the small herbal garden at the back of the house, with bees hovering over the lavender as if they were floating on a purple wave. I mentioned I would be leaving for a monastery in Italy.

– I don't think I'll be going anywhere for a while, Mary said.

– Don't you want to travel?

– I do, but there's so much to do around the house first.

– Maybe when you're done, you could come visit me in Italy.

– That would be great. You'll be Italian by then.

– Si, italiano, I said.

Mary was the only one of her family who adjusted easily to wealth. She wore clothes similar to those she'd worn before Eleanor died, saw the same friends, lived a similar life. Gil was pleased to have a whole floor in the new house to himself, but he felt like a displaced person. Nothing in the world was quite where he expected it to be, and he was often anxious without knowing what he was anxious about.

Stanley admired the persistence of his daughter's personality, but it was not as easy for him and Beatrice to hold on to the scraps of their former lives. They visited old friends, but less and less frequently. They returned to the old neighbourhood, but their visits were sometimes awkward or peculiar, as if the place were losing its memory of *them*, as if part of a city could suffer amnesia.

Nor was it easy to establish themselves in the Glebe. Their neighbours were pleasant enough, but they were not gregarious in the way people had been on Spadina, or not as available, or perhaps it was the Stanleys who, intimidated by their surroundings, were more cautious. Whatever the reason, after almost two years, they had made no close friends. Although . . .

Stanley had grown friendly with their neighbour to the west, an odd man: tall, somewhat shy, handsome in a slightly broken way, and most unlike his name: Walter, Wally. They'd begun by nodding, whenever they saw each other. Then, one day, Stanley had asked

– How you doing?

Another day, he'd remarked on the weather. It was cold, and the drifts were four feet high.

– Yes, said Walter. It is cold.

After that, you couldn't have said who said what to whom. Their fellow feeling, if that's the word, was the result of small incursions made into the consciousness of the other until, almost unexpectedly, each grew curious about the other. There was not much, on the surface, to draw the men together. (Beatrice instinctively mistrusted Professor Barnes. She thought him suspicious, despite his tweed jackets, but she was not unfriendly when with him. Louise, on the other hand, she liked immediately and was disappointed to discover she did not actually live with Walter but, rather, on her own.) Walter and Stanley did share something essential, however: one was a man proud of his directness and simplicity, the other was one who had discovered simplicity by accident, after the complications of his life had almost undone him. In effect, they were both men who wanted no more from life than what they had. In this, they were unlike most of those who lived on 3rd. And so, they were, potentially at least, good neighbours.

Beatrice did her best to settle into the Glebe. She frequented its shops, grocery stores, and cafés. She and Stanley walked about the neighbourhood from Bank to Bronson, Sunnyside to Gladstone. They became familiar with the Glebe, without taking pleasure in its oddities (an apartment building with French balconies looking out over a compact, almost English park) or its surprises (a Jamaican baker who made health bread) or its beauties (the intense quiet of a summer evening, a timid bat making its bewildered way along and above the canal).

In fact, Beatrice and Stanley had become exiles in their own city: never quite at home, missing the place they had come from, which, though it was no more than a few miles away, was now unfamiliar. Ottawa had become foreign, but it was not foreign enough. So, Beatrice tried to convince Stanley that travel was what they needed, that the wide world held some solution to their discomfort, that it would put their home in perspective. (Not to mention that it was appealing to imagine herself and Stanley standing before the Sphinx or the Great Wall or the Grand Canyon.) At first, Stanley did not find the idea of travel enticing. He wanted less change, a world that stayed the same, but then . . .

On All Souls, Beatrice and Stanley had set out with Mary to see a film by Federico Fellini: *E la nave va*. They had set out early, because Beatrice wanted to spend some time in an antique dealership off

Sussex. It was just as well they'd left when they did. At four o'clock, the Market was filled with people and Sussex Drive was almost impassable. They stopped and asked a young woman about the occasion.

– It's a parade, she said.

– For what? asked Beatrice.

– Saudi Celebration Day. There's a parade and fireworks.

The procession was wonderful. From where they stood, there were, on the street before them, two rather pale young men on horseback. Nothing peculiar about that, save that the men were not Mounties. Their hair fell in tawny ringlets, long at the back. They were exotically dressed (red leotards, umber dresses, gold doublets) and their horses were caparisoned. One of the youth held a long sword, gold with two black bands, elaborate designs on the blade; the other held up a peculiar object, Middle Eastern no doubt, that was like a chalice with a conical lid, gold studded with jewels.

Definitely not mounted police.

Then came a boy on a white horse. He wore red leotards, but he had on the most unusual gold spurs, spurs so long they looked as if they could have punctured the horse. On his head, there was a crown of a rough metal along the side of which there were gold circles in which there were alternating squares of purple or red stones, the whole topped by long, triangles of gold, which stood up on the crown like broken glass.

After that, there were countless men and horses. Some of the men were bare-headed, but most wore red toques. All walked side by side, in silence, in a determined crush towards wherever it was they were going. All were on Sussex Drive, with the Château Laurier, the Parliament Buildings, and the river behind them so that, for a moment, Stanley was confused. What had become of his city? He recognized the buildings behind the procession, knew the street well, knew where the river was, though it wasn't visible from where they stood. But the costumed men were so unusual, it seemed for a moment they had been superimposed on Sussex or that Sussex was poised beneath them. In any case, they did not, initially, make sense together: Sussex and the Saudis. And yet, it was like pineapple and chocolate. Once you've tasted them together, you can better appreciate the sweet and citrus of the pineapple, the bitter and coffee of the chocolate. For the duration of their march, the Saudis made the city both more like itself and less so. Ottawa was dissolved in the Middle East, which was dissolved in Ottawa. Stanley and Beatrice were happy to stand in the street, watching the parade until it crossed over the bridge to Hull, to the Museum of Civilization.

The effect of the procession was deep, but not immediate. Stanley thought little of the parade, save that it had given him an hour or so of wonder, distracting them from antiques, restaurants, and movies. The oddest aspect of the parade was how quiet it had been. Parades, in Stanley's experience, were noisy affairs: bands, bandwagons, brass, whistles, bells, and voices. There was none of that here. The men in procession were quiet, and what one heard were the voices of the spectators and the clop-clop of the horses' hooves on pavement.

This added to Stanley's pleasure and he was tempted to say something positive about travel, but as he and Beatrice made their way through the crowd, the only words that came were

– We're going to miss the movie.

That night, Stanley dreamed of his mother on a rhino's back. The entire night, he dreamed of processions and circus animals. And then, towards morning, he dreamed that nothing would stay itself, that whatever he touched (a leopard, a soldier, a horse, its rider) turned to paper. A disturbing inconstancy, one might think. Yet, it seemed to Stanley, who woke as he touched a lacquered wooden table that rippled and tore, a thrilling impermanence. He'd awakened just before seven, turned to Beatrice, shaken her gently until she woke, and said

– I think we should go to Rome.

– Why, Stan?

This was something he could not explain. Perhaps his curiosity finally got the better of him. Then again, perhaps he had begun to tire of leisure. Being a man of modest wants, the pleasure he took in acquisition was, increasingly, theoretical. He did not want a new car or a new house or a new anything else. So, why not travel? Or, perhaps, some devious sense of entitlement made itself known by this longing to travel.

All interesting ideas, but . . .

The reason Stanley could not rightly explain his desire to travel was that it was something mysterious to him. Most likely, it had been in hiding. For good reason too: Eleanor had taken pains to drive all of his desires underground. The Arabian parade and Fellini's rhinoceros had touched something in him and Stanley himself was surprised to discover that the child who'd wanted to know the wide world, to read his mother's books, was still part of him. He could, of course, have suppressed this longing, but he did not, because there was no need. Instead, despite his own misgivings, despite his having suggested it would be better for the two of them to stay home, he said

– I think we should go to Rome.

Why Rome? That was easier to explain than "why go at all?" Rome because he assumed there was nothing there for him. Rome because there was no deep reason for Rome. There was reason to go to *London*. London was the city his psyche fluttered towards. London was strange (and yet it was within), London was the city of his inheritance, the city of books, and London, above all, was the city of the man who had been his father. It would have meant a revolution in his soul to have said, "I think we should go to London."

And so their travels began with a parade, Fellini, and longing for a city (London) that was not yet nameable in Stanley's soul.

50

A PARTING OF THE WAYS

W here Edward was concerned, Franklin was no longer kind. He was friendly, but distant. He was not reserved exactly, but neither was he open. It had been months since he'd invited Edward for drinks after work. The few times Edward had suggested they go for drinks, at Wim's or the Mayflower, Franklin was inevitably occupied or preoccupied. It wasn't difficult to trace Franklin's change to its source: the moment Edward had called St. Pierre and Mickleson "animals." What had possessed him to do that? If he could call a moment back, it would be that one. Franklin had summoned him for a dressing down and things had not been the same since. But no animosity could spring from anything so minor, could it?

On the other hand, the things on Franklin's mind *were* onerous. Rundstedt's departure had left a vacuum at the ministry, a vacuum that would be filled by God-knows-whom. They'd been waiting a month and there was no hint of who would take Rundstedt's place. They were all in political limbo, Franklin in particular: advisor to a minister who had resigned, kept on because he *might* be useful to Rundstedt's successor, if there were one. This limbo was, no doubt, excruciating and Edward chose to believe it was the pressure of the lull, the panic at drifting that led to Franklin's sour mood. Moreover, there were other signs that he had taken this instability to heart. Franklin was, at times, almost scattered, a touch disorganized, perhaps even slightly confused.

And then, one day, it was as if distraction or frustration got the better of him. He called Edward into the office, ostensibly to talk about Rundstedt's replacement.

– How are you, Eddy? Sit down.

And Edward, having been summoned and addressed as Eddy, had the feeling that here was a break in the clouds.

– I'm good, Frank.

– Good, good. There's news. I heard Cabinet is leaning towards a friend of the party, someone named Planchette or Rivette. Have you heard anything?

– I haven't heard a word, answered Edward. No one knows anything.

– I think it's bad news, said Franklin. Better to have a real politician than a crony.

– Yes, I suppose, said Edward. Look, why don't we go for a drink after work?

Franklin frowned.

– No, Eddy, I'm afraid not. I've got too much to do.

– A drink might help relax, don't you think?

He meant the question respectfully but, for some reason, Franklin took offence.

– That's all you think about, isn't it?

– What? asked Edward. What do I only think about?

– I've worked hard. I haven't stopped working for four years. For *more*. There's never been the same commitment from you, Edward. You've been a drag on me the whole time.

– I'm sorry, Frank. I never meant to be. I've been pretty devoted. *I* thought.

– You don't know a thing about devotion. You just do what you're told.

– I don't think that's fair, said Edward.

– You didn't hesitate to forge Mr. Rundstedt's signature, though, did you?

Edward was genuinely puzzled. He heard Franklin's words but did not understand their tone or their sense.

– What are you saying? he asked. How could I *not* have done what you told me to?

Ignoring him, Franklin took a blue folder from out of a bottom drawer and pushed it across the desk. The folder held some half-dozen documents Edward had signed in Franklin's name or Rundstedt's. There were requisitions, a memo, and recommendations.

– I *signed* those things because you *asked* me to, said Edward.

– But you didn't think twice about it, did you?

Stunned, but unsure if he'd understood Franklin's words correctly, Edward laughed.

– I'm glad you find this amusing, said Franklin.

– For a second, there, I thought maybe you were hinting I should leave.

– Well, as a matter of fact, I *have* been wondering about your judgment lately. I don't know if there's room for you here any more. It's something you should consider.

The only thing Edward could think to say was

– This is a mistake. Really, I think this is all a mistake.

Franklin looked at him as if expecting more, but what more could he say? He stood up and walked out of Franklin's office.

As Edward walked home, disbelief and a sense of inevitability fought it out. It had all sounded so reasonable. Or, rather, Franklin's tone had suggested reason, but underneath it all how little reason there was. He should, he thought, have seen this coming. Franklin had changed towards him and this change had, as he'd feared, signaled something troubled in his friend's soul. It had been a long time coming, and yet it was still incredible. He *had* been devoted. He *had* worked hard. Why should *he* resign? It seemed entirely unjust, but then the thought of justice, the naïveté of it, almost lifted his spirits. Who in the world had ever seen justice?

The day had turned its back on him. The sun was somewhere behind the tall buildings. He'd had a shock, but then a numbness gradually set in. There was simply too much for him to deal with: the possible loss of his job, an inexplicable betrayal and, worst of all, the vertiginous feeling that Franklin had perhaps never been his friend.

Faced with such overwhelming ideas, Edward's psyche seized up. Wouldn't it be better, he wondered, to kill off the things one loved, rather than risk a shattering like the one he'd just suffered. But what would that leave? It would leave something unimaginable, or at least unimaginable to him. No, he preferred the world as it was.

As he walked along Somerset, then Bronson, he thought how deep his brotherly feelings for Franklin actually ran. They were not easily dismissed. Though he knew resigning would liberate him from a poisoned atmosphere, he struggled with the idea of resignation, unsure if it would be best to abandon Franklin when Franklin was so clearly in distress. It was only much later, while distractedly turning the pages of an oversized book, that he accepted his presence only made things worse for Franklin. Something between them was irreparably damaged. Given the circumstances, the honourable thing was to leave.

The following day, Edward handed his resignation to Franklin, the moment between them as awkward as if they'd had sexual contact they now regretted.

Franklin thanked him for his service and said with (was it?) a hint of regret

– It's your decision, Edward. I hope this will work out for you.

Edward thanked him for thanking him.

– I hope it'll work out too, he added.

And as he emptied his desk, throwing countless packets of salt and sugar away, keeping an eraser in the shape of a Mountie and a pen from Iqaluit, Edward was almost overcome by sadness. So few moments in life made any sense at all. Or, rather, life seemed a constant alternation of sense and obscurity. One moment every aspect of the universe seemed clear and simple, the next all was murky. It was like walking through innumerable rooms, some of them brightly lit, some of them so dark you couldn't see your hands in front of your face. Or, perhaps, one entered the same room over and over again: sometimes it was darkened, sometimes lit. Then again, men like him came to different rooms and *imagined* them the same, while great men, men like Newton or Pericles – now that was another story. Great men could enter the same room over and over and see it anew every time, could tell one darkness from another, one light from the next. And what was it like to be great, instead of plain and faithful, as he was plain and faithful? This, he would never know.

His feelings were, curiously, like those at the end of an affair. No one emotion dominated, or dominated only briefly. He felt resentment, loss, sadness, humiliation, concern (for Franklin), concern (for himself), bewilderment, and (yes, even) a slight optimism. It is true, he was not the kind of man to make friends easily or lightly, so the situation was painful. But if he was mistaken about Franklin's friendship, there was still, as there had been since childhood, Reinhart. And that thought was consoling.

Edward sighed.

– Too bad I'm not homosexual, he thought.

– Not even a little? a voice inside of him asked.

But it was no use. He could no more fuck men than he could a house or lawn furniture. On the other hand, this barrier was only a dull aspect of himself and, so, only one of the many elements of which their friendship was composed. He did not wish Reinhart different. Why should he wish himself other? Had he been different, their friendship would have been altered, and it meant so much to him just as it was.

He had been walking towards the Mayflower and a drink when, as he approached the restaurant, he realized he didn't have the heart for drink. It suddenly seemed too early and too predictable a thing to do. So, instead, he did something he had never done before: he went to a movie on his own. He went to the Elgin Theatre, this though it was daytime and the only thing starting was called *Distant Voices, Still Lives*, which, from its poster, looked a little, what was the word? Artistic?

Yes, it looked artistic. Not the kind of thing he usually liked at all, but he went anyway, nourishing the small optimism within him.

―――――――

For Franklin, the departure of Edward Muir was a moment of mixed emotions. He had not really meant to drive Edward to resign or, more truthfully, he had not been conscious of any such desire. Why would he choose further isolation or greater unhappiness? He was not in the habit of punishing himself, and yet he had lost control.

He felt pangs of conscience when he thought about the way he'd handled matters. He had lost reason. However untrustworthy and distracting Edward had become, Franklin thought briefly of asking him back, but there was, despite the prick of remorse, an almost inadmissable relief that Edward was gone. Edward's absence might allow him to deal with the other irritants in his life: the coming departure of Mary Stanley, the ongoing silence about the fate of the ministry, the nagging suspicion that MacKenzie Bowell was the gift of a spiteful God.

But then, days after Edward had gone, as he was contemplating his own resignation and wondering what his future could possibly hold, there came a change in the weather. Rundstedt's replacement was appointed: J.P. Manchette, a lifelong Conservative who, along with his other responsibilities, would see to the completion of MacKenzie Bowell penitentiary. Franklin, if he cared to stay on, would be Manchette's policy advisor, but Manchette let Franklin know that he was not interested in the day-to-day details of MacKenzie Bowell's construction.

– I know you've been involved with all this from the beginning, so I'll leave the management to you and the quantity surveyors, okay? Dupuis? T'es francophone?

– Oui.

– Encore mieux. Je sens que t'es débrouillard. S'il y a des prob-lèmes tu m' gardes au courant. Mais, à part ça, vas-y toi même, okay?

That is, Manchette was exactly the raft Franklin had hoped for. Franklin would have a light hand in the penitentiary's construction.

There was also interesting news from the construction site itself.

The company that had won the bid for MacKenzie Bowell, Construction Potvin-O'Reilly Ltée, had managed to secure all the marble needed for the project at a discount. Someone who knew someone knew a further someone who had on hand a quantity of marble that was surplus, a surplus very close to the modest amount needed for MacKenzie Bowell. The only condition was that the marble be taken within days. This was an inconvenience, but as it was one that would save thousands of dollars, the marble was bought and brought and was now stacked in a corner of the site.

When he heard all this, Franklin felt that what he needed most was to take the place in: the river, the marble, the promontory, the land with which he'd felt such a bond.

And it was, in fact, on the day he visited the site that he would experience his deepest release, his spiritual moment.

As he approached the construction site, Franklin felt how true it was that, at times, even austere men attain pleasure, even Avvakum, say, had had instants in which, however briefly, poetry changed place with the world, so that the clouds above were like a turn of phrase, or the land an epic in which Odysseus comes home again and again.

On this day in the Gatineaus, everything came together at once for Franklin. There was sunlight and a warm breeze to melt the snow at his feet. It seemed, as he walked through the woods toward the clearing, that his behaviour (the man he had been, the man he was, perhaps even the man he would be) found justification in this one accomplishment that he had, as he modestly thought, helped into being. MacKenzie Bowell would not be all he had wanted, and yet, he was exquisitely pleased. For one ecstatic moment, it did not matter *what* he'd called into being. On the other hand, he was no artist. No, he was a socially minded man, and for him it mattered that this would be a prison: a beautiful prison, a wedding of art and retribution.

As if prompted by these thoughts, it was at this moment Franklin Dupuis "saw" Alba. He looked up from the ground along which he walked and found himself at the south-most edge of a massive clearing: miles in diametre. You could feel and hear the wide and tidy river before you saw it, a mile away, passing through the clearing on its way west. The sky above was the timid blue of early spring, and there was still snow on the ground beneath the evergreens. The most striking aspect of the scene was the marble, pallets and pallets of white marble all precisely arranged.

For a moment, Franklin could imagine he was looking onto a beautiful city; the blocks of stone heaped high enough to suggest buildings. The illusion made him feel as fever does. He was curiously aware of the hardness of the marble and the softness of the ground, as if he had bitten a pillow only to discover it was a brick. More than that, the city felt familiar, like one in which he'd spent so much time he could navigate its streets by instinct alone.

From noon until two, Franklin wandered about the clearing, undisturbed by the cold, listening to the river, walking around and among the pallets of marble, as happy as he had ever been, at home in a world of his own imagining.

51

NINETEEN EIGHTY-NINE

T hough it had been years since his mother's death, Stanley still, at times, imagined she was alive. He had, at times, to consciously dismiss her voice and presence. But the difference between himself now and the man he had been was that he *could* dismiss her, without rancour or guilt.

(Ah, what a monster the old girl had been . . .)

Months after suggesting he and Beatrice should travel, Stanley finally did what he had long been unable to conceive of doing: he made arrangements for himself and Beatrice to go abroad. The travel agent politely asked

– Where would you like to go, Mr. Stanley?

And, after some consideration, he chose Venice, largely because he liked the poster on the agency's wall, and on the understanding that they would spend time in Rome first.

Pleased that her parents had decided to travel, Mary made all further practical arrangements. She saw to their passports, traveller's cheques, and travel insurance. She went with Stanley as he shopped for luggage, light clothes and a small but powerful short-wave radio.

And it was Mary who arranged their farewell party.

You are most cordially invited to the home of
STANLEY AND BEATRICE STANLEY
128 3rd Avenue
on the evening of
July 10
at
8 PM
to wish the Stanleys bon voyage
on their European trip,
to drink to health,
and happiness

Gil would not be going with them. He might have been interested in Europe if the trip had not involved his parents, but for
now he preferred to keep company with his friends and, in particular, with his new girlfriend, Chantal. When he came into his own
money, in a year or so, perhaps he and Chantal, who had family in
Brussels, would go together and do the continent properly.

As for Mary: her parents encouraged her to come with them.
But she had only just begun to settle in her home. The house was
almost exactly as she wanted, but it needed this and that, so she
did not want to travel just yet. Besides, when she thought of
travel, it was not necessarily Europe that came to mind. François
had, one evening, mentioned how much he wanted to see South
America, Argentina in particular, and it seemed to her that
Buenos Aires is where she would choose to go first.

July 10, 1989:

The Stanleys had been living in their new house for some time,
but this was the first occasion on which they invited neighbours
(as well as friends) to celebrate the good fortune from which
they continued to recuperate. Beatrice was indiscriminate in her

invitations. Everyone on 3rd, east of Bank Street, was invited to see them off.

By nine o'clock, the first stars of the evening took their places in Cygnus and Hercules. Family and friends had made their appearance along with a dozen strangers, most of whom lived on the same street as the Stanleys, many of whom stayed when they discovered their hosts were pleasant people and generous with libations.

The guests were loud but relaxed, neither aggressive nor disagreeable. From time to time a laugh broke out, then trailed off or provoked more laughter. A wind shook the bushes at the back of the yard and rustled the branches of a willow that hung over their fence like a long-haired woman searching for something on the Stanley's lawn. Here and there, people moved together, then separated, then moved together again in other parts of the yard in what, from far above, might have resembled cell migration.

Mary had invited François. He had come with Daniel who, at sixteen, was only four years younger than Gil. Mary was often out with François these days. She had left work at the ministry and her most persistent thoughts were of her new life. What did she want from it? She was at home in her house, but what was she to do with herself, now? Was it time for children? Is that what she wanted for herself?

She lightly touched Daniel's shoulder and, to François, she said
– Il te ressemble.
– Mais non, said François smiling, il ressemble plutôt à sa mère.
– Ah, said Mary. I'm sorry I never met her.

For François, it was peculiar to stand in this backyard, next door to Walter's house. It was like a shift in perspective. He remembered gazing into this yard and wondering, the way one does, who the owners of the property were. Now, here he was with Mary, part of another world. But how mysteriously worlds came into being. As Mary spoke, he listened to her, but he allowed part of himself to drift: the moon, the evening, the sound of the city, now, unlike the sound of the city in winter, the city in summer a different instrument altogether.

And then he heard a familiar voice

– François?

and turned to see Walter and Louise, who shook hands with him as though it were natural for them all to meet here, beside Walter's house.

As he embraced Louise, François remembered an evening very like this one. He and Michelle had walked home and heard . . . what was it? The sound of a guitar playing a folk song from somewhere else, something like "Perfidia" but not "Perfidia."

– Mujer, si puedes tú con Dios hablar . . .

Perhaps it *had* been "Perfidia" after all, a song Michelle had learned from a Spanish student at the university and that she'd sung to Daniel. Strange the things that stay in mind, the past itself like a familiar but intermittently heard melody.

– Is everything all right? asked Walter.

– Yes, wonderful, answered François. I was just thinking how often I've seen this yard from your side of the fence.

– It feels different when you stand here, said Walter. Looking over the fence, it almost feels like I'm spying on myself. It's a little disconcerting.

– It must be, said François.

My parents and I arrived at nine o'clock and, though I'd intended to leave early, I stayed on past eleven, talking first to Mary and François, then Stanley, whom I had adored since I was a child, then Louise and Walter.

It was amusing to discover I was to leave Ottawa on the same day as the Stanleys, but it was Walter and Louise who were most interested in my destination.

– I envy you, said Walter. You'll be near the most beautiful things: Giotto's Campanile, Ghiberti's doors, Masaccio's chapel.

You should avoid the people, though. The Florentines are so sick of tourists, it's like they scowl for a living.

– I've never been to Florence, said Louise.

– Where I'm going isn't exactly Florence, I said, but it's not far. You two should visit me. By the time you come, I should know my way around.

– That's a great idea, said Walter. Let's keep in touch. You'll be our eyes on the Old World. Make sure you go to Siena, though. It's a beautiful city.

– I've heard it's a little . . . intimidating, I said.

– No, it's not intimidating, answered Walter, not at all. It's probably better if I don't tell you what I like. You should see it for yourself, but, if I have to mention something . . . I love the Piazza del Campo, the feel of it, being there in summer and eating persimmon ice cream. And, well, just walking along the streets, through the different neighbourhoods. The first time I went, I stayed in l'Istrice, near the old church of Santi Vincenzo e Anastasio. I was almost happy there, you know. And that didn't happen often, when I was young.

– It happens more now, though, doesn't it? asked Louise, teasing.

– Yes, said Walter, I suppose it *does*.

As if he were himself surprised.

————

Stanley, though a little uncomfortable in the clothes he'd bought, was a cheerful and interested host. As Beatrice and Louise talked about the Glebe, Stanley and Walter chatted aimlessly, the two conversations drifting gently in and out of each other.

– How did you two meet? Stanley asked.

– I'm not sure any more, said Walter. It seems like we've known each other forever.

– I know what you mean, said Stanley. I can't remember the first time I met Bea either.

– Some people are there before you know they are, said Louise.

– That's what I think too, said Beatrice.

She put her arm in her husband's. To Walter, he said

– We'll have to talk some more when we come back.

– Yes, let's, said Walter. When you come back.

He would have asked Stanley more about his and his wife's itinerary, but Walter did not want to monopolize his hosts. They would meet again. There would be time. He felt it, and there passed between them the fleeting but shared pleasure at acquaintance; and this pleasure was, it seemed, a thing to which words drifted, like snow to the side of a house. They spoke on about little matters, about *rissotti* and Amarone, until Walter said

– I think you'll have a wonderful trip.

– Thank you, Wally, Stanley answered.

———

For a few hours, it was as if a new city had sprouted up around them, their own city, one to which they actually belonged. The time would come, Stanley was almost sure of it, when this house would *feel* like it belonged to them. He'd had an enjoyable conversation with Walter Barnes and, what would you call her, his female companion? Louise. Then, he'd spoken with François. It was always a little unsettling to meet the men Mary brought round. Not that she'd ever brought many. Hadn't brought anyone in some time, in fact. But he had never learned to stop wishing for his daughter's happiness, a wish that always made him slightly anxious. Perhaps this one was serious.

After meeting François and his son, Daniel, Stanley had wandered about his own backyard greeting people, shaking his head as if he couldn't believe this was now his life, until it was midnight and Beatrice brought matters to a close, as there was still packing to be done.

When everyone had left and Gil had gone out with friends, they stayed up to wash the dishes, tidy the house, and fold their clothes into two large suitcases. They ended by playing Scrabble, a game they played on nights when they were too restless to sleep and, as always when they played Scrabble, they drank Ovaltine because it reminded Beatrice of her parents and because Stanley found it sleep-inducing.

On this night, however, sleep would not come. They were anxious, and both were unwilling to talk about their anxieties, so they spent the quiet hours on either side of their living-room table staring at their letters

N A B O N A D

(say, or)

C R I D A D S

until, at four in the morning, thinking it was still night, they retired for a few hours of uninterrupted sleep, which was all they would have for the next two days.

The excitement of travel, the thrill of flight, the thrill of landing in Fiumicino, the bright morning light in Rome, the impossibly quick rhythms of the new language . . . all of this and more would keep them awake until, at last, sleep caught up to them again.

When they returned home, at eleven o'clock, Walter picked up the book he was reading (*Flesh and Stone* by Richard Sennett), grateful that Louise had suggested they use the last of the evening to read. She returned to *Middlemarch,* but reading was not what Louise had in mind. She sat beside him on the sofa and casually opened the fly of his trousers.

– You should read, she said. Or you'll never finish.

Daring him to go on reading, if he were able.

As always, he was surprised to discover they had, in fact, made love for an hour or so. No slower than usual, not much faster. The two of them, losing track of time, had a cycle as consistent as that of the planets.

Did he lose track of her, as he lost track of time?

No, not at all.

It was just the opposite.

Certainly, in the midst of orgasm, he knew neither himself nor Time nor her, but . . . as rarely before, the actual presence of Louise Lanthier was an aspect of his own pleasure. He was fascinated by the details of her, both general and specific. The "general" were those things others might have called specific: her waist, her breasts, her hair, all things that might be measured, quantified, put in an archive labelled *Louise*. They were wonderful, certainly, but there was something contingent about them. Her physical attributes were an aspect of what attracted him, but on the journey towards her, in the years it had taken to admit to himself that he might love her, her attributes began to seem part of what belonged to her "accidentally," that this or that aspect might be altered without in the least affecting his feelings.

The "specific" details, on the other hand, were those he could not put into words, those that were both constant and shifting. (What words were there, for instance, for the taste of her?) The "specific" details, the facets that made Louise Louise, were not simply difficult to articulate, they were unnameable. It wasn't only that "there were no words," it was that "there could be no words." For him to love, to return again and again to this woman, it was necessary there be some aspect of her too specific to be named. Which meant that some aspect of Louise was foreign, not in the sense of a world to be colonized but strange and unknown as home is strange and unknown. And, of course, the foreignness of home is itself inarticulable, unnameable. An Odyssey in Ithaca.

An Odyssey in Ithaca? That sounded familiar.

Yes. Louise had said it. They were her words. She was now part of his inner life, part of a world he shared with no one but her.

How intriguing that he could meet her in the depths of himself. On the edge of sleep, drifting, he didn't so much remember as hear another handful of words Louise had spoken

– The world *is* in the senses.

The sentence returned to him unaccompanied by its context. Perhaps they'd been speaking of philosophy, of St. Augustine or Hume or, maybe, Descartes. St. Augustine, most likely, he thought. And Louise had intoned her consent: she stood with Augustine on the side of memory and the senses. He had disagreed with her. He was certain of it. He had been reading Kant (hadn't he?) and Kant mistrusted the senses, because for Kant the world was mind first, last, and inevitably, there being no world that did not pass the gateway of consciousness, no world outside of mind.

Yes, he must certainly have agreed with Kant.

And yet, lying here in the living room, on the sofa, the lights in the house still on, though it must be one o'clock (or was it two?) and he would have to get up, wake Louise, gather their clothes, and go with her up the stairs to the bedroom, he reconsidered. On this July night, wondering if he should let himself sleep, he also wondered if Kant were *inevitably* right. Or was it, instead, that Augustine and Kant, Hume and Descartes were neither right nor wrong, that their ideas were like constellations through which Reason periodically moved, like a sun, and when Reason moved through them it was possible to see Kant differently and to stand with him against Augustine.

But Augustine's time would come and Kant's time would come again. So, the world would live in the senses, and the world would not. So, there would be a time for touch, and sound, and taste . . . a time for thought, for mind, for consciousness. And Love itself, what about that? It, too, would be (at times) a habit of thought, and (at times) a truth in the body. Which was it now? He could not say. All he could say was that, on this night, with Louise in his arms, he *believed* he loved.

He had never been able to say that before.

The sun, so to speak, had entered his being, and he would have awakened Louise to tell her, but he was asleep long before the right words came to him.

52

THE PHANTOM CITY

T he farewell party for Stanley and Beatrice was the last gathering I attended. I left Ottawa the following day, on July 11, 1989, and I have not yet returned. Almost certainly, I'll return some day but, until I do, all I have are letters and rumour. I have heard, for instance, that Hull no longer exists, that the small city across the river is now called Gatineau, a change that puts a caul over my past but, well, why not? For years now, Ottawa has slowly become unreal. It's as if the city were underwater, changing in mysterious ways as barnacles, polyps, or whatever creatures exist below attach themselves to this or that facet of the city and eradicate it or darken it or cover it from view. Of course, with Ottawa, the element isn't water, it's time. Or is the element memory? I suppose it must be both. Time itself changes the city while my back is turned. And memory, as it perishes, takes with it the city I lived in, turning it to a place of imperfectly recollected monuments. Either way, whether the depredations are time's or memory's, Ottawa has slowly become, for me, a sort of phantom city occupied by the living, like an imaginary garden in which there are real toads, to steal a phrase.

Now, considering what leaving has meant to me and how important this breach has become, it's odd that I remember so little about my departure. I had decided that what I wanted in life was peace, which, as I then understood it, meant release from Mind. I chose Santa Maddalena, a Gregorian monastery, because it was in Italy, somewhere near Florence, and I thought it would bring a new perspective as well as release. So thinking, I said goodbye to my parents, not without some pain, and I left my city with no idea when I would return.

The moment was traumatic, certainly, but I *experienced* it as a kind of longing, as if leaving someone with whom I had not yet fallen out of love. I had recovered from such losses in the past. I assumed I would recover from this one. But, as I now see, the emotional pain was only the most obvious one. The loss of my city cut through every aspect of my being. No part of myself was left unhurt, but it would take years to understand the extent of the damage.

I now think the hardest part of leaving home has been the loss of coherence. I mean, all those I had known, from Stanley Stanley to Franklin Dupuis, had a solidity their stories gave them. One's friends, acquaintances, and family are held together by their trajectories, by what one knows of their trajectories: *a* happened, then *b,* then *c,* which led to *d,* etc. But all the moments in a story depend on the *place* of the story. The moments happen in a specific environment and it's that environment that gives them their weight and meaning. Once I'd left Ottawa, not only did I lose the subsequent steps in the various stories, but I gradually began to lose the meaning of such steps as I *did* know. The machinations of bureaucrats, for instance, are most feasible or most easily understood when one lives in a government town or a capital city. Otherwise, they seem inexplicable or bizarre.

My parents visit me from time to time, so their existence is concrete enough. And I've been writing to Walter, among others, on and off, for years. Oddly, Walter and I rarely correspond about him or the city. We write about medieval towers, about shepherds on stilts in Southwestern France, about spiritual concerns or European politics. In Walter's letters, I will catch only glimpses of the canal, the Rideau Centre, the Parliament Buildings. I will see Louise in an evening dress, waiting for him to finish a letter so they can go off. At some point, I heard that Walter had had his foot amputated, but this was gossip my father related and my father's gossip is rarely credible. Besides, a missing foot is the kind of thing Walter would surely mention, if only in passing.

The one I hear from most often is Franklin. Since I left, he has written me five or six times a year, though it is difficult for me to answer quite so often. This seems proof of loneliness or idleness, as we didn't know each other *that* well when I was home. There are only two subjects that really seem to interest him: his prison and the brute ignorance of the Conservative Party. He never speaks of his daily doings, his personal life, or, for that matter, of Edward and the past. Every once in a while, he will send photo- graphs of himself and someone else standing proudly before the gates of MacKenzie Bowell, as if all had gone as he'd intended. And yet, from what I can make out in the photos, the prison is dove-grey and Italianate. Not hideous, but uninspiring: two build- ings that, but for their size, would not be out of place in a neigh- bourhood of faux Roman columns and Grecian birdbaths.

As for Franklin, he has aged badly over these fifteen years. He is rail thin, his hair is ash-grey, and he has begun to stoop. If the Conservative Cabinet had killed MacKenzie Bowell at its incep- tion, there might still be something for Franklin to strive for. As it is, this prison is nothing but the shadow of a shadow, resembling his Alba the way, in his own words, a smooth pebble resembles a chicken. Nor was anyone likely to repeat the experiment that Bowell penitentiary had been, after the small fiasco that accom- panied the release to the public of Reinhart Mauer's original designs for the prison. (It was all a mistake, the revised drawings were to have been sent to the *Citizen* for an article on prison architecture. The public was outraged by the extravagance of the original designs, so much so that, even after the mistake was discovered, the public, and members of the Opposition, continued grumbling for months: "They treat prisoners better than the unemployed," "Conservatism gone wrong," ". . . reward instead of punishment.")

The sadness I feel looking at photos of Franklin and MacKenzie Bowell comes from the fact that the man is tied, inextricably, to the place, unwilling or unable to let go. His inevitably hopeful smile, as he stands before the prison, in photo after photo through the years, seems to me to be the smile of a man who is himself imprisoned.

If, as is said, man is an animal trapped *outside* of its cage, I suppose one should be heartened that Franklin has found the *inside* of his. It's a dispiriting sight, though, and progressively moreso as the years go on. At times, I feel unbearably gloomy when I think what is left of Franklin Dupuis.

I have heard that Stanley and Beatrice are healthy and comfortably installed on 3rd, that Gil has moved to Toronto, that Mary is married and a mother of two children. It is also from my parents that I learned about the death of Henry Wing, and the news affected me deeply. He was a man from whom, though I didn't realize it at the time, I learned a great deal. Not only did he introduce me to the Fortnightly, but there was about him something strikingly gentle. In school, I had learned to think of intellectual endeavour as a kind of will to power, something like scorpions in a jar, but Henry's forbearance and mildness were, by example, a strong counterpoise, and I wish I had said how much I admired him.

Yet, as the years go on, I think of my acquaintances less and less. These days, such parts of the city I can still hold in memory are what I think about most. They have the more tenacious grip on my imagination.

And what is it I remember most vividly?

A vista, in summer: the canal, at the foot of the National Arts Centre, looking south towards the Laurier Street Bridge, the black railings, the concrete walkway, the sound of the water, the sense that the water is deep, though I know it isn't, the bland buildings on the other side. There are no people. There is no occasion. The only colour that comes to mind is the green of the grass along the embankment. In other words, I remember nothing of great significance, and yet, if I close my eyes, I am able to re-enter the city, at that point, and feel myself almost at home. I will die, perhaps, in Italy, but my soul will leave the world from there, from Ottawa. In fact, I imagine my soul – always supposing I have one – mercurial, silvery and liquid, the wayward pools of it gathering a final time, upon my death, before it sublimates and I am released.

———————

Lately, I have taken to comparing my present setting to the one from which I sprang. Tonight, for instance, as I look up in the sky (it is nine o'clock), I am still surprised to find the right stars but the wrong world: the bears and monsters are rightly suspended, but where Hull should sit, there are the dark hills and the lights of Pontassieve, and where Vanier might be there is only the land: Tuscany, south of Florence.

Remarkably, many of the Italians I speak with understand my homesickness as well as I do. For instance, there is a woman here from Puglia. She is a cook and has been at the monastery for twenty years. For fourteen years, we have, from time to time, commiserated with each other or, at least, smiled knowingly in each other's direction, her smile conveying how little she thinks Tuscany fit for human life, and mine conveying how fervently I wish Tuscany were sufficient. To comfort me, or perhaps simply in friendship, she has, for almost as long as we've known each other, managed to secure for me, every Saturday evening, a pomegranate. I am not fond of pomegranate, but it is so hospitable of her, I hate to miss a Saturday-evening meal.

Curiously enough, my compatriot, my fellow Ottawan, the man who is, in some ways, closest to me, does not share my feelings. Paul Dylan, or Fra Paulo as he is known here, insists he has never felt a moment's nostalgia.

Over the years, Fra Paulo and I have spoken about most everything and I naturally feel a great affection for him. There are a number ideas we do not look on in the same way and we have had our . . . not disagreements exactly, but differences. No, that makes it sound as if our differences were disagreeable, when, in fact, they have been as fertile as some of my agreements with others, and they are almost always a challenge to my way of thinking.

For instance, one day recently as I was in Florence delivering jars of honey to churches and stalls, I was struck by something Fra Paulo had said. We had been talking about mercy and discovered that we thought of it differently. For Fra Paulo, mercy is essentially synonymous with forgiveness. He believes he's been forgiven and lives in the light of that forgiveness. Day after day, he thanks God for this, the highest blessing. Despite the unexceptional man he was, God's mercy, he says, has made him an exception, brought him closer to God.

I understand what he's saying and, yes, perhaps Fra Paulo *has* been forgiven. But this is not *mercy*. Mercy is divine and it is beyond forgiveness. I mean, the way I see it, when one has sinned, one becomes a special case. One is removed from the crowd. One stands marked before God. The sinner knows himself or herself to be apart, and lives with the knowledge that comes from being apart. Long after one has been forgiven, one goes on in knowledge of one's past transgression. Fra Paulo, for instance, constantly returns to his sins, retells them, if only to assert they have been forgiven. *Mercy,* though, when it has been granted, will be manifest as a forgetting of transgression, as the sinner returns to the fold. Through God's mercy, one ceases to be a special case, one becomes anonymous again, no longer a problem for God or for oneself. You see?

– I understand, Fra Paulo said. But aren't you just arguing about *degrees* of forgiveness.

– No, it's more than that, I said. It's not just semantics.

It seemed to me, as we talked, that mercy, when it came, would be like those moments of transport when all is one and one feels nothing and nowhere and blissfully anonymous, exactly like those moments but prolonged. One struggles to remember them, here on Earth, but in the end, it may be we can only *really* know His mercy in death.

Fra Paulo smiled.

– I've known you for twenty years now, Mark, and I wonder if it isn't the struggle you prefer, the *not* knowing. That's how I used to be too. I turned things over and over, until they meant everything and nothing. But I don't *do* that any more.

– You mean you *never* question God?

– Not often, no.

That, of course, is typical of Fra Paulo. He has said, time after time, that his faith in God is unshakeable and that he lives, with little break, in the presence of our Lord. And, yes, that *is* something I have struggled to understand. For me, the presence of God is in the very struggle to understand Him, the struggle to come to terms with His existence. I have felt Him most strongly at the moment when I doubted Him most. Doubt is the thing that calls Him to me. It is on the point of untroubled belief that I lose Him.

There's more to it than that. To be honest, I mistrust the nature of Fra Paolo's faith. What is the word for a man who, unable to control his life and world, gives up authority to a stronger party, without wondering if "control" is what's wanted? I mean, a man who has capitulated to a stronger master is not free and, given the extent of his surrender to God, it seems to me Fra Paulo is not free. He is not free, and yet Fra Paulo is at peace with himself and I am not. How did that happen? What should a monastery give if not the way to peace? I thought about these things ceaselessly, for days on end, after our conversation. Why are we here, if not for peace? But if peace comes only after capitulation, what is the point of it?

As I walked beside the Arno, thinking again about Fra Paulo's words, I considered if I had made a fetish of doubt. If God descended and granted me audience and certainty, what would I do? In my life, I have never met a proof I couldn't disprove or ignore. I *almost* believe my being would wither if it were too long with God. When I've tried to imagine paradise, I've imagined myself in a place filled with diversions, where God makes His appearances infrequently, once every one or two millennia, say, leaving enough time between visits to nourish those who are nourished by doubt, those who feel Him most intensely when they are on the verge of disbelief, but not so much time as to bring unconquerable despair. Doubt and hesitation are not accidental qualities or things I've lately learned. They are facets of my self, perhaps even ineradicable.

A year ago, after fourteen years at Santa Maddalena, my home came flooding back to me: Ottawa, a handful of my acquaintances, the circumstances that preceded my leaving. All these things came insistently back because, I suppose, after all that time, I had achieved the distance from them I needed. Over the last year, three Hilroy notebooks (blue, red, blue) have become a sanctuary for me. They hold the world that makes sense of Franklin, Walter, Louise, Mary, François . . .

As I reread these pages, pages filled with yearnings, losses, bereavement, and changes of fortune, it seems to me I have recreated the shuttle and shunt of various lives, and, in so doing, I have inadvertently described my own soul.

I have spent a year proving Fra Paulo right: I am a man of contention and disquiet, however fervently I might long for peace.

Yesterday, I helped filter and bottle the orange-blossom honey. All of this is done by hand, of course, with the honey slightly heated, so that it pours into the bottles more easily. It is one of my favourite things to work in the *fienile* after the combs have been spun and the rooms smell of oranges. Once the filtering was done, I sat at the wooden table and wrote out the labels by hand, perhaps a thousand of them, contented by the very act of printing *Miele di fiori d'arancio.*

When I had finished, I worked contentedly in the garden. There are days when I am able to work without thinking of anything in particular. These days are a blessing of sorts, but there are other days, equally blessed, when I am as aware of my surroundings as if I were seeing them for the first time: the stone wall with its wisteria in second bloom, the ordered rows of the garden, the earth beneath me, sun-faded on its surface but dark brown where a weed has been pulled up, my brothers walking about, quietly talking or, perhaps, mumbling to themselves as they carry out their duties, our monastery itself on a hill overlooking other green hills. Then there is the copse beside the chapel. It is here that those who wish it are buried when they die, their graves marked with stones from the quarry near Pontassieve, the panes of granite creating an ever-varying path among the trees. I go there often, not so much for solitude as for the cool beneath the trees and the smell of the rosemary bushes that mark the entrance to the graveyard.

Around sunset, I swept the dining hall, it being my week to clean up after the evening meal. As I was replacing a bench beneath a table, I looked up and saw Fra Paulo leave the hall. His head was bowed and he was lost in thought. I hadn't recognized him at first glimpse. For an instant, he was simply an older man in robes, his hair greying, his hand touching the side of his chin. As he left the hall, I thought how rare it is to see those we know without all the things we usually bring to seeing, ourselves unarmed, in other words, momentarily taken from who we are.

After a brief conversation with Fra Philippo, who chided me for having missed early Mass that morning, I retired to my room.

I washed my hands and face, put on my bedclothes, and sat at my table to finish translating a short poem by Rilke called "Herbsttag." It's elegant third verse is one that I have always found evocative:

Wer jetzt kein Haus hat, baut sich keines mehr.
Wer jetzt allein ist, wird es lange bleiben,
wird wachen, lesen, lange Briefe schreiben
und wird in den Alleen hin und her
unruhig wandern, wenn die Blätter treiben.

Translating is something I have come to love. The discipline is, in itself, both bracing *and* soothing. Then there is the joy that comes from weighing words: their worth, sound, and sense. Inevitably, there is self-revelation, though the object is discretion and all the effort goes into keeping oneself out of it. It always moves me to hear the language of my home through the thoughts of a writer about whom I may know next to nothing.

He who has no house will not build one now.
He who is alone will be alone for some time,
Will be wakeful, will read, will write long letters
And will wander restless along the lanes
When the leaves fall.

I am both everywhere and nowhere in this, Rilke's landscape. The man who wanders the lanes was, perhaps, Rilke. He is, perhaps, myself, now. It is all like a magician's trick, at times, this there and not-there-ness, this business of losing yourself and finding yourself in another's words. But it brings me solace and pleasure, losing and finding being the heart of whatever the journey of this life is.

So, in any case, it seems to me on this night, July 14, 2004, at 10 p.m., looking out my small window at the brilliant stars.

Sari Ginsberg

André Alexis's internationally acclaimed debut novel, *Childhood*, won the Chapters/Books in Canada First Novel Award and the Trillium Book Award, and was shortlisted for The Giller Prize. His most recent novel is *Asylum*. Alexis is also the author of a short story collection, *Despair and Other Stories of Ottawa*; the play *Lambton Kent*; and the young adult novel *Ingrid and the Wolf*, which was a finalist for the Governor General's Award. He is the creator and host of *Skylarking*, a nationally broadcast weekly program on CBC Radio 2.

André Alexis lives in Toronto.

A Note on the Text

In trying to re-create Ottawa, I have occasionally incorporated short phrases or sentences from writers whom I first read when I lived there or who have influenced the writing of this novel. Many of the quotations are from writers whose family names begin with the letter *A*. (John Ashbery, for instance, whose words are spoken by a diner at Pied de chameau. Or Anna Akhmatova, who first wrote about the past rotting in the future, or Jane Austen, whose words are spoken by the Member from Moosonee.) But there are also verbatim quotes from, among others, Emmanuel Lévinas, Vladimir Nabokov, Marianne Moore, Paul Verlaine, Arthur Rimbaud, Catherine Bush, Immanuel Kant, and, of course, Will Shakespeare (massacred, mostly, but with Francis Bacon's words – *cybele, bedizen, estuarie* – attributed to Shakespeare, for once).

The translation of the third stanza of Rilke's "Herbsttag" was done by the author.

The font used for the novel's epigraph is called Amanar and it was drawn by Pierre di Sciullo (www.quiresiste.com). Its alphabet, called Tifinar, is one of the oldest still in daily use. It is the alphabet of the Tuareg people, who call themselves, among other things, Kel Tamasheq (speakers of Tamasheq) or Imashaghen (those who are free).

The painting *Città Ideale,* ca. 1470, details from which appear on the pages introducing Books I and II, and which appears in full on the page introducing Book III, is attributed to Luciano Laurana (ca. 1420–1479). Galleria Nazionale delle Marche, Urbino, Italy.